AN
ILLEGITIMATE
AFFAIR

CAROLINE NEWARK

Matador
9 Priory Business Park,
Wistow Road, Kibworth Beauchamp,
Leicestershire. LE8 0RX
Tel: 0116 279 2299
Email: books@troubador.co.uk
Web: www.troubador.co.uk/matador
Twitter: @matadorbooks

ISBN 978 1838590 697

British Library Cataloguing in Publication Data.
A catalogue record for this book is available from the British Library.

Printed and bound in the UK by TJ International, Padstow, Cornwall
Typeset in 11pt Minion Pro by Troubador Publishing Ltd, Leicester, UK

Matador is an imprint of Troubador Publishing Ltd

For Richard

THE FAMILY TREE
(SO FAR)

Edward the First, King of England, married in 1299 as his second wife, Marguerite, the daughter of Philip the Third, King of France, and grand-daughter of Saint Louis, and had by her issue among others, Edmund of Woodstock.

Edmund of Woodstock, Earl of Kent, Earl of Arundel married in 1325, Margaret, the daughter of Lord John Wake and widow of John Comyn, by whom he had issue among others, Joan of Kent.

Joan, the "Fair Maid of Kent", in her own right Countess of Kent, Baroness Woodstock and Baroness Wake, married Sir Thomas Holand, Lord Holand, Knight of the Most Noble Order of the Garter, to whom she bore issue Thomas Holand.

LIST OF MAIN CHARACTERS

Alys	daughter of the earl of Arundel
Fitzalan	her eldest brother
Tamkin	her youngest brother
Joan	her sister
Thomas Holand	her husband
John Holand	her brother-in-law
Maud and Johane	her sisters-in-law

The Royal Family

The king	Edward III
The prince of Wales	the king's eldest son
Lionel (deceased)	the king's second son
The duke of Lancaster	the king's third son
The earl of Cambridge	the king's fourth son
Thomas of Woodstock	the king's youngest son
The princess	Joan, princess of Wales
Constanza	duchess of Lancaster
Isabel	countess of Cambridge
Richard	the prince's son
Harry	the duke's son
Philippa	Lionel's daughter
Elizabeth	the duke's daughter

Others

Edmund Mortimer	married to Philippa
Eleanor Clifford	Alys's cousin
Lady Wake	Alys's aunt
Alice Perrers	the king's concubine

Prologue

1344

The cleric approached the stairway with a degree of caution. The entrance was recessed deep within a stone archway and even the most vigilant of men might pass by a hundred times, unaware of its existence. Clutching the candle he'd been given when they'd entered the chapel, he peered upwards into the darkness.

'He's expecting you,' the old man mumbled, begrudging the late hour and the bone-chilling cold.

Treading softly, the cleric climbed the narrow steps, noticing how pale and unworn they were; this was a place seldom visited by anyone. At the top he knocked and, hearing a muffled voice from within, pushed open the heavy door.

The man he'd come to see was sitting hunched over a cup of wine.

'Sit,' he growled.

The cleric perched on a stool, his bowels churning, unsure as to the reason for this summons, fearing the outcome would not be to his advantage.

For a while they made desultory conversation: the weather, the roads, the king's latest successes in Brittany. Then, with an abrupt volte-face, his host turned to the matter of family.

'I need to be rid of her.'

The cleric shivered. This was not his province. By nature

he was a peaceable man and disliked all forms of violent confrontation, especially where women were involved.

'My lord, I do not think that is possible. She is your wife.'

'I do not keep you to tell me what is possible but to devise ways of giving me what I want. In this particular instance I want to be a free man, one unencumbered by the fetters of matrimony.'

The man's voice hadn't risen beyond its natural pitch and he spoke of ridding himself of a blameless woman who'd lived beneath his roof for what – eighteen years? – as if it was nothing more than the disposal of an unwanted shoe.

'My lord, my conscience will not permit the shedding of blood.'

'Then do it otherwise because I tell you this: the lady is an embarrassment to me. I need her gone.'

The cleric thought rapidly, trying to remember what he knew of the indissolubility of the marriage bond. He needed someone with more learning in these matters because insufficient knowledge would surely prove his downfall. At Oxford they'd told him his old teacher had slipped into retirement, eager to begin work on his great chronicle. Not far from the royal castle at Windsor, they'd said. Some small country living. Wraysbury? Yes, that was it – Wraysbury. Posed as a theoretical puzzle, one sufficiently complex to excite his interest, Murimuth might be persuaded to help.

He began tentatively, weighing each word with care, not wanting to promise what could not be delivered. 'There might be a way, my lord, but it would be difficult. And costly,' he added.

The man gave a ghost of a smile. 'I wondered when you churchmen would start talking money. How much?'

'I do not know, my lord.'

'Then I suggest you find out.'

The cleric moved figures around in his head but to no avail.

'Would the king lend support should it prove necessary, my lord?'

The man's hooded eyes narrowed to two black slits. 'Why would it be necessary?'

The cleric swallowed and wished himself away and in his bed, anywhere but here in this cold, airless room in the company of a man with murder in mind.

'I fear this is beyond the scope of the bishops. It would be a matter for the Holy Father.'

'Clement's as venal as any man.'

The cleric held his tongue, remembering that this man owned him body if not soul and he sometimes feared the lesser part had been given to God.

'And the king, my lord?'

The man gave a short laugh. 'He's in my debt. He'll be no trouble.'

The cleric gathered his cloak around him, a sudden need for the half-remembered warmth of another's closeness.

'My lord?'

'Yes?'

'What of your son?'

The eyes widened a fraction and the man looked his visitor full in the face.

'I have no son.'

1

WOKING MANOR 1374

There were some who believed the day ill-omened from the start. They whispered of blood in the sky and a muster of crows circling low above the village churchyard. Being a rational woman, I refused to give credence to this superstitious nonsense although I did admit to a feeling of unease at the raucous cawing of that whirling black mass of feathered creatures.

'Devil's warning,' remarked the steward, crossing himself and muttering darkly of witchcraft.

One of the maids began to whimper.

'Oh be quiet!' I said irritably.

I refused to accept these natural occurrences as portents of disaster but if I'd paid more attention to them, or to the earthenware bowl lying shattered on the floor of the dairy, I might have been forewarned. As it was, nothing prepared me for the unwelcome sight of my brother riding into the courtyard. He was accompanied by six men and arrived like the commander of a small invading army, mud and orders flying in all directions, his horse scattering dogs and people and chickens.

My first thought was to bar the door and have the servants say I was away from home. But I quickly dismissed the idea. Although my brother and I were not on good terms, I'd no wish to aggravate our quarrel.

1

Instead I told the steward to make our visitors welcome and then hurried up the wooden stairway to my private quarters. I could hear my brother's voice in the hall loudly demanding to know my whereabouts, followed by the softer more emollient tones of my steward. Refreshment would be offered but I knew Fitzalan would refuse; he was always in too much of a hurry.

I'd not seen my brother for two years, not since the day of our mother's funeral when he'd declared her death most advantageous as he'd no wish to have a third of his inheritance squandered on a widow's dower. There had been audible gasps from the assembled company, an anguished cry from my sister, and my father, who had loved our mother, knocked his son and heir to the ground. After that, Fitzalan and I had not spoken.

Trying to quell my feeling of panic, I dismissed my women, tidied away my sewing and placed myself by the window with a table in front of me in the form of a barricade. The room was comfortable with colourful hangings to soften the bare walls but it was not grand, not like the houses I'd been used to before my marriage and certainly not like the houses Fitzalan provided for his wife.

I heard my brother's boots on the stair and a moment later he burst into the room. He was a large man, heavy, a florid complexion and thick dark hair like our father. With unforgiveable rudeness he gave me no greeting but strode across the floor as if this was his house not mine. I wondered what he wanted. He wanted something, that much was obvious.

Instead of asking how I did, he began by reminding me who I was, as if I were a half-wit and might have forgotten.

'You are an Arundel, Alys. Your lineage comes from our father's ancient title and our mother's Lancastrian blood. You were born into a position of great privilege yet you sit here amidst your woman's bits of nonsense and forget you owe your family a duty.'

'I have always done my duty,' I said calmly. 'I married where I was bid and made no complaint. I have been a good daughter. I do not think you can fault me.'

'Fault you?' he shouted, crashing his fist onto the table and making me jump. 'It's been ten years. What have you done for your family in ten years? I'll tell you what you've done – nothing! Not one single solitary favour of any kind have I received.' He leaned closer. 'Our father didn't marry you to Thomas Holand for you to idle your time in the country picking berries like some village wench.'

'I doubt there are berries in April,' I said quietly.

I should not have spoken. I should have kept my opinions to myself.

'How dare you answer me back,' he hissed, spraying my face with drops of his spittle. 'If I say there are berries, there are berries.'

'Yes, Fitzalan; whatever you say,' I murmured weakly, wondering how long I must wait before he'd tell me the reason for his visit. A subtle man would oil the ground with meaningless compliments before edging towards his purpose, but not Fitzalan. My brother liked to jump straight in, crushing potential dissent with the solid weight of his boots.

He towered over me, practically baring his teeth.

'Thomas Holand was to be the conduit through which royal patronage flowed into our hands. But that hasn't

3

happened, has it? Our father got you the best marriage any girl could wish for yet you skulk here at Woking like a farrowing sow. Ten years and you've achieved absolutely nothing.'

'Nine years.'

'Christ in Heaven! Nine years! Ten years! What does it matter? It's still nothing. We'd have done better marrying you to Edmund Mortimer.'

Yes, I thought, you would.

My father was a shrewd man and never more so than where money was concerned. He was ambitious for his children and with an eye to his burgeoning fortune had married my sister, Joan, to the de Bohun earl of Hereford, a man with close ties of blood to the king. For me the future was to be equally glorious. No-one, not even my mother, had said anything but I was certain my father intended a match for me with his ward, Edmund Mortimer, the young earl of March. I tucked the thought safely away, bringing it out to be examined in those rare precious moments when I was alone. One day I would be countess of March and equal in rank to my sister.

But there was to be no glorious future for me. Instead it was a sad story of a foolish girl whose dreams were crushed and whose heart was irretrievably broken. I'd had no warning. It was like a storm on a summer's day that creeps up on you unawares. I was fifteen years old and hadn't noticed the darkening skies.

'You are to marry Thomas Holand,' my mother had said all those years ago when she and I were walking together in the sunlit gardens at Arundel.

The shock was immediate because I had no idea who she meant.

'But I am to marry Edmund Mortimer,' I blurted out.

I remember my mother's eyebrows rising in two delicate arches as annoyance flickered across her face at my daring to contradict her. Her voice when she spoke was cool. 'Whatever gave you that idea? Did you imagine your father had you brought back from Hertford simply to marry you to his ward?'

'Edmund is the earl of March,' I protested. 'It would be a good match.'

'And this one is better,' she said, setting her lips in a thin red line, showing me there was no more to be said on the subject and that if I valued her approval I would keep silent.

'I-I thought …' I stammered.

My voice trailed away at the hard look in her eyes.

'You are not required to think and you can forget Edmund Mortimer. The king wants him for your cousin, Philippa. They are already betrothed.'

I didn't understand what was happening. It was too unexpected, too sudden. I'd spent my girlhood dreaming of Edmund Mortimer: of his soft voice and engaging smile; of the set of his shoulders and the straightness of his back. When I should have been at my prayers I would imagine his shapely legs clad in their crimson hose which I'd seen one Christmas when he'd acted as server to those at the high table. It was true he had barely looked at me but that hadn't stopped my growing girlish infatuation for the tall fair-haired boy who I was certain would one day be my husband.

'I don't know Thomas Holand,' I said cautiously. 'Is he someone of importance?'

My mother gave one of her smug little smiles as if hugging a secret to herself. 'Thomas Holand is a fine young man. He is the elder of the princess's two sons from her first marriage.'

She waited and when I said nothing she must have felt the need to make sure I understood. 'Thomas Holand is the prince's stepson.'

So this was the prize my father had secured for me – the prince's stepson. Naturally I knew all about the prince: the flower of England's chivalry, the victor of Poitiers, the man who'd captured the king of France in battle and paraded him in triumph through the streets of London. The prince was heir to the English throne and would one day be king. And Thomas Holand was his stepson. I felt my heart give a little jolt.

My mother's eyes shone and I knew she wanted this marriage as much for herself as for me. There could be no doubt that a royal kinship, however oblique, would bring rewards, something my father would have taken into account in his dealings with the prince. Perhaps my mother was right and this *was* a better marriage.

I wriggled my shoulders awkwardly. 'We are not acquainted.'

My mother sighed in the way she often did during our conversations. 'You will become acquainted. That is what happens in marriage.'

And she was right. Thomas Holand and I did become acquainted. But despite royal kinship and the growing envy of my friends, I hadn't given him my heart and after nine years of marriage I doubted I ever would.

My brother sat down and stroked his chin. He eyed me as if considering me for the pot.

'We have a task for you,' he said at last.

I allowed my face to show nothing but wondered if *we* meant just my three brothers or was my father involved in whatever scheme they had in mind.

'What is it you wish done?' I asked guardedly.

'We've heard the prince will not recover from his sickness. The physicians are saying it is God's will and the bloody flux will do for him. Find out if that is true.'

I frowned at the impossibility of such a task. Even though he was my husband's stepfather I barely knew the prince and had only met him twice. He kept mainly to his rooms at Kennington, wracked by constant bouts of sickness and often in great pain. When I'd last seen him his face was grey with fatigue and the flesh had almost gone from his bones.

Fitzalan leaned closer. 'We need to know how long he's got.'

'Would it not be more sensible to gain the trust of someone in the prince's chamber?' I suggested.

My brother smiled nastily. 'Do you doubt the wisdom of our plan?'

'No, Fitzalan, of course not,' I said quickly.

'Women are known for poking their noses into matters which do not concern them. If you ask questions no-one will suspect you of anything other than mindless stupidity typical of your sex.'

I ignored the insult. I was used to worse from my brother and knew him for a man with a catalogue of prejudices against women.

'I doubt it is possible.'

Fitzalan ignored my interruption. 'When did you last have sight of him?'

'Shortly before the Nativity of Our Lord.'

'How did he seem?'

'Like a man walking towards his grave. But why do you need to know?'

'Because, you little fool, what do you imagine will happen if the prince goes first?'

'What do you mean, goes first?'

Fitzalan got up, kicked his chair aside, and began pacing the room like a caged beast. In three strides he reached the window which overlooked the courtyard below, paused at the sight of whatever was happening outside, and then turned to face me.

'If the king dies tomorrow, who is his heir?'

'The prince,' I replied promptly.

'But what if it is the *prince* who dies tomorrow. Who would the king's heir be then?'

I had never considered the question. 'The prince's son, I suppose.'

'Do you imagine the king will name a seven-year-old boy as his heir? Do you think any man of importance will accept a small child as his sovereign?'

'No,' I said slowly, 'but if it isn't the boy, who would the king choose?'

My brother halted in his pacing, laid his hands on the table and leaned towards me. His eyes narrowed and I tried to quell the nervousness I felt whenever Fitzalan came close.

'That is none of your concern. All you need do is discover how long we've got. Find out what the physicians are saying. Do you understand?'

My mouth was dry with fear. I had no idea what was being planned, only that my family required a piece of information which they believed I could obtain more readily than my brothers. Until then I'd thought the prince's sickness a personal tragedy for the king and his family but it seemed I was wrong.

'What of my husband?' I said, aware that Thomas would soon be home. 'What if he should discover I've been asking questions about his stepfather without his permission?'

'You will say nothing to Holand. If matters go awry there are some who will see him as part of the problem.'

I didn't ask what part of what problem. I didn't want to know. My thoughts for the moment must be on how to accomplish my task. My mother-in-law was the person who possessed the information I needed but I doubted she would tell me. She was adept at steering conversations away from personal matters concerning the prince and I was not permitted to accompany her on her visits to her husband's rooms.

'Perhaps I could write to the princess,' I ventured.

Fitzalan smiled, this time showing all his teeth. 'No need. The princess has already asked for you. Have your maid pack your things. I'm taking you to Kennington.'

I started to protest. 'I can't go just like that. I have arrangements to make. My children!'

My brother glared at me. 'If I trusted you, Alys, I'd let you make your own way to Kennington. But I don't trust you. Given half a chance you'll be hiding here in this godforsaken hole for the rest of the year. So you will come with me. Is that clear?'

'Yes, Fitzalan,' I said dutifully, lowering my lashes so that he couldn't see how I resented him ordering me as if I was his wife.

2

KENNINGTON PALACE 1374

Kennington: gloriously large, sumptuously appointed and wonderfully convenient. The ancient manor on the south bank of the river opposite the king's palace of Westminster had lain neglected for many years until it was transformed by the prince into a series of beautiful buildings designed in the new style. The house was surrounded with pleasure gardens and orchards, fine enough to rival those of the Savoy.

I thought my mother-in-law the most fortunate of women. There were few middle-aged widows with four children who could hope to marry a man of such pre-eminence as the prince. Before their marriage he had been the most eligible bachelor in the whole of Christendom, not only heir to the English throne but feted for his military exploits, wealthy beyond the dreams of avarice and famed for a legendary generosity. My friends said he had married her against the old king's advice and it was rumoured the queen had called her son a fool. When I asked Thomas if the stories were true he'd said it was none of my business, the kind of reply I'd come to expect from my husband.

To my delight, my favourite cousin, Eleanor, was waiting to greet me at the entrance to the princess's rooms. My mother had been one of six sisters and wherever I went there was a cousin to trip over. As well as Lancaster cousins, I had Percy cousins, Mowbray cousins, an Ufford cousin whose husband was a de Vere, and, of course, Philippa, whose mother had been a de Burgh. Two of my aunts had given themselves to God but the dowager Lady Wake, eldest of my mother's five sisters, still visited and was tireless in her continuing supervision of her nieces.

Eleanor took my hands in hers and kissed me.

'How is she?' I asked, shedding my damp cloak into the hands of my maid.

'Refusing to admit anything is wrong.'

'And this?' I asked, nodding in the direction of a trio of elegantly dressed young men, idly strumming their lutes.

'We keep a merry chamber here. It is supposed to remind us of the happy days we spent in Aquitaine. Three years since we returned and she still misses the triumphal progresses around the principality and the endless extravagance. I have never known a couple spend so much on buttons.'

'Buttons?'

'Yes, and jewels.'

I had heard about the jewels: hundreds of them, thousands of them, all bought by the prince to pour into his wife's lap. Sapphires, rubies, diamonds, emeralds, brooches of topaz and ropes of pearls, more jewels than I could ever hope to own.

Eleanor glanced at the three musicians who had just begun a new tune. 'It is one of her remaining pleasures to surround herself with handsome young men now that she no longer has the admiration of those hot-blooded Gascon lords with their lustful stares and wandering hands.'

'And the prince?'

'Sick. Lewis says it's worse than last time.'

Eleanor had been born a Mowbray and Lewis Clifford was her second husband. He served in the prince's chamber and must know every degrading detail of the prince's sickness. I thought it likely he'd be privy to what the physicians were saying but was unsure if he would confide in his wife. Thomas never confided in me.

'Can the physicians do nothing?'

'They try. Lewis says they bleed him till he can barely move, then starve him to the point of emaciation; and when that does no good, they use purgatives and force foul-smelling concoctions down his throat.'

I lowered my voice to a whisper. 'But God will not summon him yet, surely?'

Eleanor's look gave nothing away. 'Lewis says each bout leaves him weaker. He pretends all is well, even talks of a return to Aquitaine; but everyone knows that will not happen.'

'And the princess?'

'When he has good days they sit hand-clasped, whispering and laughing like they used to but there is no longer any commerce between them. Either he cannot or he will not.'

I glanced up the length of the room to where my mother-in-law sat gossiping with a group of her ladies. Despite being well into middle age she was undeniably still beautiful. People said that in Bordeaux she had been greatly admired, especially for her fashionable clothes. Today her gown of crimson silk brocade was cut scandalously low at the neck and displayed rather more of her magnificent bosom than I thought decent but, as Eleanor had once remarked, the only person whose approval she sought was the prince and he was past caring what she wore.

'Does she hear the rumours?' I asked.

'She cannot miss them. They flow through the gutters of the city like a tide of filth.'

'My brother says that in Paris they claim the prince's affliction is sent from God as a punishment for his misdeeds against the people of France.'

Eleanor raised her gaze heavenwards. 'A man's enemies will say anything if they think it will destroy him. Come! We'd best let you make your greeting or she'll want to know what we've been talking about.'

Eleanor tucked my arm into hers and drew me towards the colourful little group surrounding the princess.

'Alys, my dear child,' my mother-in-law exclaimed as I sank down in a respectful curtsey.

With a casual gesture she swept aside a couple of her lesser women to make room for me. Her couch was piled high with green satin cushions and at her back was a curtain of shimmering white silk.

Once I was seated she took my hands in hers. 'And how is my grandson?'

'He thrives, my lady.'

'And little Nell?'

I smiled at the thought of my clever daughter. 'She is learning to hold a needle.'

'And you, my dear? You must be longing to see Thomas.'

My face betrayed none of the nervousness I felt at the thought of my husband's return. He'd been absent for almost a year and it was easier to appreciate him quartered with the duke of Lancaster in Bordeaux than when walking naked across the floor of my chamber intent on climbing into my bed.

'Naturally I am eager,' I said, hoping I'd be forgiven the lie.

'I remember when his father was overseas in Calais,' murmured my mother-in-law, beginning another of her lengthy reminiscences of life before she became a princess. 'How I missed him. How lonely I was and how long the days were. And the nights,' she added roguishly.

I noticed her ladies smile. Doubtless they'd heard these stories a dozen times before.

'Have you received word yet, my lady?' I asked.

'Impatient?' she gave a giggle as if we were a pair of naughty girls discussing something forbidden.

I smiled thinly. 'No, my lady. That is, naturally I am anxious to see my husband but I know it is my duty to be patient and await his return.'

Even to myself I sounded more a dutiful wife than one who was loving.

She gave a deep sigh. 'Sometimes his father couldn't even wait to take off his boots.'

Mercy! His boots! If Thomas did that there'd be great dollops of mud on my embroidered bedcover. What she described was utterly disgusting and not something I could endure.

'Has the prince heard from his brother?' I asked, hastily trying to banish the thought of a booted and spurred Thomas climbing into my bed.

'Not yet. The duke of Lancaster will send word as soon as they come ashore, wherever that may be. It is not an easy journey, y'know. I can testify to that, but I pray there will be a message soon.'

'What of Constanza?' said Eleanor, half-smiling at some private joke. 'Will *she* be eager to greet her husband?'

My mother-in-law slapped Eleanor playfully on the wrist. 'I think we both know the duke will receive a glacial reception.'

'And a reminder of his duty.'

Constanza was the prince's sister-in-law, the Castilian bride the duke had married in what I'd thought unseemly haste after the death of his first wife, my cousin Blanche. It was more than a year since I'd gone to the castle at Hertford to pay my respects to the newly arrived duchess of Lancaster. I had been shocked at the icy formality of her little Spanish court where the women still wore mourning for the duchess's father, King Pedro, murdered years ago by his bastard half-brother.

'Does Duchess Constanza truly expect the duke to recapture her father's throne for her?' I asked.

My mother-in-law smiled. 'Of course she does. She lives and breathes Castile and expects him to do likewise. She agreed to marry him on that condition.'

'Forgive me,' I said, 'but I cannot see why the usurper is permitted to sit on the throne of Castile. He is a bastard. He has no right.'

The princess gave an elegant shrug. 'He may have no right, my dear, but he has the army of the French king at his back and that is what counts.'

'And Constanza is only a woman no matter that she is her father's heir,' added Eleanor.

I paid little attention to matters of politics but I knew the French king had broken the treaty of peace his father had signed and returned to arms. He was said to direct his wars from his council chamber in Paris and never took the field himself. I thought this the action of a coward but Thomas said wars were not always best fought by brute force. I didn't agree but had no wish to start an argument so had kept silent.

'Have you seen John?' my mother-in-law asked, her face softening as it always did when she talked of her younger Holand son. 'The prince swears he is never where he is supposed to be. Says I should have kept him on a leash when he was a child and taught him better manners.' She laughed. 'One day I fear my boy will disgrace me.'

I didn't like to say that John Holand had already brought disgrace to the princess's door. If he had been my son I would have had him placed in a cage. I thought him utterly disreputable. But Thomas said his brother's gambling, fighting, drinking and entanglements with his mother's maidservants were only what all young men did.

'*You* didn't,' I'd said, regarding the sober young man I had married.

When we first met I was excited by his serious looks, the smooth dark hair and deep-set brown eyes, thinking they disguised a passionate nature. But a month of disillusionment showed me my mistake. He was grave and courteous and had a smile which could light up his face but mostly he sighed in the way of an old man and the only attention he paid me was the one I'd have been happy to forgo.

At that moment a group of people came pouring into the princess's rooms, chattering and laughing. Detaching himself from the middle of a press of young women who were giggling foolishly and plucking at his sleeve, came my brother-in-law, John Holand.

'Lady mother,' he said, giving an extravagant bow and treating the princess to a wide smile and a fond kiss.

'Sister.' He bowed low over my hand, then slid onto the bench beside me and pressed his lips full onto mine. Instinctively I stiffened, drawing my elbows in and holding my breath.

John Holand was nearly twenty and knew exactly how to get what he wanted. My friends thought him wildly handsome and laughingly warned me to lock up my maids when he came visiting. My husband, in my opinion no judge of men, loved his brother unreservedly.

John gave a sly smile as if he and I shared a secret.

'No doubt you pretend it is my mother you've come to see, dear sister-in-law, but you and I know different, don't we?' he whispered.

I looked away, unsure how much he knew or if he was merely joking.

'Where have you been, John?' My mother-in-law's voice was indulgent.

He turned and gave her the benefit of his full attention. 'Keeping an eye on young Richard.'

Richard was my mother-in-law's youngest child, a fair-haired, fragile seven-year-old, the product of her marriage to the prince,. Since the death, four years ago, of little Edward of Angoulême, Richard was the prince's only son and infinitely more precious than either

Thomas or John. One day, far in the future, little Richard of Bordeaux was destined to be king of England whereas the most Thomas could expect was his father's title of earl of Kent. For John Holand, there would be nothing but scraps from the table which is exactly how it should be.

'I told the nursemaids to hurry. I knew you'd want to see him.'

My mother-in-law looked up and her eyes brightened as two young women in caps and aprons and a boy in a blue velvet tunic, appeared in the doorway.

'Richard! Come, my sweetheart! Come greet me like the noble young prince you are.'

My husband's half-brother was a delicate child with cornflower blue eyes and hair like gossamer. A halo of fair curls surrounded his face and with his pale skin and beautifully shaped lips he resembled a girl more than a boy. Oddly, he looked nothing like his father.

He let go of his nursemaid's hand and gave his admiring mother a bow and formal greeting in French.

'*Et maintenant, en Anglais,*' she said.

This time there were carefully spoken words in English, not fluent, but perfectly correct.

'Very good, sweetheart,' she said kissing him on the forehead. 'You improve each day.' She turned to me. 'Poor lamb, he likes to speak French but his cousins chatter away in English so we have been practising, haven't we my darling? Now greet Lady Alys. You remember her? She is married to your brother, Thomas.'

The child looked at me. For an instant I saw a pair of suspicious eyes before they were veiled by long fair lashes and he assumed his previous innocent expression. 'Lady Alyth,' he lisped.

'Alys,' corrected his mother.

''Aly – ss,' he said carefully.

'Very good. For that you shall have a sweetmeat.' She snapped her fingers and a tray of little delicacies appeared. 'Have you seen your father, this morning?' she asked, popping two of the sugared comfits into her own mouth before indicating they should be offered to her son.

'He grunted and told me to go away.'

'He is in pain. How I wish you had known him before he became sick. He was a father any boy would have been proud of, but now ...' She smiled tremulously and wiped a tear from her eye.

I had expected to remain at Kennington for a week before returning to report my findings to my brother, but on the third day, while the princess's women were occupied in dissecting the religious meanings hidden in a piece of truly scandalous verse, a letter came for my mother-in-law. The messenger wore Lancastrian livery and was dusty from the road. As he knelt in front of the princess and handed her a sealed packet I saw his hand shake and realised he was tired to the point of exhaustion.

She read the letter, then turned to me. 'They are returned.'

My heart fluttered. 'My husband?'

'Thomas is safe. Our payers have been answered. They came ashore at Dartmouth.' She gave a satisfied sigh. 'Alys, you must return to Woking at once to make preparations. As soon as his business here is finished I shall send Thomas home. I know the waiting is difficult, my dear, but it won't be long. Only a few more days.'

I wasn't ready for any of this. I must write to my brother. The news that I'd failed to uncover anything more than he already knew would make him angry but perhaps I could say the princess had ordered me back to Woking. Then there was the small matter of facing my husband. At least I wouldn't be here greeting him in full view of my mother-in-law and her ladies, I would be with my children at Woking. I wondered fleetingly what Thomas would think of his son, the child he'd last seen as a babe in his nursemaid's arms.

It was a mistake of course to think too much about Thomas. We had parted badly the previous year. I cannot remember how the quarrel started but I recall telling him how much I despised a man who failed to raise his sword in defence of his friends.

'Then I'm glad I do my duty,' he'd said quietly. 'I would not want to be the object of your contempt, my lady.'

Later he wanted to come to my bed and I had refused him. It was unforgiveable and something of which later I was deeply ashamed. He was leaving next morning to join the duke's army in Calais and I should have allowed him to lift the hem of my nightgown one last time. To refuse was unworthy of a wife and no way to send a husband off to war.

Any other man would have ignored my refusal and taken his pleasure no matter how much I protested but Thomas was not like that. He'd stared at me with a puzzled frown and then walked quietly away. After he'd gone I lay in the dark listening to the call of the night watch and the sound of mice scuffling under the floorboards. I had treated him badly but it was too late. My pride was too great and would not allow me to run after him and beg him to come back.

3

THOMAS HOLAND 1374

Behind our manor house at Woking the woods were full of the smell of wild garlic and the ground was smothered in bluebells. The last primroses had gone from the banks, usurped by rose-red campion and tiny star-like stitchwort. Our orchard swayed with blossom and, near the old wicker gate by the priest's house, I'd spied a wren darting into a hole in the wall with a twig in its beak.

Sunlight filled the courtyard and if I shaded my eyes I could just make out a tiny figure keeping watch on top of the stable roof. The boy sat astride the ridge, clinging to the weather-vane, and from his vantage point swore he could see beyond the wych elms at the bend in the track.

Everything was ready. The house had been scrubbed and polished. The tiny lozenge-shaped panes in the chapel windows sparkled and our ancient outbuildings had been liberally limewashed. Bed curtains and hangings had been taken down, shaken out and re-hung; fresh rushes had been strewn on the floors and even the great tapestry in the hall had been carefully cleaned and dusted. Every inch of the courtyard was swept clear and Thomas's coat-of-arms over the door was gleaming with fresh paint.

A shout and frantic waving from the stable roof sounded the alarm.

'It's them! Can't be none else.' Our steward hurried across the courtyard, almost tripping in his haste to give me the news.

'Fetch the household,' I said, trying to quell the fluttering in my belly. 'Make sure everyone is clean.'

Within moments the yard was full of men and boys and from the top of the steps came a small procession of women.

I smoothed my skirts but before I was properly prepared, the first horse was through the gate. My legs felt weak and I was as nervous as the day I'd first seen him, nine long years before.

Our hounds leapt up and down, yelping in delight, while the stable boys helped men from their saddles. Thomas looked weary but his eyes lit up like lanterns at the sight of us waiting to greet him.

'My lord,' I murmured, sinking down in a dutiful curtsey.

'My lady.' He had tears in his eyes. 'God give you good day. We are well met.'

'Indeed we are, husband,' I said softly. 'Look who is here to greet you.'

Thomas stared in confusion at the little girl holding her nursemaid's hand: Nell, last seen as a sleepy two-year-old, was now large round eyes and unruly brown curls beneath her embroidered cap.

'My lord favver.' The curtsey was not perfect; she wobbled slightly as she bent her knees but I saw Thomas's mouth tremble.

I gestured to the small boy clutching his nursemaid's skirts who stared suspiciously at his father.

'And this, husband, is your son.'

Thomas gazed in wonder at the sturdy child whose thumb had somehow found its way back into his mouth.

He seemed dazed by the sight of his children and kept blinking his eyes. 'They've grown,' he said.

Rather than conduct further conversation in front of our curious household, I led Thomas up the stairs to the solar. Once there I ordered the best chair placed by the fire. My husband stood looking about him in bewilderment as if I'd brought him somewhere he didn't recognise, although the house was just as he'd left it a year ago.

'I had forgot. It is like a miracle to be home. How welcoming you've made this room.'

I smiled, ridiculously pleased to have his approval.

'I have done everything as I should. The Lady Day rents are locked in your treasure chest, I made certain there were no outstanding arrears. Our reeve tells me the corn is sown and growing well and the wool crop looks to be heavy this year.' Thomas said nothing so I hurried on. 'You will find the house in good repair, my lord. We had to replace some tiles after the winter gales.' I knew I was talking too fast, almost gabbling, but it was preferable to long silences between us.

Thomas sighed. 'I'm sure you have done well, Alys, but tell me later, when I am rested. Come, sit with me awhile.'

He took my hand and I forced myself to let it lie there. It was odd to have a man here, taking up space in a room which had been my sole preserve for a twelvemonth: odd and unsettling. I sat on the stool at his feet and smiled tentatively at him. He didn't smile back.

'At the parliament they said the duke won glorious victories in France,' I remarked brightly. 'I was surprised when your lady mother said you were leaving Bordeaux.'

He closed his eyes. 'It wasn't glorious. We lost half our men, most of our horses and all of our honour.'

'That cannot be true,' I said stoutly, thinking how Thomas would only ever see the dark side, the very worst in any situation.

'God knows it is the truth. By the time we reached Bordeaux the men we had left were starving. They'd had no pay and no food for weeks.'

'Surely the duke could feed his army?'

He sighed again. 'You don't understand. The harvest was poor, food was scarce and the price of a loaf was beyond reason. Good men were begging in the streets for a crust of bread. It was pitiful. Those who had money bought passage home to England on any ship they could find.'

I recollected vagrants on the streets of London, men Fitzalan had said were lately back from Bordeaux, and wondered if perhaps there was a grain of truth in what Thomas was saying.

'I thought you would march into Castile?'

'So did we. The king of Navarre had agreed to let us use the passes across the mountains when the snows melted and there was a secret arrangement with the count of Foix. Even the king of Aragon let it be known he would look favourably upon the duke's enterprise.'

'Why did you not go? Was the duke not anxious to do battle with the bastard pretender of Castile?'

I thought of Constanza in her black-draped rooms, her small face like carved alabaster, clutching the relic she wore round her neck in memory of her murdered father.

Thomas put his head in his hands. 'The duke sent to England for more money. When word came that the king's council would not provide funds, he said we must go home.'

Eventually the time came for our servants to douse the candles and for my maid to prepare me for bed. I was nervous but knew I must do my duty. I arranged myself carefully against the pillows and waited. I was wearing my best ivory silk nightgown, the one I'd worn on my wedding night and recalled with shame my failings of last summer. My behaviour then had been unforgiveable but I had done penance and was now prepared to be a good and obedient wife. I would allow my husband to lift the hem of my nightgown. I would give myself to him and make no complaint.

But Thomas didn't come. It was humiliating. I hadn't expected him to wear boots like his father had, but I assumed he would be eager. After all, what husband returns after a twelvemonth away and isn't impatient for his wife?

At first I was angry but after a while an unwelcome thought crept into my mind – perhaps he hadn't spent his nights in Bordeaux alone. Perhaps there had been another woman, someone more willing than me. She would have been a widow, with firm white skin and cherry-red lips, a young woman of property who wanted a good-looking Englishman to share her bed. She would have enticed him and begged him to remain in Bordeaux and he would have been tempted. Perhaps he had wanted to stay and only duty had called him home.

He was my husband and I didn't love him but I hadn't realised how much I'd missed his presence and how lonely

I had been until I found myself weeping. As I listened to the call of a distant owl somewhere in the darkness and the familiar creaks and groans of the old house settling for the night, I sobbed myself to sleep.

We spent the long hot summer at Woking enjoying our children and reacquainting ourselves with each other. After that first night Thomas returned to my bed and, as he demanded no strange new practices and was as quietly diligent as ever, I concluded I had been mistaken about the widow with the cherry-red lips. I bore his attentions, as always, with patience, mindful of my mother's lectures on the wisdom of performing one's wifely duties.

My brother-in-law came in the company of three noisy friends and, having greeted them courteously as the lady of the house, I wisely withdrew to the solar to spend my days sewing and reading with my women. The men rode out each dawn with our neighbour's sons returning several hours later, wind-bronzed and laughing, hungry for dinner and full of their successes. I was glad to see my husband grow stronger and lose the pale shadowed look he'd brought back from Bordeaux, and pleased for him to have found friendship once more with his brother. I wanted him to be content but I also wanted him to progress and of that there was little sign.

Thomas was not ambitious, not in the way of most men. The promises my mother had made of the wonderful life I would have as wife of the prince's stepson had come to nothing. Apart from our three Yorkshire manors from the princess's Wake inheritance, all we had was the lease of our home at Woking. We had no town house in London for the winter months, no great estate in the country for the summer and Thomas refused to ask his mother for help. There were times I could have wept thinking of the life I would have had if I'd married Edmund Mortimer.

Towards the end of the summer my widowed sister, Joan, paid a visit and, once she had criticised my gowns, my hair and the way I managed my household, she demanded we took a walk by the river. She was my sister and I loved her but we had never been close. She was older than me and treated me like a dim-witted maidservant.

'Will you remarry?' I enquired.

'No,' she replied.

'Do you not miss the company of a husband?'

'I have yet to meet another man who is a delight to engage in conversation as Humphrey was. He would talk to me as if I was not simply a wife but a friend. We each knew what the other was thinking.'

'Thomas talks to me,' I said. 'I know what he thinks.'

Joan laughed scornfully. 'You, Alys, have no more idea what Thomas thinks than you do about anything else. You're a fool. You have been given a good husband and all you do is grumble. You should be kind to him.'

'I *am* kind,' I protested.

'Truly?'

From the look in her eye I knew what she meant. I felt a flush warm my cheeks.

'I know my duty, Joan,' I said quietly. 'I oblige him when he asks.'

'Do you indeed? You oblige him. If that is what you deem as kindness let me tell you that obliging a husband is not the same as being willing. Learn the difference.' She gave me a sideways smile. 'And be thankful they didn't marry you to his brother.'

'I pity *his* wife when he eventually finds one,' I said. 'I can see no advantage to a woman in having John Holand as a husband.'

'Can't you?'

'No.'

'Many of my friends would disagree. They find him interesting.'

'In what way?'

'Oh Alys! In the way a woman finds a man pleasing to her eye and wants to know him better.'

I remembered the scene in the princess's chamber with the young women plucking my brother-in-law's sleeve and laughing and how my mother-in-law had smiled indulgently.

'The princess shows him a partiality.'

My sister laughed. 'Of course she does. People say he is the image of his father and cut from the same cloth.'

I'd never bothered to think too much about my mother-in-law's first husband who was said to have been a nobody when she married him.

'Thomas says the prince won't have his father's name mentioned in his presence.'

'He is jealous,' said my sister who liked to pretend she knew everything.

'Don't be ridiculous. The prince has no need to be jealous of anyone. He is the king's eldest son.'

'The trouble with you, Alys,' Joan said, looking down her long Arundel nose, 'is that you might as well have been living in a nunnery for all you know about men.'

We walked on in silence. After a while I climbed up to the hedgerow to pick a handful of blackberries.

'I see your willingness to oblige Thomas is to have its usual consequence,' said my sister, looking with disgust at my purple-stained fingers.'

'I haven't told him yet.'

'Can he not count?'

It was well-known in our household that Thomas visited me every night and had done so since his return in the spring. Every man with a wife knew the signs of a woman with a child in her belly.

'I don't understand why I have this passion for eating fruit. It was the same last time.'

'Christmas?'

'I believe so.'

We stopped at the bridge by the mill where I spread my cloak on a grassy patch under an oak tree. I leaned back against the rough bark, idly watching a solitary duck poking about in the reeds at the water's edge. The day was warm and I was sleepy. I half closed my eyes, aware only of sunlight filtering through my lashes.

'Have you thought what would happen should the prince die first?' said Joan, idly stripping a stem of grass of its seeds.

'First?' I yawned.

'An ageing king and a dying prince.'

'I've not thought about it,' I said sleepily.

Joan sniffed. 'You must be the only person who hasn't.'

'I suppose Fitzalan sent you?'

'Of course.'

'I wish he'd leave me alone. What does he want now?'

'He wants to know who will come next?'

'Next to what?'

'For mercy's sake, Alys! Wake up!.'

I forced my eyes open and glared at Joan.

She threw a handful of grass seeds at me. 'Fitzalan is right. You *are* stupid.'

'I am not,' I protested.

'Listen! The old king had five sons. Who takes the throne when he dies?'

'The prince.'

'And if the prince is already dead?'

I frowned. 'Richard. Who else is there?'

'Exactly. Who else is there?'

I tried to remember which of the king's sons came next in line after the prince.

'The duke of Lancaster?'

'He is the king's third son. What about the second?'

'Don't be stupid. Lionel is dead. He died five years ago.'

'But Lionel had a child.'

It was like a bucketful of cold water thrown in my face. 'Philippa?'

Philippa was our cousin, a devious young woman, five years younger than me and married to Edmund Mortimer, my one-time beloved Edmund. On her wedding day she'd whispered to me under cover of a cousinly kiss, 'I know you wanted him. Alys, but he is *my* husband now.' I'd had a great urge to slap her.

'A woman can't take the throne,' I said firmly.

'No, but her son could.'

'Joan! The boy is younger than Richard.'

My sister began plaiting her grass stems into a bracelet. 'I have been told that Richard has certain disadvantages.'

32

'What do you mean, disadvantages?'

'I wouldn't like to say. You'd best ask your mother-in-law.'

She scrambled to her feet and dusted down her skirts. 'Come along. It's time to go back. Your husband will wonder what we've been doing.'

4

LONDON 1374

At the end of our idle summer, duty called us back to London. This year we had our own lodgings, a house called Coldharbour, rented from Sir Nicholas Loveyne. It stood in a riverside lane with other much grander houses and had once belonged to the prince. We could ill afford such luxury yet I found the tiny rooms and low-roofed hall, a disappointment. Thomas said he thought I would prefer a small place of our own rather than being at his mother's beck and call at Kennington. Realising he was trying to do me a kindness, I dutifully made no complaint, however much I disliked the house.

On the second day, after I had created order in our rooms, I hurried across the river to Kennington. Instead of the usual pleasant tranquillity, the princess's chamber was in uproar. My view was blocked by a dark press of men's backs filling the doorway. By leaning sideways I could see the familiar figure of Eleanor and my brother-in-law, John Holand. But centre stage, striding across the floor and in full voice, was a man I didn't know.

'It is outrageous,' he thundered. 'The king of England is supposed to be my friend. He promised me help. I was given a sealed and sacred oath.'

'Britto dear,' soothed the princess, as I slipped silently into a seat beside Eleanor. 'He sent you a thousand men. What more could you expect? He kept his promise.'

So this was the princess's son-in-law, John de Montfort, duke of Brittany, married to Thomas's sister, Johane. He was an imposing man, no longer young, with the dark eyes and narrow nose of a born schemer.

'How was I supposed to explain to the king of France the presence of a thousand Englishmen rampaging around my duchy, eh?' he bellowed, his voice, if anything, becoming louder and more strident. 'I sent Monseigneur Charles a gift of fish to appease his anger. I told him it was a mistake, that these men arrived uninvited, that they would be gone as soon as the weather improved. I was contrite. I declared myself his vassal in all things. But he didn't believe me. He accused me of double-dealing.'

'Are we surprised?' whispered Eleanor.

The duke of Brittany sat down heavily on a chair next to the princess and put his head in his hands. 'What am I to do? Lancaster and I were to lead an army to the duchy. We were to drive back the forces of the Bourbon and Monseigneur Charles. Instead we went on a great march to Aquitaine.'

The princess laid her hand possessively on her son-in-law's arm. 'You know the danger to us, *mon cher,*' she breathed in her most seductive voice, low and intimate. 'Aquitaine cannot be allowed to fall. If it is menaced in this way, how can it survive? Our friend, the king of Navarre, will be unable to defend himself against his enemies. The bastard Trastamara will overrun his lands, take his fortresses, control the passes across the Pyrenees. The ships of Portugal and Castile will attack Bayonne and Bordeaux; the armies of the French king will march through the valleys of the Garonne and the Dordogne. Soon everything the prince and I achieved in our years in Aquitaine will lie in ruins.'

The arguments raged for most of the morning until the duke of Brittany decided to go and visit the prince in his chamber. Perhaps there, he would receive a more favourable reception for his plans for were not he and the prince old friends?

'Poor Britto,' sighed my mother-in-law as the disgruntled figure disappeared in the direction of the prince's apartments, followed by a jostling throng of men. 'Regrettably he is not like his mother. What a woman she was! Fought like a wildcat. Cut off her skirts and rode out against her husband's enemies. And when all seemed lost – what did she do? She sent a chest of gold to the king of England and pleaded for his help.'

'Did he give it?' I asked, liking the thought of a woman who would take up a sword instead of obediently sewing seams and scolding her maids.

'But of course,' said the princess. 'You must remember, Alys, that in those days our king was young and handsome and courageous. He took his army across the Narrow Sea and rescued the duchess. It was an act of great gallantry.'

'The story didn't end there,' added Eleanor.

'No indeed. The king brought the duchess and her children back to England.' She paused and gave me a little smile. 'A chivalrous deed?'

'Most certainly.'

My mother-in-law demurred. 'Let us wait and see. The duchess was a beautiful woman of strong passions as we already know. They say she eyed this good-looking

Englishman who was her saviour and decided she wanted him for herself.'

'The king would not betray his marriage.' I said stoutly. Then I considered the long reign of the king's concubine, Dame Alice Perrers, begun while the queen was still alive, and didn't know what to think. Even kings, I supposed, could be tempted.

'Who knows?' said the princess. 'Perhaps he did, perhaps he did not. Maybe it was he who desired her and she rejected him. No-one knew for certain but within a six-month, the duchess was taken to one of the king's northern castles and it was given out that she had gone mad.'

'Poor lady. What happened to her?'

The princess shrugged. 'I believe she is moved at the king's pleasure but is still alive. It is a tale I told my daughters, Alys, to warn them of the dangers of unbridled lust. How a wife can be seduced by the allure of forbidden love and not realise the danger until it is too late. The flames of passion blaze as bright as the noonday sun but if you stretch out your hand, the heat will scorch your fingertips and fire will burn you up.'

It was only a story from the past but I felt certain there was an uncomfortable truth here which I had somehow failed to grasp.

Next morning there was no time to ponder on the princess's story as I was required to attend Aunt Wake. The Lancaster cousins had been summoned to dine with our aunt at the Savoy palace which meant taking extra care with my appearance. I spent so long hesitating over which gown to wear I was in danger of being late.

There were eight of us at this private dinner: my Ufford cousin, the dowager countess of Oxford and mother of young Robert de Vere; my disagreeable cousin, Philippa, freshly risen from her birthing chamber at Usk; fourteen-year-old Mary Percy; Eleanor; three young Mowbray girls, daughters of Eleanor's brother; and me. Joan had returned to Essex to the endless task of managing her late husband's estates and Eleanor said her own sister was making merry elsewhere with her new husband – her third!

I smiled sweetly at Philippa and dipped her a little curtsey, perhaps not as low as I should considering she outranked me but Aunt Wake was not looking.

'Alys!'

I swear the old woman had eyes in the back of her head. I tuned slowly and looked as innocent as I could.

She raised her finger. 'I suppose since marrying that Holand boy you have forgot how to behave as a lady should. But I won't have it. No niece of mine is so unmannerly in my presence. Greet Lady Philippa properly.'

I gritted my teeth and ignoring Philippa's grin, made a proper formal greeting of exactly the correct degree. The old lady harrumphed, fixing me with a cold eye as she allowed herself to be settled into her chair by two of her women.

There was to be no casualness at this dinner, no ignoring of any of the proper rituals which accompanied a meal and no idle conversation except as directed by Aunt Wake. First our hands were washed by a couple of elderly grooms bearing ewers of warm water scented with rose petals, then a lengthy grace was said by my aunt's chaplain, who snuffled and coughed over every other word. We waited patiently, half-dead with hunger while the first dishes were brought in from the kitchens by a succession of bent old men.

'We must congratulate our dear Philippa on her success,' said my aunt, wiping the tips of her fingers with great deliberation. 'A boy, a Mortimer heir and a healthy one, so I hear.'

Philippa glanced sideways to make certain I noticed how she was favoured. 'My husband is particularly pleased with me, my lady. He says our little Roger is a true Mortimer. He has composed a verse in my honour.'

'Oh fol de rol!' Our aunt was clearly not impressed by Edmund's gallantry. 'The sword is to be preferred to the pen, my girl. You remember that.'

She waved away the dish of poached figs and turned her attention to me.

'And is your Holand husband also composing verses now you have given him a son, Alys?'

'No, my lady. My husband is not inclined to use his pen.'

'Not inclined to use his sword either, from what I hear,' she said with needles in her voice. 'The only good word anyone had to say about the father was that he could fight. But not the son, eh?'

I knew Aunt Wake had not approved of the princess's first husband. And who could blame her? Everyone said the man was a rogue, though Thomas spoke of his father with great affection.

'Perhaps no-one will need to use their swords now the king's council has agreed to make peace with France,' ventured Lady de Vere from her seat at the far end of the table.

'Peace?' said my aunt sharply. 'No-one has said anything to me about peace. Whose idea is this?'

'I told you,' Eleanor soothed. 'The duke has proposed a treaty of peace with the French and the Holy Father's representatives are in agreement. They believe the princes of England and France belong to one cousinhood and should live in amity. In the spring they wish for a meeting of envoys to see if an accommodation can be found.'

'I thought our men were to sail for Brittany?' Philippa laid aside her last morsel of cinnamon pear and looked across the table at Eleanor. 'My husband tells me he and the earl of Cambridge are to lead an army of four thousand men. That doesn't sound like peacemaking to me.'

Philippa might think herself well-informed but Eleanor, being in the princess's company, knew everything.

'It is not an act of war but a move designed to frighten Monseigneur Charles and his brothers to the treaty table,' she said. 'Britto believes he will succeed in wresting his duchy back from under their noses while they dither.'

We argued about the possibilities of peace and listened while Aunt Wake warned us yet again of the dangers of over-mighty clerics. Each time we dined with her we heard the same story. Many years ago she had successfully ruined one of the king's bishops who had menaced her; she liked to remind us of what a dangerous opponent she could be when roused.

The meal was drawing to a close, Aunt Wake's minstrels began strumming an old-fashioned melody. We were comfortably relaxed, gossiping quietly when our aunt's voice cut through the air like a lash.

'What is this I hear about Lady Swynford?'

'Who?' Lady de Vere looked up in alarm.

The others shook their heads, clearly not knowing who the old lady was talking about.

'I believed her a godfearing respectable woman, fit to have charge of the duke's children. Is it true what my ladies tell me, that she is his harlot?'

I smothered a smile at Aunt Wake's outspoken description. Margaret Mowbray giggled into her fingers.

I knew Katherine Swynford though it was many years since I'd last seen her. We had both served my cousin, Duchess Blanche, in those faraway happy days before my marriage and before the tragic death of the duchess. I'd heard of the death of Sir Hugh Swynford and how the duke, in his kindness, had given Sir Hugh's widow the position of governess to his own three motherless children.

'The king has a concubine so why not the duke?' remarked Philippa.

'I doubt the duke would allow his paramour to lead him by the nose as the Perrers woman does the king,' said Lady de Vere, choosing a more elegant word to describe Lady Swynford's position.

We gossiped shamelessly about the king's concubine, the dreadful Alice Perrers, and once we had torn her to shreds our aunt quizzed Eleanor on the state of the prince's illness.

'Is he like to die?'

There was a gasp from the youngest Mowbray girl at Aunt Wake daring to speak of such a thing followed by a long silence where nobody was willing to say what we all thought.

'So what will happen?' Our aunt's breath was coming faster and her chest heaved with the effort of talking. 'I shan't live forever. God will call me to account one of these days but I never thought I would outlive the victor of Poitiers. The bishop's tell me his punishment is God's judgement but I cannot believe it will end with that little milksop.'

'What will end?' said young Mary Percy, not understanding the conversation at all.

'By the Virgin, child! What do you think I mean? The king is gone in his senses, the prince is dying by inches and who is going to protect us from our enemies? Pretty little milksop?'

She meant the child, Richard. And it was true, he was nothing but a sweet boy with flaxen hair. He couldn't rule. Yet if the worst happened, someone would have to.

Aunt Wake, with a great effort, leaned forward in her chair and placed her wrinkled old hands flat on the table.

'You take heed of what I say because I've seen it all before.' She spat the words out as if they were cherry pips. 'I've seen a king pushed from his throne and a man with not a drop of royal blood rule the land. I've seen a woman go whoring to get her hands on the reins of power and an innocent murdered for knowing another man's secrets. So don't tell me it can't happen. You girls with your newfangled ideas, you know nothing.'

She collapsed back against the cushions, panting, and Eleanor called for one of her women but Aunt Wake waved away all help. 'I'm not ready for the grave yet,' she croaked. 'Leave me be. I curse the day my brother died, God bless his perfect soul. He would have known what to do.'

It was fifteen years since Duke Henry had died of the plague and still his sisters mourned his passing. I remembered how my cousin Blanche had turned her shocked face into her husband's tunic when they had brought her news of her father's death and how, for weeks, the castle was draped in black and filled with the sound of women weeping.

As we were leaving, Aunt Wake drew me to one side and thrust her whiskery chin close to my ear.

'Watch that husband of yours, Alys. Nothing good ever came out of that family. Turncoats and scoundrels the lot of them. Let nobody tell you any different. I was seventeen when the grandfather betrayed my father's brother, the man who had raised him up to riches. The foremost earl in England, my uncle was, and the old king took off his head like it was a turnip. All because of that Judas.'

'That was a very long time ago, my lady. I was not even born.'

'Lancastrians have long memories. And if you think what the grandfather did was not sin enough, consider the father: a scoundrel; a rogue. Seduced my husband's niece when she was little more than a child and married her in secret. Forced four children upon her before God saw fit to deliver her from his clutches.'

'The princess speaks kindly of her first husband,' I protested weakly.

'Bedazzled she was. Just you be careful that you don't burn like she did. Good for nothing hedge-creepers, the lot of them.'

She ranted some more about the dreadful and iniquitous Holand family until Eleanor said it was time to go. The bells for Vespers were echoing up the river and the princess would be wondering where she was.

'She's a slippery woman,' grumbled Aunt Wake, as I made my farewell.

'Who, my lady? Who is slippery?'

'The mother, the princess. Favours her little milksop. Anyone can see that. Favours him above all others. Calls him her lamb. I've heard her. You should be careful she don't cheat your husband. There's many a firstborn who never sees his inheritance. You ask your brother.'

My brother! She couldn't mean Fitzalan. She must mean my youngest brother, the esteemed, recently enthroned, bishop of Ely. My brother Tamkin had been plucked from his studies at La Oriole last year and, to my utter amazement, given the valuable diocese of Ely. Such ridiculousness when he was three years younger than me and twice as stupid. But Thomas said I must accept with good grace that my father's wealth and his long-standing friendship with the king could achieve such miracles.

Unlike Richard, who was the darling of his mother's chamber, I'd had little time to savour the joys of being the youngest child. I was barely two years old when my brother Jack stole my place in the nursery and a year later the horror was compounded by the arrival of Tamkin.

In the domain of the Arundel nursemaids, where our mother seldom ventured, my brothers were fussed over and called sweet lambkins. They would pinch my arms and stamp on my favourite poppet but no-one chastised them. Tamkin was fortunate to look as innocent as a newborn babe. He could, at will, blink tears into his huge round eyes and some foolish woman would scoop him up saying she was sure he didn't intend such meanness to his sister. Then, having assured herself that he was unhurt, and with

44

a reproachful sideways glance at me, she would cover his face with tender kisses and tell him yet again what a lovely boy he was.

I knew he was at Westminster so next morning sent a note with one of our men asking if he would visit. To my immense surprise it took him less than a day to respond.

In true episcopal magnificence he swept in with an entourage of richly-dressed young men, cluttering up our tiny courtyard, making it look even smaller than it was.

'Well?' He looked around in surprise at the lack of splendour. He must be used to far grander surroundings than a narrow dark hall with no glass in the windows and no ranks of gleaming silverware on display. 'Why the summons?'

He had grown sleekly plump, swollen with his own self-importance and it was hard to reconcile this imposing young man in his bright-coloured silks with the hair-pulling tormentor of my nursery days.

I smiled sweetly. 'I need your advice, my lord bishop.'

'Spiritual or temporal?'

Oh, how pompous he had become! I felt like slapping his face.

He had seated himself on the best chair where Thomas usually sat and was sipping a cup of wine. I could almost feel the shudder as he swallowed. From the pained expression and the wrinkling of his lips, he was clearly accustomed to better.

'There is a matter which is puzzling me, brother. Is it possible for a man to be disinherited? I thought with your years of book-learning at Oxford, which you so thoroughly enjoyed, you would know.'

I was well aware Tamkin had hated his time with the scholars at La Oriole, finding no outlet for, what he considered, his remarkable talents. He had complained bitterly to our father but his protests had been in vain.

He eyed me with cunning interest. 'Worried for your husband?'

I ignored the question.

'Is it possible?'

'*De donis conditionalibus*,' he pronounced, looking down his nose at me. 'A man shall not have the power to alienate his lands from the heir of his body if the deed of gift of the original donor wills it otherwise. In other words, if a *feodum talliatum* exists, then the heir of the body must inherit.'

'I wish you wouldn't speak in Latin. You only do it to irritate.'

He grinned, for a brief moment my aggravating young brother, before the eminently punctilious bishop reasserted himself.

'The mother is *suo jure* the countess?'

'If you mean is it she who is possessed of the lands and the title, then yes.'

'What I mean is, in law, is the title hers by inheritance and not that of her first husband?'

'The title came from her father, through her brother. My mother-in-law is the king's cousin; I doubt her first husband would have expected to rise so high.'

'And is your husband the eldest son of his mother, the legal persona from whom the title now flows?'

'Yes.'

'Legitimate?'

'Don't joke about such matters.'

He furrowed his brow, producing a fearsome expression which I suspected was practised in front of a mirror and designed to strike fear into the members of his flock.

'One never knows, sister. It is surprising what secrets lie hidden in even the greatest of families. Men are silenced, documents mislaid, clerks bribed to alter words on a roll of parchment. A man's memory can be purchased for a handful of silver and no-one is any the wiser.'

'Thomas is legitimate,' I said firmly.

'And the estate is intended to pass without interference of the present holder?'

How was I supposed to know? The law was his concern, not mine.

'I presume so. I do not think it would be otherwise, not for an earldom.'

'Then he will inherit. The law is so framed as to make it impossible for a legitimate heir to be disinherited. Think what chaos there would be otherwise. Disobedient heirs would find themselves cast out and replaced by self-serving, toad-eating lickspittles. Any fool would have licence to insinuate himself into the good offices of another and gather up a fortune. Just imagine: every rich man on his death bed, having cleansed himself of his earthly sins, would be troubled by knaves and ne'er-do-wells, desirous of stealing the heir's fortune from under his nose.'

I said a quick prayer and thanked Our Lady it was not thus and that Thomas's inheritance was safe. There was no way the princess, or anyone else, could deprive him of what was rightfully his.

We spent a little time talking about our father who was proving increasingly infirm, and of the estates in Hampshire which Tamkin was managing for him. I could see he relished his role as my father's right hand and wondered if he regretted his position as a younger son, notwithstanding the acquisition of his bishop's mitre.

'It is a good marriage you have, Alys,' he said more kindly as he rose to take his leave. 'Our father was careful. He wanted the advantages to our family that your marriage would bring and I'm certain your husband will have his title and his lands before long.'

But the more I thought about our impecunious state, the more I worried. Thomas was twenty-four years old and there was still no sign of the promised earldom. I guessed the estates of the earldom must be vast and they would all pass to Thomas. One day we would be rich but when would that day come?

'What year did your parents marry?' I asked Thomas that evening as we sat companionably by the fire listening to one of the boys strumming his lute.

'The year of the great pestilence. My mother said it was as if the world had come to an end. There was nothing but plague pits and the stench of death.'

'And when were you were born?

'The following year. A sign of hope and God's forgiveness.'

Something was terribly wrong but I couldn't think what. Thomas was legitimate, not that I had ever doubted it. My father would have made certain of such an important matter before agreeing to our marriage. He would not have wanted the stain of illegitimacy to blight the future of my children. So what was it that wriggled away at the corners of my mind and kept me awake while my husband slept silently by my side, as quiet and composed in sleep as when he was awake?

The day had barely begun and, despite damp seeping into my slippers, there was pleasure to be gained from the early morning air. Beyond a jumble of rooftops on London's bridge the sky was brushed with the faintest wash of lemon. But this deceptive promise of warmth and sunshine could not last. Rain was in the offing.

Across the river, on the Southwark shore, a solitary boatman pulled in at the bishop's wharf. A lone figure huddled in a deep-hooded cloak stepped out of the boat and hurried up the path. I wondered who had business at the bishop of Winchester's house before dawn and whether the bishop himself was in residence. It was possible Edmund might be there, just across the river from where I stood. Philippa had boasted of a friendship between her husband and the bishop.

The bishop of Winchester was an influential man and it was obvious that Edmund was as skilled at making useful connections and furthering his fortunes as my husband was not. If Thomas had made the bishop's acquaintance, he had never said.

A dog barked and the peace was broken. From every ward in the city, from Cripplegate to Broad Street, from Farringdon to Vintry and from Billingsgate to Queenhithe, came the clanging of bells. Like the buzzing of honeybees rising from a skep, the streets of London began to stir and hum.

I retraced my footsteps through the garden and up into the gloomy hall, deciding as I walked, that I would spend the morning improving our house. Gazing at the bishop of Winchester's grand buildings had made me more dissatisfied than ever with what we had.

I was on the dais in the hall directing the hanging of one of the tapestries donated by my mother-in-law and wishing it was a few feet longer, when my brother-in-law arrived.

I avoided his eyes as I greeted him.

'I am sorry your visit is wasted; Thomas is at the Savoy.'

My hands wouldn't stop trembling so I moved behind the table and hid them in the folds of my skirts.

He grinned. 'I didn't come for Thomas. I came for you.' He walked round the corner of the table and ran his eyes across my morning's handiwork. 'Is that one of my mother's?'

'It was a gift,' I said stiffly.

'I wasn't accusing you of thievery, pretty Alys.' He smiled and put his fingers on my sleeve. 'I have someone who wishes to meet with you and has requested I act as your escort.' I forced myself to stand absolutely still, suppressing an instinctive desire to move away from his touch.

'Someone who wishes to meet with me?' I was instantly suspicious.

'Is that so surprising? Surely you are much sought after. You must have hordes of people queuing at your gate, asking if you will put in a good word for them with my lady mother?'

It was a mark of how ill-favoured we were that nobody bothered with us. Why ask Thomas Holand for something when he can't even ask for himself? That is what they would think. They would wonder why he had not been given his earldom and presume he must be in some degree, unworthy. If there had been signs of promise, the prince would have offered rewards. But he hadn't, so there was clearly nothing to be gained from befriending the stepson. He did his duty but it was a duty that any man could do. No, they would conclude, don't bother with Thomas Holand.

'Did you see people queuing?'

John laughed cheerfully. 'I sent them away. I wanted you all to myself.'

He was very sure of his charms, this brother-in-law of mine. I wished I had some other claim on my time so that I could get rid of him but I had to admit to being curious.

'Who is this person who wishes to make my acquaintance?'

He smiled like a man who believes he has already won the battle. 'A great lady and a near neighbour. She has heard of you and cannot wait to make your acquaintance.'

I hesitated. What could anyone have heard about me?

'It is not far,' said John persuasively. 'We'll be back long before Thomas returns.'

I was unwilling to spend time in his company but curiosity about the great lady was stronger than caution. I called my maid to bring my warm cloak. Scuds of rain were pitting the water on the river. The wind had got up since morning and the all-pervading smell of fish was blowing up from the quays.

We rode along the riverside lane away from the din and bustle of the bridge towards the imposing gates of a fine house. It was built high with a view across the river to the priory of St Mary Overy on the edge of the Southwark marsh. The livery of the men on the gate had royal leopards quartered with the fleur-de-lys, denoting a member of the king's family, but I had no idea who lodged here. It did not belong to the king. It was not one of the prince's houses and I doubted it belonged to the duke. Perhaps it housed the earl of Cambridge who must have a grand house somewhere in London.

John marched confidently past dozens of men up the wide steps and into the hall. Guards stood aside, men threw open doors and I knew at once he had been here before, and often. No man treated another man's house as his home, bowed to by the man's servants and certain of his welcome, unless he was well-regarded, almost one of the family. I passed my damp cloak to my maid and followed the steward who had come to escort us to the private quarters.

'Juan! You are back.' A pretty girlish voice called from the far side of the room and a young woman came tripping across the floor. I recognised her at once. She was Isabel, countess of Cambridge, Constanza's younger sister, married to the king's fourth son.

'Countess,' I murmured, curtseying low, wondering what she wanted with me.

She dimpled prettily and greeted me in return.

'You are right, *mon cher,*' she said slyly to my brother-in-law. 'She is *bella, bella. Muy bonita.*'

'Lady Isabel! I shall make you pay a forfeit if you do not speak English,' admonished John. 'You remember what we agreed yesterday? No French and most definitely no Castilian; only English. You ladies will vouch for me, will you not?'

The half dozen young women sitting clustered together on their cushions, blushed as my handsome brother-in-law looked in their direction. Their gowns shimmered in pale shades of russet and green, cut in the latest fashion with tight sleeves and low at the neck. Isabel herself shone in a luscious creation of rose-red silk, designed to emphasise the slimness of her waist and expose the tops of her creamy white breasts. The room was full of suppressed excitement and, remembering the gloom of Constanza's sober household, I was amazed at the light, the gaiety and the carelessness of her sister's surroundings.

Isabel tucked my hand into the crook of her arm and pulled me close. 'Juan, he tell me so much about you. He thinks you are *el copo de nieve.*'

The giggles from her women told me that a *copo de nieve* was not a term suited to a dutiful married woman.

'Thank you, countess.'

She lowered her voice to an intimate whisper. 'No more, countess, please. Only Edmundo call me countess in that chilly way. But he is my husband and like to remind me how important he is and how I belong only to him. So, no *condesa.* You must call me Isabel as do my friends.'

'If you wish, Isabel.'

She smiled. 'Now we too can be friends. Tell me Alys, what does your fine husband, Tomás, do all day long? Does he make plans for war like my Edmundo? Such a dull business, war. All talk of ships and sieges and chests full of arrows. They spend money on bright shiny armour and great sweating horses but never spare a thought for we poor women left behind in our loneliness.'

'My husband does his duty as he is commanded.'

'All this talk of duty. How dull!' Her pretty mouth twisted in distaste. 'You are like my sister, *la duquesa*, who speak of nothing but duty. Do your duty, little Isabel. Pray for this, give thanks for that, another hour on your knees, little Isabel, so you may show proper contrition.'

She leaned closer so that her scented breath felt warm on my face. 'I wear dusty black for six years, Alys. Six years! First in piteous sorrow for our exile from *Castilla*, our homeland which we love. Then in yet more piteous sorrow for the death of our most beloved father, Don Pedro, *el Magnifico*. If Edmundo do not make me his wife I would still be shrouded in black.'

She pouted and gave a merry laugh. I wondered what the earl thought of this frivolous little wife who condemned duty and considered entertainment as the sole reason for her existence. I guessed she was an expensive wife. Now that novelty had become the everyday, did he wish for a more dutiful companion, someone more like her sister? But two children within two years did at least speak of a woman who knew her duty in the marriage bed.

She made me sit and asked about my house, my children, my sister and my cousins. She touched delicately on my relationship with my mother-in-law, bewailing the loss of the queen who she was certain would have been a loving mother to her had she been living still. She giggled over Dame Alice Perrers. She thought her very *intrigante* and asked was I frightened of the king, her father-in-law who had patted her knee in a most familiar way at the tournament.

'He is an old, old man and yet he is king so I am kind to him. I tell him what a great man he is which make him smile and make Dame Perrers angry. I like to see her eyes flash and know that I am safe because I am Edmundo's wife and she is just *la puta*.'

I tried not to laugh.

'How shall I entertain you, *mi amiga*?' said Isabel, speaking to me but flashing a hot glance at my brother-in-law from under her long black lashes. 'You like to see my *ninos*, my little ones? Up, up, ladies.' She gestured with her arms. 'No more idleness. Time to work. I shall study like a dutiful wife and you shall entertain my newest and dearest friend, Lady Alys.'

She ushered me into the care of her women, who fluttered around me, pulling me out of the room past young pages who stood by the door, down steps, across a courtyard, into what I presumed were the nursery quarters in the old part of the house.

As I was drawn through a third archway and along a narrow covered passageway I murmured to the dark woman at my side, 'Should not one of us remain with the countess?'

She gave me a surprised look. 'No, no, *Senora*? It is time for the *condesa* to study. She learn the words of your language so she can converse with the lord, the king, and his friends. She say she must do this in private. She send us away. She say we laugh at her and make her *nerviosa*. She say Senor Juan does not laugh. She say he is most attentive.'

The young woman at my other side, said slyly. ' *Oh si, muy atento*,' and collapsed into giggles.

I could say nothing to these women who were not mine to order but as they tripped gaily up two shallow steps into a brightly-lit room, I felt growing irritation with my brother-in-law for bringing me into this household where there was no proper order.

'See, *Senora*.'

The dark woman touched my arm.

The little boy holding his nursemaid's hand looked just like his father, the earl. He was a pudgy infant with pale eyes and none of the charm of my own children. He took two uncertain steps on his own, looked up, wavered and collapsed onto the floor with a thud. The younger women laughed and ran to pick him up.

'*Eduardo*,' they crooned. '*Pequeno Eduardo*.' This was followed by numerous kisses and a stream of what I took to be baby words in Castilian before they put him down. He immediately put up his arms to be lifted up again.

'Oh *Eduardo, Eduardo*,' one of them murmured with a mischievous glance at her friends. 'So like his *madre*. One kiss, it is never enough.'

This caused peals of laughter amongst the women. Even the nursemaids, who had looked none too pleased at having their fiefdom invaded, broke into smiles. I was horrified at their lack of respect for their mistress but then I was horrified at Isabel's behaviour. I wondered if her husband knew what she did.

What did she do? What was involved in studying with my brother-in-law? Forfeits? Rewards? I shuddered to think what might be going on behind those closed doors whilst we were admiring Isabel's children.

'*Bebé*,' said one of the nursemaids, picking up an infant, so swaddled I could barely see her face beneath the folds of white cloth. Two big dark eyes and a solemn expression. This was Constance, so named for her aunt, the duchess; another child with none of Isabel's finely-drawn features but with the heavy nose and jaw of her father. Poor child.

Isabel's ladies insisted we played games with the little boy. They rolled a cloth ball along the floor and encouraged him to crawl after it. Like all infants he never tired of playing the same game time and again but I considered him far less advanced in his learning than Nell, who at this age had been toddling round the hall, happily scrambling onto her father's knee. Thomas would settle her comfortably against his chest with one arm holding her tight, and to amuse her, would play games with his fingers.

Constance was eventually rescued by the wet-nurse and borne away to be fed in peace and quiet at the far end of the room.

'Should we not return?' I suggested.

'The boy, he come when the *condesa* wish us to return.' The dark woman smiled at me. 'Tell me, my lady. Your husband, *Senor Tomás*, does he look like *Senor Juan*? Does he too have eyes like jewels?'

'And lips like …?' said her friend.

'Shh!'

'Has he fingers like *aranas*?'

'*Aranas*?' I enquired, not understanding the word.

The woman's fingers crept along my sleeve in imitation of what – a mouse? A spider?

I could not imagine what they'd seen or what secrets of Isabel's they knew but whatever they were I wanted none of them. Secrets were dangerous, that much I did know.

It was a long time before one of the pages came hurrying up the steps.

'*La condesa* say, come,' he said, spinning a coin into the air and catching it expertly in his other hand.

'Who gave you that?' I spoke more sharply than I should.

He dropped his head and looked at his shoes. I was a lady and he recognized the tone of authority even though he didn't know me.

'The English *Senor Juan*, my lady.'

'For what service?'

He thought for a moment, then grinned, an insolent look on his young face. 'For closing my eyes, my lady.'

5

BERKHAMSTED 1376

The gardens at Berkhamsted stretched ahead of us, grey and cold like a mist-shrouded plain. Bushes, which last summer would have blazed with colour, were frosted white. Above our heads, thin black branches entwined themselves into delicate curling patterns. It was a chilly Christmas, fifteen months since my visit to Isabel and twelve months since I'd last seen the princess, a year in which my life had crumbled into pieces.

Mt sister-in-law, Maud squeezed my gloved hand. 'It is not like last Christmas.'

Indeed it was not. Last year Thomas and I were celebrating the birth of another son, our little Dickon.

'Were you jealous?' asked Maud.

What in God's earth did she mean? Jealous? Of whom?

'I thought when your friend Lady Swynford was invited to Otford for the festivities you might have minded the king didn't think of Thomas.'

Oh yes; of that I had been jealous. A year ago I'd thought to pity Lady Swynford for throwing away her reputation on an ill-advised liaison with a married man, yet she was the one who doubtless pitied me. She had been honoured by spending a private Christmas with the king while I had been all but forgotten.

When the duke took Lady Swynford to Otford for

Christmas to present her to his father, I had burned with envy. She was given wonderful new gowns and reportedly sat at the duke's side in the same way as Dame Alice Perrers sat with the king. Although she was not the duke's wife, she was his duchess in all but name, whereas I was not even a countess. I was plain Lady Holand and looked as if I would remain Lady Holand for the foreseeable future.

'A court of fools and concubines,' John had sniggered when he'd heard about the king's festivities.

But this year was a very different Christmas.

Ahead lay the narrow pathway which led to the vineyard, an ornamental archway which in summer would be covered in my mother's favourite white roses.

'Shall we go further?' said Maud putting her hand on the gate latch. 'Or turn back?'

'Lady Swynford has given the duke another son,' I said bleakly, feeling the accustomed stab of pain where the wound was raw, still fresh and bleeding.

Maud leaned across and placed her cold lips gently on my cheek.

'Oh Alys, I have never been a mother so I cannot understand the pain of losing a child. My mother says it is the worst of all losses.'

'Yes, it is,' I whispered and dropped my head so that she wouldn't see my tears.

Dickon had died when he was eight months old, when the sky overhead was blue and no-one was thinking about death. It was not a plague year and there'd been no sign of summer fevers. Shafts of sunlight shone through unshuttered windows, gilding the walls and painting slabs of yellow on dusty floors. Every room in our home was filled with warmth but nothing could warm our little son who lay swaddled and silent in his cradle. I snatched him up and tried frantically to kiss life back into his soft blue lips and waxen cheeks. But it was too late. His tiny body was limp in my arms and the transparent eyelids didn't even flutter. His soul had already flown to God.

'He is with your mother,' said Thomas, choking on the words and folding me tightly into his arms. 'May God keep them both safe from harm.'

We buried our baby in the church at Woking and when I stopped weeping, Thomas carried me and our two other children to Pleshey, to my sister's house, where I wept some more.

'I have heard that Constanza's boy will not live,' said Maud as if that was some consolation. 'The birth in Bruges was to be a crowning glory for the duke; a son born into a time of peace-making while the eyes of the princes of Europe were upon him. But it seems the child is sickly.'

Poor Constanza. I didn't care for her but I wouldn't wish this pain on any woman.

'And Isabel?'

'Have you not heard?'

I shook my head. 'I have been in Essex. I have heard nothing.'

'A catastrophe. The earl returned from Brittany to find she had a belly on her like a brood mare. The city was alive with gossip. She hadn't told him there was to be a child and, slow-witted though he may be, he's not completely stupid.'

'Did he accuse her?'

'Nobody is saying but I've heard he took his belt to her and locked her in her rooms. Eleanor says her women have been dismissed and the earl has taken Isabel with him to Bruges. He has put her into the care of her sister.'

'And the child?'

'Regrettably, a boy. The earl might have been generous enough to overlook the birth of a girl, but not a boy. A boy will carry his name and could possibly inherit.'

'Is he certain it is not his?'

Maud laughed. 'That is the joy of it. He cannot be certain because it is rumoured she was lying with both of them: her husband and my idiot brother. In truth, the earl knows nothing. We all saw those kisses she gave John last Christmas but thought it just foolery. Nobody knows if it went further, least of all the earl. Isabel swears she is innocent but the earl doubts her word and threatens her with a convent. My brother has, sensibly, made himself scarce and is saying nothing. Let us hope the child grows up to look like the earl.'

I recalled John and Isabel flirting shamelessly, whispering private jokes to each other, giggling like two unruly children. When asked to dance for the prince's enjoyment, Isabel, instead of holding her partner's eyes in the turn as she should have done, gazed provocatively over her shoulder at John until no-one in the hall could have been unaware of her interest in my brother-in-law. No wonder there was gossip.

'Marriage is such a difficult matter,' I said slowly. 'A woman has no choice.'

Maud trailed her fingers across the rim of the frozen fountain bowl frowning at the shrivelled plants at its base.

'This time I fully intend to make my own choice, My mother thinks otherwise. But while she is busy with my stepfather, I shall find a new husband and he won't be like Courtenay.'

'They won't let you,' I said, thinking how impossible it would be for the princess to allow Maud the freedom to choose.

'The king's daughter chose her own husband.'

I smiled. 'Lady Coucy is her father's favourite and, in his eyes, can do no wrong. He would have agreed to her marrying his cook if it made her happy. I doubt your mother will view your decision with the same enthusiasm.'

But Maud was not to be deterred.

'She chose my father even though her family were against the marriage. She may be old and have forgotten the pleasures of love but surely she must remember what it is like to be young.'

I smiled at Maud's description of her mother. Admittedly, the princess was not as she'd been when she'd married the prince. I had attended my cousin Blanche that day in the royal chapel at Windsor and remembered the enchantingly beautiful woman dressed in red cloth of gold with her hand on the prince's arm. Now there were wrinkles on the famous peach-soft skin and threads of silver in her golden hair but admirers laughed that the plumpness of her breasts and the increased girth around her hips merely added a touch of voluptuousness to her already over-ripe beauty.

'I truly believe your mother is ageless. When was she born?'

We had reached the foot of the steps. With one hand Maud took hold of the velvet padded rail. 'She says she came with the king. Her birth was the feast day of St Michael in the first year of the king's reign. She claims it was an auspicious beginning.'

'She is right. How many women could hope to marry the man they love and in doing so become a princess?'

We had reached the top of the steps. Maud seized my hand and pulled me into a alcove.

'She didn't love him,' she said, fiercely.

'But I was told …'

'Forget what you were told. Think what it was like for her. My father was dead. Half the men in England were eyeing her for her fortune. You've never been a widow, Alys, so you don't understand. It is like being a prize cow in the marketplace with every man aiming to snatch the halter. Everywhere I go I see men wondering if it might be worth forcing me into marriage.'

'How could they force you?'

'Abduction. That is why I accepted the Courtenay's offer and returned to my mother's care. I was frightened to stay in Devonshire. Here I have family to protect me. My mother had no-one.'

'Surely the king would have kept her safe?'

'He doesn't care for my mother. She may be his cousin but I doubt he'd have lifted a finger to help her. He certainly did not want her to marry his son,'

This was odd. I'd been told the prince's family encouraged the match and how the prince had always loved the woman he called "his own true Jeanette". Yet here was Maud telling a very different story.

'My cousin Blanche said it was a fairytale romance, two childhood sweethearts reunited at last,' I ventured.

Maud gave an unladylike snort. 'I remember the winter my father died. The prince rode up to our gate like the captain of a besieging army before my father was cold in the ground. He demanded access to my mother. He was very insistent. He told her she was his Poitiers, his second Crécy and he was going to marry her no matter what his father said. Could you love a man who compared you to a battle?'

I smiled. 'And yet she *did* marry him.'

Maud sighed. 'She did it for us, to give us a stepfather who'd make our lives splendid. Thomas was given you which was a better marriage than he expected. I got Courtenay and Johane got Britto. Not so splendid for either of us as it turned out.'

'You would have been countess of Devon had your husband lived,' I said, squashing all thoughts of my own situation because now I knew a much greater pain than being without a title. Some treasures cannot be purchased no matter how rich and powerful you are. They are God's gifts. Our lives lie in His hands and we none of us know the hour.

It was January and we had returned from our chilly Christmas at Berkhamsted to an even chillier London. There were frost ferns on the solar windows and flurries of snow rushing along the length of the Thames. Across the river on the Southwark shore, the bishop's house was completely hidden behind a veil of misty white, while sloping rooftops on the bridge were gathering bonnets of snow. Few boatmen ventured out on the water but there were usually barges close to the bank making their slow way along to the quays.

On the second morning, with the snow easing, Thomas set out for Westminster on a matter concerning a boundary dispute at one of our Yorkshire manors, one which was proving troublesome. He had not been gone more than a few hours when, most unexpectedly, my mother-in-law arrived. Instead of making for the stairs to the upper floor to see her beloved grandchildren, she suggested we made use of Thomas's room.

To one side of the narrow hall at Coldharbour was a small room which my husband habitually used to conduct his business. To be truthful, having so little property and with few offices or employment, there was precious little business to occupy his time. But we had both agreed he needed a private room away from the noisy chatter of the hall. It would be unthinkable to entertain the duke or the bishop of Winchester, with hounds nosing in amongst the rushes and trestle tables and benches crashing around them.

The timber frames on the walls were somewhat crooked but once the princess's "miracle tapestries" were in place, the room shone with a deep rich glow. She had made us a gift of them three years ago, saying the memories woven into their soft silken folds were too painful to bear but she thought they might give me pleasure. We hung them either side of the tiny window where they covered the unpainted plaster nicely. It was "the marriage at Cana" and "the miracle of five loaves and two fishes" which greeted me each morning when I opened the door.

Fortunately the fire in the tiny hearth was alight and the room warm as I had no wish for my mother-in-law to consider me remiss in managing my household. I had been a poor enough wife to Thomas these past months without having him accuse me of not providing his mother with proper hospitality.

'I had forgotten how beautiful they were,' said the princess, pausing on the threshold with her hand flown to her throat.

To my surprise, she had tears in her eyes.

I offered her the comfort of Thomas's chair and made to fetch a cushion from the settle but she stopped me, taking my hands in hers. Her fingers were cold but I was struck once again by the delicate softness of her skin. reminding myself to ask what salve she used. The heat of the room caused a deep musky perfume to rise from the velvet skirts of her gown, so reminiscent of my mother that, for a moment, tears pricked the back of my lids.

'Alys, my dear,' she said quietly. Her face was serious but her eyes were kind. 'You must be brave.'

It was as if all the blood in my veins had turned to ice and I couldn't move. Thomas had spoken those same words on the day our son died – "Alys, you must be brave."

'Thomas?' I whispered.

'No, my dear. It is not Thomas. He is quite safe. He is with the prince. It is your father. A message came this morning from Arundel, from your brother, the bishop, and was brought to Kennington. I said I would come and tell you.'

'My father is dead?'

'Dying. A matter of days, the letter said.'

I put my hands to my face to hide the tears which filled my eyes. This was not because I had been close to my father but because he was part of my family and I'd been taught that family was all we have this side of the grave. I loved him with humility and reverence, as a daughter should. He had been away on the king's business for much of my childhood but whenever he was home he was not unkind and, with his riches, had purchased for me what he believed was a good marriage.

'I must go to him.'

'Of course you must. Thomas is making arrangements. But Alys, dearest child, before you go there is something I need to tell you.' She signalled to the man at the door. 'Bring Lady Alys some wine.'

She sat me gently in the big chair and she, herself, took the stool. Once the wine had been served she ordered everyone out of the room and the door closed. She watched me drink and then very quietly began to speak.

'It was a lifetime ago when I first met your mother. We were in Flanders, serving the queen and I was far from home. Your mother was kind to me when others were not and we remained friends until the day she died. I loved her dearly. I loved her as you loved her. We had no secrets from each other so you will know that what I am about to tell you is the truth.'

There was nothing the princess could tell me about my mother that I did not already know. I knew her as well as any daughter can know the woman who gave her birth. It was to my mother I had turned when Thomas first left me to go to the Aquitaine. I had wept and she had comforted me. She had explained the difficulties all women must face in marriage and had told me secrets that I hadn't known before. She kept nothing from me. We were as close as sisters.

'You knew that your mother was first married when she was a young girl?' said the princess. 'You were acquainted with your Beaumont half-brother?'

I thought of the bright-faced young man who occasionally visited my mother, who had ruffled my hair in a brotherly way.

'Yes, and it is through his widow's good offices that we are fortunate enough to have this house.'

'So you knew that when your mother met your father she was a widow?'

'She told us how her Beaumont husband had been killed in a tournament and she'd gone to Walsingham to pray to Our Lady to bless her with the gift of another husband.'

The princess's eyebrows rose slightly as if this surprised her which was odd. She must surely know the story of my parents' most uncommon encounter. The miracle which befell them at the shrine of Our Lady at Walsingham was our favourite nursery game: me in my sister's old silk gown and Jack and Tamkin belted with swords and scabbards. There would be much sighing and swooning and declarations of love before I allowed Tamkin to wave his wooden sword about and kiss me. Then, our shaggy hound, who was much too elderly to do more than give a single piteous look of protest out of his rheumy old eyes, was dressed in a cloak and cap, borrowed from one of the grooms, and made to play the priest. We didn't know the words of the marriage vows and the nursemaids must have despaired at our unseemly behaviour, but we children had tremendous fun.

I smiled, remembering the happiness of those long-ago days.

'It was love at first sight.'

'A *coup de foudre*,' agreed the princess. 'Exciting but dangerous.'

'They were happy together.'

'Indeed they were. It was a good marriage from uncertain beginnings.'

I didn't know what she meant. Nothing about my parents' marriage was uncertain.

'Did she tell you what happened at Walsingham?' my mother-in-law asked.

'She kissed the blessed shrine of Our Lady's milk and when she turned, standing there in a pool of golden light, was my father. She took one look at this handsome man and knew she wanted to marry him. For him, it was the same. Love's arrows loosed from Cupid's bow, struck together.'

'That is what she told you?'

'Yes,' I laughed. 'They were so impatient to marry that before they left Walsingham they had planned everything, even the dishes for their wedding feast and the list of people they would invite.'

The princess nodded. 'Yes indeed and there were a great many obstacles to overcome in this planning.'

Obstacles? What did she mean? What obstacles?

The princess paused for a long moment. I could hear my heart beating and the slap of wet snow against the closed shutters; a muffled rumble of a wagon passing and the sound of running feet and a scream from somewhere on the riverbank. Then nothing.

'Your father was already married. He had a wife.'

I felt as if a jugful of cold water had been thrown down the back of my neck.

'A wife?'

My mother-in-law must have noted my open mouth and the shocked look on my face. She said wryly, 'I didn't think your mother had told you that.'

A wife? How could my father have had a wife? He was planning to marry my mother.

'I don't understand. What sort of wife?'

'The sort of wife who stands in the way of a man marrying the woman he wants. An inconvenient sort of wife. But a wife who was very real indeed.'

'But who was she? Did she die?'

'No, my dear, she did not die. However obliging that might have been of her. However much your parents may have wished for such an event, your father's wife did not die.'

'You are mistaken.'

The princess put her arm round my shoulders and must have felt me shiver. 'What does a clever woman do to bind a man tight when otherwise he might slip away?'

I shook my head. I didn't know even though I considered myself a clever woman.

'She takes him to her bed, Alys. That is what she does and that is what your mother did. She took your father to her bed and whispered to him of the advantages she could bring to him as his wife. She was a daughter of the earl of Lancaster and greatly loved by her family. Her brother was the king's greatest war commander and her great-grandfather had been king of England. Your father didn't need much persuading.'

'But you said he was already married.'

'The woman was a Despenser. She was of no use to him.'

I knew the name; a disgraced family who, many years ago, had over-reached themselves.

'The woman was not the only problem, Alys.'

'I thought you said ...'

'There was a child, a son, a fine young man nearly full-grown. A son who would inherit. A son who would one day be earl of Arundel.'

I didn't believe any of this. A wife. A son; a son who would inherit. It was ridiculous and the princess was foolish to think I'd believe such a parcel of lies. She was mistaken. But I looked at her steady blue eyes and knew it was I who was foolish and I who was mistaken.

'What happened?' I whispered.

'Your mother demanded that your father get rid of the wife and the son. She wanted it to be as if the marriage had never been.'

I felt sick. 'She wanted them killed?'

The princess gave a glimmer of a smile. 'I doubt your mother would have wanted the blood of an innocent woman and her son on her hands. What she demanded was an annulment of the previous marriage. This was her price for agreeing to marry your father. She wanted no trace left of the first wife and particularly not of the son. She intended her own Arundel son, when she had one, to inherit the earldom.'

'And my father agreed?'

'Your father wanted to marry your mother. She had done her work well and after that first night your father was convinced he must make her his wife. With her family connections she was eminently suited to be countess of Arundel and she had already proved her

72

desirability as a woman. He was no fool but they do say that when a man is led by lust and greed, good sense is trampled underfoot.'

I could feel the sure foundation of my life crumbling. My parents had become two people I didn't recognise: my father an adulterer, prepared to cast off a blameless wife of many years without a moment's hesitation because he preferred another woman. And my mother, a Salome. She had entranced my father and asked, not for half a kingdom or a prophet's head, but for the lives of his wife and his child. They might not be dead by my mother's hand but she had destroyed them nonetheless.

'What did my father do?'

'He approached the king for help and between them they petitioned the pope for an annulment of your father's first marriage. They were fortunate. The Holy Father was inclined to favour the English king and, of course, your father's purse was stuffed with gold. Your father swore an oath that he had never consented to the marriage. He had been a boy at the time and later had only lain with the Despenser girl because he'd been beaten.'

'Not much of an excuse,' I said thinly. 'Was he believed?'

'He was. Fortunately for him, those dried-up old cardinals at Avignon with their shrivelled loins forgot what it is like to be a lusty young boy of fourteen and no-one enquired too closely how your father could have been forced time and again into the marriage bed if it was not his desire. His word was enough. He got his annulment and before the summer, your parents were married.'

'What happened to the Despenser woman?'

'She was bought off with a few manors. And with a daughter of Lancaster resolved to be rid of her she was wise enough not to make trouble. She knew it could be dangerous if she did.'

'And the son?'

'Bastardised. He protested bitterly to the king and to Pope Clement but was silenced with a settlement.'

'Why are you telling me this?' I cried. 'Why could you not have left well alone?'

I wished I didn't know. I wished the princess had never told me. I would rather have remained in a state of ignorance than know what my parents had done.

The princess was remorseless. 'I have told you because once your father is dead, his firstborn son will want his revenge. He will come for what he considers rightfully his. You must warn your brother. If your mother didn't tell *you,* I doubt your father told your brother. The two of them will have decided to keep this secret from their children.'

I thought of Fitzalan and his pride in the family name; of Tamkin, bishop of Ely, with a position in the Church; all five of us rewarded with brilliant marriages built on my mother's steely determination and my father's baseless lies.

But the princess was not finished with me.

'The legitimacy of your brother's claim to the earldom, indeed the legitimacy of the birthright of every one of your parents' children, is at risk if this son of your father decides to make trouble. You must tell your brother if he wishes to be earl of Arundel and inherit his father's riches, he may have to fight.'

Legitimacy! The word opened a chasm of sharpened knives beneath my feet and I began to tremble. It couldn't happen. Not to us. Our parents were protective of our honour. They would not have left a legacy of such unimaginable horror for their children.

6

ARUNDEL CASTLE 1376

I had hoped to arrive at Arundel by midday but just beyond the priory at Hardham my mare cast a shoe and we had to turn back. By the time a new shoe was fitted the wind had already got up, blowing sharp spatters of rain straight into our faces and driving ragged grey clouds in a wild race across the sky. The captain of my escort sniffed the air and pronounced in his slow Sussex drawl that we should expect snow before dusk.

'Best hurry, my lady,' he said, as if it was likely I might decide to linger on this lonely stretch of track.

I shrugged myself deeper into my hood, trying to ignore the aching fatigue in my bones and the insistent snatching at the folds of my cloak. At this time of year the hours of daylight were short and we had already been three days on the road. But it was not only the urgency of my journey which made haste essential, I had no desire to seek another night's uncomfortable lodgings.

Just when I thought I could not bear my physical discomforts a moment longer, the lead man gave a shout. Not half a mile ahead, standing stark against the darkening sky, rose the familiar outline of my childhood home, the castle of the Arundels.

We rode wearily up the hill from the town, turning our heads away from the sleet which whipped our frozen cheeks, and, with profound relief, plunged into the darkness of the narrow gatehouse entrance. In the courtyard, torches were already lit, and welcoming hands helped me from my horse before ushering me up the steps to the hall and into my sister's arms.

I noted the absence of black mourning. 'Is he ...? '

'Still alive.' She held me tight and kissed my cold mouth. 'But I fear it will not be long.'

'And our brothers?'

'No word of Jack but the others are here. Fitzalan arrived yesterday, cursing the snow, the state of the roads and the duke's misguided peace-making in equal measure. And that was before he started on poor Lizzie for giving him yet another daughter.'

I followed her, forgetting my aching bones and my longing for dry clothes in my haste to see my father. We hurried through well-remembered rooms, up shallow steps, past a twisting stairway which gave access to what had once been my mother's solar, through to the little presence room guarding my father's private chamber.

In the hushed silence beyond the door, the fire had charred to embers. The lamps burned low, lending a softness to the surroundings. The magnificent tapestries, which many years ago he'd brought back from Bruges, merged into shadow, but heavy crimson bed curtains warmed the grey face of the man who lay beneath the furs.

His eyes were closed and his breathing was shallow. His hands were crossed quietly on his breast, between his fingers, a jewel-encrusted cross. This was Richard Fitzalan, earl of Arundel, earl of Surrey; beloved husband, father, brother, grandfather, master and friend. The man who had clawed his way back from disaster to rebuild the fortunes of the Arundels and was now one of the richest men in England. He had held our family together and shaped the destiny of each one of his children. To me he had been unfailingly kind but to others, I knew, he had been ruthless. This was the man who had cast off an unwanted wife and bastardised his firstborn son at my mother's request. All for the benefit of me and my brothers and my sister.

The end came two days later.

'*In manus tuas Domine,*' murmured my father's chaplain as he leaned over the unmoving body. '*Commendo spiritum meum.*'

A tear rolled down my cheek and beside me I heard my sister gently sobbing. My brothers knelt on either side of the bed, their heads bowed. Behind them stood dozens of my father's men, their hats held in their hands. Most were weeping because they loved and respected my father and with his death, a great man would be gone and none of them knew what would come next.

That night my brothers stood vigil over my father's body where it lay in the tiny Arundel chapel, while Joan and I knelt praying for the salvation of our father's soul. By the time a pale grey light in the sky towards Angmering heralded dawn, we were exhausted.

'Four years ago we did this for our mother,' I murmured. 'Do you think she is waiting for him?'

Joan looked up. 'We know nothing of what lies beyond this life other than what the Church teaches us.'

I got to my feet. Every bone in my body ached after a cold night on my knees and my throat was parched raw.

'Our cousin, Eleanor, says priests are not gatekeepers and a woman may speak directly to God.'

Joan struggled up, hanging onto my arm to give her support. 'I've also heard her say our bishops have too much power.'

'I doubt Tamkin would agree.'

Joan gave the glimmer of a smile. 'If I pray to Our Lady am I speaking into the void? I was taught we need priests and bishops to ease our pathway to God and prayers are only heard if offered to Him by one of the Holy Saints. Now, I do not know what to think.'

'Nor I. Until I lost my baby I rarely thought about what lies beyond this life. I accepted what I was taught and tried as best I could to obey the rules of the Church. I'm sure some bishops are avaricious and over-powerful but I cannot believe such wickedness is widespread. Besides, with the marked exception of my husband who cannot be bothered to bestir himself, all men seek profit for themselves.'

On the fourth day, in response to my increasingly frantic requests, Fitzalan agreed to a family council. We met in the little chamber above the chapel, well-known as the safest and most private place in the whole castle. The only approach was a narrow stairway which could be held by one man with a sword, and the room at the top had no windows, no chimney and no privy chute. It was a chill and airless place, dusty with lack of use, but for our purpose, it was ideal. It was completely secure and our conversations could not be overheard.

'I hope this is important,' said Fitzalan, swirling his cloak round his legs as he sat down.

For a moment, seeing my brother's impatience and knowing him quick to anger, I hesitated. Suppose the princess was mistaken.

'Don't be a bully, Fitz,' said Joan, who treated her nursery playmate as an unwanted irritant. 'If Alys says this is a matter of urgency, you can be certain it is.'

We sat round the small table, four Arundels bound together in blood. Of our brother, Jack, supposedly somewhere in Dorset, there was still no word. I wanted to believe we five were the only children our father had left behind but sadly I knew different.

I bit my lip and began.

'Our father had another wife.'

'What do you mean "another wife"?' said Joan, immediately alert. I had refused to tell her anything and now she was demanding plain speaking.

'He had a wife when he asked our mother to marry him.'

There was a moment's silence. Fitzalan turned to look at Tamkin and then at Joan.

'Who told you that?' he said slowly.

'The princess. She had it from our mother.'

'She is mistaken,' said Fitzalan with a degree of anger in his voice.

'She meant our father had once been married but the woman was now dead,' corrected Tamkin. 'It is a common enough occurrence but odd he never mentioned it.'

'The wife was not dead. The princess said she was still living.'

'She died soon after.'

'No, she did not die. She stood in the way of our parents marrying. Our mother told our father to get rid of her.'

'How dare you mouth such a foul slander against our mother,' yelled Fitzalan. 'She was a good and gentle creature. She would never have asked our father to do something so wicked.'

Somehow I had handled this badly. My brother didn't believe me.

'She was not asking for her to be killed. The princess said our mother wanted our father to seek an end to his marriage.'

Tamkin narrowed his eyes like a penny clerk. 'And who was this wife? Do you have a name?'

'If she ever existed except in the addled mind of that demented fishwife,' spat Fitzalan.

Joan laid her hand over his arm. 'Have a care, Fitz. You should not speak ill of the princess.'

I turned to Tamkin. 'She was a Despenser. The princess said she would have been of no use to our father.'

'No more she would if she was a Despenser,' murmured Joan.

Fitzalan stood up, banging his shins in his haste. 'I am not going to waste time listening to this foolishness. I have work to do.'

'Sit down, brother,' said Tamkin firmly. 'We need to hear the rest.' He nodded to me to proceed.

'Our father promised to seek an end to his marriage. Our mother was insistent. I don't fully understand what it means but she said there must be an annulment.'

Tamkin sat forward in his chair. 'Ah, so that was it! I understand now. Our father had contracted a childhood marriage. He and this Despenser girl would have been under age and the betrothal was unconsummated. It is not uncommon but strange it was forgotten.'

'Of course,' said Fitzalan, dropping back into his chair with a sigh of relief. 'A marriage planned by our grandfather when our father was a child; an ill thought-out arrangement left to gather dust. I'm not surprised our father forgot.'

'No,' I said quietly. 'It was not an unconsummated betrothal; it was a full marriage.'

'How can you possibly know that?' Fitzalan thrust his angry face in front of mine and banged his fist on the table.

For a moment I was too terrified to answer but, knowing the story must be told to the end, I gathered up the last remnants of my courage.

'There was a child.'

'What!' Fitzalan was up on his feet again. 'Are you out of your wits? Are you saying my father and this Despenser girl had a child together?'

His face was drained of colour and I saw fear creeping into his eyes.

'Yes.' I waited for the next question and when he said nothing I knew he was afraid to ask.

'What was it?' said Joan in a half-strangled voice. 'Did it die?'

'It was a boy. A son. A strong healthy child who grew into a strong healthy young man.'

'I'm not listening to any more of this nonsense,' yelled Fitzalan. 'If our father had married this girl and made a son on her he would have told me. I am his heir. He would not have left me in ignorance.'

Joan pulled on Fitzalan's sleeve. 'Sit down, Fitz, and listen.'

Fear was swirling round the chamber as one by one they began to realise the implications of what I'd told them.

'Are you certain it was an annulment?' said Tamkin.

'What does it matter what it was as long as he was rid of the bitch. Christ's teeth! Why did this happen now?' Fitzalan turned away and started fiddling with his beard, the way he always did when worried.

'it was most definitely an annulment,' I said.

I waited for Tamkin to explain how an annulment worked for I was uncertain. He remained hunched in his chair, chewing his knuckles and frowning.

'Tam?'

'Oh yes. An annulment. Most unusual in these particular circumstances. I don't think I've ever heard of such a thing. There's not been a single case like it brought to the bishops' courts as I recollect. Are you quite certain it was an annulment?'

'The princess was muddled. The Despenser woman died. It's obvious.' Joan had already decided the matter. There would be no sifting of evidence when Joan was meting out justice; a swift look and a man would be judged innocent or guilty as charged.

'The princess was quite specific. It was an annulment. Our mother insisted.'

Tamkin stood up. 'The matter is easily settled. There will be a record somewhere. Our father's clerks are meticulous in their filing. I've had plenty of evidence of that this past year. We'll get them in and they'll find it in no time.'

'Good idea.' Fitzalan was up on his feet as well. 'Tam and I will search the record room with the clerks.'

'No!' My brothers had been on the threshold when Joan's voice made them stop. 'Do you want every man in the castle knowing our business? This is a private matter, something we must do alone. If you involve others they will talk and before morning everyone will know. This must be kept amongst ourselves until we know more. Alys and I will help.'

If I thought finding a single document would be simple, I was mistaken. As the hours passed our fingers became blackened with dust and traces of ink, and our eyes were strained from reading endless pages of faded script. By the time the bell rang for Vespers we had examined every roll in our father's registers and hauled out hundreds of documents relating to leases and purchases and grants of wardships. Yet we had found nothing. With undisguised fury, Fitzalan banged down the lid of the last box he'd been searching and called a halt.

'You've had us chasing a phantom. There's nothing here. There never was. It was a pack of lies from start to finish.'

'It must be somewhere,' I said. 'The princess was not lying and our father would not have burned such an important document.'

'Perhaps it is at Reigate or in one of the Shropshire houses,' said Joan, rubbing her face, making herself look like a wild creature of the forests with great black patches around her eyes.

'No,' said Tamkin. 'I agree with Alys. If the document exists, it is here. Our father would have understood its importance and kept it with him at all times or placed it in the custody of someone he trusted.'

'I disagree. I'll waste no more time,' said Fitzalan. 'I'm for my bed. Are you coming, Tam?'

I sat back on my heels in complete despair. What if the document wasn't here? What if the princess's story was false and the document had never existed? But in my mind there was no doubt she had told me the truth. If we hadn't found what we were looking for in the record room, my father must have placed it safely somewhere else in the castle.

That night, in my sleep, I was revisited by the terrors of my childhood: a demon hound with dripping jaws, prowling below the castle walls; the dark corner at the turn of the stairs where an assassin lurked, knife and noose at the ready; a shapeless fiend shuffling and breathing behind the bed curtains and a sharp-fanged serpent coiled between the linen sheets. Worst of all was the memory of a big hairy man and a room, ice-cold, black and silent – the treasure chamber of the Arundels.

Long ago, a distant Lord of Arundel, needing to hide his wealth from his enemies, built himself a tower. The outer walls were twenty feet thick and the only way to reach the top was through a narrow passage and up a steep winding stairway. There were no arrow slits and no torch brackets and the air smelled of dead people.

Once, as a six year-old child, my father had gripped me by the hand and led me up the stone steps to the room at the top. With an oppressive silence whispering in my ears and this strange man's sweating, bearded face looming down out of the darkness, I had been terrified. My father had sworn me to secrecy and, in fear of eternal damnation and the flames of Hell, I had never told anyone what I'd seen, not even Tamkin. In the years which followed I remembered the treasure chamber of the Arundels as the most inaccessible and frightening place on God's earth.

The door to the passageway was hidden behind one of the rich hangings in the place where our father had conducted his business. Dozens of men must have passed in and out of this room over the years without realising the significance of "The Moneylenders" in the far corner where the wall bulged inwards. But the joke would not have been lost on our father who revelled in the power of his wealth. When I'd asked my mother why he gave his money to other men, she told me, "Money needs to work for a man and your father has an eye for our advantage."

Tamkin lifted a torch from its bracket while I pulled aside one corner of the heavy cloth which hung ceiling to floor. We stood in silence while Fitzalan undid the lock. The door was built low into the wall and we had to bend our backs to get through. The air smelled stale and by the time we reached the foot of the stairway I was beginning to wish I'd had the foresight to bring a candle.

As we climbed higher into the well of darkness, the stone walls pressed closer and tentative fingers of creeping cold brushed the back of my neck. I thought I had cast off my childhood fears of demons with dripping fangs and black leathery wings but when an unseen creature slithered over my foot and a cobweb floated across my face, I almost screamed.

The door at the top was barred, chained and bolted. Fitzalan took a long time with his bunch of keys but after much rattling and scraping and cursing, there came a hideous creak and the door swung open.

The treasure room was smaller than I remembered, just a windowless chamber with bare rounded walls. It was full of wooden chests and huge canvas sacks, with a table, a stool and, tucked into one corner, a low pallet bed. There was no hearth, no candles and the cold ate into your bones.

'By Christ!' said Fitzalan. 'The old fox kept this well-hidden. He never once mentioned it to me.'

Tamkin placed the torch in the single wall bracket and looked about him in amazement. The chests with their heavy ironwork: the flaps, the bars, the bands and plates, the hanging locks with hidden keyholes, and the loops and pins and lengths of chain, seemed somehow insignificant compared to those of my nightmares. As a child I had wondered how they opened and what might be hidden inside. My mother had chests for her robes, but not like these. My mother's chests were roped when full and carried to the wagons but I never saw any of these chests bumping along the road to our other homes at Lewes and Reigate.

After some fumbling with the keys on Fitzalan's belt, up went the lid of the first chest.

'Oh, mercy!' gasped Joan.

She slid her hand into the thousands of dull gold coins which filled the chest to the very brim.

'By the saints!' Fitzalan was almost lost for words.

'A fortune,' said Tamkin.

The last time I had barely been able to peep over the edge of the chest and had not understood the significance of what I'd seen. Now I could sit on the lid if I wished and most certainly knew the value of the contents.

Two more chests and a sack opened: gold plate, cups, bowls, silverware, a jewelled crucifix and yet more coins.

'A prince's ransom,' murmured Joan, letting the coins trickle through her fingers. 'I wonder where it came from?'

By the time we reached the last chest and unroped the final canvas sack, we'd still found no sign of any documents and I was losing faith. They were not here. I was mistaken.

Tamkin rifled through the remaining gold and silver plate and shook his head. 'Nothing.'

'I knew it,' spat Fitzalan.

''Wait! What's that?'

Joan pointed to a small wooden coffer, squeezed against the wall and almost hidden from sight by two larger chests. It was easy to miss in the gloom. Faced with the quantity of other treasure, a man in a hurry would not have noticed the little wooden box.

With much difficulty, because the coffer was wedged tightly, my brothers pulled it out. The keyhole was tiny but Fitzalan had a key on his ring which slid in surprisingly easily.

We craned our necks as he lifted the lid. The rolled documents lay inside, neatly piled one on top of another, almost filling the coffer. They were unsullied with not a single speck of dust to be seen.

Fitzalan picked up the first one and it was quickly apparent that we'd found what we were looking for. It was a thick page of the softest parchment, beautifully illuminated; at the top in flowing letters of red and gold: "*Clemens, Episcopus, Servus Servorum Dei.*"

'Clement, Bishop, Servant of the Servants of God,' I whispered, in awe of the words and the man for whom they were once written. 'It is from the Holy Father that was.'

Tamkin, as the only one of us fluent in the reading of Latin, quickly translated.

'The marriage between Richard, late the son of Edmund, earl of Arundel and Isabel, late the daughter of Hugh le Despenser, knight of the diocese of Hereford, having taken place when the said Richard and the said Isabel were not of an age to consent, and the said Richard and the said Isabel having at the age of puberty expressly renounced their vows, the later consummation of that marriage, having taken place under duress, the said Richard being forced by blows to cohabit such that a son was conceived and born, is hereby declared to be null and void for lack of proper consent.'

'It was true.' Joan shook her head. 'It did happen.'

Fitzalan looked over Tamkin's shoulder. 'When was this written?'

Tamkin's eyes ran to the bottom of the page just above the corded metal seal.

'December. *Anno Domine* ... the year of our parents marriage.'

'Our mother got what she wanted,' I said quietly, half-wishing we'd not found the letter.

'There's more,' said Tamkin. 'The bull refers to six manors having previously been settled on the said Isabel for the term of her life and in addition, provision to be made for the son of the said Richard and the said Isabel born out of wedlock.'

'The Despenser woman and her brat couldn't complain of shabby treatment, could they?' said Fitzalan. 'Not

89

exactly cast out into the wilderness as the princess would have us believe. A reasonable settlement.'

'Do you think so?' Joan looked as bleak as I felt.

Was it really this easy for a man to rid himself of an unwanted wife? He may have been my father but he had not treated this woman well.

My brothers had their heads together, examining the rest of the contents.

'These are grants of property,' said Tamkin. 'The manor of High Rothyng, to Isabel, late the daughter of Hugh le Despenser, knight … for the duration of her life … and the reversion …'

'And this one?' said Fitzalan thrusting a bulky roll at Tamkin.

'Prittlewell near Great Wakering.'

'And this?'

'Ovesham in Matching.'

Tamkin ran his eyes over the remaining documents. 'Six manors, all in the county of Essex, just as the papal bull said. Granted for life to Isabel, late the daughter of Hugh le Despenser, the reversion to Richard, earl of Arundel or his heirs upon her death.'

'And the son?'

Tamkin picked up the next roll and began to scrutinise the contents. To me this looked like another papal bull, the same flowery script and corded seal.

'A dispensation for the marriage of Richard, earl of Arundel and Eleanor, daughter of Henry, earl of Lancaster, and late the wife of John Beaumont, knight. Ah! I understand. It seems our mother and the Despenser woman had common kin. The Church will have ruled that

that our parents needed the Holy Father's permission to marry.'

'But why? If the marriage was annulled, why a dispensation?'

'It made no difference. Our father and the Despenser woman may not have had a valid marriage but they had been *contracted* to marry and there had been a son. See here where it says ...'

'Is this usual?' I asked. 'Was it to do with their peculiar circumstance?'

'Not really,' said Tamkin, placing the document back on the pile. 'Everyone is somebody's cousin or their great-aunt's daughter's half-sister's son and people are not only related in the temporal world but also in the spiritual one. If a man stands Godfather to a woman's child of a previous marriage, the Church regards the man and woman as kin. It is a tangle. The difficulty for any couple wishing to marry is to ensure they have discovered all their common kin otherwise the marriage could be set aside later for want of a papal dispensation.'

'And it is a good way for the Holy Father to gather money to himself,' said Joan.

'It is nothing of the sort,' said Tamkin. 'You are beginning to sound like one of those Lollards. I should mind your tongue, sister. Pope Gregory has a special hatred for heretics.'

'Ay,' said Fitzalan. 'He burns them. Women as well as men.'

The rest of the documents in the coffer were letters from the king agreeing to various grants of land to the son, born out of wedlock, of Richard. earl of Arundel; receipts for payments made to the king's treasurer; and a letter from someone signing himself "*Willelmus de Monte Acuto, Comitis Sarisbiriensis*" agreeing to the proposed marriage of the writer's daughter, Sibyl, to the son, of Richard, earl of Arundel. There was also a copy of the contract for this marriage which showed that my father had made a substantial payment as a jointure for the young couple.

Lying at the bottom of the coffer was a letter dated some years after our parents' marriage. It came from William Bateman, bishop of Norwich, informing my father that a petition had of recent been presented to the Holy Father by a man calling himself the son of the earl of Arundel. The man protested that the annulment of his father's marriage to his mother, named as Isabel, late the daughter of Hugh le Despenser, had been surreptitiously obtained. The bishop assured my father that he need not worry; nothing would come of the matter and it would conveniently disappear.

Tamkin placed the letter on top of the others.

'You understand what this means, don't you?'

Fitzalan got up and dusted his knees. 'It means we won't be troubled by this churl who pretends to be our father's lawful son. He is nothing but a bastard.'

'You assume too much, Fitz.'

'What if the son tries again now that our father's dead?' I said.

'The Holy Father is hardly going to change his mind on the matter,' laughed Fitzalan. 'These documents are our protection against any claim.'

'Don't you see?' said Tamkin, piling the parchment rolls back into the coffer. 'That is just the point. It was

Clement who granted the annulment and he's long gone. Pope Gregory might think differently. He might be persuaded to reverse Clement's decision on our father's first marriage,'

'He can't do that,' Fitzalan protested. 'It would be against the law. If a man receives justice, the matter is finished. The evidence has been examined and a verdict given. Pope or no pope, the Holy Father cannot reopen the case.'

'Oh but he can,' said Tamkin. 'The Holy Father may say he is a "servant of the servants of God" but in truth he is all-powerful. He has the authority to look at any decision made by his predecessors and rule that it was wrong. Gregory may be Clement's nephew but he is cut from a harsher cloth. If he is of a mind to reinstate this son of our father and nullify the previous bull which Clement issued then that is exactly what he will do. And what do you think that will do to all of us?'

Joan looked at me with terror in her eyes, unable to speak.

'What will it do?' Fitzalan had not as yet moved beyond the loss of his title. He hadn't realised the full horror of what could lie ahead.

'If this son is legitimate it will mean that when our father married our mother, theirs was an invalid marriage. He was already contracted to another woman.' Tamkin looked at each one of us to make certain we understood.

'But the king and queen attended their wedding. Our mother told us.' Joan looked as if she would start weeping any moment. 'How could it be invalid?'

Tamkin took her hands. 'You understand what constitutes an annulment?'

She shook her head.

93

'An annulment means that the marriage was void *ab initio*, from the very beginning. It never was a marriage. It didn't exist. Hence any child born to the couple will have been conceived and born out of wedlock and therefore is illegitimate.'

Joan frowned. 'Yes, I understand that.'

Tamkin looked uneasy. 'But if Pope Gregory reverses the annulment, the Despenser woman's son becomes our father's legitimate son and we become the offspring of an invalid marriage. Our parents were not validly married and therefore we are bastards.'

Nobody spoke. There was a long horrified silence in which all I could hear was the thudding beats of my heart. If I was a bastard no-one would recognise me. And what would Thomas say?

'But our parents had a dispensation,' protested Joan.

'The dispensation is useless if our father already had a wife. No wonder our father's other son claimed the annulment was obtained surreptitiously. Those excuses our father gave would not bear much scrutiny. The annulment was dubious. Even I can see that.'

'Well I can't,' said Fitzalan stubbornly.

'It's not a question of what *you* see, Fitz. It's a matter for the Holy Father and his cardinals.'

'Perhaps the Despenser woman's son will not do anything,' I said weakly, trying to find a straw to clutch.

Tamkin closed the lid of the coffer. 'I wouldn't count on it.'

For the next two days my brothers were busy with the necessary business following the death of a great man like my father. Messengers in black livery were dispatched through the snowy countryside to the king at Havering-atte-Bower, to the prince at Kennington and to the king's officials at Westminster. Word would be sent from Westminster to the duke and to the earl of Cambridge who were in Bruges.

Tamkin sent men to our father's neighbours and letters to the stewards at Reigate, Lewes and our Shropshire manors, telling them the sad news. Fitzalan, meanwhile, was dealing with arrangements for the funeral and, as Joan doubted he had thought of the women, she sent word to his wife Lizzie, to Jack's wife in Dorset, and to our father's sister, Aunt Latimer. I, with little else to occupy my time, penned a private note to the princess which went with the dispatch to Kennington. I thought to write to my husband but could think of nothing to say.

Late on Thursday evening, when Joan and I had finished the unhappy task of sorting the last of my mother's clothing which my father had kept in a chest in his bedchamber, I wandered off in search of Tamkin. I had decided to leave for Woking next morning and wanted to know if he would arrange an escort for me. I found him checking an inventory.

'What's to do, Alys?'

I smiled and sat down beside him. When he wasn't playing the bishop, I found Tamkin pleasant company and was fond of him. Our shared years together in the nursery had forged a bond which was stouter than most. I never felt as close to Fitzalan or Jack as I did to Tamkin.

'I thought to leave for Woking tomorrow.'

'Sensible.'

I picked up a weighty-looking document.

'Is this it?'

'Yes. Our father's final wishes. Edward St John brought it to me; he had it in safekeeping.'

I tried to read the words but my Latin was not good enough so I handed it back to Tamkin.

'You are to get his third best coronet.'

I gave a hollow laugh. 'I doubt that will be of much use to me. Eleven years of marriage and I am still plain Lady Holand. '

'Patience, Alys.'

'It is all very well for you to preach patience. You were made a bishop in the cradle whereas I despair of Thomas getting his earldom.'

Tamkin returned to his study of our father's will and testament.

'In death he wishes to be buried next to our mother. And look!' He pointed to the bottom just above the wavering signature of a man who must have known he was dying. 'He says to his executors, "Be good to my children".'

At that I started to weep. As I rubbed away the hot tears with my fingers, I didn't know if I was crying for my father or my mother or for those of us they'd left behind to deal with the legacy of their shabby dealings.

Tamkin put his arm round me and pulled my head down onto his shoulder.

'Don't cry. When I return to Westminster I shall find out what I can. There is nothing to worry about. This man may not even be alive. And if he is, he's well gone into his middle years. Perhaps he won't make trouble.'

'But if he does?' I sniffed miserably.

'Then we'll meet it together.'

He placed a brotherly peck on my cheek and patted my arm. 'Go to bed, Alys. Say your prayers and forget all this. Go back to Woking tomorrow and leave everything to me.'

7

COUSIN PHILIPPA 1376

A heavy snowfall shortly after my return created ripples of anxiety throughout the household. Drifts blocked the track to our neighbour's house and wherever we looked, ghostly white mounds of snow obliterated traces of once familiar fields and hedgerows.

This year we had prepared ourselves as if for a war siege but before we fell to eating the rats and the horses, an early thaw set in. An unfrozen bowl of water and a slight breeze blowing from the west were the first signs of better times. By noon the eaves were dripping. Within days the Wey breached its banks, rushing floodwaters washing away two forgotten eel traps and the old rickety bridge near the priory. But after a week all was returned to how it had been before and the snow and its aftermath, just unpleasant memories.

In the solar five of us gathered around a sulky fire, trying to ignore the seeping damp and secretly rubbing our chilled fingers beneath our covering sleeves. The maids dutifully poked needles in and out of a pile of torn household napery, a task I hated and which I'd been happy to pass to someone else. Lying across my knee was a new gown for Nell, cut from one of my mother's old skirts. It was very plain but with a little left-over silk thread and some careful thought I had managed to embroider a pattern of tiny leaves along the hem.

I dreamed of warm days, of primroses peeping out from under hedgerows and of a haze of bluebells filling the woods. This spring I would take my daughter along the path to Fox Hill and show her how to place one of the tiny blue thimbles on her thumb, close her eyes and make a wish.

To my cousin Blanche, the bluebell was the flower of humility and constancy but to my one-time friend Amy Melbourne it was something much darker. Every May Day Eve she would place a single flower beneath her pillow, telling us girls that magic woven by the fairies would reveal her husband-to-be as she slept. One year I tried it for myself. All night long I dreamed of Edmund. But the magic was malign, as I should have guessed. Before the bluebells came again I found myself married to Thomas.

I glanced in despair at the girl sitting next to me whose crooked stitches would have disgraced a five year-old. I had taken her into my household at the request of a neighbour. She was a lumpish child of eight with fair hair and a pale face, heiress to her late father's single manor and greatly in need of polishing. Her mother, who had recently embarked on a second marriage, was only too glad to be rid of the girl and after two weeks spent in my household I could understand why.

We were singing a familiar song which required little skill or attention when we heard the sound of a horseman in the yard. The girl jumped up and clambered up to the window to peer outside. She rubbed the tiny pane of glass which was misted but, in her haste, failed to see who it was.

'Sit down,' I reprimanded. 'A lady waits quietly for some man to tell her who has arrived. She does not prance around like a lamb in springtime.'

The girl scowled but obediently returned to her seat and bent her head to her stitching.

We did not have long to wait. From beyond the door came the solid clomp of a pair of heavy boots and within moments our steward appeared, out of breath from climbing the stairs.

'The countess of March is fast approaching and seeking shelter, my lady.'

Philippa! Now, what did she want? My cousin never did anything without careful planning so this was certainly no casual passing by. The last I'd heard, she was at Usk having been safely delivered of another daughter. I had sent a note of congratulation but the loss of my own child was too raw for me to do more. She was, I presumed, on her way to join Edmund in London, unless he too was passing by.

'Is the earl expected?' I tried not to sound eager but my heart skittered at the thought of Edmund, here at Woking, under my roof.

'I do not think so, my lady. I was told it was the countess.'

'How many in the company?'

When he told me the number, I did wonder how we would manage to feed them but of course Philippa, as countess of March, would travel in style and could hardly be expected to arrive with just two old men, a girl and a broken-down hackney.

'Warn the kitchen. The Lenten fast is still a month away so they will expect meat. Make sure the cook has sufficient spices and bring out the best wine for the countess. And send up a boy with more logs.'

I looked down at the skirts of my dark wool gown, worn as a tribute to my dead father. I considered having my maid lay out fresh clothes but decided a battle of brocades and damasks with Philippa was not worth the effort. I did, however, call for my best slippers.

'Cousin,' I said, smiling warmly.

Philippa greeted me, her eyes measuring the quality of my hangings and estimating the value of the silverware on display before she was half-way across the hall.

'It is very cosy,' she said. She meant small.

'We think so.'

'Of course our hall at Usk is enormous and vastly impressive. Do you not find this room rather dark? The ceiling is very low.'

She brushed her hand across the board, pretending to examine Thomas's silver bowl but most likely looking for evidence of dust and grime. With practised ease she swirled her magnificent fur-lined riding cloak round her skirts so that the velvet billowed in deep green waves, then treated me to a small triumphant smile.

Whatever test she had prepared for me, I knew I had failed.

'Let me take you to the solar,' I said smoothly. 'You will find it more to your liking and it is not horribly draughty the way castle rooms can be. You must take refreshment. We have some fine wine from Bordeaux.'

Once she had divested herself of her cloak and had her fingers washed, Philippa regarded my plain dark gown with interest.

'Has somebody died?'

'My father, God rest his soul.'

Her hand flew to her mouth. 'When?'

'Three weeks past.'

'Oh Alys, I am sorry. I know what it is like to lose a father. I was hardly more than a child when mine died. I barely knew him. We are so very alone when our parents are gone, I more than you as I have no brothers or sisters to fill the void.'

'I thank you, cousin, your prayers are welcome.'

'This winter cold is dangerous for the old. It weakens their resolve and lays them open to all kinds of ills. I worry for my grandmother shut away in her convent. I hear she is very frail.'

'I doubt my father was frail, merely tired of this life and missing my mother. I am sure God's command was welcome. I know he made a good death.'

While sipping her wine, which she had sniffed carefully before tasting, Philippa's eyes roamed around the solar, noting the still-smouldering fire, the plain wooden settle and the bare painted walls where I had only two hangings. As if to emphasise what she saw as a lack of material comfort, she shifted restlessly in her chair and I cursed myself for not offering her a cushion. At the far end of the room the huddle of my curious women, supposedly occupied with their sewing, kept staring at the elegant visitor in her extravagant clothing. I was unsure whether to reprimand them or not.

Instead I called for the children to be brought. I thought it might be entertaining to watch Philippa compare them to her own and doubtless find mine wanting in some degree. But to my amazement she was tender with them.

'Gweetings, m'lady,' piped Nell, grasping the skirts of her gown and giving a bob in the way she'd been taught.

'Sweet,' murmured Philippa. 'Like a little songbird. My Elisabeth must be a year younger but let us hope they will be friends as you and I are.'

'I hope so too, cousin,' I said, warming to Philippa. Perhaps I had misjudged her. 'And this is Tom. He is barely four.'

My son let go of his nursemaid's hand and regarded this brightly-dressed woman he didn't know with a straight gaze, just like his father's. He was a brave child and for once his thumb wasn't stuck in his mouth. 'Lady,' he pronounced. He was not a great talker, unlike his sister who insisted on speaking for him.

Philippa surprised me by calling the children to her knee and talking in words they could understand. She patted Nell's head, calling her a good girl and when she stoked the soft skin of Tom's cheek, he rewarded her with a big smile and another 'Lady.'

She looked regretful as the children were taken back to the nursery. 'Your Tom has that sweet baby smell and hair like soft down. I would have the older two with me but I leave them at Usk because Edmund fears for their safety in the city. There is so much sickness, even in the winter months. And Roger is particularly precious.'

'Naturally,' I agreed. 'As your husband's heir he will always be most precious.'

Philippa looked round to see who was listening but by now the others had their heads bent to their sewing, allowing us some privacy. 'Have you had word of my uncle, the prince? I hear he is close to death,' she said softly.

'He was a little recovered at Christmas but mostly he lies in his bed or in a litter, too weak to stand or even sit,' I said.

'Is there no hope?'

'We pray for a miracle.'

'But it is slow in coming.'

'Indeed.'

'And young Richard – he is well?'

'In good health.'

Philippa demurred. 'I thought him a fragile child, such pale skin and so very slender; a strong puff of wind might blow him away. I have heard he is not strong.' She paused, arching her eyebrows enquiringly. 'Perhaps some blight?'

'Blight?'

Philippa shrugged. 'You know how people love to gossip.'

There was clearly a piece of information Philippa wished to impart but was holding just out of reach, hoping to make me beg.

'What are people saying?'

She glanced at my women once more and lowered her voice still further.

'I should pay no attention. I am sure it is nothing. There are some who love a scandal and if there is not one to be had they will twist a man's words until they have invented one.' She smiled blandly. 'When I was told, I refused to believe such a monstrous accusation. I said it was a nonsense and doubtless came out of a quayside tavern. You know how men with nothing better to do, gossip about their betters. If I believed half the tales I was told …' She gave a little laugh. 'But you know what they say about smoke? Silly really, smoke and fire.'

'What is the story?' I said wearily, wondering why Philippa made such a mystery out of every bit of tittle-tattle she heard.

'No, it would be wrong to repeat ill of her in this way. It is not as if it could be true.'

'Ill of whom?'

'You promise not to tell? I would not want her to think I'd give credence to such a pack of lies. But you never know, do you? I've always thought her a wonderful woman. As a child I was taught to revere her.'

'Who are you talking about, cousin?'

'Why the princess of course.'

It was odd the way the princess's name surfaced in every mystery which floated past. I was still trying to puzzle out what it was that had eluded me about her marriage to Thomas's father. There was something not right in what I'd been told but I was unable to fathom out what it was.

'What have you heard, cousin? Whatever it is I very much doubt it is true.'

Philippa rose from her seat and pulled me by the arm. 'Come over here. I cannot say such a thing so close to your women. They might hear. Maids have ears like priests in the confessional when it comes to secrets. One little whisper and they know every thought in your head. Come by the chest.'

I obliged her but felt foolish hiding in the corner. She stood on tip-toe because she was smaller than me and whispered, 'The Holy Father intends to proclaim young Richard a bastard.'

'What!'

The others looked round in alarm at my raised voice and Philippa clutched my arm. 'Shush! Keep quiet! No-one must know. My husband had it from a man who'd been in Bruges.'

'I don't believe a word of it.'

'The man swore it was true. He heard it from a Frenchman who served the bishop of Amiens.'

'A Frenchman? It's a nonsense.'

'But what if it's true? What if the boy *is* illegitimate?'

I laughed nervously, thinking of the secrets we'd discovered at Arundel.

'It is impossible.'

'Is it?'

'You know it is. Do you imagine the prince fathered a child on some Gascon woman?'

'It is nothing like that.'

'So what is it? Did the princess lie with a lover unbeknown to her husband? Because if that is what is being said I can tell you most definitely it is not true. She would never commit such a sin.'

'That is not what is being said.'

'So what *is* being said?'

'The marriage is unsound. She is not the prince's wife.'

I felt the cold slap in my face as the past jumped into the present.

I chose my words carefully. 'I was there, cousin. I saw them married.'

'That is what is so odd. They were married in front of witnesses so how could she not be his wife?'

'You should not pay heed to this kind of nonsense. You do see it is nonsense, don't you?'

Philippa looked up through her lashes, a trick she'd perfected as a girl and now used to great advantage. It made her look vulnerable and from what my friends said, eminently desirable to men.

'It could be so,' she said quietly.

'No it could not.'

I felt a quivering inside. I knew that long-buried secrets were best left alone, not dug up into the unforgiving light of day. But Philippa was like a dog with a fresh meaty bone, one she refused to abandon.

'If the Holy Father says there is a defect in their marriage, what do you imagine it could be?' she asked.

'There is no defect. The prince and princess have been married for fourteen years and there has not been the slightest breath of scandal concerning their life together. I am afraid your man in Bruges is mistaken. Besides, what would anyone gain by making such a claim?'

Philippa opened her eyes wide and smiled.

'The king, the prince and then who? Richard? A child with a dubious claim?'

'By the Virgin, cousin! Stop there! Say nothing else. You are close to talking treason.'

Philippa put her head on one side and regarded me coolly.

'Perhaps you should warn your husband, Alys. It may be time to consider whether keeping close to his half-brother is the wisest of choices.'

Fortunately at that moment, the steward announced the household was assembled for supper. I was able to cloak my astonishment with the politeness required of me as lady of the house.

I escorted Philippa down to the hall and sat her on my left, leaving Thomas's chair empty. All through what seemed an interminable meal we made conversation but said nothing of any importance. We discussed the drought of last summer and the scandalous appearance of Dame Alice Perrers at the Smithfield tournament wearing the late queen's jewels. At last it was time for some music.

While my minstrels played a tune I'd brought back from Berkhamsted there was ample opportunity to consider my cousin. Philippa was not all she seemed: proud of her position as the king's eldest grandchild and devoted to the memory of her father, Duke Lionel; seemingly meek and mild like a springtime morning but overtly triumphant when she married Edmund, knowing I had wanted him. She was slyly ambitious; every bit as ambitious for Edmund as I was for Thomas and seemingly far more successful.

'You won't say anything, will you, cousin?' she'd said as we'd walked down the stairs to supper together. 'Don't tell Aunt Wake. She lectures me on the sin of gossiping. I am a married woman with three children but she treats me as if I was five years old.'

Philippa was not careless and never said anything she didn't mean to say so why mention Aunt Wake?

Our aunt had a hundred tales from the past: the beautiful lady who failed to capture her husband's heart because of his infatuation with a man he called his brother; the nobleman who escaped through walls forty feet thick and flew through the air like a raven; the king who lived on after death, walking the pilgrim ways in atonement for his sins; and the queen who abandoned duty for love and lived to pay the price. She told us of a long-ago king who'd hanged his wife's lovers from the bed rails and of the wily baron who'd raised a rebellion and tried to steal a crown. Aunt Wake knew everyone's secrets. I wondered if she knew the princess's and … Oh mercy! Did she know my mother's?

Next day, Philippa, played her role as the grand lady magnificently, thanking me for my hospitality and hoping we would meet at Windsor for the St George's Day celebrations. As her cavalcade rode off in the direction of London, I wondered why she'd come. Was it to find out what I knew or was she giving me a warning? She had not come simply to pass on gossip, of that I was certain. It was far more likely she was searching for information. If she wanted to discover something about the princess's marriage, who better to ask than her dearest cousin, Alys.

What did I know of the princess's two marriages? Aunt Wake had said the princess married the dreadful Thomas Holand when she was little more than a girl – twelve years old she'd said. The princess herself told me she'd waited ten long years for a child. Yet Thomas said his mother was married in the time of the great pestilence and he had been born the following year. However hard I tried I could not reconcile these three statements. Someone was lying.

The pestilence came after the king's victory at Crécy. The old men said It was brought by the French hostages who'd filled the king's houses. Crécy, as every child knew, was fought in the twentieth year of the king's reign. Maud said her mother had been born in the first year of the king's reign, nearly fifty years ago, twenty years before Crécy.

There was deliberate deception here but why and by whom? Why was Philippa so interested in the princess's marriage? And what was it that Aunt Wake knew?

It was a cold day when we buried our father. We placed his body beneath the paved floor of the Benedictine priory church at Lewes next to our mother just as he had asked. I had not realised how strong was the bond they'd forged that day at Walsingham until I saw him destroyed by her death. Since losing her, the passing of each season brought him renewed suffering.

I watched as his body was carried in procession from the castle chapel to the priory church where he would rest for eternity next to the woman he had so dearly loved. As my brothers made their slow way down the hill behind the black-draped coffin, rain swept in from the west, drenching the black silks and drooping plumes of the horses, soaking the thousands of mourners who stood heads bowed in silence, and running in rivulets into ditches all the way down to the Cockshut stream. It was as if all Heaven wept for my father yet the seas were not filled no matter how many tears were shed.

It was in the aftermath of this sadness when I couldn't stop weeping that Thomas told me he'd been honoured by the king. He sat me down beside the fire and explained how he was to become a member of the king's most noble order of chivalry, a garter knight. At first I couldn't believe what he was saying. I had waited such a long time and been so often disappointed in him. I'd thought I was married to a man who would never make progress and would for ever be left languishing in some dusty forgotten corner, unnoticed, unappreciated and unrewarded. Wealth and glory would pass him by because he wouldn't make the necessary effort.

'A garter knight?' I smiled through my tears.

'Yes. Along with brother-in-law Britto and one of your Percy cousins.'

'Oh Thomas.' I put my hand up to his face and stroked his cheek, noticing with surprise how smooth his skin was: no nicks, no cuts, a sure sweep with the razor.

He captured my hand in his and brought it slowly to his mouth. The heat of his lips scorched my upturned palm and from somewhere I felt the faintest of flutters within my belly.

'You are pleased?' he asked gently.

How could he think I would not be pleased? He would be one of only twenty-four specially chosen men to join with the king and the prince each St George's Day, to celebrate and honour the saint under whose emblem they fought. The duke and the earl of Cambridge were members of the order but my own father had never been honoured and neither had Edmund.

This was a wonderful gift and I found myself suffused with joy. I wound my arms around my husband's neck, wanting to show how proud of him I was, how happy he had made me. He started in surprise as I pressed myself carefully against his chest and grazed my mouth against his. I kissed him once, twice and smiled as his lips slowly parted against mine.

'Alys?'

'Hush,' I murmured and kissed him again.

He sighed and I felt him begin to quiver beneath my touch.

I was not vain and shallow like Philippa, but a man who was a member of the most noble order of chivalry would surely be considered worthy to receive his title. It was probable that at this very moment arrangements were being made and documents drawn up. A lengthy list of manors to add to our three in Yorkshire, and the princess would yield up beautiful moated Castle Donington in Leicestershire where we could take the children. We would make the splendid castle overlooking the river, our main home, spend our summers there. We would bid farewell to the smoky solar and low-ceilinged hall at Woking and visit only occasionally – perhaps in springtime to see the bluebells flowering. Or Thomas might lease it to someone else, a man who wished to be his friend. There was so much we could achieve once we were rich.

As my husband tightened his grip on my waist and whispered nonsense into my hair, I knew it could only be a matter of a few weeks before I was countess of Kent. I would take my rightful place amongst the other noble ladies at court, women such as Duchess Constanza, my sister Joan, and Lady Coucy, the king's daughter. Everything my mother had promised me on that long ago day in her garden at Arundel would finally come true.

The St George's day celebrations at Windsor were every bit as magnificent as I had imagined but the gossip was lewd, almost treasonous at times. Nearby was a group of wives from the shires who knew nothing about how women should dress. Their gowns had been fashionable some years ago: too high at the neck, loose with belts round the waist instead of slung low on the hips. None of them had bothered to pluck their eyebrows and their hair was in a style favoured by the late queen, wound round their ears like a ram's horn. I wondered which of their neighbours they were dissecting with such undisguised glee.

'Poor lady. Most cruelly used.'

'Shut away while he rides around with his whore.'

'My cousin says she's utterly shameless. You can practically see her duckies.'

'No!'

'Yes. She has one of those new-fangled corsets, pushes them over the top of her gown. And she wears fox tails attached to her buttocks!'

'I'd not know where to look.'

'I'll wager your husband would.'

Gales of coarse laughter ensued.

'My cousin heard he took her with him to visit the king.'

Eyes widened and mouths dropped open as I realised who they were discussing: Lady Swynford.

'You'd never think great folk'd behave like that and them thinking themselves so grand.'

'Those set above us think themselves untouchable.'

'My cousin's husband says the fornicator reckons to climb higher still.'

'Higher?'

'Shush!' The heads moved closer together and I could no longer hear what they were saying.

Joan pulled on my sleeve. 'By the time those old crows have finished, Lady Swynford will have no reputation left. It's hard to know who they despise more: her or the duke. I'd not fancy the chances of either of them trying to ride through the streets of London at the moment. Crowds can turn ugly when they're roused and Londoners loved the Lady Blanche. The duke is a clever man so why does he continue to keep such a woman?'

'Perhaps he loves her.'

Joan laughed. 'Oh Alys! When will you learn? Love between a man and a woman exists only in stories. In this world there is only lust and marriage. Nothing else.'

'What about our parents? They loved each other.'

Joan took my hands in hers. 'You think so? Lust, greed, calculation and impatience. And when lust waned – liking, respect and duty. What more can any man and woman expect from marriage?'

'If marriage it was,' I murmured.

Joan glanced round, making sure no-one was listening. 'Tamkin says the Despenser woman is dead.'

'Is he certain?'

'He said if we were inclined we could dig up her bones from beneath the chapter house floor of the Austin Friars in Broad Street.'

I felt a wash of relief.

'And the son?'

'Fitzalan has sent his men to take possession of the manors in Essex.'

'So the son is alive?'

'Protected by his mother's Despenser kin, it seems.' Joan gave a bright smile. 'Now, little sister, forget our troubles. Today is for celebration. Let us enjoy ourselves.'

After three frenzied days the celebrations were over. Summonses had been received for the king's parliament which was to meet at Westminster before the end of the month and as this was the first parliament for nearly three years, no-one could afford to be absent.

A low morning mist hung over the wharf, hovering a hand's breadth above the wooden boards, as I embarked onto the princess's barge for our journey downriver. The brilliant sunshine of the last few days had disappeared and it would be a chilly journey to London. I was glad of my cloak with its lambswool lining and hood trimmed with squirrel fur.

Maud's conversation trailed away on the damp air, lost in the swirling grey waters sweeping in our wake, but it was of no matter for her words were inconsequential: 'A young man of good birth. He glances over his shoulder at me. Oh Alys, he is so handsome.'

I wasn't listening, preferring instead the hushed exchange between the princess and Eleanor. Theirs was a theological discussion on the nature of sin and forgiveness and I wanted to hear the princess's thoughts. I already knew Eleanor's. Every argument with her ended the same way. She would cast aside all bishops, throw them from their palaces and cleanse the pathway to God. To Eleanor and those like her, clerics who profited from their positions, men such as my brother and the wealthy bishop of Winchester, men who grew fat on the superstitious fears of rich and poor alike, were to be despised. In private, she denied Pope Gregory as father of the princes of Christendom and was, I thought, in the gravest danger of being branded a heretic.

Today the dispute turned on the prince's sickness and how it was that no amount of prayer and supplication in any form had pleased God to alleviate his continued suffering. The question was the same as the one Joan had posed that cold morning in the chapel at Arundel – are our voices heard or are they lost in vastness of the void?

'He is of the Royal House of Luxembourg.'

I turned my head.

'Luxembourg?'

'Count of Ligny and St Pol,' Maud sighed.

Her prattling was endless: one of the king's hostages, captured near Calais, sent to England. no notion as to how his ransom would be paid. But his smile. 'Oh Alys, if only you could see his smile.'

The day grew warmer and I began to recognise familiar landmarks: the great London stone on the riverbank at Staines, the tiny huddled rooftops marking the village at the mouth of the Wey, the pretty chapel at Kingstown and, by mid-afternoon, the royal manor house at Sheen.

And still the princess anguished.

'Some say it is punishment for what happened at Limoges but that I cannot believe.'

Eleanor's words were soothing. 'Nor should you. The prince did what was necessary and God gave his approval.'

'I worry for Richard. He is too young to take his father's place.'

'There is still time. And you will not be alone. There will be help in carrying the burden. The prince will have made provision.'

'But what if …?'

Maud touched my arm. 'I *shall* marry him. I am quite determined.'

Ahead of us the familiar walls of the king's palace at Westminster shimmered rosy and gold in the reflected light of early evening and I wondered for the hundredth time that day how Maud could be so stupid as to fall in love. It would not please the king to have his son's stepdaughter embroiled with one of his prisoners and if a new husband was not found for her by the end of the year she might take matters into her own hands. And what would happen then?

Thomas was waiting for me at Coldharbour. After the solemn ceremonies at Windsor and his ignominious performance at the tournament afterwards when he'd been unhorsed by his brother-in-law, he had gone straight back to London. He said he wished to make the house ready for my arrival.

'You are not too weary to welcome your first guests?' he enquired as he escorted me into the hall.

My heart sank. I had no appetite to see anyone. My ears were still ringing from Maud's insistent chattering and the princess's mournful predictions of what was to come. Besides, who would be so thoughtless as to visit so late in the day? – his brother no doubt. Who else could it be?

My husband gave me a small smile, took hold of my shoulders and turned me round. 'See!'

Standing in the shadows at the edge of the hall were my two sleepy children: Tom grinning with pleasure at this unexpected evening treat and Nell in nightgown and cap, her dark curls peeping out, and her little slippered feet.

I knelt on the floor and Nell came running into my arms.

'I sent for them before I left Windsor,' said Thomas. 'I knew it would please you.'

8

AUNT WAKE 1376

After three weeks of waiting, the man I had sent to discover the whereabouts of my aunt, returned with news. The dowager Lady Wake, he reported, had quit her home at Bourne complaining of damp seeping into her bones. She had removed herself and her household to London. The steward left to care for the castle said it was the stench of the privy pits which had driven the noble lady away; either that or the east wind off the marshes which was something cruel this year. The lady, he confided, had leased a residence in the outer precincts of the house of the Grace of the Blessed Mary outside Aldgate, professing a desire for proximity to the religious life of the nuns. But his informant thought it more likely the noble lady was missing London gossip.

For two days I pondered over what to do. Eventually I decided to write a simple note stating my intention to visit. Next afternoon, dressed in a suitably sober gown and together with one of my women and an escort of two well-armed men, I made my way through the crowded streets towards Cornhill, along Leadenhall Street and out under Aldgate.

To my left, amidst a patch of green, was an ancient church where a small knot of people were gathering. To my right, bathed in the soft spring sunshine of late May, were the mellow walls and rooftops of what must be the house of the Grace of the Blessed Mary. This was the home of the Minoresses, sisters of the order of the Grey Friars, dedicated to poverty and holiness. Near the convent gate, a striped cat pursued its solitary business, padding silently along the top of the wall, oblivious to our presence but causing calls of alarm from the branches of a nearby tree. We alerted the porter and, having instructed my escort to wait outside, I passed through the wicket gate into a small paved courtyard.

There was serenity here, next to the convent gardens, away from the stink and bustle of the city streets. I understood why Aunt Wake would prefer this peaceful retreat from the world to a grander house near the river. As an elderly woman concerned with her own salvation and that of her kin, she would wish to make her peace with God before she died. What better place could there be than here where she could enjoy the simplicity of a religious life and doze away her final days.

I made my formal greeting to the old lady who sat bolt upright in her chair but when I rose it was to an icy glare. 'You've taken your time, my girl.'

'Forgive me, my lady. It is but three Sundays since I arrived at our house and I have been occupied with my husband's affairs.'

'Is that so. No time for your mother's family? I suppose like the rest of 'em you're only here to ask questions. Why should I tell you girls anything, eh?'

Aunt Wake had become more crabbed and disagreeable with each passing year but it did no harm to flatter her a little.

'I only wish to ask your advice, my lady.'

'Advice eh?' A tear oozed out of the corner of her left eye and trickled down her parchment-like cheek onto her whiskery chin. 'One time everyone wanted my advice. Now all they want are my memories.'

She wiped away the tear with a cloth.

'How is that husband of yours?' she barked before I could speak. 'Made anything of him yet? Bad blood there but better than young Mortimer. Too ambitious, the Mortimers. Told my sister so. Don't give her to the Mortimer boy, I said.'

I found I was trembling. Had Aunt Wake interfered? Had my father been going to marry me to Edmund but instead had given me to Thomas?

'I would have been happy to marry Edmund Mortimer.'

'Happy? Don't be such a fool. Marriage is not designed for happiness. Marriage is duty – duty and loyalty. Happy? You're as foolish as that child, Philippa. Prattling away about her so-called royalty.'

I wanted to ask had Philippa been here before me but Aunt Wake was too busy reminiscing about Philippa's father, the king's second son.

'Giant of a man he was. Pretty face but no brains. Made a mess of his life. Couldn't cope with the Irish. The king made a mistake sending him. Thought he could do it but he couldn't. No perseverance. You remember that, my girl. Perseverance and loyalty, that is what's needed in a man.'

'Yes, my lady.'

'No-one believes in loyalty any more. Every man for himself, these days. The curse of the Mortimers. Follows father to son. Disloyalty and betrayal. The seeds of destruction. You remember that and do your duty.'

'Yes, my lady. I am aware of my duty both to my family and to my husband.'

She gave me an appraising look out of her sharp old eyes.

'So? Let us walk in the garden and you can tell me why you've come. As no-one comes for the pleasure of my company I presume there is something you want. Here, give me your arm.'

One of Aunt Wake's women came fussing, holding out a fur-lined cloak and wrapping a woollen cloth around my aunt's neck. There were ribbons to be tied and clasps to be fastened and a hissed conversation over the suitability of my aunt's shoes. When, at last, the old lady was ready we edged very slowly outside into a tiny courtyard garden where white-pebbled pathways formed a pleasing pattern between low box hedges. Nothing was in bloom but the air smelled sweet.

After a few steps Aunt Wake stopped, breathing heavily. 'Well? What is it? What d'you want?'

I spoke clearly. 'I have been given a secret and I do not know whether to tell my husband. I was told to counsel my lord to take a course of action which he would not otherwise take.'

My aunt looked amused.

'I would have thought you'd had your fill of secrets by now. I hear your brother has been poking around in the house of the Austin Friars.'

The warmth of embarrassment flooded into my face.

'You know?' I blurted out without thinking.

She jerked her head for me to move forward again.

'Of course I know. Would you think I wouldn't?'

'But how?'

'Your mother told me. Oh, not at the time, but later. She had this sin weighing heavily on her soul and lived in fear of God's retribution. I was her eldest sister. Who else would she come to but me?'

'She repented?'

Aunt Wake turned her creased old face to me and laughed. 'Not her. She regretted she'd not had the stomach to rid your father of the woman and the boy at the very beginning. Cursed her tender heart but knew it was too late to remedy the situation.'

'I cannot believe that of my mother,' I protested. 'She was a good woman.'

'And you think good women cannot do bad deeds? What a foolish child you are. I was born in the time of the first Edward and I have known many a good woman whose hands were stained with blood.'

'But she was my mother,' I cried. 'I knew her.'

'Oh child, child, we all carry the propensity to sin within ourselves. Evil beckons like a candle flame in the dark; seduces you with the promise of light and warmth but when you stretch out your hand there is nothing there but the pain of burned fingers and scorched sleeves. Like Our Saviour, your mother was tempted. But she was a daughter of Eve and had no strength to resist.'

I swallowed hard and tried not to think of my mother wanting to murder an innocent woman and her child. She would have planned how it could be done: cowbane, mandrake, monkshood, devil's herb; plants which could kill, yet grew innocently in the fields or in a woman's garden.

'Now,' said Aunt Wake more gently. 'What is it you have been counselled to tell your husband?'

'He should not cleave to his brother's side.'

Aunt Wake raised her eyebrows in surprise.

'The boy, Richard,' I added in case she thought I meant John Holand.

'Ah, yes. Pretty little milksop.'

'I do not understand. What does it mean?'

'What else was said?'

'The boy is not his father's trueborn son. He is not legitimate. There is a defect in the marriage.'

Aunt Wake did not look surprised. She regarded me calmly.

'And what do *you* think?'

'I cannot see why anyone would say such a thing. Who would spread such a malicious slander?'

There was a long silence.

'*Cui bono*?'

My Latin was not good but I understood the meaning: who benefits?

'Well?' said my aunt when I didn't reply.

I stumbled hesitantly over my words. 'If the boy is not trueborn, the prince has no legitimate son. If he has no legitimate son, everything will pass to his next brother when he dies.'

'And what is it that the prince possesses which is so desirable that a man might risk the salvation of his immortal soul to make his own?'

'He has great wealth.'

'What else?'

I shook my head.

'By the Blessed Virgin, child! Where are your wits? The throne! The prince is his father's heir. So ask yourself again: *Cui bono*?'

'The duke would take the crown?'

'You believe he would rob his brother's son?'

'No. He is a good man, loyal to his brother and to the princess. He would never do such a thing.'

'Even though we know good men can do bad things. But – *Cui bono*? Who else?'

I thought of Philippa at Woking – the king, the prince and then Richard, a child with a dubious claim. Those were the words she had spoken. If Philippa's father were alive he would come next after the prince, not the duke. The second son and Philippa his only child. And she, herself, had a son.

Aunt Wake smiled. 'I see you have remembered.'

'Is it possible? Surely a woman cannot take the crown?'

'Ask your brother. I hear the bishop is a great one for his books. I do not pretend to have the answer to such questions. I've seen three Edwards and thought to live to see a fourth but if it is not to be …' She shrugged her bony shoulders. 'A child on the throne will bring trouble and a woman even more so. If I were you I would counsel my husband to sharpen his sword and keep his wits about him.'

She grasped my arm. 'I was born into a time of bloodshed, child, but the third Edward has brought us peace. He has waged his battles beyond the seas while here we grow fat and idle on the profits of war. But it cannot last. Read the prophecies! Evil times are coming and it is best to be prepared.'

As we stepped back into the warmth of her rooms, she pressed my hand. 'Ask your husband to tell you about William Montagu.'

When I reached our house there was an unfamiliar horse in the yard.

'The master's brother, my lady,' said the groom who took my bridle.

This was unwelcome news. What did John Holand want?

When I walked into the hall he was lying flat on his back on top of a table, his arms folded behind his head.

'Sister!' he said propping himself up on one elbow.

'What are you doing?' I said sharply, not wanting him to imagine I welcomed his presence.

'Looking at your ceiling.'

'That is a ridiculous answer. Why would anyone spend their time looking at a ceiling?'

I'd not been alone with him since the day we'd visited Isabel and was annoyed to find myself discomforted by the memory.

John gave a lazy smile as if he knew what I was thinking. 'Edmund Mortimer says your ceilings are too low. He criticises the oppressive nature of your beams. I was wondering if it was true.'

I could feel the heat rise into my cheeks at his casual mention of Edmund.

'Edmund Mortimer has never, to my knowledge, set foot in any of our houses. He knows nothing about our ceilings.'

My brother-in-law rolled himself off the table and stumbled over to where I was standing, upsetting one of the benches on the way.

'But you wish he did, don't you?'

'You're drunk.'

'And greetings to you, sweet Alys.'

He leaned forward and kissed my lips. His mouth was hot and I could taste sour wine on his breath.

I took one step back. 'Why are you here? Why are you not at the parliament?'

'Oh, the parliament! Has my brother not told you?'

'Told me what?'

'The commons are hungry. They smell blood. They have sharpened their knives and have an enemy in their sights. The place is in uproar.'

'The commons are there to accede to the king's requests. That is their purpose.'

He laughed and took a step closer. My back was against the board where we displayed Thomas's best silver bowl. I could feel the hardness of the wood pressing into my flesh through my thin woollen gown.

'The commons think otherwise, sweet Alys. They have demanded a ...'

'Demanded? The commons?' I was shocked.

'It is an attack on the king's councillors who take bribes and skim money for themselves. The commons say why should they pay taxes to the king when the money is stolen by others? They cite fraud, embezzlement, malfeasance of every kind. And in the wee small hours of the morning, when you and I are tucked up safely in our beds, they whisper to each other of witchcraft.'

'Witchcraft?'

'Dame Alice Perrers. She has grown rich on the king's generosity. The hedgerow knights ask how the victor of Crécy can be in thrall to a common whore. They suspect enchantment. And be assured, they will find enough to have her burned twice over.'

'The king would never allow that; nor the prince.'

'The king is too old and the prince too sick. The commons are dealing with the duke. He is angry beyond anything I've yet seen.'

He reached out and caught my wrist.

'The commons have the support of your good friend, Edmund Mortimer. I wonder what the little turd hopes to gain by such a thing?'

At that moment I heard the sound of boots on the steps. I wriggled out of John's grasp and was trying to compose myself when Thomas walked in followed by his brother-in-law.

'Your grace,' I murmured dropping a deep curtsey, confused by the presence of the duke of Brittany in our hall.

'Lady Alys, there is no need. I am a duke without a duchy, a man not worthy of the title.'

'No duchy, your grace?'

'Bartered away by the duke of Lancaster at Bruges. If the English peacemakers have their way the French king will keep what he has already taken. My towns and fortresses will be gone; all that will be left to me will be Brest, Auray and a pension.'

'Britto,' said Thomas quietly. 'All is not yet lost. The duke has merely agreed to a truce for another year. Peace must surely be preferable to more fighting?'

'For you, my friend, perhaps, but not for me.'

'And your duchess?' I enquired, thinking of Thomas's sister.

He gave a lopsided smile. 'I shall bring her back to England and deliver her to her mother.'

I tried to forget John Holand's words, but that evening, when our visitors had gone, I asked Thomas if what his brother said was true.

'Yes. The commons are in an ugly mood. There is no money in the king's coffers for furtherance of the war and the commons want to know where it's gone.'

'It is not their business to call the king's councillors to account.'

'They have made it their business. They have demanded Lord Latimer and his son-in-law are brought to trial and that Dame Perrers is banished from the king's side. They want a say in who advises the king and if they don't get what they want, they won't agree to the tax.'

He poured me another cup of wine and drew his chair next to mine. There were just the two of us in the circle of firelight and it was getting late. After all this time the routine was familiar: the wine, the closeness, the gentle touch on my arm and the suggestion that I might call for my maid. My husband was a man who preferred an orderly life and the preliminaries rarely varied.

'Thomas, what do you know of William Montagu?'

He blinked in surprise at the question.

'The earl of Salisbury?'

'You know him?'

'He is a garter knight, past middle age, but not a man I know well.'

'Have you served with him?'

'Twice. He is a magnificent captain but has an uncertain temper and is known to hold grudges. He has no liking for me but there are others he dislikes more, his own brother for one. People say old man Salisbury was a stalwart man, close to the king, but the son is without his father's easy ways.'

'Is he close to the prince?'

My husband considered my question as if trying to recall a past when his stepfather was young and vigorous and not the sick man of today.

'They fought together but there is constraint, some bar to friendship. A past quarrel maybe? Montagu is always quarrelling.'

This told me little: an ill-tempered man, past his prime, a good soldier but not well liked. Nobody's friend. The last of the logs shifted on their bed of ash as I felt the touch of my husband's hand on my upper arm. I held my breath and didn't move.

'Will you call for your maid?'

I sighed and looked at my hands in my lap. 'If it is your pleasure.'

9

THE PRINCE 1376

It was night. I was half-asleep, my face pushed deep in my pillow and the folds of my nightgown wrapped firmly round my legs. But my feet were bare and they were cold. From down in the courtyard came the sound of a violent knocking. This was followed by men's voices, lights flaring in the darkness and the noise of running footsteps. Thomas was out of bed with a dagger in his hand before I even realised he was awake.

'Stay there,' he ordered, pulling on his robe as he ran for the door.

He was back within minutes, calling for his shirt, his tunic, his boots.

'I have to go,' he said, throwing his robe to the floor.

He came to where I sat shivering on the edge of the bed and took my face between his hands. His voice was surprisingly unsteady.

'They have taken him to Westminster. He is dying.'

'The king?'

'The prince.'

I kept my hands where they were, thrust into my sleeves.

'Will you go to Westminster?'

'No, to Kennington, to my mother. Help protect my brother.'

'What would you have me do?'

He looked surprised. 'Stay here. My mother has no need of you.'

Within moments he was gone. I heaved a sigh and slid my feet back under the covers.

It was impossible to believe the prince was dying. He'd been dying every day of every week for the past five years. His sickness was the one enduring constant in our lives, as ever present as the waxing and waning of the moon. Once he'd been the mightiest warrior in England, famed as the prince who'd vanquished the French king at Poitiers. All I remembered of him before he became sick was the triumphant husband smiling on his wedding day.

What would happen when he died? Who would the king name as his heir? With three grown sons, would he really name a small boy to wear the crown of England? It did not seem possible.

I thought of Aunt Wake who was old enough to remember the evil times when fear and rebellion stalked the land, with cousin pitched against cousin and father against son. She said the king had brought peace. He had given us law and order here in England and glorious wars across the Narrow Sea. There was not a single household in England which didn't boast a fur coverlet or a rich tapestry or a piece of gold plate seized from some French town, and the men loved him for it. But he was old. The good times were gone, there were no more victories to be had and the prince was dying.

Reluctantly I got myself out of bed and called for my maid. Once dressed I called for our steward. There was much to be done and done quickly.

'Send one of the men out for black cloth.'

He raised his eyebrows in surprise at my instructions and waited for further information. I would not tell him it was the prince. He probably thought it was the king but let him think what he liked.

'We shall need a tunic for each of the indoor servants and enough cloth for arm-bands for those in the kitchens and for the outside men. And my women will need new gowns.'

'And the hall, my lady?'

'That also. And make sure it is done this morning. Once word spreads every cloth merchant will put up his prices.'

Thomas didn't come home that night and sent no news. Our steward said the city was alive with rumours: the king was dying; the prince was dying; they were both dying and, may God protect us all, it is the plague returned.

For two days my women and I stitched seams and hems until our fingers were pricked raw and our eyes red from squinting in the cheerless gloom of the solar. I thought longingly of the sunlit chambers of the Savoy palace; there, a woman could sit stitching all day long by the great glass windows and never need a candle. It was unworthy but sometimes I envied Lady Swynford the luxury in which she now lived.

After supper on the second day, with still no sign of Thomas, my brothers arrived with Joan in tow.

'Thomas isn't here,' I said as they stamped noisily into the hall bringing with them clouds of dust and a warm ripe smell of city streets. Fitzalan and Jack, being heavy, were sweating profusely but Tamkin was his usual cool sleek self.

'Thomas isn't here,' mimicked Fitzalan with a sneer. 'By Christ! Of course Thomas isn't here. That's why we've come. We'd hardly be wanting to break bread with that crawler.'

'Fitzalan!' Joan laid a hand on his arm. 'This is not your sister's fault.'

'What has happened?' I said, feeling the old terror rise in my belly. 'Has he made a move?'

"He" meant only one person between the five of us and my first thought on seeing my brothers was that our father's other son was ready to expose us in some way.

'Joan patted my arm. 'There has been nothing. This is something else.'

'Where can we go?' enquired Tam eyeing the servants busy clearing away the remains of our meal and folding up the napery. 'We need somewhere private.'

I led them into Thomas's room where the only listening ears were woven in silk and the mouths of the multitudes fixed on the wall were mute and would tell no tales. Fitzalan promptly dropped into Thomas's chair and stretched out his legs. His boots were scuffed and looked in need of some care.

'I knew this would happen. He made them swear an oath.'

'Who? The king?'

'No, you little fool – the prince. Blood of Christ! Where does that leave *us*?'

I looked at Tam.

'It seems once the prince knew he was dying he called the king and the duke to his bedside. He had them swear

133

a solemn oath to care for his son and uphold the boy's rights. There were witnesses. That's how we know.'

You see!' yelled Fitzalan. 'Uphold his rights!'

'What does that mean?' I said.

'Mean? Mean? I'll tell you what it means. It means a mewling brat with a crown on his head and us bending our knee. And you don't need the Holy Father and his coven of cardinals to tell you what will happen then.'

Joan sighed. She would have endured these rants all the way from her house to mine. 'Perhaps the king will confound your expectations, Fitz. He may live for many more years.'

'And the royal bag of bones may drop dead tomorrow. Which will you take as a wager, sister?' said Fitzalan, rubbing the back of his hand across his sweating brow. He looked ready to expire with the heat.

Tam pushed me gently into a chair. 'As long as Aunt Latimer's husband had the king's ear, we'd no reason to worry. If our father's Despenser son tried anything we could be certain of the king's support. Any attempt to petition Pope Gregory would fail.'

'What happens now? Thomas says Latimer is likely to face trial. He could be executed.'

'What happens to Latimer is unimportant. The king's days are already numbered by the Almighty. We need to gain the favour of whoever comes next.'

'Is that what the prince meant? Was he asking for Richard to be made the king's heir?'

'He'd not need to ask,' Joan said. 'Surely the crown follows father to son: the king, the prince, the prince's son.'

'The king will choose his own heir,' growled Fitzalan. 'That is how it's always been. You ask anyone. And why would he choose that little pansy?'

'A deathbed promise is binding, isn't it, Tam?' I said. 'Once having sworn, the king could not change his mind.'

My brother looked doubtful. 'That depends.'

'That depends! Bloody lawyers' words,' muttered Fitzalan. 'Why can't you say it plain? It don't matter what promise the prince has wheedled out of the two of 'em; it'll be the king's choice. Let's hope to God he don't choose Cambridge.' He laughed. 'Or his own bastard. I'd not put it past him. Christ alone knows what that Perrers whore has been whispering in his ear these past years. I'd burn her tomorrow if I had my way.'

'That is impossible,' I said. 'You cannot have a bastard on the throne. It would be unthinkable. There must be a law or a charter of some sort; something to say how a king should be chosen.'

We all looked at Tam.

'Nothing is written,' he said. 'The king's father was king and his father before him but there is evidence of them naming their son as their heir. I've searched the ancient texts in our libraries and the last time the crown failed to pass from father to son was in the days of the Lionheart.'

'That was many lifetimes ago,' said Joan.

'Nevertheless, that is where we must look for a precedent.'

'Oh yes,' sneered Fitzalan. 'Let us all look for a precedent as if that will make a penny's worth of difference.'

'What happened to the Lionheart?' I said, ignoring my brother's rudeness.

Tam shrugged. 'When the Lionheart died, he had no children; the crown passed to his younger brother, John.'

'So the throne will go to Lancaster,' growled Fitzalan. 'I knew it. He'll get his hands on it one way or the other.'

'Wait,' said Joan, watching Tam. 'There's more.'

'Even though the Lionheart named his brother, John, as king hereafter, there was another claimant – a boy, Arthur, son of John's dead brother, Geoffrey, duke of Brittany. If Geoffrey had lived, *he* would have been king after the Lionheart, not John. '

'I've heard of King John,' I said. 'But nobody has spoken of this Arthur. What happened to him?'

'We have no idea. The barons preferred John. There was an order for Arthur to be imprisoned and nothing more was heard of him. He disappears from the records.'

'Murdered?' said Joan.

'Possibly. Who knows?'

'Cousin Philippa!' I cried aloud, all of a sudden realising the relevance of what Tam had just said.

They looked at me as if I had lost my wits.

'Cousin Philippa. Don't you see?' I said. 'If her father had lived, he would be king after the prince, not the duke.'

'Lionel has been dead these past eight years.'

'Philippa is his daughter.'

'By the blood of Christ! A woman? You're not seriously suggesting we let a woman sit on the throne? That is lunacy,' said Fitzalan.

'Fitz,' said Tam, warningly. 'Alys is your sister, not one of your servants.'

136

'A woman cannot rule,' said Joan. 'No-one would stand for that. But could a claim pass through a woman to her son? I remember our mother talking of such a thing.'

'It is possible,' said Tam carefully. 'The king declared himself king of France in such a way. His mother, Queen Isabella, was daughter of the Iron King. Her brothers were dead and had left no male heirs. The throne of France was vacant. The Valois claim descended from a brother of the Iron King and was considered inferior to our king's. But the French preferred the Valois.'

'So it *is* possible,' I said. 'Cousin Philippa *could* claim the throne in the name of her Mortimer son.'

'A Mortimer on the throne?' said Fitzalan. 'Don't make me weep.'

'You are forgetting the prince's son,' said Joan. 'The princess would not allow anyone to push her little lamb from his rightful place. She has waited a long time for this.'

Fitzalan was looking at me. 'What a waste it was marrying you to Holand. With the prince gone there will be no advantage to us in your marriage.'

'My husband is the boy's brother,' I protested. 'He can still be of use.'

'Your husband will roll over at the first sign of trouble,' said Fitzalan.

'Why did you come here if only to insult my husband?' I said, angrily. 'And who says there'll be trouble?'

'Of course there'll be trouble. Mortimer's already gathering his allies. I wondered why he had his lickspittle attack the Crown. Now I know.'

'Who's he got?' enquired Joan, ever practical.

'Percy; bishop of Winchester; bishop of London; some

137

hedgerow knights and a collection of burgesses who don't like Lancaster. Stafford; possibly Clifford though I think he'll stay loyal to the boy. Maybe de Ros and the Greys of Ruthin. Pembroke might have supported him had he lived.'

'So would my husband if he had lived,' said Joan. 'When it comes to a show of arms, the Marcher lords stick close together.

'What of your son-in-law?' said Tam to Joan.

'Young Woodstock?' Fitzalan laughed. 'Ferocious little puppy, ain't he? Runt of the king's litter but the sharpest teeth of the lot.'

Thomas of Woodstock was the king's youngest son. He had married Joan's elder daughter for her de Bohun fortune but was seldom seen without a scowl on his face. My sister didn't like him.

'Greedy,' said Joan, bluntly. 'He'll have his eye on the boy. He won't take kindly to Mortimer pushing in but I doubt he'd welcome the duke holding the reins of power either.'

'The Londoners don't like Lancaster,' said Tam. 'Mortimer could have support there.'

'Londoners love the princess,' I said remembering the cheering crowds along the riverbank each time we rowed down the Thames with my mother-in-law's standard flying. 'They will want Richard.'

'They may want the boy but it won't take them long to realise who's putting words into the boy's mouth.'

'The prince won't leave his son unprotected,' I said, thinking of the men who filled the princess's rooms at Kennington.

'Let us be clear about this,' said Fitzalan. 'Lancaster can raise an army ten times greater than anyone else in England. If he wants the crown, he'll take it. At the point of a sword if necessary.'

'I do not believe he wants it,' said Joan.

Fitzalan roared with laughter. 'Where've you been, sister? Lancaster's had his eye on the crown from the moment he was born.'

The sky next morning was washed the colour of a dunnock's egg, a perfect spotless blue. Surely not a day for dying? If I stood on tiptoe I could just make out the newly-built church of St Michael's on Crooked Lane, towering over the lay-stalls and slaughter grounds of the Eastcheap butchers. Across the river on the Southwark shore, a boy was moving sheep onto a small plot of land next to the bishop's wharf and in the hay meadows towards Lambethmoor, the grass shimmered in the heat. As I watched, the bishop's barge slipped silently away from the quay with three men huddled under the canopy. The bishop's standard flew from the prow, an unexpected flash of brightly coloured red.

At noon, with the heat still rising, one of Thomas's men arrived to escort me to Westminster. I called for the children and explained I was going to the king's palace because their grandmother's husband was sick.

'Is he old?' said Nell.

'No, not really. But he may die.'

I watched my daughter as she considered this intriguing fact.

'Shall I pray for him? I could speak to Our Lady. She would ask God to save him.'

I smiled at the simplicity of childhood. Once I too had believed that my prayers would bring me what I most desired. But that was to misunderstand the nature of prayer. And I had been disappointed.

As we travelled upriver I glanced over to the Savoy. The massive walls gleamed a pure, unsullied white, an impressive sight to anyone passing by; but the duke's flags drooped miserably. They hung limp in the sultry air, waiting with dutiful resignation for the breeze which would come with the turning of the tide. A body of men in Lancastrian livery lined the landing stage but in the gardens there was no sign of Lady Swynford.

Considering the gravity of her husband's situation I was surprised to find my mother-in-law in her rooms, sitting calmly amidst the growing chaos, a piece of embroidery held lightly in her hands. She looked up and smiled. There was a tightness at the corners of her mouth and her eyes were peculiarly bright. She looked very much as if she had been weeping.

'Alys, dear child. Thank you for coming.'

I kissed her and sat down beside my cousin, Eleanor, who looked even closer to tears than the princess. Her fingers were twisting themselves into ever more complicated knots. The only other lady in attendance was a mutinous-looking Maud. Her eyes were downcast and she failed to look up at my arrival.

'She's been told that under no circumstances will she be allowed to marry this count of wherever,' whispered Eleanor softly.

'Ligny and St Pol.'

'Wherever. It doesn't matter because the princess will not allow it.'

Poor Maud. No wonder she looked miserable.

'Is he really dying?' I said in the quietest of voices so that only Eleanor could hear.

'Yes. The men of his household have been summoned to say farewell. His friends have been arriving since dawn. You would not believe how many have asked to see him; not just trusted companions from his years in Aquitaine and men who've been with him since boyhood, but elderly knights, half-blind, half-deaf, who remember him from Crécy. The doors to his chamber are open so that anyone can approach, just as he ordered. But it is a dreadful sight.'

'Is your husband with him?'

'Day and night this past week. He says the prince is in great pain but bears it bravely.'

'The king?'

'Yes. And the duke.'

'Will the princess go?'

'In a little while she'll take Richard to say farewell and receive his father's blessing. Then she will leave the bishops to do what must be done. After that,' she shrugged in a gesture of helplessness, 'we wait.'

An hour later Eleanor's husband arrived to escort the princess and her son to the prince's chamber. Lewis Clifford's face was white with fatigue and I could see that he too had been weeping. As my mother-in-law rose she turned and asked me to accompany her.

'Come with Eleanor as far as the door. I might have need of you both if my resolve fails.'

141

It was an honour to be asked but the scene in the prince's chamber was worse than I'd expected. My father had died peacefully in his own room with his children kneeling at his bedside. He had repented his sins and made his peace with God. It was a good death. There had been almost no sound and his final breath had been a little sigh, nothing more.

Here, despite a hundred candles pouring light and warmth into the chamber, and fragrant herbs burning in the censors, the darkness and stench of death were overpowering. From the bishop of Bangor's lips came a constant murmuring of prayers for the dying. But beneath the supplications, struggling to be heard, were a series of agonising groans from the man in the bed. Whatever the eulogists would say in the days to come, the prince was not going peacefully to God. He was fighting his demons every inch of the way.

The king, supported by two of his body servants, was weeping openly. The duke knelt at the bedside, holding his brother's hands. Not since the death of my cousin Blanche had I seen such misery in the duke's face. But it was natural; he was losing his favourite brother. A chasm of ten years separated them but they had always been close. Thomas said there was genuine love and no two brothers could be closer.

I watched as my mother-in-law approached the bed and gently pushed young Richard forward. The child's face was hidden from view but his slight recoil at the sight of his father was obvious to everyone. The prince raised his head and tried to grasp his son's arm but didn't have the strength. His head fell back and his hand collapsed uselessly onto the cover. He opened his lips but the words were mere whispers, too quiet for anyone to hear.

In a voice choked with tears, the duke explained to Richard what his father wanted: for the boy to do his duty at all times and honour his father's promises. The dying man's groans became more agitated. The duke repeated the words, urging Richard to kiss his father and make his promise. The child turned in panic to his uncle and for a moment I sensed a connection between them as the duke placed his hand on Richard's shoulder to give him courage.

The child's neck was very small and wisps of fair hair curled softly round his ears. He raised his pale blue eyes to his uncle. I thought how easy it would be to snap that tiny neck and crush those fragile bones; how easy to destroy this child who was his brother's heir. What a temptation for an ambitious man wanting to step into his nephew's place.

The duke stroked his fingers absent-mindedly along the child's collar bone and up to the hollow at the base of his neck. I could see the fluttering of the boy's pulse and the brushing of the duke's thumb across the delicate whiteness of his skin. Then the group of people surrounding the bed moved closer and my view was blocked. I could still hear the droning voice of the bishop and the low voice of the duke urging Richard to kneel and receive his father's blessing and from every corner of the room, the perpetual sound of muffled weeping.

Later I accompanied the princess and young Richard back to the princess's rooms. The boy was weeping and clutching his tutor's hand but everyone pretended not to notice. His father would have been horrified at his son's lack of bravery but his father was not here. His father was dying.

'It is finished,' said my mother-in-law bleakly. 'There is nothing more. Tomorrow is the feast day of the Holy Trinity and he will cease to fight. He will submit.' She gave a small smile. 'I never imagined our life together would end like this. On our wedding day he promised me he would win every battle, that loving me had made him invincible. But he had forgotten the lessons of the past: death conquers all in the end.'

'He was a brave fighter,' said Eleanor.

'Yes, he *was* brave; some said foolhardy, others said he was lucky. He believed his causes to be noble and that God would reward him with victories. But after Castile he met an enemy he could not outrun and in that moment he faced the dreadful truth that God had deserted him.'

I sat there not knowing what to do. I had expected my mother-in-law to pray but she simply sat in silence, doing nothing.

After a little while she asked Eleanor, 'Has William been?'

'Yes, this morning.'

She nodded, satisfied, as if some final piece of a puzzle had fallen into place. 'I hoped he would.'

'Who is William?' I whispered to Maud.

'How would I know?' she muttered.

We knew many Williams but could this one be William Montagu, the good soldier, not well-liked?

Hundreds of the prince's friends had arrived since dawn, all of them in tears as they came to say farewell to a man they never believed would end his life like this. He had led them to glory and now he was leaving them. If death had to come before a man's allotted time, and which of them knew the hour, they would prefer it to be gloriously on the battlefield, not in squalid sickness and despair. There was no triumph to be had in meeting God like this. The Church might call this a good death but it humbled a man.

He died next day. We wore our freshly sewn mourning garments and our steward reported the price of black cloth in the shops had shot up. As I had predicted, everyone was demanding clothes of the deepest, richest black.

Each man in our household now boasted a new black tunic or armband and even Nell had a small black gown which she hated. We hung the hall with the remaining lengths of cloth, covering the brightly coloured tapestries and making the room even darker than before. When an evening breeze from the river found its way through the shutters, the draught made the black drapery stir slightly, shifting uneasily as if possessed by some spirit of its own. Tom was afraid and began to cry.

Bells tolled night and day as an unstoppable tide of mourning swept through every parish in the city. The prince had been the flower of England, the hope of his countrymen. No-one could quite believe he had gone. Nobody expected the son to die before the father, the heir to die before the king. It was against the order of the Almighty's great plan. In side-street taverns, men bewailed their loss in drink, saying all hope had gone of defeating the French now that the prince was no more. In every church, priests preached sermons of the prince's glorious deeds, of his piety and of his acts of kindness.

His body was placed on a bier in Westminster Hall where it would lie in state until his funeral. An endless stream of Londoners poured out of the city along the road past the Savoy. They moved slowly up the steps and through the black-draped hall where the air was heavy and cold, murmuring prayers as they went, every one of them in tears. Four knights stood guard at the corners of the bier. The only glitter in the darkness was the prince's shield, his helm, his breastplate and his arms, and the hundred beeswax candles burning steadily in their sconces, lighting his way to eternity.

10

COLDHARBOUR 1376

Amidst the horror of the prince's death, the brutal business of the parliament dragged on. Lord Latimer was arrested and his person placed in the charge of the earl of March, Edmund Mortimer. My aunt's husband and John Neville, his son-in-law, were to be stripped of their offices; Richard Lyons, the London merchant, was to be imprisoned for life and Dame Perrers, the king's avaricious concubine, widely suspected of witchcraft, was to be ordered from court.

'Will they burn her?' I asked my sister.

'Probably,' she said, 'if the duke doesn't step in to save her.'

'Do you imagine it hurts very much?'

'To be burned alive? For sure. They say the skin bubbles before the flesh begins to roast.'

Three weeks after the prince's death, Thomas returned from Kennington with his brother. They shut themselves in Thomas's room. It wasn't long before one of my husband's men came for me.

I waited hesitantly on the threshold, wondering why I'd been summoned.

'Close the door, Alys.'

I kept my eyes on my husband.

'Is this necessary?' said his brother.

'Yes,' said Thomas firmly. 'Alys knows Lancaster's woman from before and she's friendly with Mortimer's wife; they are cousins.'

John flashed a brief grin. 'I was not aware friendship could flourish on such stony ground.'

I ignored him. I had not forgotten his last visit.

'What has happened, husband?'

'Our brother, Richard, is in danger.'

'Mother Mary! How? From whom?'

'The king has yet to name him heir to the throne,' said John. 'The commons are demanding he should be next but there has been no word from the king. Just silence.'

'We fear his mind may be being poisoned by others who are promoting their own interests,' said Thomas gloomily.

'Those who would also like to poison our brother,' said John.

'That could never happen,' I said, thinking of the tasters employed by the princess, and the men who patrolled the kitchens at Kennington. Every morsel of food placed in front of young Richard passed through the hands of at least a dozen of the princess's men before it reached the child's lips. Wine was inspected and duly sipped before leaving the ewery and the brewing of ale from the palace stores of malt and barley took place under the watchful eyes of three men.

'There are rumours,' said Thomas.

'There are always rumours,' I said, trying to make light of it. 'It is what people do: gossip, embroider tales, make meals from a single crumb. London is the worst place for rumourmongers.'

'These are very specific rumours. They name the duke. It is said he sees himself as heir to the throne now the prince is dead. He wants the crown for the House of Lancaster. First him, then his son, Harry.'

'But husband, he swore to uphold Richard's rights. He won't go back on a death bed promise.'

Thomas exchanged a look at John, who nodded his head as if agreeing with what I should be told.

'Pope Gregory has threatened to call into question our brother's legitimacy,' said John. 'He claims the prince's marriage to our mother was defective.'

I feigned surprise though this was not news to me. I had not yet told Thomas of my brothers' visit or of what Philippa had said.

'There is information coming from Flanders,' said Thomas. 'The duke has struck a deal with the French king. He will not defend his brother's son against the Holy Father's accusation of illegitimacy. Once his father is dead he will take the crown and make peace with France. In return, the French will withdraw their armies back across the Pyrenees leaving the way open for the duke to march into Castile and fly the leopards of England over the fields of Spain.'

'That is a calumny,' I said hotly. 'The duke is loyal.'

John leaned forward. 'D'you know what the French king's brothers do at Bruges when they are alone, after they have finished feasting on roasted quail and baiting the English envoys?'

I shook my head. I had not the slightest idea. Something evil no doubt. Everyone knew the brothers of the carpet king were creatures addicted to killing, whose word was not to be trusted.

'They plot how to take the crown of France when their brother, the king, is dead. They look at his small sons, just eight and four years old, younger than Richard, and laugh at their feeble limbs and shrill piping voices. They wonder if it would be better to jerk the strings of a child king and make him dance to their tune or if they should contrive an accident. They plot and doubtless their thoughts run to unguarded wells or little vials of poison. All men are greedy for power, sister. Why would you imagine the duke any different?'

I looked to Thomas to tell me John was lying but he just shrugged his shoulders. 'It is true, Alys. The duke may offer friendship but who knows what he is thinking? And if Richard is put out of the succession or God forbid, harmed, what will happen to us? That is why we need *you*.'

'Why me?'

'You must go to your friend, Lady Swynford. Find out what the duke has been saying to her.'

'Passion loosens a man's tongue, sister, or did you not know,' said John slyly.

'The duke has declared he would never harm his brother's child.'

'Of course he has,' John laughed. 'He'd hardly admit he was planning to do away with the boy. A little subtlety is required here, sister. If you wish to discover the duke's secrets you will have to act clever. But I am sure you can do that, can't you?'

Before I could answer there was a knock and Thomas's man put his head round the door. 'A man from Kennington, Sir Thomas. He's asking for you.'

Thomas heaved himself up. 'I won't be long,' he said, making for the door.

'He's not asked,' said John idly as soon as Thomas was out of hearing.

'Asked what?'

'About the Kent title, the estates. That is what you want to know, isn't it? He has not asked our mother and he never will. It is not in his nature. He will simply wait his turn like an obedient pup.'

I knew it. After the garter celebrations at Windsor I had thought I would be countess of Kent but nothing happened. The princess failed to offer anything and Thomas had not pressed for what was his due. As John said, it was not in his nature. He was too weak, too trusting, too lacking in ambition for advancement; too idle to think of improving our lives.

John was watching me closely. 'Now our mother has control of her inheritance she won't let it slip from her grasp. You might think that with her dower from the prince she'd be well provided for and would need nothing more. You might think those manors would come to Thomas. But you'd be wrong. They won't. They belonged to her father and are far too precious for her to grant them to Thomas who, you have to admit, seems rather uninterested. Besides, all her attention at the moment is focused on our little brother. Everything will be done for Richard and Thomas will be forgotten. I think you will have to make do with Woking for some time yet, my sweet Alys.'

I tried to remember my cousin Blanche's training: keep your face serene, do not let your thoughts intrude upon others, never inflict your sorrows or your anger on those close to you. But my lips began to tremble and unwanted tears of fury and despair quivered on the tips of my eyelashes.

'You are wrong,' I whispered.

John leaned forward and very gently brushed his finger across my eyes. I closed them. His finger stroked my cheek and traced the curve of my lips.

'If they had married you to me, sweet Alys,' he said in his softest voice. 'Think what we could have achieved together. Those three fat Yorkshire manors and all the money your father provided for your marriage portion would have been just the beginning. I shall travel far because I am a man like our father. I want more.'

'Thomas is perfectly content with what he has,' I said uncertainly.

'I know. He tells me he finds you a most obliging wife.'

'What else should a wife be but obliging?'

'And what else should a man need but a wife ready to oblige him?'

'He is a good husband. I respect him and do my duty.'

John's lips curled in the semblance of a smile. 'Oh, I'm sure you do, sweet Alys. I'm sure you do.' His smile broadened. 'I'm sure you are indeed a most dutiful and obliging wife.'

I thrust to the back of my mind my husband's impatience when I had been anything but a dutiful and obliging wife in those bleak dark months after our baby died. I had turned away from him and denied him any comfort. I had remained with my sister in Essex until he had come and fetched me back to Berkhamsted.

'Thomas voices no complaints.'

'We both know Thomas is not a man to complain. He

is perfectly content to stay at home and sit by the fire. But that is not the life for me. Shall I tell you what I am going to do?'

I shrugged. 'You will tell me whether I want you to or not.'

'With my little brother Richard's help I shall become the most powerful man in the kingdom. I shall make my wife a countess or maybe a duchess. I shall clothe her in silks and satins and buy her a ruby the size of a pigeon's egg. And when the music stops and the lamps expire, I shall take her to our marriage bed and show her exactly what it means to be a dutiful and obliging wife.'

I sniffed. 'I pity her.'

'No you don't,' he grinned.

We both heard Thomas approach the door and I instinctively looked away from John. If my pulse was racing a little faster than usual, Thomas would never know.

He came in slowly, composed, unruffled, and sat himself down.

'I have to go back to Kennington. The duke is coming to swear our mother.'

I looked up in alarm. 'What for?'

'Before she is allowed to receive her dower. the king requires her to swear an oath that she will not remarry.'

'She will never remarry,' I said with certainty, thinking of the princess's red eyes and the fond way she had always talked of the prince.

'Nevertheless she has to swear.'

'Do you need me, brother?' said John, leaning back in his chair and stretching out his legs. He was wearing one of the newly fashionable short tunics which exposed most of a man's legs. He had well-shaped calves and black suited him; unlike Thomas who looked like a half-starved crow.

Thomas smiled. 'I think you should come with me. Our mother may want you there.'

Next day, the man I had sent to the Savoy palace, returned late. He hovered at the doorway, too frightened to approach any nearer, scuffing the toe of his left boot awkwardly against the heel of the other and refusing to look me in the eye.

It seemed he had been delayed on his errand, an unavoidable delay I was to understand, not intentional, by no means; and when he reached the Savoy, the Lady Swynford wasn't there. No sign of her anywhere. Her rooms were as empty as the tomb. Even the little girls were gone. If only he'd not met those scurvy knaves preaching how the duke was kissing the arse of the carpet king and selling the young prince's birthright for a mess of Spanish pottage, he'd have seen the fair lady for himself. But when there were men telling him how the Frenchies would soon be sailing their cursed fire-ships up the Thames, he'd got to stop and listen, didn't he? M'lady'd not like to be burned in her bed, would she?

I was not impressed and told him so.

'The duke's leman's gone to Kenilworth, m'lady,' he said in a wheedling tone, clearly hoping this nugget of information would appease my anger at his failure to deliver my message. 'They'm saying the duke has a rare care for her and wanted her safe. She left at first light and took her women with her.'

''And the children?'

154

'Gone to Kenilworth, m'lady, all but my lord of Lancaster's son and the Swynford boy.'

So Lady Swynford had been sent to safety.

That evening I told Thomas.

'Do you wish me to follow her north to Kenilworth?' I thought fondly of my visits to the great rose-red castle with my cousin, Blanche.

He gave a thin smile. 'No, Alys. That will not be necessary. I want you to return to Woking with the children and spend the remainder of the summer there.'

'May I not be of use here?'

He put his hands on my shoulders. 'There is nothing you can do now Lady Swynford has gone. Let the children enjoy a summer in the country.'

I had forgotten how solemn he could be, how serious. His brown eyes were steady as he gazed at my face.

'Are we not safe?'

Most husbands would have immediately reassured their wives that yes indeed, of course they were safe, there was no danger at all, not the slightest, not to a woman and her children. But not Thomas. Thomas was too truthful to employ easy lies.

'I do not know,' he said.

He put his arms round me and pulled me towards him. I remained perfectly still, not particularly liking the closeness but mindful of my duty as a wife to enjoy my husband's embraces.

'I doubt if anyone would regard me as a threat to their ambitions. It is not as if I have an army of followers to call on, not like the duke or Edmund Mortimer.'

'You must have some,' I protested, thinking of the

hundreds of men who filled the courtyards and fields at Arundel each time my father issued a summons.

Thomas shook his head. 'Alys, I have no vast estates with dozens of men owing me fealty like the duke does. I fear the stolid peasants of Woking with their pitchforks and flails cannot equal the wild men of the Marches when it comes to a fight. You have never seen a battle but I have.'

'Our men could fight.'

'Not against those who have practised for years with axes and hammers and enjoy shedding blood. Fighting against the French at the king's command is our duty and we know God is with us because our armies win great battles; but to slaughter one's fellow Englishmen cannot be part of God's plan. Nor, I am certain, is it the king's desire.'

'You must surely have friends who would fight with you to keep the throne safe for your brother,' I persisted.

'There are very few I could count on to march with me if it became necessary,' he said soberly. 'But whatever happens you can be certain I shall defend Richard to the last. He is my mother's son, as am I. It is my duty to protect him.'

He held me away from him and gazed sadly into my face. The smile when it came was barely a smile at all but I knew what would come next. He placed one hand softly on my sleeve, hardly disturbing the thin cloth which covered my arm.

'It is late. Will you call for your maid?'

Next day, with Thomas's permission, I went to make my farewell to Aunt Wake. I'd not seen her since the spring and felt guilty at my neglect. For all her interfering ways, she was an old lady and could not be long for this world. Apart from Philippa's ailing grandmother shut away in her convent at Bruisyard whom I hadn't seen since I was a small child, Aunt Wake was the only one of my mother's sister's alive. I could not imagine our lives without her.

I did not expect to find anyone I knew at the house of the Grace of the Blessed Mary other than my aunt and was more than a little surprised to see a familiar figure in the garden. It was a warm afternoon, full of drowsiness and the buzzing of insects. The walled garden with its pebbled paths and low box hedges was drenched in sunshine and full of the delicate perfume of roses. Sitting comfortably on a velvet cushioned bench next to my aunt, was my cousin, Philippa.

She was quite at ease, watching a tiny lapdog with a soft plumed tail which had curled itself into a ball in a bed of lavender. She looked up at the sound of my footsteps and her finger went straight to her lips.

She nodded towards Aunt Wake who sat wrapped up like a parcel in a warm woollen cloak with a scarf wound loosely round her neck. Her head drooped forward onto her chest. Judging from the grunting wheezes issuing from her half-open mouth and her tightly closed eyes in their web of leathery wrinkles, she was fast asleep.

Philippa eased herself off the bench and came over to where I stood by the archway.

'Visiting?' she enquired with a lift of an eyebrow.

'Like you,' I replied with a sliver of a smile.

We were two experienced combatants eyeing each other, looking for a weakness to exploit to our own advantage, unsure whether the other wished to join battle

157

or merely rattle her weapons of war. It had ever been thus. As girls we were little wildcats, spitting insults at each other: I was older, she was prettier; my father was the king's closest advisor, hers was his son; and when I hissed that we Arundels were wealthy beyond anything she could possibly imagine, Philippa had given me a silly simpering smile and told me that she got to sit on the king's knee.

But of course that was not the root of my dislike of her now that I was a grown woman. The truth was that I had wanted Edmund for myself but he had been given to Philippa. I was unable to forgive her for her good fortune and she was unwilling to let me forget.

She stretched slightly, arching her neck and hollowing her back. It was a common enough pose for a woman who'd been sitting for a long time but I understood what she was doing. The light silk cloth which had a tendency to cling to the body if cut on the cross, accentuated the swelling, ensuring that I, like everyone else, could see that she was carrying another child. Another little Mortimer for Edmund. Philippa was proudly displaying her easy fertility.

She looked down her nose at the flatness of my own waist, raised her eyebrows and smiled.

'I am returning to Usk,' she said, wanting to see my reaction to her news. 'Our child is due by Martinmas and my husband wishes me safe at his castle before the roads become treacherous. It is a comfortable place and our second son will be born there.'

Another plump goose for the St Martin's Day feast, I thought meanly. I hoped she would choke on it.

'I congratulate you, cousin,' I said, not meaning a word of it.

She flashed a small smile of triumph and acknowledged my good wishes with a slight dip of her head.

'Are you not concerned about leaving your husband alone at this difficult time?' I enquired sweetly. 'His responsibilities as earl marshal are onerous. I thought you might consider it your duty to stay at his side.'

Philippa had an answer for everything.

She took my arm and walked me a little way along one of the paths so that we were out of Aunt Wake's hearing. 'You have to understand, cousin,' she said, her voice as smooth as honey. 'The prince's death has changed everything. My grandfather will soon be an irrelevance, consigned to the grave and to history. The grey-beards will mourn his passing and talk a lot of nonsense about his legacy and how greatly he will be missed, but that is only men like old Courtenay of Devon who must be eighty if he's a day, and sour-faced grumblers like the earl of Salisbury. The truth is, their time is past. Ours is just beginning.'

'The prince's death changes nothing,' I retorted. 'His line lives on. His son is the heir and will take the crown. My husband assures me it will happen.'

'You think so?'

'Parliament will demand it.'

'That may be so but it is my grandfather's choice. The men in the parliament can speak their minds and make as many demands as they like but only one man's word matters and that is the king's.'

'The king will be guided by the duke.'

'The duke is a fool,' spat Philippa. 'He poured blood and treasure into a war which has impoverished England

and led our army to ruin. His foolish peacemaking destroyed our prospects of victory and left men like the duke of Brittany and my husband near destitute. Nobody is making up our losses because your precious Lord Latimer and his coterie of friends have stolen it all.'

'The king listens to the duke,' I protested.

But Philippa was adamant. 'The duke has been humiliated by the commons. They have savaged his reputation and torn him to shreds. He is sulking like a schoolboy and now the king has better advisors. My poor grandfather may be in his royal dotage but he will be guided by his new council and they are men who are not afraid to tell him the truth.'

'Men like your husband?'

'Yes indeed. Edmund heads the council and you will see his wishes prevail. He will not be like your aunt's husband, Lord Latimer, of that you can be sure. Edmund is wise. He has taken advice from his good friend, the bishop of Winchester, who always has our best interests at heart.'

'Is that so?'

'And the bishop does not care for the company that some of your husband's kin keep, cousin.'

'What kin?'

'He disapproves of those who follow heretical mouthings. You should warn your mother-in-law. She would be well-advised to cleanse her stable of men like Lewis Clifford.'

Our aunt's imperious voice cut across the garden. 'Who is that? Who are you talking to? I will not have you gossiping. Come here. Let me see you.'

Reluctantly we moved back to where Aunt Wake was sitting bolt upright, wide-awake and greatly annoyed.

'Nobody told me you were coming,' she said indignantly as I made a demure curtsey.

'I sent a message,' I explained.

'Nobody gave it to me,' she grumbled. 'Must have got lost. People are always losing things. Why are you here? What were you talking about? I will not have private conversations taking place right under my nose without my permission. Do you understand?'

'Yes, my lady,' Phillipa and I chorused obediently.

She looked at us each in turn as if our words were writ large on our foreheads. 'Hmph! Don't need to ask what all that was about,' she snapped. 'That look on your face says it all, young Lady Philippa. Don't think because I live in the care of the sisters I don't get to hear what's going on. I know what your husband's been doing and I tell you, it's got to stop.'

Philippa fluttered her eyelashes. 'I could not possibly tell my husband what to do, my lady. He might beat me.'

Aunt Wake choked on her laughter. 'Oh fol-de-rol, girl. I wager you give as good as you get with young Mortimer. Everyone knows he's wet behind the ears for all his grand posturing. You are the sharp one, always have been.'

'My husband is head of the new council. He is highly valued,' protested Philippa.

Aunt Wake sniffed and looked unimpressed. 'Fancies himself, does he? Sees himself as a man with power at his fingertips? And doubtless you encourage him.'

Philippa opened her mouth but Aunt Wake didn't wait for Philippa's reply.

'Been telling him how your claim is stronger than the duke's, have you? Boasting of how that father of yours was a second son and the duke just a third son. Filling his head with nonsense. Well, you listen to me, girl. I once knew a man who thought to grab power for himself when he had no right to it. Saw it lying there and thought he could steal it. Stole a king's wife as well.'

Aunt Wake stopped and clutched her throat but when I tried to help her she waved me away.

'Don't fuss,' she wheezed as she heaved great gulps of air.

'What happened to the man who stole the king's wife?' asked Philippa.

'Came to a bad end with a noose round his neck and so will young Mortimer. You tell him from me that his name is cursed. No son of a Mortimer will ever sit on the throne of England. You tell him that.'

I shot a glance at Philippa to see the effect of Aunt Wake's words but she was still smiling serenely as if nothing of importance had been said.

'And now, ' said Aunt Wake, turning to me. 'What are *you* doing here?'

Later, after we'd been dismissed, Philippa said, by way of farewell. 'It was nonsense what she said. Whoever heard of a man stealing a king's wife and grabbing his throne? Not I.'

'But you *will* tell Edmund what she said?'

'Why should I?' she said, beckoning her groom with a wave of her gloved hand.

'I would if I were you,' I said stoutly.

'But you are not me, cousin,' she replied, quick as a flash. 'You may wish you were, but you're not.'

By the time I returned to Coldharbour, the chests were packed and last-minute arrangements for my journey were complete. My belongings were neatly stowed away and two men had been sent ahead to ensure the house was ready for my arrival. The children were wild with excitement at the thought of returning to Woking. I found Nell in the nursery telling a wide-eyed Tom of the mysterious creatures who lived in the wood behind the house.

'A dragon! It breathes fire and burns people.'

'I've not seen your fire-breathing dragon,' I said, lifting her up. She was still of a age where I could scoop her into my arms but each day she was heavier and her legs grew longer. She was fast losing her baby plumpness and beginning to look like a little girl.

'You haven't been looking prop'ly, lady,' she replied in all seriousness, wriggling out of my grasp. 'Me and Tom are going to find it and kill it and then you'll be safe for ever and ever.'

My husband came into the nursery, smiling at the sight of me and the children. Nell, now fully aware of proper manners, dropped him a small curtsey and murmured, 'M'lord.'

Little Tom smiled broadly at his father and ran straight into his arms. Thomas swung him up, held him against his chest and ruffled his hair. The nursemaid blushed as well she might. Tom was quite old enough to know he should greet his father with a small bow before expecting hugs and kisses and it was the woman's duty to teach him these things. I sighed. It was an endless task trying to instil anything into these women.

We went back down the steps and through the hall to Thomas's room where he had laid out various packages for me to take to Woking. There were letters for our near neighbours and a list of repairs to be done before the winter. I sat down on the stool next to the table.

'Any news from the house of the Grace of the Blessed Mary?' he asked as he gathered everything together, tying the letters with a narrow black ribbon.

I drew my finger across the surface of the red cloth which covered the table, making little circles.

'My cousin, Lady Philippa, was visiting.'

One circle overlapped the next and then a third and a fourth. A small winged insect alighted at the far end of the table and began inching its way towards my finger, then, thinking better of its plan, scuttled hastily down the table leg to the nether regions where it couldn't be seen. There was no noise apart from the slight movement of my finger over the woven threads of cloth, a gentle intake of breath and the familiar rustle of parchment.

Thomas raised his eyebrows. 'Did you discover anything?'

'No more than we knew before. She believes she has a claim through her father. When I mentioned Richard she smiled as if there was something I didn't know, some great secret. Is there?'

'Is there what?'

'Some secret? Something I don't know? Something nobody is telling me?'

Thomas picked up the neatly tied letters and put them to one side.

'You are my wife. Alys. I have no secrets from you. Everything I know, you know. Does that satisfy you?'

'Yes,' I said, still unconvinced.

'Any other news?'

'She tells me she is with child,' I said continuing my pattern.

Thomas didn't speak but I knew what he was thinking. He came up behind me and I felt his fingers touch the stuff of my gown.

'And you? It's been a long time since you came back to me at Berkhamsted. We have …'

Yes, we had. Most nights we had. Most nights I had lain silently beneath him while he took his pleasure and thought of the unkindness of fate. I had thought of Edmund and how our togetherness would not have been like this.

I looked down at my slippers, noticing that one of the ribbons was loose.

'I am sorry to be a disappointment to you,' I said quietly, thinking of Philippa, flushed and pretty with triumph.

He pressed his lips to my hair. 'You are not a disappointment, Alys. You are my wife. I care for you.' With his fingers he turned my face to his. 'And we have tonight.'

11

A YEAR OF WAITING 1376-7

The children and I had a wonderful summer. The sun shone from a clear blue sky and each day we walked in the meadows by the river and played lengthy games of hide and seek amongst the bushes. On hot afternoons I would sit comfortably in the shade of an old oak, my back resting against its weathered trunk, while my children crouched on the bank looking for minnows below the surface of the water.

There were lazy days when the children would lie curled up on my lap while I told them stories, remembered from when I was a girl; and adventurous days when we removed our shoes and stockings and dabbled our toes in the shallow pools near the old priory mill. We splashed each other until we were soaked and then sat on the little plank bridge in the sunshine, swinging our legs backwards and forwards above the slow-moving waters.

When it was time for to cut the corn, I took the children along the hedgerows and taught them the country songs of my childhood as we picked blackberries and elderberries and bitter-tasting sloes for the winter. Our fingers became scratched and Tom was horribly stung when he tried to pick a nettle, but by the end of the day our baskets were overflowing with fruit. As the sun began to dip lower in the sky, we trudged home with our purple fingertips and full bellies, tired, hot and sticky, but wonderfully content.

Once the autumn gales arrived, bringing showers of rain from the west, our expeditions ceased and I began to think nostalgically of London. Thomas wrote letters but told me little except that he was well and we were in his prayers. Apart from our elderly neighbours who called twice and stayed overlong, there were no visitors.

It was some time after the feast of St Michael when I decided to stop hiding away and pay a visit. Mindful as always of my safety, I summoned a man with a weapon to accompany me, and headed along the towpath to the Newark priory.

The priory stood to the north on what was a pretty little island, with a stream at its back. The canons who lived there were our nearest neighbours of any consequence.

'Lady Holand,' exclaimed the elderly prior with a beaming smile. 'Our day is blessed indeed. To what do we owe the pleasure of this visit?'

He hitched his robes and settled himself comfortably in his heavily carved chair. I noted the exquisite tapestry hanging on the wall, a new addition since my last visit. But I wasn't surprised because the priory was rich and no expense was spared when it came to decorating the church or the prior's private accommodation.

We were old friends, the prior and I, and fish from the priory ponds often found their way onto our table to be reciprocated with gifts of a haunch of venison or little London delicacies.

'Have you news?'

He raised his eyebrows. 'None of any importance. The miller has a bad case of boils but that is hardly of interest to you, dear lady. And a widow at Pyrford claims to have witnessed the great stone move. She says she saw it dance up the hill to the church of St Nicholas.'

I smiled. 'A miracle?'

'I know, I know. We are told Our Lord chooses the most unlikely of us sinners to manifest His presence but if you knew the woman … well, let us just say, I have my doubts.'

'No other news? Nothing from the bishop?'

The priory church, dedicated to the Virgin Mary and to St Thomas the Martyr, came under the auspices of the bishop of Winchester. He was a rare visitor and I'd never seen him set foot on the island.

'We have been praying daily for the soul of the king's son so recently gone to God. I hear the interment is to be at Canterbury.'

'My husband will be there with his brothers.'

'Ah!' said the prior, rubbing his fingers together as he contemplated the unknown future. 'Sir Thomas's brother is the heir, I presume.'

I shrugged my shoulders. 'Nobody knows. It is a great worry. I thought you might have heard from the bishop. Some requirement for special prayers perhaps?'

He spread out his hands. 'Alas, no. I have heard nothing. The boy is very young to take on such a burden, poor child. But if he is called upon, God will give him strength.'

He regarded me steadily, doubtless noticing the pallor in my cheeks and the trembling of my fingers.

'Lady Holand. If you are worried, I suggest you put your trust in God. That is not just the man of the Church speaking but your friend. Go back to your little ones and care for them. Let men sort out these matters. At the moment there is nothing you or I can do but pray for a propitious outcome.'

Five weeks later the prior sent a note telling me that instructions for prayers for the king in his grave illness had been received from the bishop and that the great stone at Pyrford had remained resolutely unmoving despite several visits and numerous blessings. Also the miller's boils had reacted favourably to treatment with onion, a remedy heartily recommended by the priory's apothecary.

I heard nothing from Thomas or from my mother-in-law but, with the first frost, my sister arrived bearing a cheese.

'You didn't tell me you were coming,' I said crossly. 'How were we to know you were not an enemy?'

Joan calmly removed her gloves and patted her mare's neck. 'Your boy on the roof had gone to sleep,' she pointed out. 'By the time we reached the gate, your porter knew who we were. Besides, who would regard a middle-aged widow journeying peacefully with a small escort, as a threat?'

I gave her a hug, wanting to cling for comfort but telling myself I was being foolish.

'Is the king recovered?'

'He is but he had us all frightened. His physicians announced it was an epostyme. Someone said he had made a will and everyone thought he was going to die. The duke rushed to Havering and apparently ordered Dame Perrers back to court to give his father comfort; even after the scandal of her marriage.'

'What marriage? I've heard nothing of a marriage?'

'You,' said Joan dismissively. 'are becoming a real country wife. What do you talk about down here?'

'Country matters: the harvest; our neighbours' doings; whether Sabina Doxeye's heirs have a claim to the Twichen land at Pyrford.'

'Dull, dull, dull!'

'Perhaps.'

'You don't hear court gossip?'

'I hear nothing.'

'Well sister, I would not want you to remain in ignorance. It appears that at some time this past year Dame Perrers got herself married to William de Windsor, the king's man in Ireland. The vile little schemer has been organising favours for de Windsor ever since, as well as sleeping in his bed.'

'Did the king know?'

'He does now.'

'Is he angry?'

'Distraught. But he forgives her. In his eyes the woman can do no wrong. He blames de Windsor entirely and swears he will see him suffer. He has already cancelled the lucrative posting which Dame Perrers arranged for her husband and is said to be planning further punishments. The man will be lucky to escape with a spell in the Tower.'

A sudden shower of hail rattling onto the yard sent us scurrying for shelter and we ran laughing up the steps to the safety of the solar. Joan threw off her cloak and looked around at the bent heads of my women who were industriously sewing. I knew they'd been at the window until they heard us coming up the steps but I could hardly blame them and, except for my neighbour's fat daughter who was still a disappointment, they were all good workers.

I sent for refreshments while Joan told me the rest of her news.

'After Canterbury, the duke took revenge on his enemies. He is not a man who forgives easily.'

'Or forgets the names of those who cross him.'

'Indeed. The bishop of Winchester should have been more careful. The duke called a meeting of the grand council and its first act was to condemn the bishop on a charge of misconduct whilst a minister of the crown.'

'They condemned the bishop?'

'Yes. He is forbidden to come within twenty miles of the court and has been deprived of all his temporal possessions.'

Images of the glorious palace across the river from Coldharbour floated into my mind: the gold-painted private barge, the hundreds of servants and the pomp and splendour which accompanied the bishop wherever he went.

'He will have nothing left.'

'Exactly,' said Joan, holding out her fingers for the groom to pour the water. 'He has had to dismiss his personal household and disperse the scholars of his new college in Oxford. With no income he has been thrust back into holy poverty.'

'But where will he go? How will he live?'

Joan used the napkin to dry her hands and shrugged. 'He will wander from house to house seeking a roof over his head. But no-one will take him in. What advantage would there be in a disgraced bishop for any man?'

'Edmund Mortimer is a friend. He will take him in.'

'Edmund Mortimer is unable to be a friend to anyone,' said Joan. 'From the moment he instigated that commons' rebellion, he was a marked man. The duke has persuaded the council to relieve him of the office of earl marshal. They said he could go to Calais to inspect the fortifications if he liked but the little turd chose not to suffer that humiliation. He resigned. And you can't really blame him, can you? They'd have had him banished to Ireland next.'

As I picked up the bowl of late pears to offer them to Joan, I felt a sudden pang of pity for poor Edmund. I would happily send Philippa over the Narrow Sea to Calais, and not just to inspect the fortifications. But not Edmund.

'What of his creature?' I enquired. 'The man who spoke out against our aunt's husband at the parliament?'

'Mortimer's steward? He has been arrested and taken to Nottingham Castle. Lord Latimer is to be brought back; and his son-in-law, John Neville.'

I shook my head. Everything was being overturned and the duke had shown the commons and their supporters just how powerful he really was. It was as if the last parliament had never been.

'What about the cheese?' Joan suggested.

My mind was full of thoughts of Edmund who was now unfavoured and unloved. I had a sudden desire to take his head in my lap and stroke the tendrils of the soft fair hair that I remembered so well. Philippa would have no time for a husband who was not in the ascendant, of that I was quite certain, but if he had been mine ... if only he had been mine.

Joan's Essex cheese usually boasted a white crumbly sharpness but this one was different. The rind hid a deep golden centre which was very smooth and sweet on the tongue.

'It's beautiful. How did you make it?'

'A widow from Gloucester gave the secret to her sister-in-law's cousin who is kin to one of my women. She uses Our Lady's bedstraw. Puts it in the milk until the milk curdles. It's as simple as that.'

'I'll slit open my mattress this very night,' I said smiling. 'I'll have the dairy filled with your cheeses.'

'I think you need the fresh herb; in flower of course, otherwise you won't get the colour.'

'For shame! I shall have to wait till next summer.'

Joan lent forward and whispered quietly. 'The king is to make young Richard, prince of Wales and have him proclaimed as his heir. The duke persuaded him it was time. He said the prince was gone and the king must look to the future of his family.'

I closed my eyes and whispered a silent prayer of thanks. Once Richard was declared the king's heir, there would be no further possibility of danger and I could return to London.

'So we shall be safe.'

'Fitzalan thinks there is more danger yet to come and our troubles may not be over. But for the moment the duke has arranged a Christmas gathering at Westminster Palace and plans to present young Richard as heir.'

'And then we wait.'

Joan nodded. 'Nobody says anything but everyone knows we are waiting for the king to die. It's like being entombed in a long night of darkness, waiting for the sun to rise and day begin.'

'Let us pray it is a fine dawning.'

'Amen to that.'

She picked up the last fragments of cheese and smiled. 'And your husband bids you to return with me to London.'

I gave her a gentle push. 'How mean you are. You could have told me that first. Here I was, hoping and praying he would allow me back, and there you were, keeping it a secret.'

'He wanted to come himself but I persuaded him I was perfectly capable of escorting my sister and her children to London.'

'He wishes me to bring the children?'

Joan leant forward. 'I think it is the children he wishes to see, not you.'

I gave her another push, harder this time. She put up her hands and fended me off.

'What he actually said was that he could not wait to see you again.' She paused. 'He is very loving for a man, isn't he? *Trés amoreux.*'

'Is he? I wouldn't know. I have no-one to compare him with. I've only had one husband.'

Joan gave me a sideways look and said. 'You should be careful, Alys. Good husbands are like tender plants, they need warmth. Neglect Thomas and you will live to regret it.'

If anyone was neglected it was me. I had no title and a husband with no ambition. If he was anxious to see me doubtless it was only because he was finding his bed cold.

'Thomas doesn't complain,' I said.

'Does he have a woman?'

'No,' I said indignantly. 'Of course not. He has no need.'

'Not even when you are as you are now?'

She gestured to my belly where evidence of Thomas's attentions of early last summer were obvious to any woman who knew what to look for.

'Thomas is a faithful husband and I, as you see, am an obedient wife.'

'Hmm,' said Joan, cocking her head to one side. 'Unlike Constanza's sister.'

A prickle of distaste slithered down my spine at the mention of my brother-in-law's former paramour.

'What have you heard?'

'A rumour that she's entertaining John Holand again.'

'He wouldn't be so foolish.'

'Maybe not,' smiled Joan, 'but *she* would.'

I thought of Isabel dancing across the floor, peeping through her eyelashes at my brother-in-law; stroking her fingers along the silks of his sleeve and whispering in his ear. I remembered how she'd smiled at him in front of the assembled company that Christmas before my baby died and how each time she caught sight of him, her face lit up with joy. She had loved him; possibly she loved him still. But she was a married woman and not free to love. As a royal wife she was not permitted to favour anyone other than her husband.

'Has her sister said anything?'

Joan pursed her mouth. 'Duchess Constanza hides herself away at Hertford with her Spanish ladies. She only comes to the Savoy if the duke insists. I hear from her English women that since her son died she has lost interest in his company.'

'She is a cold woman.'

'And he is a passionate man. He and Lady Swynford are well-matched. It is a pity they cannot marry.'

My shocked face must have told Joan what I thought because she laughed. 'It was a jest, Alys. Only a jest.'

'You'll be telling me next it's a pity the king cannot marry Dame Perrers.'

'Now that,' said Joan pulling me out of my chair, 'would be an abomination. If it were a possibility, which of course it isn't, I would truly fear for the consequences. Just imagine: Alice Perrers as queen!'

The duke was true to his word. The extravagant Christmastide celebrations at Westminster were utterly splendid with feasting and entertainments to rival anything we had enjoyed before. On the day of the Nativity the duke presented Richard to the assembled company as heir to the throne and the kingdom. In front of everyone, he knelt before the slight figure of this fair-haired ten year-old boy and swore to accept him as his sovereign. Men cheered and stamped while the king peered vacantly through his rheumy old eyes and asked plaintively where Dame Perrers was.

Richard, dressed in silver and white, was seated next to his grandfather at the high table until the king became too weary and shuffled off to his nearby palace at Sheen. There was little sign of the duke so it was Isabel's husband, the earl of Cambridge, who was to be found lolling in pride of place next to his nephew, drinking too much and examining with great interest the expensive gifts given to the new heir by those wishing to gain his favour. The youngest royal uncle was also sprawled at the table, encouraging Richard to reckless gambling. Young Woodstock was a quarrelsome young man who didn't like losing and probably thought a child would be easy to beat. But Richard was a skilful player with the dice and before long had his uncle bankrupt.

'I see my son-in-law is losing again,' laughed Joan in my ear. 'That won't please him. I pity my daughter having to live with such a brute but she seems content.'

'And your other daughter, Mary?'

Joan sniffed. 'The king has given her wardship to my son-in-law and he has put her with the nuns. He is hoping she will find a vocation.'

'Surely a good marriage would be preferable?'

'He wants control of the whole of my daughters' inheritance, not just half,' explained Joan. 'He is insufferably greedy.'

On the last day of the Christmastide revels, we wore masks and laughed our way through the ridiculous antics of those chosen to pay forfeits by our mock Twelfth Night king. The ungainly young man with the thatch of yellow hair was one of the duke's squires. He was clumsily garbed in a fur-trimmed cloak with a tawdry crown on his head and allowed to sit on the canopied chair where Richard or the duke usually sat. His duty was to issue whatever orders he liked, to anyone, high or low, and if his hapless victim could not comply he would devise a suitable forfeit.

As the evening progressed his demands became more and more extreme. For failing to catch a city wife in a game of tag round the benches, an elderly knight from Northamptonshire was made to crawl on all fours, braying like an ass, whipped with a holly wand by one of the Percy girls. Next, fourteen year-old Robert de Vere had to stand on the table dressed in just shirt and hose, singing for his supper while the assembled company pelted him with cinnamon comfits. As the forfeits became wilder, women sent their young charges to bed, the better to enjoy themselves. I noticed with surprise, the number of couples who took the opportunity to slip away into the shadows.

'You look pale,' said Eleanor, removing her mask. 'What's wrong?' She regarded me as my nursemaid did when I was a child and had torn my gown. 'It's horribly hot in here. Let's go down to the courtyard garden at the back? It will be icy cold but better than this stuffiness.'

Reluctantly I allowed myself to be drawn away from the others, through the warren of rooms and covered passageways which made up this part of the king's palace of Westminster. At the bottom of a short fight of stairs and through an empty echoing chamber to where Eleanor found a door leading out onto a cloister and a small courtyard garden.

'See!' she whispered as we stood together on the flagstones at the edge of the pebbled path.

I looked up. Above the shelter of the pantiled roof was a square patch of darkness. A thousand stars filled the heavens, scattered across the black sky like tiny pinpricks of light.

'The children say each star is an angel with a candle,' said Eleanor quietly. 'I wonder if it is so.'

'I used to think they were diamonds and that was what made them glitter.'

178

At that moment we heard a rustle on the far side of the cloister garden. Somebody was there, hidden in the furthest corner. There were two of them and they were too busy with what they were doing to notice us. The woman's voice sighed with pleasure as the shadowy figures moved closer and merged. There was a gasp, a smothered laugh and more sighs and the torchlight caught the flash of a bare shoulder and a woman's gown – dark crimson and silver. Then a gentle susurration as the rich brocade was crushed by her companion. The man's voice was low and insistent.

It was wrong to stay but there was a horrible fascination in watching what they were doing not ten yards away from us, half-hidden in the darkness. It was disgusting, and we were no better than the village girls at Woking when they peeped through the bushes on Midsummer's night while the men took their pleasure with whomever they had enticed under the hedgerows.

I was certain Eleanor recognised the gown as belonging to Isabel and the identity of her ravisher as none other than my brother-in-law, John Holand, but neither of us moved. We heard their soft languorous moans warming the cold night air, the sighing and the increased urgency of their gasps as my husband's younger brother rutted away with the royal wife who should have known better. From their careless behaviour, they surely believed they were unobserved but the noise seemed over-loud in the quiet of the garden. I could hear my heart beating and was aware of Eleanor's soft breathing next to mine but there were no footsteps, no voices or movements other than ourselves and the two lovers in the shadows. All of a sudden there

179

came a muffled cry and then silence. A moment later there were sounds of a scuffle, a cascade of giggles and a friendly slap.

'Eleanor,' I whispered. 'Let's go. We can't be found here.'

I pulled her arm and we slipped back through the door.

'That was …'

'I know exactly who it was,' she said.

'What shall we do?'

'Do? We do nothing. What is there to do?'

'But my brother-in-law will get himself killed if the earl finds out.'

'Then let us hope he remains ignorant.'

'And Isabel? What will happen to her?'

'Convent,' said Eleanor shortly. 'She was lucky last time, the earl believed her. He won't believe her a second time.'

'Perhaps we should tell my mother-in-law.'

'No,' said Eleanor swiftly. 'She has enough to worry about.' She sighed. 'When she married the prince she had no idea it would end like this. But then, when she married Thomas Holand she never thought he would die so soon.'

'How old was she when she married Thomas Holand?'

Eleanor looked at me sharply.

'Should that be a matter of interest to you?'

'No, but it's odd. My husband told me she was married in the year of the great pestilence yet I have heard different, that she married when she was a girl of thirteen.'

Eleanor stopped and put her hands on both my shoulders and looked hard into my eyes. 'If I were you, Alys, I should stop asking questions.'

'Why?'

'It would be safer. I wouldn't want anything to happen to you. Do you understand?'

She looked so serious I was suddenly afraid.

'Eleanor, what is it about the princess's first marriage? Why should it not be talked about?'

'Alys, I want you to swear you will ask no further questions.'

'But Eleanor!'

'Swear it,' she hissed.

'Very well,' I replied sulkily. 'I swear.'

'We will not discuss this again and you will forget this conversation. Do you understand?'

'Yes, Eleanor.'

But how could I forget such a conversation? I would not discuss it with anyone but I couldn't forget and it didn't stop me wondering what my mother-in-law was hiding and why it was so important.

One evening towards the end of January a great company of Londoners dressed in fanciful costumes paraded across the bridge and made their way along the river bank towards Kennington. With darkness falling, their blazing torches lit up the sky and the noise of singing and piping and banging of drums as they approached the palace walls was enough to wake the sleepiest page curled up in the ashes of a hearth. This was, I was told, a special tribute to Richard, but it was odd to see the duke retreat into the shadows and allow his nephew to step forward and receive the men who had come to see the little heir to the throne. The mummers presented gifts and, with no urging from his mother, Richard bade them welcome, ordered wine for the men and called for the minstrels to strike up a tune. Then he settled down to the serious matter of gambling.

'I hear you have been asking questions,' murmured my mother-in-law.

Inwardly I cursed Eleanor and was glad the darkness hid my blushing face. 'I'm sorry, my lady, I didn't mean to pry.'

She gave a low laugh. 'You have nothing to apologise for, my dear. It is natural to be curious. Would you like me to tell you what you wish to know?'

'Yes please.'

'It is very simple. I was young, only thirteen, and fell in love. But Thomas Holand was not a man my family would welcome. He was poor and had no title, no prospects of any kind. But we loved each other and so we married secretly. I told no-one.' She smiled at the memory; I could hear it in her voice.

'You were very brave,' I said.

She laughed. 'Brave? Foolish? Call it what you will but when my family discovered what I'd done they were outraged. They locked me up and wouldn't let me see my husband. It was a dark time for me and as you can imagine I was heart-broken. Thomas had no money and no way of getting me back. We were completely cut off from each another. It wasn't until some years later after my mother and my uncle were dead and Thomas had the bishop of Norwich wed us publicly, that the king recognised our marriage and we could be together.'

'The year of the great pestilence?'

'Yes, the year of the great pestilence. A truly terrifying time. We went to sleep each night not knowing if we would wake next morning.'

'But you survived.'

'Yes, we survived and the following year our first child was born.'

It was so simple. I wondered why no-one had told me before.

She leaned over and kissed my cheek. 'There, now you know.'

'May I ask you a question?' I said shyly.

'Certainly.'

I felt awkward asking but knew I needed to rid myself of any lingering suspicions.

'The rumours from Bruges?'

'Ah yes.' She shook her head as if in amusement. 'Again, very simple. The prince was so anxious to marry me he was careless over the dispensation. You knew, of course that the he and I were cousins? My father was half-brother to his grandfather.'

I nodded. This I had always known; my mother had told me.

'What no-one remembered until later was that my mother also had distant ties of kinship to the prince's family. Not wishing there to be the slightest doubt about the validity of our marriage we applied to the pope for a second dispensation. It was readily given but you see how this might give rise to speculation on the part of a mischief-maker.'

Of course. As my mother-in-law had said, a simple mistake, a moment's carelessness but quickly put right.

How foolish I had been to doubt her and how wise she had been to tell me the truth.

The city was an uneasy place that winter. The council had removed some of the Londoner's privileges, giving the mayor no say in matters of public order. People were angry. Up Crooked Lane, a tall man, dressed better than most, stood on the steps of St Michael's each morning, shouting insults about the duke; and down by the quays a woman was heard openly urging men to give the duke a day of reckoning. "We'll show Lancaster what we think of 'im and 'is liberties. Rip out 'is guts and burn 'em in front of 'is eyes," she screamed. The men of our household reported such incidents as commonplace.

We were perfectly safe behind the high walls of Coldharbour but Thomas was taking no chances.

'There is talk of burning the Savoy. I want you and our unborn child out of here.'

'But Thomas …'

'I shall send you to Pleshy, to your sister's house.'

When I looked doubtful, he wrapped his arms around me and said, 'Alys, please do as I say. I could not bear to lose you both.'

I was touched by his concern and thought how kind he was. He might not be the man I desired but he was kind. If only he were ambitious. If only he was more like Edmund. Or his brother, John. But he wasn't.

She was a girl, an easy birth. My sister stood godmother and we named the baby Joan in her honour. Thomas send me a gift of a brooch and wrote diligently each week. His letters were not gossipy like those of Eleanor who told me how a mob had forced the duke and Lord Percy to flee from the house of Sir John d'Ypres and across the river to Kennington. In the panic to escape, the duke had bruised his shins while rising from the table which did not please him one bit. He was all for hanging, drawing and quartering each one of the mob until the princess intervened and calmed everyone down. In the end a deputation was sent across the river to talk to the Londoners and a full-scale riot was narrowly averted. Thomas merely wrote that there had been trouble but everything was now resolved. He conveyed his thanks to my sister for my care and told me how much I was missed.

Once I was fully recovered from the birth, little Joan was dispatched with her wet nurse and nursemaid to Woking to join her sister and brother in the nursery and I returned to London and my husband.

12

DEATH OF A KING 1377

In London everyone was holding their breath. No-one was sure what would happen next and during those weeks of indecision we all waited. Easter came and went and still we waited. When the king appeared at the St George's Day ceremony at Windsor to knight his youngest son and his two grandsons, Richard and Harry, everyone said how old and frail he looked, how this must surely be the last time they would see him, how it couldn't be long until the summons came. But the days passed and still he lingered and still we waited.

Charters were signed and orders given; men went to Bruges to escort the duke of Brittany back to England, and a party of Londoners who went to Sheen reported the king as befuddled, not in his right mind. And still he lingered. The end of the truce with France drew near and preparations were made for a great expedition to be led by the dukes of Lancaster and Brittany; ships and men were ordered and at Kennington we continued to wait.

One day in the early part of June, my mother-in-law asked me to accompany her on a private visit. She didn't say where we were going and, to my surprise, she didn't order her private barge with the duck-down cushions and gold-fringed canopy. Instead we boarded a common boat with hard wooden seats and a plain canvas cover, the sort a low-born knight might use, one which would not merit anyone's attention. There was no fluttering standard and no body of liveried oarsmen, merely a few of her more discreet servants, close-mouthed but, I noticed, well-armed in case of trouble. I was her only companion.

'I do not want this visit known,' she explained. 'I chose you because you are not inclined to gossip. You are my dearest daughter-in-law and I can trust you.'

I nodded obediently, wondering where this clandestine adventure would lead us and why nobody else must know.

The river swirled and eddied with the tide, ripples of dark brown and blue, with white splashes from the dripping oars as we slid silently through the water. We passed the palace of Westminster and were quickly out into open country. Beyond the banks of rushes at the water's edge stretched marshland with little islands of stunted trees and occasional villages consisting of nothing more than a few mud huts. I saw the squat tower of a distant church and the rooftops of some misshapen houses clustered at the mouth of a wide stream whose slow-moving muddy waters were quickly lost in the faster-flowing waters of the Thames.

I dozed in the gentle morning sunshine until my mother-in-law announced that we had arrived. I looked up. This was the king's royal manor house of Sheen, a beautiful little palace set amidst the summer meadows, right on the banks of the river. At its back rose a low wooded hill of oak and lime and stands of beech and to the side lay a flowery pleasure garden and a neat little orchard enclosed by a white fence.

'Follow me and say nothing,' she said. 'Remember, this is a private visit.'

I followed the hem of her dark cloak, keeping my eyes lowered, not looking to either side although half of me longed to stare at the glittering wonders. We passed from room to room, past lines of liveried servants, up steps and through more rooms until at last we found ourselves in front of an imposing pair of gilded doors, guarded by four men-at-arms. With a few murmured words from my mother-in-law, the doors opened and we passed through.

I was immediately struck by the silence and the gloom. Very few candles were lit and the only people in the room were an elderly priest kneeling at the bedside, a single servant standing in the shadows and a modestly-dressed woman holding the hand of the man in the bed.

Could this be all that was left of the king of England?

The woman turned and I saw the hard glittering eyes of Dame Alice Perrers, the king's concubine, the woman hated up and down the length and breadth of England; branded as a witch, an enchantress and an avaricious, grasping whore. Without her glorious gowns, her furs and her jewels she looked quite ordinary, rather plain if I was being honest, and it was hard to believe she had exerted such influence over the king for nigh on fifteen years.

She hesitated and then curtsied. 'Princess, what a surprise!'

My mother-in-law's face was unreadable. 'Ask Dame Perrers to accompany you outside, Alys. I wish to speak with his grace, my father-in-law, the king, in private.'

'He can't speak to you,' said Dame Perrers. 'He is beyond speech, but he will probably know you. Not that you have visited him very much in his sickness. I thought a good daughter-in-law would care for her late husband's father but then what would I know, coming from the gutters as you have told me on many occasions.'

She turned and gazed fondly at the king. 'You know me though, don't you, my lord? You don't forget.'

The king's hands moved slightly and one side of his face twitched convulsively. A single tear trickled slowly down his furrowed cheek and was lost in his beard which lay tidily combed on the embroidered cover.

'I told them to send to France for his daughter. He'll want to see her but I doubt if he'll be pleased to see you. Never much liked you, did he? Weren't the wife he wanted for his princely boy?'

My mother-in-law's face remained impassive under this torrent of rudeness.

'Dame Perrers,' I said. 'Please come with me and allow the princess to make her private farewells to his grace.'

She shrugged and leant over and kissed the king's forehead.

'I won't leave you again,' she whispered. 'I'll be back.'

I ushered her through the doorway into the outer chamber where the air was fresher and the light brighter.

'No need to feel sorry for me,' she said before I had time to speak. 'He's given me plenty. I'll be alright. No call for jointures and dowers when you've got a good man, and king or no, he is a good man.'

'He is the king,' I said simply. 'It is part of his kingship.'

'He is dying.'

'And you betrayed him,' I said. 'How could you do such a thing as to marry?'

She gave a deep throaty laugh. 'You imagine any of them will look out for me when he's gone? You think

189

they'll be generous? Let me tell you, Lady Holand, I have plenty of enemies, men who will gladly see me destroyed. A woman like me needs a protector and who better than a husband.'

'It was cruel.'

'It was necessary.'

She watched me with some amusement. 'Being a man's concubine is no different to being his wife, your hardest work is done in his bed. But you know that already, don't you, Lady Holand? Everything else is simple. You flatter, you keep him company, you entertain his friends; you smile even when you bear his children alone and in pain. The bishop of Winchester regards me as the devil's own instrument, an unprincipled slut. But that is just the Church censuring those they do not understand. What would they know of love and a man's desire?'

'You're nothing but a common whore.'

'That is where you are wrong, Lady Holand. I am a wife, just like you; and when it comes to whoring aren't all women the same under the skin. Which one of us has not lain with a man, not from desire, but out of duty? Not for love but for the rewards we will reap?'

'I was married in the sight of God.'

'And you think God turned his eyes away when the king first took me to his bed? I was seventeen years old, Lady Holand, a virgin, and I did as I was bid. As you did. As all young women do. A man tells us what we must do and we obey.'

I turned from her and walked to the window embrasure and sat on the tiny seat. I would not lower myself to argue with Dame Perrers.

190

'What of Lady Swnford? I hear she has another child?' she continued.

I chose to ignore her, instead peering through little panes of glass at the garden below: early roses, neat banks of scented lavender and clove-pink gillyflowers; low hedges of pale green box and a trellis smothered in trailing blossom, marking the entrance to an allée. Two men walked across the garden and disappeared into the allée. Moments later a small dog scampered after them. It was very peaceful.

After some while I heard the door open. I turned to see my mother-in-law framed in the doorway. She looked at Dame Perrers who curtsied, a small secretive smile on her face. Neither of them spoke and after a moment my mother-in-law indicated that we were leaving. I followed her as we swept through the maze of rooms and down the steps and out under an archway into the bright sunshine. It was only as we took our places on the seat beneath the plain canvas canopy that I saw she was weeping. Instinctively I put out my hand and covered hers.

'I looked at him and saw my end,' she said. 'I saw what I am and what I shall become.'

Awkwardly I stroked the back of her hand with my fingers. 'Not yet, my lady, not yet.'

'You never knew him,' she said as tears trickled down her cheeks. 'He was the father I never had. All those years ago, in that other life, he would sit me on his knee and call me his little Jeanette. So handsome, so glorious; golden-haired and bejewelled, so kind and so strong. Was it any wonder that I loved him?'

She stared across the fast-widening gap between boat and riverbank, at a couple of ducks dabbling industriously near the landing stage and an army of small black moorhens scurrying for shelter in amongst the reeds.

'He loved me,' she said quietly. 'Once upon a time in that other life, he loved me.'

'Of course he did; you were like a daughter to him.'

She smiled and tried to wipe away the tears.

'He never forgave me.'

'I'm sure that is not so,' I said stoutly. 'What could you possibly have done that was so unforgiveable?'

'I lied to him. I married without his permission and when he tried to save me, I threw his so-called help back in his face.'

'But, my lady; that is what a father does. When a daughter disobeys, at first he is angry, he shouts, he threatens, perhaps he lashes out with his fist. But later, when he has had time to reflect, he forgives. He loves her so he forgives her.'

She smiled thinly. 'A father, maybe.' She paused. 'But not a lover.'

A great chasm of silence engulfed the space where we sat. I had surely misheard. A lover?

She laughed at the expression on my face. 'I have shocked you.'

'No,' I said, desperately trying to make sense of what she had just said. 'I am not shocked.'

'Of course you are, Alys. And rightly so. Looking back, I too am shocked.'

'You are?'

'Of course. He was my royal cousin and I was little more than a girl. He should never have given in to temptation.

In so many ways it was an unforgiveable sin. But I am also shocked at myself for having enjoyed the occasion as much as I did and for wishing there had been more.'

'How old were you?' I asked, curious, realising how little I really knew about my mother-in-law. I thought I knew the kind of woman she was but clearly I didn't.

'Fourteen? Fifteen? I forget.'

'But your husband?' I gasped.

'Which one?'

If she had been fourteen she would already have married her beloved Thomas. Her family had kept her away from him, yet they had allowed this seduction to take place. I didn't understand how any of it could have occurred.

'Did you tell them?'

'No. Husbands are not understanding in that way. Besides, what could I say? "My cousin seduced me but I was willing". No, I was not inclined to tell them and you are the first woman I have told. I have no idea why I feel the need to unburden myself, except that today I saw death in the face of a man I had once loved and knew I would never see him again.'

I murmured some words about God's forgiveness.

She smiled. 'It is too late for forgiveness, Alys, and too late for regrets. I had hoped for some kind of absolution but it has been denied me. All that is left is penance for past sins. We have to live with our failures and I know you will tell no-one. Eleanor would tell Lewis but you, I am certain, will not tell Thomas, will you?'

'No, never.'

No wonder the king hadn't wanted her for his princely boy; no wonder there had been such stiff formality and mutual wariness between them these past years and no wonder that now, when death was creeping ever closer, she was consumed with guilt and sadness.

He died two weeks later. I was not at Kennington when they brought the news but that evening Thomas told me how everyone in the room knelt to Richard to make their obeisance and how delighted his little brother had been.

'He particularly enjoyed having his uncles on their knees. You could see the gleam in his eyes. Imagine what it was like for him: three grown men who throughout his life had been telling him what to do and what to say; all of a sudden, there they were, kneeling on the floor in front of him, their heads bent and their hoods in their hands. And the others: Burley, Clifford, de Vere, the men of the household; everyone.'

'You?'

'Of course. He is my king even though he is my little brother.'

'It hardly seems real.'

'But it is and do you know who was the first to drop to his knees?'

'The duke?'

'No. Harry.'

Cousin Harry! Poor Richard. What a long hard road lay ahead of him. Harry, at ten, was already an energetic jouster-in-the-making, a born leader with a following of young Percys and Mowbrays, learning to wield a sword and take a turn at the quintain. But Richard was not like his cousin. The only sport he cared for was hunting. If you gave him a hawk, a clear day and an open view, he was as good as any man.

'I doubt Richard will be the kind of king to lead an army,' I mused.

'He won't need to.'

'Not yet, he's too young. But he'll grow. And what then?'

'Let us hope that whatever happens he will grow in wisdom. Our mother has allowed him to draw much too close to Simon Burley and Robert de Vere. Naturally a boy must pay attention to his tutor's words but Burley has filled Richard's head with fanciful notions of a prince's self-importance. And de Vere is nothing but a creeping toad, constantly telling Richard how wise he is and how clever. They praise him beyond what is good for him.'

'I'm sure they do no harm.'

Thomas began rubbing his fingers together and hunched his shoulders inwards like a bedraggled heron caught in the rain. I wanted to tell him to sit up straight but he was my husband and it was not my place to say such things. Instead I let him carry on worrying about his little brother.

'Burley hovers over him like an over-anxious nursemaid and de Vere is forever in his company, flattering and fawning like the worst kind of lickspittle. A king should not have such intimate friends. A king needs to be even-handed.'

'Even-handed? What king was ever even-handed? And since when were you an expert on kingship?'

He smiled. 'I read, Alys, or haven't you noticed? No, you probably haven't.'

I returned to my mourning robes, my crow-black cloaks and veils, my shimmering silk gowns and embroidered leather gloves; all the colour of deepest ebony. I laid aside my ivory-coloured satin slippers in favour of a more serviceable dark pair and explained patiently to Nell that wearing the hated black gown was necessary now that the king was dead.

Our steward saw to the re-hanging of black cloth, once again hiding our bright tapestries and plunging the hall deep into stygian gloom. The drapery billowed and swayed but this time young Tom informed me he wasn't frightened. 'It's only the wind,' he declared, clutching my hand. 'It won't harm us.'

That first morning as my maid laced my gown and straightened the heavy folds of my skirts, I felt as if nothing had changed and I had been wearing black all my life. But while here in England we were making preparations for the funeral of a dead king, the men of France and Castile were making preparations for war.

In the last days of June when the honey-sweet scent of woodbine drifted through the hedgerows and the swallows twisted and turned as they swooped through the skies, the enemy beached their ships beneath the walls of Winchelsea and proceeded to burn their way along our south coast. The town of Rye became an inferno and Hastings was utterly destroyed. There was nothing left for the survivors but blackened piles of smoking rubble and dozens of men with their throats slit lying in the ashes of what had once been one of our greatest seaports.

I could have borne the carnage if this had been all, but it wasn't. A week after that first assault, the French attacked my brother's town of Lewes. Here the walls were undefended and the people unprepared. Fortunately my sister-in-law, Liz, and her daughters were safe in London. The enemy captured the prior and two of his knights and then marched their way up the river valley to the gates of the priory. They celebrated their triumph by burning the town and stealing our casks of wine before sailing away on the next tide. It was shameful and horrible and I must admit that I wept.

In the eleven days after we buried old King Edward, the duke arranged a splendid coronation for Richard. Of the people in my family, only Aunt Wake had been alive when King Edward was crowned and she was past remembering anything unless it touched her person.

Richard was to lodge one night in the Tower as was the custom. On the day before the actual coronation he was to ride in procession through the city streets, past the Savoy to the palace at Westminster, accompanied by all the great men of the realm.

London was packed for the occasion: merchants, apprentices, stableboys, servants, beggars in rags, hooded friars, shopkeepers, fishwives, young women dressed in their best and tradesmen of every kind and description. Expectant faces crowded upper windows of houses along the route and walls groaned and creaked as more and more people clambered up, hanging onto poles and corbels to get a better view. There wasn't a single step where people weren't crushed together like stalks of corn in a sheaf, clutching their neighbours and craning their heads to see what was going on.

People had come from every part of the city, from Bishopsgate and Broad Street, from Cripplegate and all the way from outside the walls at Clerkenwell. Since before dawn the men of Kent and Essex had been swarming into the city. They poured across the bridge and through the gates, pushing and squeezing themselves amongst the crowds, grabbing bread from baker's trays and pies from market stalls. Others had travelled for hundreds of miles, spending days on the road, eager for this moment, wanting to see the new young hope for England. They were hungry and thirsty and footsore but nobody wanted to miss a moment of the fun.

Richard's London was a city glittering with silver and gold. The streets shone with fluttering coloured ribbons and brightly painted banners. The great conduit tower in the market at Cheap flowed with wine and at every corner, the London guildsmen provided displays of mock castles. Choirs of boys dressed as angels sang to entertain the crowds and to please their king. The noise was deafening.

The procession was led by the commons dressed all in white: the squires, the knights, the aldermen, the mayor and the two city sheriffs. Then came the duke and Lord Percy with their wands of office, cutting a swathe through the crowds, making way for Richard's other two uncles and the troupes of musicians with their flutes and drums and trumpets. The musicians were followed by the men of Bordeaux, the Gascons, the Germans and the men of the London wards clothed in their luxuriously-furred robes. But however rapturously these men were received by the crowds, everyone was really waiting for the young king. They had lived so long in the shadow of death that when they saw Richard dressed in silver and white, his horse led by a knight of his chamber and followed by his earls, barons and knights all in due order and robed in white, they could hardly contain their joy.

As the procession wound its slow way through the narrow streets and out under Ludgate, little girls in white dresses darted out of the crowd, tossing petals and imitation gold coins over the boy king on his high horse. Wine flowed in abundance and the people of England cheered and sang and danced and drank until the sun disappeared behind the rocky hump of Lambethmoor and those with nowhere to go for the night, lay down to sleep in the gutters. The joyful celebrations lasted until well after midnight and by morning it was said you couldn't find a single sober man or woman in the whole of London.

Next day in the abbey, in the most solemn of ceremonies, with the assembled nobility in attendance, Richard was anointed with holy oil by the archbishop of Canterbury. The crown was placed upon his head and a new dawn had broken.

It did not seem possible: little milksop, king of England.

Two days later my mother-in-law called a family council in her private rooms at Kennington. She was gathering together her Holand children but had asked that I should accompany my husband.

As I looked at the bright faces of my sisters-in-law, I knew precisely what they were thinking because their thoughts mirrored my own. Now that Richard was king, his brothers and sisters could expect rewards, favours, significant marks of recognition. I had been told it was what kings did in the aftermath of a coronation whilst basking in the warm glow of everyone's admiration. No-one could possibly resent a king who gave his kin their just rewards and nobody would doubt his right to make such gifts. It was what men expected.

After the coronation banquet Richard had rewarded Simon Burley by making him his master of falcons and keeper of the mews at Charing Cross. Greater rewards had been given to others. Richard's uncle, young Thomas of Woodstock, Joan's son-in-law, was now earl of Buckingham; Richard's old tutor, Sir Guichard d'Angle, was earl of Huntingdon; and my Percy and Mowbray cousins who, as my mother had once said, liked to think they ruled the north, became the earls of Northumberland and Nottingham.

Naturally decisions about ennoblement had been taken by the duke and my mother-in-law. Richard was far too young to have an opinion but it was he who belted on the ceremonial swords and kissed the men on both cheeks and received their fealty. I had expected Thomas to receive his earldom at the same ceremony but of course, a brother was special. His would be a grander and perhaps a more private affair.

My mother-in-law was dressed, as usual, in the bodice-hugging blue gown which was her favourite. If she had asked for my advice I would have suggested a looser style, more flowing, cut higher at the neck, but I knew she enjoyed displaying her magnificent bosom and narrow waist and was probably unaware of the growing plumpness of her arms and her hips which caused her flesh to bulge and the silk to wrinkle and crease; so I said nothing. She had made no change in her dress because of her new role as mother of the king, which surprised me. However, I had to admit she looked wonderful, like a lovely dewy over-blown rose, a little past its best but, nevertheless, still beautiful. Even after two husbands and six children men's eyes were drawn towards her wherever she went and this was not simply because of who she was.

She sat in the large chair at the head of the table with Thomas at her side and John, Maud, Johane and me arranged in front of her. She looked at each of us in turn and smiled.

'You are my dearest children; yes, you too Alys. I never want you to doubt that my affections for you are anything other than the genuine love of a mother for her children. There has not been a single moment in my life when I have ceased to love you and you have always been amongst my greatest blessings.'

I could feel Maud's body tense and noticed a slight trembling of Johane's fingers which caused her to stuff her hands in her lap.

'Now that your brother is our anointed king, I know you have expectations,' continued my mother-in-law. 'It is natural.'

I shifted slightly on the hard seat, hugging the knowledge that soon Thomas would have his title and his lands and we would be wealthy and admired. This would be our moment.

'All of you understand the burdens that Richard carries and if you paid attention to your lessons when you were younger you will remember that accusations of favouritism are particularly dangerous for a king, especially for one as young as Richard. Many people are waiting for him to make a mistake and it is our responsibility, yours as well as mine, to ensure that mistakes are not made.'

We nodded our heads, murmuring in agreement. But she was not finished.

'The year I was born, Richard's great-grandfather was pushed from his throne because he rewarded his favourites too highly and men became jealous. He took no notice of a growing tide of discontent and paid the price for his foolishness. It is an object lesson to all men who think they are untouchable simply because they have been chosen. I shall not allow that to happen to my son.'

'But we will get something?' said Johane, looking straight at her mother. 'You can't give us nothing.'

'You have a husband to give you gifts, Johane, if you think you deserve them.'

'I don't have a husband,' said Maud. 'Since Courtenay died, I've had no-one to give me gifts. So I will get something, won't I?'

My mother-in-law smiled. 'My dearest Maud. How you have suffered. Yes, you shall have something. What would you like?'

Maud blinked in surprise. 'I hadn't thought,' she lied. 'An annuity perhaps?'

'Would you not rather have your heart's desire?'

'My heart's desire?'

'Which would be?'

Maud gasped. 'The count of St Pol?'

Her mother laughed. 'We are in discussions with the count to see what can be arranged. I am promising nothing

202

but we shall do our best to advance Richard's cause whilst not forgetting your own.'

'Oh!' Maud squeaked, grasping my hand tightly. 'Thank you, dearest lady mother.'

'What about Thomas and me?' said John.

He was trying to look unconcerned but I knew his situation was parlous. Like most young men he spent freely without thinking too much about where his money came from. When his purse was empty he borrowed from friends or from the moneylenders. If the prince had not been sick he would have found John a wealthy wife but instead my brother-in-law was an impecunious young man who badly needed a position to give him a good income. He was depending on Richard to rescue him.

'You, John, are to be one of Richard's chamber knights,' said my mother-in-law. 'He needs a member of our family close, to keep an eye on what is happening and I know you will take good care of him. There will be many new faces and men who seek positions may turn out to be less than scrupulous. I shall be relying on you.'

A chamber knight was a prestigious position but would bring John little income and would not, I thought, suit him. He was a man of action and would not enjoy strolling around in the company of his ten year-old brother and his lordly young friends.

John bowed his head, acknowledging the gift but struggling with his disappointment. Clearly he had expected more.

'And you, Thomas.' My mother-in-law gazed fondly at her firstborn. 'You are to be appointed custodian of the royal forests south of the Trent. You will replace Sir John

Foxley and receive the income commensurate with the post.'

Custodian of the royal forests! Custodian? Not even Justice of the Peace! I put a hand across my mouth to stop myself from saying what I thought. My mother-in-law glanced over and must have read the dismay in my face because she placed her hand upon Thomas's. 'You will not have to wait forever, my son, but now is not the right time. You must see that.'

'Of course I do,' said Thomas without the slightest quiver of disappointment. 'It is a generous gesture and I shall endeavour to carry out my duties responsibly in accordance with my brother's wishes.'

My mother-in-law smiled at my husband's humility. 'I think you will find it preferable to appoint a deputy to manage your day to day duties. It is what most men in your position do. The income of course will come to you.'

It was Johane who voiced what I was thinking. 'Why are we being treated so meanly, lady mother? It is unfair. The four of us are royal kin. It is not as if Richard has a string of other brothers and sisters waiting to be rewarded. Surely Thomas and John should be given titles; and Maud and I should each be given gifts of money. When my brothers sit on the royal council ...'

'Thomas and John will not be members of the royal council,' replied my mother-in-law firmly. 'This has already been decided. It would not be a sensible move.'

'If they are not on the council they will have no influence.'

'Not in that way.'

'We were first. We were your children before Richard was born. Surely that counts for something?'

'I'm sorry you feel like that,' said my mother-in-law smoothly. 'But it never does to appear grasping. A little patience now will bring greater rewards in the future. Wait and see.'

Thomas, as always, took his mother's part. 'You have no need to speak for me, Johane. I am perfectly content with what I have been given.'

'So am I,' beamed Maud, lost in a haze of happiness at the thought of a betrothal with her French count.

'Well, I'm not,' said Johane. 'And neither is John.'

My mother-in-law sighed. 'Bad behaviour does not reap rewards. If you and John feel you have been ignored or treated badly perhaps you should look to your conduct rather than blame others.'

Johane opened her mouth and then shut it again.

'What about you, John?' said his mother to her second son.

'Me?' He shrugged. 'There is no point in wanting more than a king offers, is there? Naturally we all know that none of this is Richard's doing. It is the duke and yourself, lady mother. You make the decisions. But doubtless there will come a time when our brother will speak for himself. So I shall be his closest supporter and in the years ahead perhaps he will be inclined to offer me more. I do have a fancy to become a duke.'

'You?' said Johane. 'A duke? You might as well whistle for the moon. Our mother will never allow that.'

'Then I shall find a duchess to marry.'

The thought of John marrying a duchess, even if he could find one, was so ridiculous we all dissolved into laughter and the difficult moment passed. But John's laughter, like mine, was tinged with anger and hurt. I knew we would have him pacing the floors of Coldharbour before long, complaining of ill-treatment.

'Come,' said Thomas. 'It's time we left our lady mother to her work.'

I felt a grumbling disappointment as we pushed back our chairs and made to leave the room. There should have been more. Johane was right.

'Alys!' My mother-in-law's voice made me turn. 'Stay please. I wish to talk with you.'

As soon as the door closed she began to speak.

'Did you think I had forgotten you?'

I blushed. 'No, my lady. I have no expectations.'

She raised her eyebrows at this patent untruth but let it lie.

'What you must understand, my dear Alys, is that gifts come in all guises, some clearly displayed for all to admire, others not quite so obvious. What if I were to tell you that I have received a report of a trespass?'

I frowned. 'A trespass?'

I had no idea where this was leading. What did a trespass have to do with me?

'It appears that a certain man and his servants have broken the closes and houses at High Rothyng and Ovesham and assaulted the servants of the lord who rightfully owns these manors.'

I caught my breath. I knew those names. They were the manors given to my father's Despenser wife when my father annulled their base marriage. They were compensation for a casting-off and also a bribe. But they were to be hers only for the rest of her life.

'At Yenge Margarets and Wolfhamptom, these same men took fish and at Childscanfield they took money and goods.'

I felt a cold knot of fear squirm in my belly. This was a warning of what was to come now that the old king, was gone. The Despenser woman might be dead but Richard would not be able to protect my family from this bastard son of my father who was trying to blacken our name. Pope Gregory might choose to disregard my father's annulment and even now my father's base firstborn son could steal my brother's earldom and all of our inheritance. We would be impoverished and bastardised, as he had been and I could not bear the shame and the loss.

'Does my brother know?' I whispered, wondering what Fitzalan would do if he was stripped of his title and lands. Where would he go? How would he live?

'I'm sure his stewards have informed him. Would your steward at Woking not tell you if such a calamity had happened?'

Yes, of course Fitzalan must know. But Mother of God! What were we going to do?

'Alys, listen.' My mother-in-law reached out and laid her hand on my arm as if to reassure me. 'What I wanted to tell you, my dearest Alys, is that you do not need to worry. Before the end of the year I believe your father's bastard will find himself in the Tower.'

'The Tower?'

'Yes. And there he will learn the error of his ways. Men remember things differently when they are faced with a prison cell, however comfortable their accommodation may be, and the thought of a hangman's rope inevitably loosens a man's tongue as well as his bowels. I think any belief in his right to share in your father's inheritance will quickly be forgotten. I suspect he will be more than happy to put his name to any agreement put in front of him. Don't you?'

She smiled at the relief on my face and patted my hand. 'There. Now at last I have made you happy. I know today was a disappointment and you expected more for Thomas but you must trust me in this.'

'I do,' I said fervently. 'Oh, I do.'

'And now, my dear, return safely to Woking and take care of that new grandchild of mine growing in your belly.'

I opened my eyes wide and stared. I had told no-one about the baby apart from Thomas.

'There are no secrets in this family, Alys,' she laughed as she kissed me. 'Surely you know that by now?'

13

THE UPRISING 1381

There was great pleasure to be had in travelling the pilgrim road from Canterbury to London on a warm summer's day, the larks singing high above and the sharp smell of salt blowing in off the estuary. Inside the royal coach a feeling of lightness filled the air and the hundreds of people tramping towards us, singing and laughing as they went, ensured the road surface was gloriously flat. They were mostly men and women on their way to the holy shrine at Canterbury who waved cheerfully at our little cavalcade, doubtless recognizing my mother-in-law's brightly coloured banner.

It was five years since the prince had died and four since Richard had become king, yet this was the first time I'd been asked to accompany my mother-in-law on her annual visit to her late husband's tomb. We had stayed five nights at Wickham Brewes, a pretty manor house in the valley of the Little Stour. It now belonged to Thomas but was used by his mother as if it was still her own personal property. She had little consideration for my feelings as she directed the servants and made herself comfortable and I found myself having to bite my tongue.

I was now countess of Kent but that didn't mean I was the recognised lady of Wickham Brewes and it certainly didn't mean we were rich. Thomas had been given the post of marshal of England and a paltry annuity for which he was pathetically grateful; but we were far from wealthy.

'Happy?' my brother-in-law had murmured into my ear at the feast following the lavish ceremony where Thomas received his earldom to add to his title of marshal of England

'Hardly,' I snapped. 'What good is a single manor and an annuity of thirty pounds.'

His hand touched my waist in that horribly familiar way he had.

'Stop it!' I hissed.

He laughed. 'Why? Is this not what women like?'

I was a little afraid of him on that particular day because he was drunk and I was well aware he could be violent. The day before I'd seen him make one of the maids laugh and had later found the girl sobbing in a corner with a livid bruise on her face and her gown disarranged.

He leant his head conspiratorially against mine and whispered into my ear. 'You don't know what you like, sweet Alys.'

He had been watching me carefully, noticing every quiver of my lips.

'Has Isabel tired of you?

The scandalous affair between Constanza's sister and my brother-in-law still blazed brightly but was politely ignored by most people. Her husband was too stupid to notice, my mother-in-law looked the other way and Thomas said it was none of his business.

'By no means.' John lowered his voice to a whisper. 'But a man needs variety and I find you most appealing.

210

Motherhood has improved you greatly.' He removed his hand. 'You are lusciously ripe, my dear sister.'

'If you don't stop, I shall tell Thomas.' But I knew it would be impossible to describe to my husband what passed between me and his brother.

John laughed. 'Thomas will believe me. And remember, sweet sister, I always get what I want in the end. I trample on those who get in my way.'

It was hot and airless in the hall but I had shivered at the thought of being trampled on by my brother-in-law.

The coach rattled and lurched sideways. Johane clutched Eleanor and then returned to the quarrel she'd been fomenting for most of the journey.

'I do not see why,' she said in the thin whiny voice women employ when trying to get their own way.

'You know perfectly well why,' sighed my mother-in-law. 'The prince was Richard's father and if I do not go, people will wonder.'

'Why care what people think?'

'Once people start to wonder, strange notions enter their heads and I won't have more foul rumours spread about Richard.'

Johane scowled. 'You never visit *my* father's tomb.'

I gave a little gasp. Mentioning the princess's first husband was always inadvisable as I had discovered. My mother-in-law's eyes flashed like splinters of glass caught in the sunlight as she leant forward. Her face was barely inches from her daughter's.

'You know nothing. Do not dare to criticize me, daughter. You would do well to look to your own behaviour.

A wife should be loyal and she should be at her husband's side whatever the hardships. That is what I did and what you, too, should do.'

The whole court knew Johane had refused to return to her husband and why, but few had any sympathy for her. Wives were expected to be dutiful. When you married you became part of your husband's life and left your own family behind.

Last autumn, when the carpet king died, Britto had torn up his everlasting treaty with the English and made peace with the new French king. It was shocking and there was only one person more furious than Johane and that was my sister's son-in-law, Thomas of Woodstock, earl of Buckingham. He had marched from Calais to Brittany to join with Britto in attacking the bridge over the Loire at Nantes but when he'd arrived, instead of a battle, he found to his disgust that he was being asked, most politely, to leave the duchy and take his army with him. The Bretons had overnight become friends of our enemy and the English were no longer welcome.

'I shall never speak to him again,' Johane declared. 'He is no husband of mine. I shall never allow him into my bed.'

'I thought it was your husband who had abandoned your marriage bed?' said Eleanor in that innocently mocking way she had.

'I shall stay in England,' Johane announced. 'He can beg, he can go down on bended knee but I shall never go back. Never.'

I pulled the curtain to one side and tried to see through the tiny window but the way ahead was hidden by a thick grey cloud of dust kicked up by the horses' hooves. The coach rocked as we hit another unexpected rut and my mother-in-law put out a hand to steady herself and then laughed.

'Pitfalls for the unwary! A woman's life is full of them.'

It was true: pitfalls, losses, failures, death.

My brother Jack, ever a risk-taker, had not expected to die whilst sailing to Brittany, yet a sudden storm, a wrong decision, a ship on the rocks and he had drowned. Aunt Wake with nothing but a summer rheum yet she had slipped away, grumbling and complaining to the bitter end.

And how did I explain two more daughters? What had I done to deserve that? Each time I had prayed for a boy and each time there had been disappointment. Thomas, content as always, told me that two more little girls in the nursery at Woking was a joy he could not have hoped for, but then he had no understanding of what was important.

The coach lurched and veered and then came to a sudden, rattling halt. A horse screamed and a man cursed. Outside, there was noise and commotion and the coach rocked wildly as something banged on the side.

'What is happening?' cried Eleanor.

The noise grew louder. It was the voices of men, a huge crowd of men; men shouting and yelling. There must have been hundreds of them to make so much noise. Eleanor dropped to the floor and covered her head with her hands as if vainly trying to hide. Johane crouched low, shut her eyes and began exhorting Our Lady to come to her aid. Only my mother-in-law and I remained upright in our seats.

'Do not be frightened, Alys.'

'I'm not,' I lied.

'Think of your children and be brave. Put your trust in God.'

The door opened and there was the captain of our escort, beads of sweat covering his forehead. He looked scared.

'It's a mob, my lady,' he said, panting for breath. 'Hundreds of them. They've come up behind us and they're armed. They're saying they want to speak to you.'

'Speak to the king's mother?' Johane lifted her head. 'That is outrageous. Make them get out of our way.'

'Too many, my lady,' said the man. 'They're quiet for now but I'd not like to offer violence. Things might turn nasty for yourselves.'

The mob must have known who we were from the royal banner and my mother-in-law's colours emblazoned on the coach doors. But what did they want?

'I shall speak to the leaders,' said my mother-in-law, looking not the least bit frightened. 'Have them brought here.'

Almost before the captain had withdrawn himself, two burly men, surprisingly clean and tidily dressed, presented themselves in the opening. They were so large they blocked out the light.

'You know who I am?' said my mother-in-law, in the same voice she used when addressing the duke.

'Yes, lady,' said the taller man. 'Ye be the princess. Ye be our little king's ma. They'm say he be the bly of ye. A fair young prince.'

To my amazement my mother-in-law dimpled at this compliment and rewarded the man with a smile.

214

'Tell me what it is you want of the king?' she said softly as if speaking to an intimate.

The totality of these ruffians' demands was unbelievable. "Evil counsellors" was how they described men such as Archbishop Sudbury, the king's chancellor, and Sir Robert Hales, the king's treasurer; good men who had served Richard loyally but whom the mob wanted handed over to them to answer for their offences against the common folk. What offences did they imagine men like this had committed? Rape? Extortion? It was ridiculous. But mostly they hated the duke. "Justice" was the word they used but I could see they meant to kill him. Their blood lust was up and they needed a victim.

'Stop yer yarping!' shouted the tall man over his shoulder at his comrades who were pressing closer and calling out rudely to the two men at our door.

'Thank you for bringing me your worries,' smiled my mother-in-law. 'I promise you I shall see justice is done. I shall inform the king of what you have said and tell him you crave an audience. I am certain he will agree to see you.'

She extended her gloved hand in a gesture of friendship, but the smaller man, the one with the pock-marked face and dark red jerkin, seized it, pulled her towards the door and planted a rough kiss on her mouth.

'What am ye doing?' shouted his friend, elbowing the lout out of the way. 'Ye'll get un ballowed.'

The captain of our escort had not noticed the man's impertinence as his eyes were on the increasingly restless crowd surrounding the coach, but my mother-in-law simply smiled sweetly, thanked the ruffians and asked that our party should be allowed to proceed.

Outside, the crowd retreated to a grey dusty field at the side of the road, still growling in discontent while the tall man stood on top of a tree stump and shouted instructions. By now, both Johane and Eleanor were back in their seats. We heard the captain give the order to move off and the coach lurched forwards.

'Why did they do that?' said Eleanor in a voice which shook slightly.

'They have grievances,' said my mother-in-law.

'*I* have grievances,' said Johane. 'But I don't riot and assault people.'

Her mother smiled. 'It is the new tax. They say four pence is unjust. They do not believe it is Richard's doing and they look to him for a remedy.'

'They should go back to their homes and obey the king's laws,' muttered Johane.

'Thank God, the duke is in the north,' said my mother-in-law. 'He is safe for they certainly mean to kill him.'

'Kill the duke?' squeaked Johane.

'Indeed, what else did you think they meant? And if we do not make good speed and reach the Tower as quickly as possible they might decide to kill us too.'

We raced through the night with the men of Kent, their longbows and cudgels and their unquenchable thirst for vengeance, only a few miles behind us. We crossed the bridge at Rochester but didn't stop; it would have been much too dangerous to stop. Outside, owls screeched into the summer darkness as we rumbled on and within the coach nobody spoke.

A dull red glow lit up the night sky and before long we

passed a house on fire. The thatch was already destroyed and smoke billowed in great clouds from the guts of the house, spreading out across the nearby fields. Flames roared as a great balk of timber in one of the outbuildings collapsed and all the time, with every turn of our coach's painted wheels, I could hear the persistent throbbing drumbeat of danger.

By the time we reached the outskirts of London, great crowds were massing in the fields around Southwark. I hadn't seen this many men since the days of Richard's coronation. But in those days the crowds came to cheer and make merry whereas these men sought violence. On the far side of the river were thousands more and it was obvious the hordes behind us were not the only ones coming to London to demand a meeting with the king. The men of Essex were also on the march.

We crossed the bridge at a rattle and entered the Tower where we found Thomas with Richard and John and the young men of Richard's household. Hovering behind them, looking more than ready for a fight, were my brother Fitzalan, one of my Percy cousins, the earls of Salisbury, Warwick and Buckingham, and the mayor of London, William Walworth.

Thomas greeted his mother, then quickly took my hands. He held them tight against his chest as if reassuring himself that I was real and wouldn't disappear.

'I prayed for your safety,' he said, quietly so the others couldn't hear. 'It was all I could do. When I heard the rebels were moving out of Kent I knew there'd be trouble. I was sick with worry. I wanted to come but couldn't leave my brother.'

'Naturally not,' I said a little stiffly. 'The king's safety comes before all else.'

I was not as clean as I would have wished and longed to retire but my mother-in-law was talking to Richard so I had to stay. He was telling her of his plans to speak to the crowds.

'Is it wise?' she said. 'They are very angry.'

'The archbishop assures me they do not wish harm to me personally. He says they should be appeased. He believes any other way is inadvisable.'

'What other way is there?'

'Force, my lady.' This was the mayor speaking. 'This is no rabble. These men are organised and they are dangerous. Many served the king's grandfather in the French wars. We taught them to fight and we taught them they are invincible. Now some mad hedgerow priest has stirred them up and they fancy themselves equal to the lords. They need to be shown they are not.'

'What do you think?' said my mother-in-law to Thomas.

My husband chewed his lip and, as usual, hesitated. 'I agree with Archbishop Sudbury. We should make these men see reason, not attack them.'

Mayor Walworth snorted. 'There's bloody thousands of them, begging your pardon, your grace. They've not come for a picnic. Invite them to parley and they'll stick a knife in your guts.'

'De Vere?' Richard turned to his closest friend, the expensively dressed seventeen year-old son of my Ufford cousin who was idly fingering his dagger.

'I gave you my opinion, your grace. These men are scum. I favour force.'

'I agree,' said the earl of Buckingham who, as Richard's uncle, expected his advice to be taken seriously.

'Won't work,' said the earl of Salisbury with admirable bluntness. 'Not yet, leastways. As I said before, if Walworth favours a bloodbath we'll have to draw a little poison first. Go and speak to them, your grace, by all means. But be careful.'

This was William Montagu, the man whom nobody liked and who appeared to discomfort my mother-in-law. Her lowered eyes didn't look anywhere near him while he spoke and, though perfectly polite, he never looked at her. But whatever anyone thought of the man himself, I thought his advice sound. Thomas said he was a good commander and it was obvious he had brought a soldier's mind to the problem.

Richard didn't ask Harry his opinion. He ignored him. The boy stood in the shadows with his guardian and his tutor, looking scared, as well he might. He had good reason. The rebels wanted his father's head but everyone knew that if they couldn't have the duke they might well settle for his son. At his side, like a faithful hound, was Lady Swynford's eldest boy, whose eyes watched Harry.

We were hopelessly outnumbered and might not withstand a full onslaught by the thousands of men outside the city walls should they decide to attack. We needed help but our armies were far away, fighting in Scotland with the duke who had no idea of the danger we were in. The council members made suggestions but Richard was no longer a child and they couldn't take the final decision. That was the king's privilege.

Eventually Richard said he would take the barge downriver to meet with the rebels.

My mother-in-law was prostrate with worry.

'I didn't keep him safe all these years for this,' she wept. 'He's not old enough. He won't know what to do. They'll kill him.'

'I was no older when I held the fortress of Auray for my husband against the French,' said Johane. 'You didn't concern yourself with *my* safety so why worry about Richard?'

'Duchess!' hissed Eleanor. 'Be quiet! Your comments are not what your lady mother needs. Have some compassion or be silent.'

Johane opened her mouth to reply but closed it again quickly when she saw the look on Eleanor's face.

By noon the party returned having not disembarked. It had been reckoned too dangerous. There were thousands of rebels on the shore shouting out their demands and the archbishop wisely counselled Richard not to move.

'They're no longer satisfied with having just the duke and the archbishop and treasurer Hales,' said Thomas miserably 'they're asking for more. They have a list.'

'Who else do they want?'

'The keeper of the privy seal, the chief baron of the exchequer, the chief justice, a royal tax collector named John Legge and nine others.'

'What has this John Legge done that he is so hated?' I asked.

Thomas shrugged 'You don't need to know.'

I turned to his brother.

In the press of people John Holand slid his hand round my waist. 'It is said, sister, that Master Legge is a man of great diligence when it comes to carrying out his royal duties. That is why they want him. A churl says, "my daughter is but thirteen years old, master, and need not pay the tax." But the girl has a bold look in her eye so Legge puts his hand up her skirts just to make sure.' He laughed. 'The girl doubtless enjoys the experience but the father does not. By the blood of Christ, I wish I had his job!'

He disgusted me, but before I could say anything, Mayor Walworth came down from his lookout position. The rebels had broken through the gates and thousands were pouring across the bridge into the city.

I knew what this would mean. They would surge through the streets, shouting "Burn! Kill!", sacking the homes of the rich and killing anyone against whom they bore a grudge. London would burn as they torched houses and brothels and murdered the Flemings. When Thomas came and told me he'd seen the Savoy palace ablaze, I understood that the worst of my nightmares was happening and I wanted to weep.

It was a hot night and I slept fitfully, woken from time to time with the noise of screaming and crying. By daybreak most of us were exhausted and several of the maids were openly weeping with terror.

Throughout the morning the men met in informal council and by noon it was decided to offer a general pardon to the rebels. But the knights sent to offer the pardon on behalf of the king were howled down. The crowd didn't want a pardon they wanted a meeting with the king and they wanted the heads of Archbishop Sudbury and Treasurer Hales who they knew were in the Tower. Nothing less would do. After further deliberation it was decided that Richard should offer to meet the rebels outside the city walls.

Next morning I helped my mother-in-law prepare for the journey to Mile End Green, an open field a short distance beyond Aldgate where the meeting was to take place. She refused to stay in the Tower if Richard was going into what she saw as certain danger. I offered to ride with her as her lady companion as both Eleanor and Johane were prostrate with fright.

As the great outer gate of the Tower swung open and we emerged into the sunlight of the city streets, I clung tight to the reins in case I should faint. We were towards the back of our party, closely protected by several men-at-arms and accompanied by my husband. John rode in front with Richard together with the earls of Salisbury and Warwick and Mayor Walworth. Understandably, the men wanted by the rebels remained in the Tower.

My ordeal in the streets didn't last long. There was some ill-natured jostling and shouting and grabbing of bridles by men in the crowd and after a short distance we women were ordered back. The king, we were told, had decided he would ride on alone with his brothers and his advisors but he wished his lady mother to return to the Tower.

She turned white and swayed in her saddle. She was ready to refuse but Thomas persuaded her she must do as the king ordered. He wanted her safe and it would be of no advantage to anyone if he had to worry about his mother. So with a small escort of heavily-armed men we turned back. Later, I was to wish we had gone with the others because although we didn't know it, that day we were in far greater danger in the Tower than we would have been at Mile End.

It began not long after we returned. I heard shouts from down below as men streamed across the causeway and through the gates. I knew at once that the mob had broken through. I heard their footsteps as they charged from room to room within the Tower seeking out people to kill. When at last they crashed through the door of my mother-in-law's chamber, Eleanor screamed.

There must have been fifty or more of them, common men, all carrying cudgels and knives, half of them drunk. Their eyes were wild with lust for violence. They laughed when they saw us. We were nothing but a bunch of feeble women and they wanted some sport.

That evening, after it was all over, Thomas took me to our room and sat me down. He looked uncomfortable and rather grey in the face.

'I should never have let you go back without me.'

'There was nothing you could have done?' I said. 'There were far too many of them. The guards were overwhelmed. Besides, as you said, your brother's safety must be your first concern.'

'But if I had been here …'

'They would probably have killed you,' I said bluntly.

His hands which held mine began to tremble and I wished he would let me be.

'Oh Christ! Did they …?'

'No,' I snapped. 'My honour is in tact.'

'But your clothing?'

The front of my gown was torn but I'd thought him unconcerned by my dishevelled appearance.

'Oh they pushed us around and pawed at your mother

and made free with a couple of the maids who wouldn't stop mewling.'

'Made free?'

'For pity's sake, husband. What do you think I mean? If the stupid girls had kept their mouths shut as your mother ordered, they'd have been left alone. But they were crying and pleading and asking to be spared. They threw themselves onto their knees and put themselves into danger.'

'But you are unharmed?'

I thrust away the memory of foul leering faces and filthy hands, the man who rolled on the royal bed, the rancid smells and slobbering mouths, the grasping, the pulling, the mauling and the threats.

'Yes,' I said shortly. 'I am unharmed.'

'They killed the archbishop,' said Thomas. 'Cut off his head. He was in the chapel, praying, but they dragged him out. Oh Christ, Alys! They butchered him like an animal.'

'And Harry?' My voice quavered.

It wasn't that I wasn't shocked at the killing of the archbishop but I hadn't known him personally. Not like Harry, I knew Harry.

'They wanted to kill him. They killed Appleby, the duke's family physician, and wanted Harry too, but one of the guards said to leave the boy alone. Said he was nought but a lad.'

'Lady Swynford's boy?'

'Safe.'

'The others?'

'They took Hales, the treasurer. I've no idea how many more. It's like Eastcheap slaughter ground out there on the hill. They set up a block. We saw it but couldn't get near. Oh Christ! Poor Sudbury. Someone said it took eight blows to take off his head.'

Thomas looked as if he was going to vomit and I'd already seen enough of that today to last me a lifetime.

'What happened at Mile End?' I said, wanting to talk of something else.

He wiped his sleeve across his eyes and shook his head. 'Just as we expected. They made their demands. Complained they were mightily oppressed and asked the king to set them free.'

'Ridiculous,' I muttered.

'Richard agreed to their demands.'

'He did what?'

'He had it proclaimed that they could have the head of any traitor adjudged by law and that he would give them their freedom.'

'Was he out of his mind?'

'No, he was drawing poison.'

'And is Richard to meet with them again?'

'Yes, tomorrow at Smithfield.'

Naturally it proved the right thing to do because by the end of the following day, the danger was over. The rebel leader, one Master Tyler from Kent, was dead. He had been killed by the mayor's men when the churl made some futile attempt on the king's life during their meeting. And Richard was the hero of the day. He had ridden straight for the rebel lines shouting that he would be their captain. He offered them mercy and said if they followed him they could have everything they wanted.

Like the fools they were, they believed him. If they had

watched him grow from a boy and seen the slyness and the petty cruelties that I had seen; if they had known of his vanity, his pride and his delight in his royalty, they would never have accepted his word. But they hadn't. They were stupid, addle-headed, cloth-eared dolts, who had listened to a priest prattling of casting off the yoke of bondage and who had no idea of the proper order of God's estates.

That night Thomas held me in his arms and stroked my face.

Our bed, once the curtains were drawn, was an airless place and I found it difficult to breathe. I had to admit it was comforting to be held but I wished he wouldn't weep.

'I nearly lost you,' he said, his voice choked, his eyes full of tears. He laid his wet cheek against mine and whispered, 'Don't leave me, my dearest wife.'

I moved my head and looked into his soft brown eyes, eyes so like young Tom's with their thick black lashes and straightforward gaze.

'Why would I leave you, husband? Where would I go?'

He laid his mouth on mine and kissed me very gently, brushing my lips like a lover would. 'I love you,' he whispered.

I didn't reply. I was fond of him but I didn't love him and he knew it. But he also knew I was always ready to do my duty. I never refused him and had ceased to mind much what he did in the privacy of our bed. If his pleasure took a long time, I didn't complain, there was always something to think about. Sometimes I wondered what my life would have been like if I had married Edmund but I tried to be a good wife to Thomas however much he failed me as a husband.

In the days that followed, the rebels discovered just how much they were mistaken in their king. The earl of Buckingham and my Percy cousin were dispatched to Essex to put down the remainder of the revolt while Thomas was sent into Kent with a strong guard to enforce the peace and re-establish royal authority. Meanwhile, I went with my mother-in-law to Chelmsford with Richard.

For a fifteen year-old boy, he was surprisingly vindictive. He showed no mercy at all to the rebels and if he'd had his way he'd have hanged the lot of them. He wanted them to live in misery. 'Rustics you were and rustics you shall remain,' he said to a deputation who came seeking redress.

Thirty-one men were executed and the hedgerow priest was given a traitor's death. I loathed the smell of sizzling innards and found the whole episode nauseating but Richard's eyes gleamed with satisfaction as the preacher's suffering was prolonged for as long as the executioner could manage. The man's skill in holding death at bay was very commendable and I hoped he would be well rewarded but wished I didn't have to watch.

Throughout the summer Richard progressed on his visitations in Essex and Kent, ensuring that his orders were being faithfully carried out and showing nothing but contempt for those who had dared to insult his royal dignity.

'He doesn't need me any more,' said my mother-in-law in a voice tinged with sadness. 'He is a man. I have raised him to be a king and these past months he has made me proud. But my task is finished. Once he is safely married I shall retire to Wallingford.'

14

QUEEN ANNE 1382

'Anna.' I tested the unfamiliar name on my tongue. 'Anna, queen of England, daughter of the Imperial House of Luxembourg. How strange it sounds.'

'Anne,' said my brother-in-law, draining his cup and inspecting the dregs. 'Queen Anne. If she is to be queen of England, she must carry an English name.'

I had no idea why this unknown sister of Wenzel, king of Bohemia, had been chosen when Richard had received offers from almost every ruling house in Christendom. Why had he not preferred an alliance with the Visconti dukes of Milan?

'What is she like?'

I knew that everyone in England would judge Richard's bride on her looks. Too tall, too short, too fat, too thin, and they would laugh at her.

John smiled provocatively. 'She is a young woman. They are all the same, aren't they?'

He was being deliberately difficult. He knew perfectly well what I meant.

'Is she beautiful?'

'Oh that! She's a plain little scrap of humanity but smother her in velvet, put a crown on her head and you won't notice.'

'I hardly think it matters what she looks like,' said Thomas stiffly.

How like a man! After four and a half years of waiting, of course it mattered.

'What does she bring to the marriage?' I asked.

'Not much from what I hear,' said John, beckoning for more wine. 'You weren't very successful with your negotiations, were you, brother? By Christ!' he screwed up his face. 'Where did you get this gut-rot from. It tastes like cat's piss.'

'Bordeaux,' said Thomas, peaceably, 'and the negotiations with the Bohemians were perfectly satisfactory, I thank you. We extracted the concessions we needed and as you know perfectly well, it wasn't about money but about putting pressure on the French.'

'Which won't work. Everyone knows it won't work and by the time Richard has finished lavishing gifts on Wenzel and his cronies he'll be paying for the privilege of marrying his own wife.'

Thomas had spent the early months of the previous year in Bruges finalising not only arrangements for the marriage but also the treaty of perpetual co-operation between the two kings. The English envoys had agreed that the dowry which Anne would bring would be decided later. A grave mistake and an embarrassment because Wenzel proved to have no money and required a loan and a grant from the English Crown. John was right; Richard *was* buying his own wife.

'I hear she nearly drowned.'

'How you women like to exaggerate. It was nothing.'

'That's not what Eleanor Clifford says.'

'There was groundswell in the harbour and her boat broke into pieces. But she was already ashore so no harm was done.'

'A bad omen, nonetheless,' said my husband gloomily.

'I should worry more about the lack of a dowry rather than bad omens,' said John. 'I believe the Crown's coffers are almost empty and yet Richard is heaping gifts on his new Bohemian friends as if he owns all the riches in Christendom. I said we should have taken the Visconti offer. The duke of Milan is fabulously rich and regrettably our brother Richard is profligate.'

Thomas looked even more miserable. 'I know. He doesn't concern himself with where his money comes from.'

'No more he should,' I said in Richard's defence. 'He is the king. He has a chancellor and a council and a parliament to do that.'

John's eyes slid sideways to mine and gave me a conspiratorial smile. 'Ah, sister, how you always rush to a man's defence. I wish I had a wife like you.'

'I just wish you had a wife,' I said sourly. 'Then we wouldn't have to suffer you at our table criticizing my husband.'

Thomas put his hand on my arm, warning me to be quiet while John threw back his head and roared with laughter.

'I'll be gone soon. Then you'll miss me, you know you will,' he said.

'Is it time?' said Thomas.

'Yes. Tomorrow she leaves Leeds Castle and by now the good citizens of London will have her entry arranged so wish me God speed. I must go. I shall bid you farewell.'

He leaned over and kissed me on the lips, lingering just that little bit too long for politeness but Thomas didn't notice; he was too busy sniffing the wine.

'Farewell, sweet sister,' John whispered. 'Keep safe.'

Four days later, Richard and Anne were married. The wedding was dazzling and the coronation of Anne as queen and the celebrations afterwards, even more splendid. This was what Richard did best, this display of his magnificence. He strutted like an exotic peacock in tight-fitting, high-necked satin jackets decorated with fabulous beasts and sewn all over with precious stones, his deeply-dagged sleeves trailing gracefully to the floor. He wore long red damask gowns lavishly trimmed with miniver and beautifully embroidered tabards of crimson velvet studded with pearls. And on everything he displayed his personal emblem of the white hart.

To my surprise, Richard was delighted with his bride. He showered her with gifts. He clearly wished to please her and she in turn smiled and dimpled and was seemingly entranced by this tall young man who was now her husband. Just watching them together in those early days, I could see that theirs was going to be a supremely happy marriage. The grumblers, and there were plenty of those, men who had expected more from this union than simply a king's happiness, wisely kept their own counsel.

'Don't they look wonderful together,' breathed Joan, as we sat together beneath my mother-in-law's canopy.

'Yes,' I said, remembering a time when I had looked at someone like that, when I believed that I, of all girls, had been uniquely chosen to live a life of everlasting happiness.

It hadn't happened and now Edmund was dead. He'd died in that rotting graveyard they call Ireland, not long after Philippa was taken. I had long since come to accept that my interest in him was both ridiculous and an embarrassment to all of us but the memories I held were still precious.

I was not the only woman in mourning for a lost love that spring. The duke had terminated his sinful association with Lady Swynford and at every gathering of women there was speculation as to why, after so long, he had cast her off. Blinded by desire until God opened his eyes was the verdict of most of my acquaintances.

It was a small scandal but people quickly forgot there had ever been a time when Lady Swynford had ridden at the duke's side. Few gave a thought to the discarded concubine and her four little bastards living in faraway Lincolnshire but I observed the duke looking old and tired and unhappy. He was ever courteous to his wife and she responded by smiling at him. I doubted there was much affection in their marriage after what had happened but one of her women, my some-time friend Amy de Melbourne, told me they now shared a bed.

As the days grew hotter and the nights more stifling I became weary of the constant round of tournaments and feasting. An invitation from my mother-in-law came as a welcome reprieve and in early August I travelled to Wallingford to keep her company. Eleanor had gone with her husband to see their eldest son ride in his first tournament at Windsor and my mother-in-law said she was lonely.

Her pleasure in her retirement was no longer a glittering entertainment with hundreds of guests but a gentle walk in the Queen's Mead. The field was surrounded on one side by a low stone wall covered with ivy and moss, and on the other by a row of beech trees with smooth grey trunks and sweeping branches of bright green leaves. Sunlight trickled through the leaves making patterns on the ground. Around the base of one tree, undisturbed by the shifting patchwork of light, a solitary blackbird was busily digging for food.

The air around us was heavy with the warm sweet scent of summer and our shoes made hardly any imprint on the close-scythed grass beneath our feet. The sun was hot and above our heads the sky stretched away like an endless canopy of seamless blue. I felt deliciously indolent.

My mother-in-law leaned heavily on my arm and I was aware once again that she was no longer young. She used juice of lemon to lighten her hair and pastes to redden her cheeks and hide the pouches beneath her eyes, but nothing could disguise her increasing girth. Her flesh was as soft and dimpled and rosy as ever but her gowns bulged and strained where previously they slid smoothly over her wonderful figure. She was, in all ways, twice the woman she had been when I first met her.

She was fretting over Richard and Anne. 'They seem devoted to each other.' She sounded doubtful.

'I'm sure they are. It is a good marriage.'

She gave an uncertain little laugh. 'Tell me I am being a stupid old woman but I had hoped for more.'

'More?'

'Oh, it is nothing. All mothers worry about their children's marriages. It is one of the burdens we carry. We give birth to them, we raise them and we let them go but we never cease to worry. Have you given thought to your young Alianor?'

I smiled. 'She has spoken to you?'

'Oh yes. Last month. "Lady Grandmother," she said. "I am twelve years old and nearly a woman."'

I smothered a laugh. 'Nearly a woman?'

'That is what she said. "I am nearly a woman and I do not wish to be called Nell any longer. It is a childish name. I wish to be Lady Alianor." I kissed her and told her that of course I would call her Lady Alianor if that is what she wanted.'

The children were growing up fast. Our eldest daughter was with the queen, one of her favoured little maids, learning how to be a young lady just as I had done all those years ago with my cousin Blanche; while Tom had begun his education in his Uncle Richard's household. The three younger girls would soon be too old for the nursery. And I longed for another child.

'I thought of the Mortimer boy,' my mother-in-law said.

'Edmund's son?'

'Yes. The inheritance is substantial. It would be a good match for your daughter. And, for you Alys, it might bring peace.'

I blushed as I always did when she talked of Edmund.

'I shall speak to Richard. He will hold the inheritance until the boy is of age and, as you know, the wardship and marriage is in his gift. There will doubtless be competition for such a great prize but I think Richard will be pleased to do this favour for his brother. The price should be manageable and Thomas must know how valuable a marriage it would be.'

A young man in dusty clothing with a leather pouch slung across his chest, was walking towards us across the grass and I recognised him as one of Lewis Clifford's men.

He fell to his knees and proffered a letter. 'Your grace, Sir Lewis Clifford bade me bring this to you.'

'Thank you, Robin. Have you eaten? You look hungry.'

'No, your grace, I travelled without stopping. I'm afraid I'm rather travel-stained.'

My mother-in-law smiled, the skin around her mouth wrinkling into soft creases which caused her chin to quiver. 'You look as handsome as ever, dear boy. A little dust never harmed anyone. Now go to inside and get some food. I'll send for you later if there is a reply.'

The man scrambled up and hurried off back the way he had come.

My mother-in-law broke the seal and looked at the letter. 'I wonder if ...'

She gasped and stood perfectly still. Her face was white with shock and her eyes, huge. She had aged ten years in an instant as if struck down by an enchantment.

'No!' she whispered in the smallest of voices. 'It cannot be true. God would not be so cruel. Not after all these years. Have we not been punished enough?'

'What is it?' I said, fearful for the children. 'What has happened?'

'Oh, Alys!' Her eyes were full of tears. 'Oh, Alys!'

She was trembling and I thought she might faint. I looked around for somewhere to sit and saw a small turf seat in the shade of one of the trees. I took her arm and gently led her across the grass and made her sit down.

She read the letter again and then thrust it into my hands.

'It never ends. Never. Have we not paid sufficiently for our sins?'

I smoothed out the letter. It was written with all the usual flourishes and formalities in the neat hand of a clerk.

"Sir Lewis Clifford wishes to inform your grace, the King's Mother, the Princess of Wales, that on this dread day of the Feast of the Most Miraculous Transfiguration of the Son of God, our Lord Jesus Christ in all His Radiant Glory ... the son and heir of Sir William Montagu, Earl of Salisbury, Lord of Man, Lord of the Isle of Wight ... has been summoned to God as a consequence of mortal wounds sustained in a joust of peace."

The letter was signed and sealed that same day at Windsor by Lewis, but someone, probably Eleanor because I thought I recognised her hand, had scribbled underneath, *"The father's lance hit the son full tilt and knocked him from his horse. The boy died within the hour."*

My mother-in-law sobbed uncontrollably, her shoulders heaving, her hands over her eyes; tears trickled from between her fingers. I couldn't understand her distress. She barely acknowledged the earl amongst her acquaintances and had never, to my knowledge, met the son. I had more reason to weep as the boy was husband to one of my brother Fitzalan's daughters. I had seen him once, a sallow-faced young man with little to recommend him other than his position as heir to his father's earldom.

I put my arm around her shoulders and gathered her against me, feeling the heavy warmth of her head where it rested on my breast. Her tears soaked the front of my gown. I murmured words of comfort as I would have done to my little children.

I knew her so very well: all her secrets, all her joys, all her fears. She was as dear to me as my own mother had been. She was generous to everyone but had opened her heart to me, her daughter-in-law, in a way I was certain she had not done to anyone else. I felt a warm glow when I thought of how I had been chosen to share her most private and intimate secrets. I could not have felt closer to any other woman, even my sister.

After a long while her sobbing ceased and she raised her face, blotched and streaked with tears, but still beautiful.

'He waited such a long time for his son,' she said quietly. 'All those years of hope denied. He was very angry. But it was God's punishment for what we had done.'

'I don't understand,' I said. 'What had you done?'

She stared unseeing at the grass, the wall and the river beyond. In the distance, a pair of swans glided slowly by and a child with a dog ran along the far bank calling out into the still summer air.

'He didn't know, you see. He didn't know. It wasn't his fault yet he has been punished more than me. It cannot be just. His only boy. His only, longed-for boy. What did he ever do to deserve this?'

I had no idea what she was talking about. Something concerning the earl of Salisbury, a man she barely knew. Then I remembered how her father-in-law, the king, had ignored her; how he had coldly turned his face away from her, his son's beloved wife. The earl of Salisbury had done the same in the Tower. But surely she had never …? An unwelcome thought crept into the corner of my mind.

'Tell me,' I said, not wanting to believe the enormity of what threatened to engulf us both. 'Please tell me what it was that you did.'

She held onto my hand, stroking my fingers absentmindedly.

'I never meant you to know,' she said. 'There are so few now left who were privy to the truth.'

And then she told me. It was the final piece of her story. I thought I had known it all but of course I hadn't. This explained everything else and she had kept it hidden from me all these years. Had she thought I would be disappointed in her or had she simply been too afraid I would reveal her story to someone else?

'William Montagu was my husband.'

I couldn't prevent a small gasp. This was not what I had expected.

'He was my husband for nine years.'

'Nine years!'

I tried to compute the numbers in my head. Nine years. Married at twelve to Thomas Holand. The great pestilence. The first child. Marriage to the Prince. Nothing fitted into place. There was too much story and too few years. When had any of this happened?

She must have seen my bewilderment because she smiled sadly and gently completed the puzzle for me.

'After I married Thomas, I told you how my family kept us apart but that is not all they did. My mother told me

238

that my marriage to Thomas would never be recognised either by the Church or by the king. She said I had been deceived by a wicked man for his own evil purposes, the marriage was a fraud and I was a fool. For two days she beat her truth into me and when she had finished and I was weeping in terror at the sin I had committed, she told me I must marry William Montagu.'

'But how?'

'Nobody knew, you understand, nobody but my mother and she kept her own counsel. She wanted the Montagu marriage and told no-one what I had done. The king was in favour of the match as were the Montagu family. I was the king's cousin, a prize for their heir. I would bring them ever closer to the king and that was what they wanted. My mother told my uncle I was ready to do my duty and within a week William and I were wed.'

'And he didn't know?'

'No. Not then. Not for a long time.'

'When did he find out?'

'Seven years later.'

'Seven years!'

'Yes.'

'And there was no child?'

'No.'

I listened as she told me the rest. How Thomas Holand had captured a valuable prisoner on the French campaign and sold him to the king, and how he had used the money to retrieve his wife. He had presented his case to the Holy Father and asked for justice. It took two years during which time she had continued to live with William Montagu.

'The bishop of Norwich came and took me away,' she said. 'The Holy Father commanded that I should be returned to Thomas.'

'And Sir William?'

'Our parting was unbelievably painful. He was angry.'

'But you didn't love him?'

'No, not at all but as you must know, Alys, you cannot lie with a man without feeling something, without worrying afterwards how he does. I knew William's private terrors and his hopes and that did not cease because I left.'

'What did he do?'

'She gave a small smile. 'He remarried, the daughter of Lord de Mohun, and they had a son. At last he had what he wanted.'

'And you never met with him again?'

'I see him at feasts and tournaments, in the company of others, but we never speak.'

Shadows were beginning to creep across the grass and a slight breath of cool air drifted slowly across my face lifting the tiny tendrils of hair which had come loose from their pins. The day which had started so well, in so much golden brightness, was beginning to fade and die.

'It wasn't that I didn't trust you, Alys, but the very existence of William Montagu threatens Richard. As long as William is alive, men might remember. There would be those who would say that, with a husband still living, I was not free to marry the prince.'

'But you had a dispensation.'

'Nonetheless, doubt would be cast on Richard's legitimacy.'

'Does he know?'

'I have told him. Naturally he was greatly distressed. A boy does not like to hear of his mother's – what shall I call them? – her marital adventures. He was angry but unsure where to direct his anger. He said it was like fighting phantoms in the dark. At the moment he is confused and bitter, but give him time and he will understand and forgive. Apart from William and I, all the others in this miserable tragedy are dead. William was blameless and Richard loves me too much to be angry with me for long.'

'Does Eleanor Clifford know?' I said, suddenly jealous.

'Yes, she knows. Not because I told her but because her first husband was Thomas's friend. He witnessed much of what happened.'

'Did the prince know?'

Of course he knew. When he realised he was dying, we discussed what must be done. I have given all the papers to Richard: the annulment of my so-called marriage to William, the documents relating to my marriage to Thomas, the records of the inquisition post mortem and the dispensations the prince obtained both before and after our marriage. I have impressed on him how important these documents are and how they must be kept safe because without them he cannot prove his right to wear the crown. Together we selected a pretty box with a lock and placed everything inside. I told him he must keep it with him always.'

The look she gave me was one of great sadness.

'And the others,' I said quietly. 'My husband. Does he know?'

'No. Nobody knows except for those very few who still remember. It was such a long time ago. People who were alive then are dead now or are too old to care.'

She had been a girl when it had happened and now she was becoming an old woman. As she said – such a long time ago.

'Let us go back.' I took her by the arm and helped her to rise. 'Perhaps you should go to Windsor; it's less than half a day's journey. It might bring comfort to Sir William to know you share his grief.'

She smiled crookedly. 'He wouldn't want that. Some wounds, my dear Alys, leave scars that cut too deep, scars which a woman, no matter how well-meaning or how contrite, can never hope to heal.'

I wondered how much else there was that she hadn't told me, what other secrets lay scattered around in her past, what other men there had been. Naturally I would never trust her again. Not now, not after this. I still loved her but I couldn't trust her.

Talworth Manor was undeniably small, a few acres of unkempt grassland bounded by a poorly managed piece of woodland and a muddy stream called the Hogsmill. The land sloped gently down to the south which meant the buildings were bathed in pleasant autumn sunshine which softened their rather untidy appearance. To my surprise the house was well appointed with a chapel, two halls and six chambers as well as the usual kitchen, brewhouse and bakehouse. But the private rooms were narrow and low-ceilinged letting little daylight through their tiny windows and as I investigated further I found a distinct lack of fireplaces. The larger hall retained its central hearth, a disgustingly old-fashioned means of heating which resulted in smoke-filled rooms and blackened beams.

'What d'you think?' enquired Thomas, anxious as ever for my approval.

I swallowed my disappointment. This was no Castle Donnington, not even a manor as grand as Woking, which was not really grand at all despite its pretensions.

I gave him a bright smile. 'It is lovely. And closer to London than Woking.'

'My mother wanted you to know how important you are to her.'

Was Talworth Manor a reward for my silence? If so I wondered what else we might be given. I thought how wise I was to reassure my mother-in-law of my discretion.

'Your mother has made a suggestion for our daughter,' I said, suspecting my husband already knew but wanting him to know I was in his mother's confidence.

Thomas didn't answer but pushed at the fallen leaves on the path with the toe of his boot. 'Richard has dismissed Chancellor Scrope.'

Scrope was the man who had replaced poor Archbishop Sudbury as Richard's chancellor. A red-faced Yorkshire lord, experienced in royal service, whose northern speech and blunt manner were said to hide a sharp mind.

'Why, what has he done?'

'Refused to carry out Richard's wishes. Said the king is not acting as a king should but like a fifteen-year-old boy.'

'He *is* a fifteen-year-old boy.'

'Where matters of state are concerned, he is a king.'

'Is it serious?'

'Very. It appears Richard has granted lands from the Mortimer inheritance to his personal friends. He is giving away what should come to young Roger Mortimer.'

'He can't do that.' I protested, imagining the royal dagger carefully filleting my prospective son-in-law's inheritance.

'He can. He shouldn't, but he can. As king, he believes he may do what he likes.' Thomas took my arm and began walking back towards the house. 'He had documents drawn up settling lands on de Vere and Burley and when Scrope refused to countenance the transfers, Richard dismissed him on the spot.'

'Can you not do something?' Even as I asked I knew it was useless. Thomas would let this injustice roll over him in the way he let so much else pass him by.

'The Mortimer inheritance is not the worst. When the old king died he left a list of his bequests. It was Richard's sacred duty to carry out his grandfather's dying wishes but instead he has given manors intended for a religious house to Simon Burley and his brothers. His behaviour is shameful.'

'Will there be trouble?'

'I fear so. Others are already grumbling about his extravagance and how he listens to no-one other than Burley and de Vere. Your brother Fitzalan complains how little lordlings like Ralph Stafford and Tom Mowbray have more of the king's ear than he does. Claims he is ignored.'

'Can the duke not do something?'

'It seems not. Either he is unable or unwilling.'

'Or too wrapped up in his plans for conquering Castile.'

A week later Richard appointed Sir Michael de la Pole as his new chancellor. I heard the news when I paid a visit to my brother's London house.

'The man's a sheep farmer's son,' stormed my brother. 'He is not worthy to hold high office.'

'The father was a wool merchant not a sheep farmer,' said Joan.

'Sheep farmer? Wool merchant? What's the difference? The man's a parasite. Look at them all! Pole, Mowbray, de Vere, Stafford, Burley – crawling like cockroaches over the king with their greedy claws outstretched. And what does his grace do? Shovels favours onto them. A nice fat manor here, an office of profit there. Then he comes whining to parliament wanting our money. He should bloody well learn to live off his own.'

'Why are you so angry?' Joan said. 'You have your earldom and you have guardianship of the Mortimer boy.'

'A pig's arsehole! What use is the boy's person? What I need are those Mortimer lands and the king's making me dance for them. Says he must consider Warwick, of all men. Then I hear Northumberland and Neville are also on his list. By the blood of Christ! What do I have to do? I am treated like a turd. And by a poxy boy.'

Fitzalan's wife, Liz, crept into the room in the manner of an apologetic servant, bobbing a brief curtsey to her husband and sliding onto the bench beside me. She was clearly no higher in my brother's favour than she was before she gave him his long-awaited son and heir. Doubtless he blamed her for the death of his Montagu son-in-law as well as his other problems.

'You mustn't speak ill of the king like this, husband,' she said softly. 'It is dangerous.'

'Dangerous is it, madam? I'll say it to his face one of these days. I won't be treated like this. Christ! Why did the prince have to die and leave us with this arrogant little whelp on the throne?'

15

CLARENDON 1384

The seasons slipped one into another; autumn to winter to spring and then summer again. As dead leaves once more covered the paths and an early frost nibbled at our windows, the king finally decided the Mortimer estates should be shared amongst my brother, my Percy cousin, the earl of Warwick and Lord Neville. The price for his generosity was the enormous sum of four thousand pounds. Nobody was happy except Richard, who, according to my brother-in-law, had promptly commissioned a large sapphire ring for Robert de Vere.

No decision had been taken about young Roger Mortimer's marriage and the boy continued to live in my brother's household. I fretted but there was nothing I could do. I had other things to concern me. In the summer I had discovered I was carrying another child.

'This time it will be a boy,' I declared defiantly.

'I will be just as happy with a girl,' said my husband, easily pleased with small pickings. I couldn't believe he was indifferent.

'Don't you want another son?'

'I want whatever you have – son or daughter. All I pray is that you are safe and the child, healthy.'

But Our Lady heard my pleas and on the Feast of the Epiphany, as snow flakes swirled outside my chamber and frozen drifts piled high against the walls, our third son was born. It was an easy birth and he was a fine healthy child.

'May I name him?'

'Certainly,' said Thomas, all smiles and contentment.

'Then I choose, Edmund.'

'For my grandfather.' My husband smiled at the newest occupant of the Holand family cradle. 'What a wonderful idea. My mother will be delighted.'

Edmund was a placid baby and gave no trouble and as he grew I was pleased to see that his eyes were a dazzling blue, just like those of the young man I had once loved, after whom I had named him.

When Edmund was barely three months old and still at his most adorable I was summoned back to my duties as my husband's wife and countess of Kent. The queen, as was her privilege, desired my company at Clarendon Palace for the duration of the spring parliament. Thomas, unsurprisingly, desired me to warm his bed. But I was oddly touched by his letter.

"My dearest companion and truest sweetheart," he wrote. *"It has long been accepted that a wife should have respite from her husband's attentions for a period of forty days after the birth of a child but it has been twice that long since I have had the pleasure of holding you in my arms. If it was in my nature to command you, I would order you back to my side, but as it is, I humbly implore you to return to me. I miss you at bed and at board more than words can*

247

*say and would dearly welcome an early sight of you.
Give my blessings to our little daughters and to our
newborn son."*

I read it twice and then wiped the tears from my eyes and
gave orders for my departure the following day.

It was mid-afternoon when I arrived at Clarendon and
the light in the queen's chamber was a muted silvery-
grey. It streamed through the etched glass windows and
flooded the rose-coloured tiles which patterned the entire
length of the floor. On one wall was a fireplace filled with
blazing logs. It was flanked by two marble columns with
an overmantel carved with images of the seasons. My
mother-in-law had told me many times of the wonders of
the queen's rooms at Clarendon, of the blue-washed walls,
the vaulted ceilings and the glowing window of Our Lady
devised from pieces of coloured glass, but I had never
imagined them to be quite so beautiful.

Anne was a pleasing young woman, not beautiful,
but dignified, with fine dark eyes and a pale smooth
complexion. She wore the latest fashion in horned
headdresses as did all her ladies. It was an odd sight
because three years ago they would have netted their hair
in golden cauls as my mother-in-law did, but not now; now
every stray hair was tucked away and hidden, showing off
their broad white foreheads and their delicately plucked
eyebrows.

As I walked towards the raised dais my eyes slid
sideways, looking for my daughter. She sat in a shallow
alcove with three other girls of her own age, all giving the

appearance of busily sewing whilst secretly peeping up from under their lashes to see who had come to visit the queen.

I swept a curtsey and Anne smiled.

'Countess, greetings. And how is your little son?'

By now her English was nearly as good as her French and she was eager for conversation, insisting I sat next to her on one of the velvet cushions. I was pleasantly surprised at how widely read she was and more than a little disconcerted at the depth and breadth of her learning. We talked of the radical ideas of Master Wycliffe which clearly interested her although she told me she feared some of his teachings verged on the heretical. But when she began delving into the intricate arguments of *De Regimine Principum*, I found myself floundering.

'A king mediates the flow of God's favour to his people. Is that not so?'

'Certainly it is.'

'And he cannot allow heresies to multiply or his kingdom will wither.'

'That is also true.'

'And proper obedience to the king is the sole foundation of all peace and quiet within the realm.'

'Of course.'

'Therefore countess, why is your brother so disobedient? The king tells me the earl insults him to his face.'

I thought we were discussing philosophy and the rule of princes but all of a sudden found myself wrong-footed and under attack.

'What has my brother said?' I hoped Fitzalan had kept a watch on his tongue and a rein on his temper but I feared he might have forgotten both.

'The earl says the country stands in peril because of lack of good government and that it is the king's fault if there is decay.'

My brother was possibly right but an utter fool to have said it.

'I'm sure he is wrong, your grace.'

'Naturally he is wrong. The king told him he lied in his teeth. But that is not the point, is it? Who are these men in my husband's kingdom who do not bow before their king, who have not learned proper humility and think themselves as mighty as their lord?'

I tried soothing words: how Richard was loved by all his subjects, not least by those of high birth; how he had grown to manhood in the shadow of the most dreadful of events, yet proved himself worthy. But Anne was not persuaded.

'The king suspects his royal uncle, the duke of Lancaster, covets his throne.'

Her words were sharp as needles, jabbing my flesh, drawing droplets of blood.

'That cannot be true, your grace. The duke is loyal. I know it.'

'The king does not.'

Her small red mouth pursed in displeasure. She was a tough little thing for all her sweetness and her beguiling smiles. I was beginning to wish I had remained with my younger children at Woking. I told her how steadfast an influence the duke had been for Richard in the time of his father's sickness and how he had guided him safely through those early years of his royalty; but I could see Anne's views had already been formed by her husband.

If Richard considered the duke treasonous then so did she.

A woman moved silently across the floor, the folds of her dark green gown brushing the tiles. She was thin with black slanting eyes and a full red mouth. Untrustworthy, I thought.

'It is time, your grace. Everything is ready.'

Anne rose.

'Thank you, Anezka. I must change my gown for supper, countess, but please to stay and talk with your daughter.' She turned her head to the knot of younger girls. 'Alianor, you may remain for a few moments and listen to what your lady mother has to say.'

My daughter blushed at being singled out for attention just as I used to do when I was young. She murmured that she would follow the others once she had done her duty. It was obvious she adored the queen.

'Are you well?' I said once we were alone.

I barely knew what to say to this daughter of mine who had strayed so far from my care; but young Alianore found no such difficulties and chattered happily of her life with her new friends in the queen's household.

'They do not share a bed in the way you and my father do,' she remarked.

I felt a sudden coldness in my belly and quickly put my finger to my daughter's lips.

'Shh. Tell me quietly. What you have seen?'

'The king is brought to the queen's rooms each night in his night robes and they are put to bed. But as soon as the candles are out and the others leave, they rise to pray together. Then they sit by the fire and talk; afterwards they pray some more. He stays for hours and it is dreadfully dull.'

'What do they talk about? Is it love talk?'

'Oh no! Mostly about God's forgiveness and how a man may achieve spiritual perfection. Last night he read her passages from *The Life of the Confessor* which she said she had never fully understood. They spent a long time discussing whether there were hidden meanings within the words.'

'Does he do anything else?'

'I don't think so.' she blushed prettily. 'I know what a man is supposed to do. But I have never seen the king do that.'

'You're sure? 'He doesn't do things ... things a brother would not do? Does he remove any of her clothing?'

Holy Mother of God! Here I was interrogating my little daughter on what she had seen in the royal bedchamber when she was of an age where she could have no understanding of the sordid dealings between a man and a woman.

'No, nothing like that. He holds her hand to help her rise from her chair and when he bids her a good night, he kisses her on her lips. But that is all I have seen.'

'Where is the king's valet?'

'He waits outside.'

'And you are there all the time?'

'Yes. The queen likes me to be there. She says she chose me specially. I sit in the shadows and when the king leaves I help her into her bed.'

'I expect the king returns to the queen later when you are asleep.'

'Perhaps,' she said doubtfully, 'but I sleep on the pallet in her room so surely I would know?'

'Does the lady they call Anezka not wait on the queen at night?'

'Anezka Launcekrona?' My daughter sniffed. 'No, she looks after the queen's jewels and makes eyes at the king's men. I am the one who is there in case the queen wakes. But she doesn't, she sleeps like my little sisters do, without making a sigh and I am sure the king never comes back.'

She tipped her innocent little eyes to mine. 'Is it wrong?'

I stroked her cheek. 'No dearest, it is not wrong but it is dangerous to talk of such matters so you must tell no-one. Can you do that?'

She nodded. 'Mother, may I ask you something?'

'Yes, of course you may.'

'I know the king and the queen are different from us because God has chosen them, but if they do not lie together will God still bless them with a child?'

'Hush,' I said. 'Do not talk about it. Do not even think about it.'

The following evening I sought out my husband. I had barely seen him since my arrival and had heard nothing of what was being discussed at the parliament. I was not surprised because parliaments, as Fitzalan said, were concerned with the raising of monies for the king's needs, and must therefore be exceedingly dull affairs.

After enquiring of several servants, I discovered Thomas with his brother, in a small room near the chapel.

Two empty jugs of wine sat on the floor and the third looked well on its way to joining them.

'Sister!' said my brother-in-law, joyfully. 'Have you come to join in our revels?'

The room smelled sour and I thought my husband looked drunk.

'Thomas?'

He lifted his gaze to mine and smiled. 'Wife! What a pleasing sight. Were you looking for me?'

Not as drunk as I had thought. His speech was clear, his face, though a little flushed, looked the same as ever.

'How goes the parliament?'

'Badly.'

'Very badly,' John yawned. 'The king plans to execute his uncle of Lancaster. He believes the duke is plotting to take his throne.'

This might have been a joke but with John you could never tell.

'And is he?'

John shrugged. 'I doubt it.'

'The duke is loyal to Richard,' said Thomas. 'Richard is his brother's son. The duke regards serving him as a sacred duty. Even the lure of the English crown would not allow him to commit a treason.'

'So why does Richard suspect him?'

'Because he's a suspicious little prick,' said John rudely. 'Men babble to him of plots hatched by the duke and he is frightened because he knows about his grandfather's last will and testament and what it says.'

'And what does it say?'

Thomas glanced towards the door and lowered his

voice. 'If Richard dies without a son, the throne must go to the duke. Old King Edward wanted matters settled because Richard was so young.'

'And because he distrusted Edmund Mortimer,' added John. 'Didn't want him moving his arse close to the throne with his infant son.'

Thomas nodded in agreement. 'The king ignored any claim your cousin Philippa might have had and determined the crown should never pass through a woman.'

Poor Philippa! All her hopes and her devious plans would have come to nothing even had she lived.

John rose to his feet, pulled out a chair and pushed me into it. 'Not much time left for the duke, is there? Won't be long before little Anna gets herself with child. Then any hopes he may have will disappear like smoke on the midnight air.'

'Is it true?' said Thomas. 'There are whispers coming from the queen's women. Is there to be a little prince for England?'

'Our daughter has told me certain things.'

'Concerning Anne?'

'Yes.'

'Oh joy!' said John, rubbing his hands together and leaning close. 'Tales from the queen's bedchamber. How delicious! I love tittle-tattle. You women are so gloriously indiscreet in your conversations.'

Thomas frowned at his brother's levity. 'What does our daughter say?'

I was dreadfully embarrassed at having to repeat Alianore's confidences with my brother-in-law in the room but I kept my gaze lowered and picked my words with care. When I had finished there was a moment of complete silence and then John began to laugh.

'Oh poor little brother Dickon! I always did wonder and now we know.'

'Wonder?' I said. 'What did you wonder?'

'Whether he knew what to do with that little cock of his.'

'Perhaps it is Anne,' I said, blushing furiously. 'Perhaps she is unwilling.'

'After two years?' laughed John. 'She may not be much to look at but she's young and knows her duty and no man with blood in his veins waits two years for a reluctant bride; two hours more like.'

'I think it more likely our daughter is mistaken in what she has seen,' said Thomas stiffly.

I turned to him. 'You have read *The Life of the Confessor*, husband; what does it say about marriage?'

'The Confessor and his wife disavowed the demands and temptations of the flesh and chose to live in a state of spiritual unity. There are some who consider a chaste marriage enables a wife to bring her husband closer to God. But surely our brother had a woman before he married?'

I knew this was what happened. Boys were not expected to perform in the marriage bed without experience. It would be unthinkable for a prince to be left in a state of ignorance.

John shrugged. 'I wasn't privy to what went on in his chamber. Old mother Burley had charge of him and guarded access to his lord and master like a jealous husband. If there was a young woman, it was done without my knowledge. Christ knows what the old fool taught him.'

'He was a good tutor. The prince valued him highly,' protested Thomas.

John gave a sly smile. 'There was always de Vere,'

'Impossible!' said Thomas quickly.

I touched my husband's arm. 'What is impossible?'

Thomas sighed. 'There have been whispers about Richard and Robert de Vere but they need not concern you.'

'What kind of whispers?'

'Oh sister,' said John, honouring me with one of his most charming smiles. 'I do not like to say this to a chaste young woman like yourself but it is said that our little Dickon is a cocksucker.' He gazed straight into my eyes. 'You know what that is, don't you? You've heard of such men?'

'Hold your tongue,' said Thomas angrily. 'Your language is foul. To even think such a thing is treasonous. Besides it is untrue.'

John swung round. 'How would you know? Did you crawl under the royal bedsheets to see what our little brother got up to?'

'No, but de Vere chases women. Everyone knows that.'

'Exclusivity may be our little brother's taste but I doubt if de Vere would shrink from getting on his hands and knees for his king; not if he could lap up a few more offices as a reward for his dutiful compliance.'

Thomas brought his fist down on the table making me jump. 'Be silent this instant! My wife is not accustomed to hearing such talk.'

John leaned closer, his mouth twisted into an unpleasant half-smile. 'There's plenty your wife's not accustomed to, brother. Perhaps I should take it upon myself to give her a lesson.'

Thomas was out of his chair in an instant and had John up against the wall, held by the collar of his shirt. 'I trust you did not mean what you said,' he hissed into his brother's face, 'because if you did I will smash your head open.'

I sat there, transfixed by the sight of my husband threatening to use his fists. I had no idea he could be so combative. I'd always believed him a cowardly man.

John shook himself free and held up his hands in a gesture of peace but as Thomas moved back, John swung a punch which caught his brother full on the mouth.

I screamed. Within moments they were on the floor, half-killing each other.

'Stop it!' I cried, but they didn't stop. They fought like a pair of feral beasts, snarling and scratching, punching, gouging and trying to throttle each other; knocking over chairs and stools, kicking out and crashing against the table legs. One of the two jugs on the floor rolled over and hit the wall, shattering into a dozen pieces while the other ended up in the corner of the room. I looked round wildly for help and spied the half-empty wine jug on the table. Without pausing to think twice I picked it up and threw the contents over them both.

'Christ's blood! What was that?' spluttered Thomas, sitting up.

John, red wine dripping down his face, held his hand over his right eye. 'God's truth, brother! I didn't know you could fight like that? I thought you were a peacemaker these days.'

Thomas glared at him. 'Not where you are concerned.'

'You are both a disgrace,' I said. 'Look at you!'

'Look at the state of the realm,' laughed Thomas. 'The king hates the duke, the duke hates the king and the earl of Arundel hates everyone.'

'And only you and I are friends,' laughed John.

I knelt down and used Thomas's shirt to wipe the blood from the corner of his mouth.

'Does it hurt?'

'Not now,' he said, holding my wrist and smiling into my eyes, the quarrel all but forgotten.

'What about me?' complained my brother-in-law who had scratches on his cheek, a reddening bruise on one eye and whose shirt was ripped to pieces.

'If you want caring for, go find yourself a wife,' I said crisply.

I knew exactly why he wasn't married. He was a good prospect and could easily have netted himself the daughter of a wealthy lord. But he was ambitious. He was waiting for his duchess. In some matters he was cleverer than Thomas who would never be a great man and would always settle for small rewards. But I needed no lessons from John Holand. There was nothing he could teach me.

All through that summer and into autumn we watched the duke and the king eyeing each other uneasily, each believing the other was planning their murder. Thomas said rumours were rife that Richard's friends were plotting to arrest the duke and have him arraigned for treason before the chief justice. But the duke removed himself to Pontefract and nothing happened. When he returned to

Sheen for a meeting with the king, he came with a heavily armed escort and, it was said, wore a breastplate beneath his robes.

The kiss of peace between uncle and nephew was chilly and it wasn't until the princess came out of her retirement to plead with them both that an uneasy truce was agreed. I was not privy to what she said to the duke but I was present when she told Richard he must cease listening to flatterers as their advice was by its very nature false and full of self-interest. It was not right for him to be at odds with his royal uncle. As king, he needed the duke's support.

If dissension within her family was not a sufficient burden for the princess, the sad news from Brittany nearly crippled her. Duchess Johane, dispatched two years earlier, unwillingly to her husband's side, was dead. Her death had been sudden and unexpected and the loss of her younger daughter was almost more than my mother-in-law could bear. Usually so resilient, she visibly crumpled and nothing Eleanor or I could say gave her any comfort. Maud was sent for and that Christmas, she and Thomas spent many hours talking and praying with their mother.

Winter was cruel, the coldest for many years, but it suited my mother-in-law's mood. The princess who eventually emerged from her months of mourning was older, more thoughtful and less inclined to frivolous entertainment than the merry widow I remembered from my early years as Thomas's wife.

By late spring there were persistent rumours of French forces massing at Sluys which, as Thomas patiently explained, posed a threat to our towns on the south coast. There were also alarming reports of the arrival in Scotland of a large army of Frenchmen. As a result of this intelligence, and for once following the advice of his council, Richard ordered a muster in late July at the town of Newcastle upon the Tyne. To my great surprise and against all my expectations, he was taking his men to war against the Scots.

16

THE ROAD TO YORK 1385

The priory of Wilberfosse on the road to York was poor; that much was abundantly clear: poor, decaying and miserably small. The cloistered buildings adjoining the old stone church were in urgent need of repair and only the abbess's house was in good order. There was a tiny herb garden growing some unidentifiable north country vegetation and an orchard with a few stunted trees. The wall separating the sisters from the sinful world outside was high but to me there seemed little difference between the place of prayer within and the endless dreary greyness without.

'I'm sorry, my lady,' said the royal official who had been charged with sorting out our accommodation. 'The sisters swear there's no more room. They say they're already sleeping in the stables and the infirmary is stuffed full with the queen's women.'

I sighed with annoyance. 'How much further to York?'

'A good half-day's ride, my lady. We've not yet reached the bridge over the Derwent.'

'And nowhere to sleep.'

'You could try the brewhouse, but if I were you, my lady, I'd seek out Sir Thomas. He's likely got a pavilion and would gladly welcome his wife. I know I'd be mortal pleased to see mine.'

Outside the priory gate, tents were springing up like midsummer mushrooms, covering every available patch of dry ground. In the lee of a dripping awning some cooks were getting to work with their fires and the smell of food made my belly rumble. This was a vast encampment, close on four hundred wagons blocking the road and thousands of men and horses crowded onto the verges.

I thought the North a dismal place. Since leaving Lincoln we'd seen just two villages, neither of them anything more than a collection of hovels. There'd been few signs of life at the ferry crossing at Winteringham and not a solitary animal or bird as we traversed the moor. Here, apart from the ruins of an ancient tower dwelling and the isolated priory by the beck, there was nothing but bleak sodden countryside. It stretched away from the road, dotted with ponds and patches of marshland, for as far as the eye could see. There were no trees and no houses, nothing that would bring comfort to any woman.

Followed by my maid I picked my way through the morass of men and their belongings until I spied the Kent colours flapping wetly on the pinnacle of a blue and white striped tent. Inside I found my husband.

He was pleased to see me and quickly offered me his straw-filled pallet for the night.

'I hardly think there is much comfort to be had there,' I remarked eyeing the narrow soldier's bed with distaste.

'I could wrap my arms tight around you and we could lie close.'

'I think it would be preferable if you took the floor.'

'As you wish,' said Thomas in the tone of a man who knows when he is defeated.

He bade me sit in the best travelling chair and had wine brought but, as we often did these days, we soon fell to arguing.

'He is not a coward,' protested Thomas.

'I never said he was a coward.'

'Look how he faced the rebels at Smithfield. That was not the behaviour of a nithering.'

'Husband, I merely remarked that as a boy he didn't enjoy fighting. He would hide behind his nursemaid's skirts at every opportunity.'

I remembered Richard as a sly pincher, not a fighter.

'I'm sure you are mistaken, Alys. Besides to take up arms is expected of a king.'

'True.'

'Richard wants an opportunity to win his spurs and must lead his men into battle.'

'Of course he must,' I said. 'I understand that.'

'The men do not see him as a coward. They see him as his father's son. They want him as their leader.'

What the men wanted, with the sole exception of my husband and possibly the duke, was war; preferably glorious war like those French campaigns of long ago fought by Richard's father and grandfather. What they didn't want was a shameful slide into ignominy with perpetual talking at the treaty table. They wanted war not peace. War would bring conquest, and conquest would bring rewards for those who fought. Peace would bring nothing but lives spent huddled by the fireside with endless re-telling of ancient battles.

'How is young Roger doing?' I asked, thinking we might talk of something else.

'Well enough. He's brave; inclined to rashness but he'll learn.'

Last summer at my mother-in-law's request, Thomas was finally able to purchase the wardship and marriage of Edmund's son but to my horror it had cost us six thousand marks. Every time I looked at the slight fair-haired boy who bore an unfortunate resemblance to his mother, I remembered those piles of coins and hoped he would prove worthy of the investment.

I put out my hand and touched the walls, surprised at how sounds of rain and wind could be muffled by heavy canvas. But it wasn't warm and I shivered, pulling my cloak further round my shoulders. At home, the trees would be shimmering in a soft golden summer haze; bees would be buzzing in amongst the roses and the air would be balmy. Here in the North it was cold and wet and miserable and windy.

We endured a lengthy wait and it wasn't until well after dark that we supped on a scant meal prepared by our cook.

'Only one night together in our pavilion,' remarked Thomas, sadly.

'The king has ordered the queen and the women to remain safely at York,' I replied, thinking with pleasure of the promised luxury of St Mary's Abbey and not minding in the slightest that my husband was setting off to war without me.

All of a sudden from outside came the noise of a commotion and, with no warning, John Holand burst through the doorway. He was dirty and dishevelled, as if he'd been fighting again. His shirt was torn and his cloak covered in mud. His eyes were over-bright and his face was as white as a dead man's shroud. He looked wildly around him and shouted at the servants to get out.

'What's the matter?' said Thomas, starting up from his chair.

'I've killed Stafford.'

'Christ's blood!' Thomas's chair tipped over and fell to the ground.

'I didn't mean to kill the fool. Just frighten him.'

'You've killed Ralph Stafford?'

'Yes. Stafford. Richard's friend. Oh Christ! He'll string me up for this.'

I dropped my cup and the wine spilled over my skirts. Ralph Stafford was heir to the Stafford earldom. He was young and he was merry and, at this moment, other than Robert de Vere, the man who stood closest to the king. How could he be dead?

'You're certain he's dead?'

'Of course I'm certain. He was down in the mud, spewing up blood. Ran onto my sword. I heard him scream and the sound as he fell. His boot was caught in the stirrup but the horse didn't run. I had a torch brought to see who it was. Oh Christ! What shall I do?'

I exchanged a frightened glance with Thomas. This was the most dreadful news. To kill a member of the king's inner circle was bad enough but to kill one of his closest friends ... Richard would never forgive this.

'Where did this happen? Where were you?'

'About a mile back. Where the road dips. '

'Thomas thrust a cup of wine into his brother's hand. 'Tell me exactly what occurred.'

'I don't know,' said John, running his hand through his hair so that it stood up in damp spikes. 'Some damned row. His men and mine. Arrows were loosed. A couple of men died. Nothing serious but I wanted answers from Stafford.'

'And you were angry?'

'Of course I was bloody angry but I wasn't going to murder the man over a couple of churls who couldn't hold their drink.'

'So how come he's dead?'

John sat down and put his head in his hands.

'I don't know. It was almost dark. Rain was whipping against my face. I was riding fast and he came out of the shadows. I drew my sword. I thought he was someone out to kill me.'

'So you struck the first blow?'

'No. No. He was on my sword before I knew it.'

I could see it clearly. My brother-in-law, at the best of times rash and impetuous, raising his sword in anger against an enemy only to discover, too late, that it was no enemy at all and he had killed the king's friend.

'Were there witnesses? Anyone with Stafford?'

'What? Yes, of course. He had half a dozen men with him.'

'Thomas.' I touched my husband's arm. 'He'll have to flee.'

'I'm not going anywhere.' This sudden spark of defiance was stupid but typical of John. 'It wasn't my fault. Stafford should not have been there. He should not have approached me like that. What was I supposed to think?'

'It doesn't matter what you thought or what Stafford thought, Richard will not hold an inquisition into your motives or why you were both out on the road after dark. All he'll see is his friend lying dead and you with a blood-spattered sword in your hand. Alys is right. You must go.'

'I can't.'

'You must. Go now before Richard is told. He'll have you killed if he catches you. You know he will.'

John appeared dazed by what he'd done and by what he must now do.

'Where shall I go?'

'East. To the shrine at Beverley. Dress as a pilgrim. Go into sanctuary until his temper cools. Richard won't dare break sanctuary, of that you can be quite certain. It's only a few miles from where we crossed the Humber. It won't take you long. You remember the ferry?'

'No!' I said, thinking quickly. 'He'll expect you to go east.' Both men turned in surprise. 'Go west. Make for the Holand lands in Lancashire. You'll be safe there.'

'She's right.' Thomas took his brother's arm and raised him from his chair. 'Go west, through the hills. Go now, John. Delay and you're a dead man. Tell no-one and don't come back.'

I lifted a finger to John's blood-smeared forehead and traced the sign of the cross, then placed my mouth against his cold lips. 'I pray you stay safe, brother. We would not want to be without you.'

For a moment he hesitated, then flashed a brief smile and disappeared out into the night.

Thomas sat down and stared at the flapping door and

the blackness where his brother had been only moments before. 'What shall I do?'

What indeed? I tried to order my scattered wits and make a plan. It was obvious Thomas was incapable of reasoned thought.

'Wait. Do nothing. It may just be that Stafford lives or that the others didn't see who killed him. Wait until we know more.'

But the morning brought dreadful news. The body of Ralph Stafford was carried by his men to the king's lodgings and when Richard saw what had become of his friend he raged like a man possessed by a dozen devils.

He had Stafford's men dragged in front of him to tell their story and when the murderer, John Holand, could not be found, Richard began to scream. He would have his brother disembowelled; he would cut off his head and impale it on London's bridge; he would put out his eyes, slice off his private parts, cut out his tongue and chop off his hands; he would flay him alive and if anyone was in any doubt what he thought of this man he had once called "brother", he would show them by personally ripping out the murderer's traitorous black heart. There was no talk of a trial, only revenge.

'Send word to your mother,' I said to Thomas who was in tears and shaking after an hour-long audience with Richard. 'She is the only person who can make Richard see reason. Ask for her help. Plead with her to intercede on John's behalf.'

'My mother?' He seemed bewildered by the idea.

'Yes, your lady mother. I will go if you give me permission.'

'You?'

'Yes.'

'But it is a week's journey away. You cannot ride that distance on your own.'

'Husband, listen to me. Any messenger you send will be stopped by Richard's men. You know that is true. But no-one will suspect a woman. I shall tell the princess what must be done in a way that no letter can.'

It took much pleading but within two hours I was on my way with my maid and an escort of a couple of brutish-looking youths who were mightily displeased at being removed from their duties in the baggage train. Despite their doltish appearance, Thomas assured me they were trustworthy and handy with a club. They would deliver me safely to Wallingford.

Amidst the chaos which overtook the camp after the discovery of Ralph Stafford's body, I hoped no-one would notice the four of us slip away. We could have been anybody: two overgrown louts, a whining girl and her mistress, all dressed in dark clothing, with a couple of bundles strapped to the horses, making their way to the edge of the encampment.

I cast a glance behind me as we passed the last wagon, one full of long wooden boxes of arrows. The canvas covering was roped partially across and I could see the head of a small boy who must have crept inside to sleep in the dry. The old man, meant to be on guard, was dozing against one of the wheels and didn't open his eyes as we rode past. No-one was watching us.

The day could have been full of bright sunshine making us easily visible to Richard's men who would be out searching for sign of my brother-in-law or anyone bent on favouring his escape, but luck was with us. A low damp mist rose up from nowhere and within moments blanketed the whole of the moor. I could just make out the track, marked as it was by the deep ruts and hoofmarks of yesterday, but no-one could see us. We were completely hidden.

We kept our heads down and rode as fast as we could towards the ferry crossing. I had no idea how long our journey would take but John's life depended on how quickly I could reach Wallingford. I needed to find my mother-in-law because she was the only person on God's earth who could save John, the only person who could prevent Richard from killing his brother.

17

It was dusk by the time we reached Wallingford. The last of the daylight was fading from the sky behind the castle walls as I clambered wearily out of the barge onto the wooden jetty. Darkness was gathering and the steps already lay deep in shadow. I could see a man with a torch hurrying to discover who the unexpected visitor might be.

'My lady? Oh! Countess, it's you! But we had no warning. Did you not send word?'

'Forgive me, no; I had no wish to alarm the princess. Tell me, is Lady Clifford in the castle?'

'She is, my lady.'

'Will you find her and ask her to meet me alone in the hall. Make sure the princess is not told.'

He was a sensible man and asked no questions, merely dispatched the boy at his heels to run back up the steps with a message for Lady Clifford.

'What has happened?' Eleanor's eyes were huge with fear. 'Is it Richard?'

I kissed her. 'No. Richard is well. It is John Holand. He is in the greatest of trouble.'

Once I had shed my cloak, I told her what had happened on the road to York and what the princess must do. 'Richard will hang John if we cannot persuade her

272

to intervene. She is the only person he would listen to. Thomas says he has never seen the king so angry. When they brought him the news about Ralph Stafford he was out of his mind with rage.'

Together we hurried through the hall and up the stairs.

'She must leave at once, Eleanor,' I urged, almost tripping over my feet in my haste to reach my mother-in-law's chamber.

'She cannot. To travel north would kill her.'

'You don't understand. She must. If she doesn't it will be too late and Richard will have John killed.'

'No, Alys. It is you who do not understand. She cannot possibly undertake a journey of that length. She is a sick woman.'

I stopped and stared in disbelief. Surely, surely I had not come all this way for nothing? I had been so certain that my mother-in-law would make Richard see sense. She would be able to persuade him that he must not commit this dreadful act of revenge. John was her son. She could not let this tragedy happen.

But the moment I saw the princess I realised Eleanor was right. A journey of that length *would* kill her.

She sat by a little fire, a vast bloated figure who barely resembled the woman I'd last seen only a few months before. Then, she had been merely a woman of faded beauty, overly plump, ageing and tired; now each breath she took seemed an effort too great for her heaving rolls of flesh. I watched as she struggled but the moment she saw me her eyes sparkled and her lips curved in the loving way they had always done.

'Alys, dear child,' she said after I had told her what had happened and she had wept and then sent for Lewis

Clifford. 'Do not go back. Stay with me. There is nothing more you can do. You have done enough.'

I noticed how her hands were swollen as if fattened for the pot, the fingers reminiscent of huge white slugs. She found difficulty in grasping the arms of her chair and, when Lewis arrived, hid her hands carefully beneath the folds of her skirt. I gave a sad smile at that little piece of vanity thinking how even at this time of personal crisis she was still a woman who needed the admiration of men.

She had me repeat my story to Lewis, questioning me closely on exactly what both John and Thomas had said and what I had heard of Richard's rages against his brother. When they had wrung every last piece of information from me, she sent me away to get some rest while she and those closest to her remained talking through the hours of darkness, deciding what should be done.

At first light Lewis Clifford and a small party of the princess's men left Wallingford with instructions to make haste before it was too late. They carried with them letters for all her sons and a personal plea to Richard to be merciful. I wasn't privy to her exact words because she had been closeted alone with Lewis at the end but I knew her thoughts.

The lads from the baggage train who had escorted me safely to Wallingford, I sent back to Thomas with my thanks, a handful of coins for their trouble and a private note for my husband. They might be useful to Lewis on the journey and if not he could always send them on their way alone.

'He is so like his father,' the princess cried as we watched them leave.

'John?'

'No, Richard.'

I glanced at Maud who stood beside her mother. She had been with the princess for most of the summer while her husband, the handsome count of St Pol was absent. I knew how worried she was.

We turned and walked slowly back inside with my mother-in-law supported by Maud and Eleanor. They appeared to carry her whole weight, which was not insubstantial, and I wondered if she could even stand on her own. I wanted to weep when I remembered the light-hearted, fleet-footed woman she had once been, the beautiful widow who had captured the heart of a prince.

'You have never lived with a man who possessed an ungovernable temper, Alys,' she said, pausing at the foot of the stairs to catch her breath. 'I have, and I learned early in my marriage to the prince to avoid angering him.'

Maud said very quietly, 'I was frightened of him but I was only a child.'

Her mother patted her hand. 'He loved us and he was generous but he was a proud man and expected our loyalty and obedience in return.'

'He was greatly enamoured with you,' I remarked. 'Everyone said so.'

'Yes, he was, and equally determined that I should be greatly enamoured with him. In his eyes my previous marriage was of no importance and my first husband was no rival.' She sighed as if the remembering of those days was too much for her to bear. 'You should understand,

Alys, that from the time he was a small boy the prince knew exactly what he wanted. I was everything he desired in a companion and he presumed I felt the same about him. He was heir to his father's throne: rich, handsome, intelligent, courageous; well-liked by his friends and greatly admired by women. Why would I not have desired him as a husband above all other men?'

She laughed but I sensed an emptiness in her laughter. 'He and I had known each other since we were children and our bond was strong. We had been raised together in the royal nurseries and had been as close as brother and sister. You have no idea what a wonderful childhood we shared. It was beyond his comprehension that I could have desired Thomas more than I desired him. He never asked and I never said anything of my feelings for my first husband. Then one day we had an argument, some trivial disagreement of the kind that husbands and wives have, I forget what it was about, and I made the great mistake of telling him.'

'He was angry?'

For a moment I thought she wouldn't answer but then she replied somewhat reluctantly, 'Angry is not quite how I would put it. It was extremely foolish of me but the words were out and I could not take them back.' She hesitated as if choosing her words carefully. 'I thought he was going to kill me.'

I smiled at the ridiculousness of such a thought. 'But he didn't.'

'No, he didn't. I never told anyone what he did to me. It was distressing then and would distress me greatly now if I had to repeat it. Let us just say he made sure I understood

276

that I was his and only his and that he would allow no other man to have any part of my affections.'

She leaned forward, putting out a hand to steady herself and stared up the shadowed stairway as if the ghosts of the past were coming down to greet her. A single tear rolled slowly down her cheek.

After that we waited. There was nothing else to do but wait. We charted the journey that Lewis and his men would make through England along the well-trodden roads leading north, through towns and villages, skirting marshes and bogs, picking their way carefully through thickets in the valley bottoms and up steep-sided slopes of hills and moors. Food had to be eaten, horses needed changing and shelter had to be sought for the night.

Two days, three days, five days and we thought they might have reached York or possibly Newcastle if there had been a boat to speed the journey. But if they had ridden all that way, where could they be by now? No letters came except for the usual traffic from the king's officials at Westminster and that was mostly everyday business concerning the princess's various concerns.

My mother-in-law, once Lewis was gone, descended into a great melancholy. She said very little and when she did speak it was of times past, of her glorious days in Aquitaine with the prince and the years of happiness with Maud's father. She never once mentioned Richard or John. Mostly she slept or stared silently into the flames.

It was three weeks since Lewis's departure and we were becoming increasingly worried. Eleanor was convinced an accident had befallen her husband whilst Maud insisted her mother must be prepared for bad news. She was certain John was already dead, that Richard had caught him and horribly executed her brother.

'He was a nasty little boy,' she wept. 'I never liked him. How can he be so cruel?'

'Cruelty is many men's nature,' I said. 'It is like a poison in their veins.'

'And a man's blood can be curdled by the very thought of vengeance,' added Eleanor, which was of no help to poor Maud who merely sobbed all the louder.

'John used to be his favourite. Before de Vere came, Richard loved John best. You know what he'll do, Alys, don't you?'

I shook my head. I didn't want to think what horrors Richard might inflict on my brother-in-law if he caught him. Death would be inevitable but a death as slow and as painful as Richard could make it. I hadn't forgotten the look on his face at the rebel preacher's execution three years before and how Richard had seemed to revel in the man's agony. He would make certain that John suffered.

'He will nail John's body to the gates of York,' cried Maud. 'When he's killed him, that is what he will do. As a warning to others not to insult their king.'

'Maud, no. He wouldn't do that. Not to a man who is his mother's son, not to a man he called his brother.'

'He is a monster. See how he treated the duke, his own uncle, the man who practically raised him. Look how he threw out Chancellor Scrope for daring to voice a contrary opinion. He has discovered that he can do exactly as he likes. He is the king and Simon Burley has taught him that kings are all-powerful. He told Richard that to be a great ruler you must command obedience. You mark my words, Alys, he will make every single one of us Holands pay the price for what John has done. He will cut us off from his royal favour. I will no longer be his sister and Thomas will no longer be his brother We will be publicly shamed and sent from court. Thomas will lose everything.'

I felt the blood in my veins turn to ice-water and an emptiness fill the pit of my stomach. If Richard turned against Thomas there would be no-one to protect us. The duke and my brother were no longer welcome in Richard's presence, they no longer had the king's ear, and my mother-in-law didn't have the strength to protest.

Time crawled by, the days shortening by a candle-width, sunshine weakened by low mists rising daily from the river. The servants moved silently about their duties and the musicians at the far end of the room played low, sorrowful tunes as if we were already in mourning.

Then on the eve of the feast day of St Dominic, Lewis and his men returned from the North. Empty-handed.

'We caught the royal party before they crossed the border,' he said, kissing the princess's hand which in her panic she had forgotten to hide from view. 'The army is headed for Edinburgh but the campaign is not going well.'

'And Richard?' said my mother-in-law, her hand now at her lips.

'The king is well, my lady. He is in good spirits and sure of success.'

'And my other son? What did he say about John?'

'He won't listen, your grace. Forgive me.'

'But my letter?'

'I gave him your letter; I told him what you said and the private words you wished for his ear alone, how you begged him to show pity because John is his brother.'

'And will he? I am his mother and it is a small request?'

Lewis looked more and more uncomfortable at having to report the failure of his mission.

'I do not think the king will be merciful, my lady. After he had read your letter he said there was nothing you, as his very dearest mother, could do or say which would change his mind. Murder had been done and justice must prevail. He spoke of justice and the rule of law as if they were of the utmost importance but I sensed he was not interested in justice so much as in avenging the death of Lord Stafford's son.'

'And John?' Her voice shook and her eyes were slowly filling with tears.

'No word, my lady. The king has men scouring the countryside around York but they've found nothing. They've been to Beverley where they discovered the scoundrels involved in the original skirmish hiding in sanctuary, but there was no sign of your son. Lady Alys's husband says his brother is likely in Lancashire and begged me not to tell the king.'

'But Richard *will* forgive? He is not a monster to kill his own brother? He is no Cain who would kill his brother, Abel?'

Lewis shot a glance at Eleanor who moved swiftly to the princess's side.

His voice was full of compassion. 'I pray the king will forgive your son but he is fixed on taking revenge. His tone to me was that of a reasonable man but the words he spoke were dreadful. I fear greatly for what may happen.'

'But John is my son. He is the king's brother. Does that count for nothing?'

'I fear not, my lady. The king said that a man who dared to slay the king's friend is not worthy and can no longer be considered as his royal kin. He said the Scots would soon feel the power of the king of England's fury and once he had dealt with them, so would John Holand.'

A little sigh escaped my mother-in-law's lips and she slipped sideways in her chair. The book she had lying on her knee, fell to the ground with a thud. The curly-haired lapdog hiding beneath her skirts yelped with fright and fled for the doorway, its tail between its legs.

'Mother!' screamed Maud.

Eleanor crossed herself and dropped to her knees beside the princess while I found myself too shocked to move. Only Lewis had the presence of mind to call for the servants and send for the princess's physician.

We had her carried to her bed where she lay like one already dead, laid out beneath the covers of crimson silk, her eyes closed, not breathing.

While the men pushed each other aside to get closer, shouting for more light, more room, more warmth, I leaned over and placed my cheek close to her lips. At first there was nothing but then, very gently, the slightest movement of air. There was hope. She was still alive!

The physician arrived with the usual self-importance of such men. He sniffed the princess's breath, consulted his books and his charts, muttering to himself how the humours were clearly more unbalanced than before but that as the moon was not passing through Gemini it would be most unwise to draw blood.

His recommendation was to rub her limbs with a specially-prepared salve made from mare's tail and juniper berries. This would relieve the swelling which had most certainly caused her collapse and when she opened her eyes, we should have her take an infusion of watercress collected from the headwaters of a chalk-bed river. If there was further discomfort, he said, a little fresh parsley could be added. He also advised strewing the floor with young nettles, if some could be found; the aroma thus released would assist in her recovery.

'Will she wake?' I asked, having little faith in his salves and potions.

'In God's good time,' he replied. 'And if there is no improvement by tomorrow I will send to Oxford for more medicines.'

The salve was prepared and Maud and I watched two of the maids gently rub the princess's arms and legs. But she failed to wake. The sight of those swollen limbs, horribly bloated and ungainly, made me glad that my mother was no longer here to witness how her friend had aged. The fair maid of Kent who had so entranced the English court and captivated its prince, had gone forever.

We stayed by her bedside throughout the night. None of us could bear to leave her. The candles burned lower in their sconces and people came to weep quietly or to pray but the princess barely stirred. Her breathing seemed a little easier but her face was pale and her eyelids shadowed.

When the sun rose above the ridge, heralding another day, she opened her eyes and announced in a quavering voice that she felt much better. God had spared her for us. She gave a tremulous smile and apologised for frightening everyone. We really need not have worried. She would rise and attend mass as soon as her maids made ready her clothes.

'I do not believe her,' whispered Eleanor as we tiptoed away. 'Look at her lips. They are blue and her face is a peculiar grey colour. What do you think it means?'

'I don't know,' I replied. 'But she has suffered a great shock.'

I turned to Lewis Clifford who was white-faced with exhaustion, 'Did my husband have any words for me, any messages?'

He sounded almost too weary to speak. 'Yes, Lady Alys, he said to tell you that the king has stripped his brother, John, of all his possessions and that he, himself, has been replaced as earl marshal but that you are not to worry.'

I clutched Eleanor's hand. 'How can I not worry? It has begun just as Maud said it would. Richard will wreak his revenge on all of us and we will be destroyed. We will have nothing.'

'Who has replaced Sir Thomas as marshal?' asked Eleanor calmly, ignoring my distress.

'Lord Mowbray.'

'And you say the campaign is not going well?'

Lewis gave a great sigh. 'No it is not. The Scots are melting away into the hills and refusing battle as they always do and there are ominous signs of trouble within the king's circle of advisors. Robert de Vere has informed the king that the duke of Lancaster intends the Scots to do his dirty work for him.'

'Dirty work?' I said, suddenly alert. 'What dirty work?'

'De Vere has told the king that the duke will urge him further and further into the Scottish wilderness. He will assure him that victory can be his if he pursues his enemies. And when the king finds himself in the high mountains beyond the Scottish Sea he will be at the mercy of the Scots and will be killed.'

'Surely Richard does not believe this?'

'Alas, I am afraid he does.'

'You must not tell the princess,' I said firmly. 'Whatever else you do, tell her nothing of this. She has struggled valiantly to keep her family together and another breach between the duke and Richard will break her heart.'

'If it is not broken already,' said Eleanor softly.

By evening it was clear that my mother-in-law was struggling. She had failed to rise from her bed. Every time she tried she was convulsed with violent spasms and said she couldn't breathe. Her maids fluttered around offering assistance and cups of cordial but she refused them all.

Eleanor murmured quietly that we should begin making preparations.

'What preparations?'

'She will want to make her last wishes known.'

'No,' Maud whispered. 'Please no, not yet.'

I placed my arm around Maud's narrow shoulders. 'You must be brave, Maud. Your mother doesn't fear what is to come. Her beliefs are strong. She has buried two husbands and two children and wishes to set her affairs in order before she is summoned by God.'

'But I need her,' wailed Maud.

I sat by the bed in the darkened chamber watching my mother-in-law sleep. Apart from an elderly maid dozing by the hearth and Will Fulbourne, the princess's chaplain who knelt in prayer, we were alone.

When the candle was burned half down, she whispered, 'Alys? Is that you?'

'Yes, dearest lady,' I whispered. 'I am here.'

'Alys. My jewel box; the silver one in the big chest.' Her voice was very weak.

The box was only small but wonderfully embossed with images of flowers and twisted branches of leaves. The jewels inside were cushioned in a nest of dark blue velvet: three rings and a little silver coin.

With some difficulty she lifted out the brilliant emerald ring, the largest and gaudiest one in the box.

'The prince gave me this when I promised to marry him.' Her hands fumbled and she nearly dropped the ring. 'It is the jewel of fidelity and eternal love. What do you think?'

I took the ring out of her fingers before it became lost amongst the sheets and placed it carefully on the bedcover where we could admire its beauty. But she looked away, more eager to see what came next. This was a tawdry trinket, certainly nothing of value, most probably a childhood gift.

'Thomas gave me this ring on our first wedding day in Ghent,' she whispered, gazing tenderly at the little bauble. 'It is the most precious of all my jewels.'

'But, my lady,' I protested. 'It is like the fairing I bought young Margaret last Christmas; worth no more than a penny.

'Not to me. To me, it is priceless.'

She tried to slip the little ring onto her finger but when she failed she tucked it inside her nightgown next to her breast, and kept her hand pressed close.

'Do you know what that is, Alys?' Her voice had by now become so weak I could barely hear her words as I picked up the little silver coin.

I turned it over in my hand. It wasn't English. I shook my head.

'It is from Flanders. I wanted a shower of silver coins on my wedding day but Thomas was poor so he gave me this. He promised that later there would be many more.' Her eyes were gazing at something I couldn't see. 'He said that one day he would cast a river of jewels across our marriage bed.' She smiled happily. 'And he kept his promise.'

I replaced the coin in the box and gave her the last jewel, a huge ruby, the colour of pigeon's blood, set on a heavy gold band. I saw a sudden flash of iridescent blue as it caught the candlelight. It was beautiful.

'This is for you, dear Alys,' she whispered, pressing it into my hand. 'My mother gave it to me when she knew she was dying and now the time has come for me to pass it to you.'

'Oh, but my lady, should this not go to Maud?'

'No, my dear. You are the mother of my grandchildren and I know you will keep it safe. It was the ring of my father's mother, Queen Marguerite.'

I slid the ring onto my finger. The ruby: the jewel of love and friendship, of contentment and peace.

'I do not know how to thank you, dear lady.'

She shook her head as if to say that gratitude was not required. 'May it bring you a long life and much happiness, my dear Alys. But remember, jewels and riches are as nothing. Only love lasts forever. Our bodies will rot and crumble to dust; our riches cannot follow us to the grave; but our love will warm those we leave behind.'

I replaced the box where I found it and when I returned to the bedside, she had slipped back into sleep, her head dropped onto her pillow, one hand still pressed firmly against her breast.

Next morning Prior William in his black robes, hastened up from the priory to provide comfort to the princess in her final hours and later her old friend, Robert Braybrooke, bishop of London arrived. The bishop's father was distant kin on her mother's side and he and the princess had always been close. She greeted him with tears and asked for her chaplains, her clerk and the knights of her chamber. It was time and she wished to settle her affairs.

Gently and with the utmost compassion, the bishop helped her form the necessary words. She affirmed her adherence to the Catholic faith and asked that, in death, her soul should be committed to God and to the Blessed Virgin Mary and the Saints. No matter how many heretical beliefs she may have entertained over the years, at this last moment she wished it known that she was a true and faithful Christian woman of God's Church.

'My body,' she whispered, so quietly that the clerk had to lean close to catch her words. 'My body is to lie next to that of my late lord and husband.'

I looked across at Eleanor. We both knew she would lie with the prince. He had wanted her with him in death as she had been in life and had made preparations for her to follow him. Every year she had travelled to his tomb at Canterbury to honour and remember him and this, her own final journey, would be the last.

'Your late lord and husband?' enquired the clerk as a matter of form, wishing there to be no doubt, his pen poised.

'My first husband, Thomas Holand. I wish to lie with him in death.'

An anguished whisper rippled round the room. How could this be? What would the king say?

'In death my body is to be buried in my chapel in the church of the Greyfriars.'

'But?' I mouthed at Eleanor, who shook her head.

'The Greyfriars?'

'The Greyfriars at Stamford.'

'In the diocese of Lincoln, my lady?' enquired the clerk, making quite sure.

'Yes, next to my late lord and husband.'

The clerk glanced at the bishop as if waiting for some confirmation of this most unexpected of requests but the bishop merely nodded and the clerk returned to his writing.

In the end, Thomas Holand, the hedgerow knight from Broughton, was the man she chose to be with in death; not the prince who had raised her up to be the first lady in the land, who had defied the disapproval of the king and queen to marry her and who had sworn his eternal love and devotion. I could not understand how the love she had for a man she had first met when she was little more than a child and who had brought her nothing but trouble, could triumph over the honours bestowed on her by a prince of the royal blood. But I had never understood her.

She remembered each one of her three sons by name. Each received gifts of a bed, rich furnishings and clothing. Apart from the Kent and Wake lands which would pass to Thomas as his rightful inheritance, the residue of her estates would go to Richard. Provision for Maud and Eleanor, I knew, had already been made, and I had been remembered last night.

Many of those who she charged with carrying out her wishes after her death were here in the chamber: the bishop of London, Lewis Clifford, John Clanvowe, her chaplains Will Fulbourne and John Yernmouth, and her steward John Worthe. But there were others like the bishop of Winchester and Simon Burley who were absent. She asked all of them to pay her debts and reward her servants as they saw fit. No-one was to be forgotten.

After that we left her to the men of the Church who would prepare her for her final journey into the world beyond the grave.

At the end she lay motionless, her eyelids closed, her face ashen, not speaking. We watched as one laboured breath followed another until, with no warning, her eyelashes suddenly flickered. She opened her eyes and stared unseeing into the candlelight. She parted her lips and said in a very small voice, 'Thomas?'

A shallow exhalation of breath and then nothing. She had gone.

Maud turned against my shoulder and sobbed while I found myself unable to speak. For years she had loved and protected us, she had been the mainstay of our lives and now she had left us and we were alone.

Immediately messengers in black were dispatched to the king somewhere north of the border wherever he might be and also to his officials at Westminster. The princess's body was wrapped in waxed cloth and laid in a lead tomb in the chapel surrounded by candles. Everything now had to wait for Richard's return; no decisions could be taken without the permission of the king.

As soon as word of her death leaked out to the local towns and villages, people began coming to pay their respects, first in threes and fours and then in their hundreds. Watching them make their way up the steps to the castle I was reminded again of how much she had been loved by everyone, not just by her family and friends.

The days that followed were full of the sad business of sorting out the princess's clothes and personal items. Her maids were kept busy ensuring everything packed away was clean, brushed and protected from the moth. My mouth fell open at the quantity of finery in her wardrobe.

'I had no idea!' I gasped in open admiration.

'The prince liked her to look her best,' said Maud. 'He was generous with his purse, constantly sending presents of silks and furs and jewels. He encouraged her to be adventurous in the matter of fashion. If she wanted to cut her necklines lower or her sleeves longer or sew pearl buttons on her shoulders, he approved.'

'Not like that you stupid woman!' she shouted at one of the maids trying to fold a velvet robe. 'Have someone help you. It takes two people.'

'We should be finished by this evening,' I said sadly.

'What will you do then?'

'Go back to Woking, to my children, I suppose.'

'Eleanor says Lewis leaves tomorrow for Westminster to await Richard's return.'

'Will she go with him?'

'She says there is no reason to remain.'

'And you?'

'I shall seek out my husband. Perhaps travel with Eleanor as far as London.'

That morning we had received word that Richard was on his way back, having found the capital city of the Scots deserted. In the eyes of some he had gained a victory of sorts but here in Wallingford we knew he had achieved little or nothing. To the men who had wanted glory and riches, the king's campaign was a failure.

Richard would have received word of his mother's death but nothing was said about funeral arrangements or about the fate of my brother-in-law, John Holand.

18

Next morning I said farewell to Eleanor and Maud. It was a sad parting. We clung to each other in tears, not knowing when we would meet again. Promises were made to write and to visit but all three of us knew that words trip easily off the tongue and our lives were not ours to command. I stood waving on the pier until their barge disappeared, lost somewhere in the shadows of the trees past Winterbrook. Only then did I make my lonely way back up the steps.

The castle walls were awash with the warm golden sunlight of a perfect late summer's day. Across the river the last of the wheat crop was neatly stacked and the gleaners busy in the stubble. Three men and an army of small boys with baskets set out from the undercroft along the path to the orchard, singing as they went; and down in the Queen's Mead I saw the shadow of a daytime fox slink silently into a ditch.

I found myself strangely disinclined to go home to Woking where the harvest would be nearly finished and my children excited at the thought of brambles in the hedgerows and rats in the corn. I decided to postpone my departure and the princess's steward, who would stay at Wallingford until the last, seemed pleased. Perhaps my remaining presence in the castle cheered him. Without the women of the princess's household everywhere seemed empty, the rooms too big, too quiet, gathering silence and dust. Gradually, one by one, the men were leaving. The kitchens lay silent, just simple meals cooked for those of us left.

A few people came each day to pay their respects to the princess where she lay in the chapel: the Bardolfs from Mapledurham, flustered at having just heard the news; and the elderly abbot of St Pater's and St Paul's four miles upriver, recently risen from his sick bed and only now able to make the journey. Each one of them was made welcome but none of them stayed.

I wandered through deserted rooms. With no fires lit and night-time chills drifting up from the river there was a feeling of dampness in the air. Tapestries had been taken down and stored away leaving the walls as bare as the day they'd first been plastered. The chests we'd packed just two days before had been removed to the wardrobe along with the princess's woollen rugs and embroidered cushions. Tables and chairs had been carried down to the store room and only the princess's beds remained. Tomorrow, they too would be dismantled and packed away. It was as if in death, the remains of her life were unravelling.

I touched a hanging on the red velvet bed she had left to Richard. It was typical of my mother-in-law's taste: luxuriously embroidered with silver ostrich feathers and heads of leopards stitched in gold. The leopards had boughs of leaves issuing from their mouths and looked oddly passive, perhaps weighed-down by the quantity of golden thread. It was an ideal gift for a pleasure-loving young king.

In an adjoining room was the bed bequeathed to Thomas: red and gold, decorated with hatchments; no sensuous creatures, a bed well-suited to my husband. In the little room at the head of the stairs, the one with an odd-shaped ceiling, was the bed which would go to John.

I walked to the narrow window looking out across the river and wondered what had happened to my brother-in-law. It was more than eight weeks since he'd disappeared into the night. There had been no word of his whereabouts. Surely if he was dead I would know?

The fields and trees beyond the castle walls shimmered in the mid-morning haze. Nothing moved, not even a passing barge. The world outside seemed unreal, like the illuminated pages of a book. I had refused dinner, having no appetite, and was beginning to feel light-headed.

In the silence of the room I heard footsteps on the stair but I didn't move. A slight draught stirred the air as the door opened, followed by the softest of clicks as it closed.

I turned round.

His boots made very little noise as he walked across the floor towards me, just the gentle creak of well-worn leather on wooden boards. He stopped not more than a hand's breadth away from the hem of my skirt.

He had changed. He was thinner, the hollows in his cheeks testament to weeks of hard living and unknown deprivations. His eyes were deeper, less brilliant, more shadowed than before. He had the appearance of a man who had stared long into the abyss and been frightened by what he'd seen.

'I owe you my life,' he said without a single word of greeting.

I shook my head, unable to speak.

He wrapped his arms around me so that I could hear his heartbeat, a steady thud where I was pressed hard against his chest. He smelled of leather and new-cut hay, of soap and sweat and freshly laundered linen. I breathed him in as if he could fill my whole being and wondered where he'd been and who had cared for him.

He held me apart from him and regarded my face out of narrowed eyes as if weighing up what he should do. I didn't dare move. Then slowly he lowered his head so that his lips touched mine and very deliberately he began to kiss me. He kissed my lips, my eyelids, my cheekbones and the corners of my mouth. I turned my head away and whispered, 'No!' But his hand moved to my chin and with his fingers he gently brought my face back to his.

'Sweet Alys.'

His lips were warm on mine as he kissed me, each time with more determination, until the room began to spin and I began to melt, tilting my face upwards and arching my back.

I had never much liked kissing, a messy business at the best of times, with a man's mouth and his tongue all over you. But this was different. His kisses consumed me. They ate me up as if he would absorb the whole of me. And there was nothing I could do, or wanted to do, but part my lips and kiss him back.

I felt his fingers undo the ribbons of my coif and before I could protest he had the pins removed and my hair tumbling over my shoulders and into my eyes. Fine strands spread across my face. He thrust his fingers into the hair, pushing it away from my mouth, my eyes, kissing the soft spot in front of my ears, my cheeks, my forehead, my lips. all the time holding his hands on either side of my face so that I couldn't move.

'Alys,' he murmured. 'Sweetest, sweetest, Alys.'

I wanted to cry, 'Stop!' I wanted to say, 'No!' but the word which came was 'Please,' and yet again, 'Please.'

I leaned against him, quivering on his chest like a frightened animal. He slid an arm round my waist, rocking me gently as if I were a child.

'Oh Christ!' he murmured. 'You have no idea how much I want you.'

'No,' I whispered, my mouth so close to his I could breathe in his breath. 'No, please, I can't. You mustn't. What if someone should come?'

His mouth softened. 'No-one will come. I have a man at the foot of the stairs.'

His hands moved from my waist, slowly, deliberately, over my skirts down to my hips. I felt his fingers grip me through the thin woollen cloth and instead of stepping away I allowed him to draw me closer.

We stood like that, as close as we could be. I could read the hunger in his eyes.

Very gently he turned me round and pulled me to him, his arms wrapped tight, the whole of my body pressed against his from boot to chin. I felt the hardness of his desire and immediately knew a surge of panic. I had never enjoyed the sort of intimacy he would want, the sordid grappling beneath the covers, the thrusting, heaving business of naked bodies.

'Hush,' he whispered into my ear. 'Hush.'

He kissed the back of my neck, soft little kisses like those of a child, until I stopped struggling and stood quiet.

Then he set me away and began to undo the laces of my gown. With some part of me I observed how skilfully he unthreaded the narrow linen cord, wondering how many other women's gowns he had unlaced. But it didn't matter. Nothing mattered. Nothing but him and me and here and now.

I wore an old-fashioned loose-fitting gown so that when the laces were undone it slipped easily off my shoulders. I was aware of the warmth of his mouth on my back as he slid his arms smoothly round my waist and started to caress me. Through the fine wool of my kirtle, his fingers brushed the surface of my thighs, sliding across my belly and my breasts. I tipped my head back against his shoulder and must have made a little gasp of pleasure because he laughed and with an ease, surely born of practice, picked me up and carried me to the bed and laid me on top of the red silk cover.

I lay there gazing at him, too scared to move, unshed tears misting my eyes. Then without a single word, not asking if he might lift my hem or waiting for licence to proceed, he began to remove the rest of my clothing.

I was the mother of six children with a body which matched my years. There were lines and creases and roughness where, to the touch, I had once been firm and smooth like the skin of a peach. My breasts were no longer taut and round but soft and drooping like a branch over-heavy with fruit. I was not what I once had been and could not bear to see the look of disappointment in his eyes.

It took him no time at all to remove the crumpled mess of my kirtle, my chemise, my shoes, my stockings and all the while I uttered futile little mews of protest, curling myself up so that he would not see me as I was, crying that I was not the woman he thought he wanted.

I tried to cover myself but he pushed my hands away, told me I was beautiful, and began to kiss every single part of my naked body from the soles of my feet to the warm hollows behind my knees, my slender wrists and the soft beating pulse at the base of my throat. He kissed the palms of my hands and the slack of my belly and used his mouth on my breasts. He burrowed his head between my thighs and made me blush at the liberties he took with my person. But by then I had forgot that I was a woman of thirty-five years who had never much liked what occurred behind the bed curtains, because by then he had made me feel like a girl of seventeen. I felt as if this was the first time I had ever lain with a man: the first time, the last time, the only time.

Through half-closed lashes, I watched him strip off his clothes until all he wore was his shirt. I reached out for the fine white linen and pulled him down on top of me. He shuddered as I wound my arms around his neck and found his mouth with mine.

'Love me,' I whispered. 'Please, love me, please.'

He was quick, much too quick, and almost brutal in the way he took me. But the second time he pleasured me slowly and with the greatest of care until I found myself shaking and crying out with joy. I never wanted this moment to end.

But end it did.

'Will you miss me when I'm gone?' he murmured as I lay spent and weeping in his arms.

'You are going?' I whispered, my voice full of tears, my body trembling at the enormity of what had happened between us.

'Not today. Tomorrow.'

'I cannot bear to have you leave.'

He raised an eyebrow and smiled. 'I know you can't and I don't want to go but we must be sensible. And there is still tonight.'

'Oh no! Not tonight! I cannot,' I cried in alarm, thinking of the impossibility of tiptoeing around in the dark, seeking my brother-in-law's room.

He kissed my nose and then my mouth. 'Yes you can, sweet Alys. I shall come to your room when the castle is asleep and I shall make love to you again.'

'What of my maid?'

'Send her away. Or would you rather I didn't come? Shall I make love to your maid instead?'

He was running his finger between my breasts, moving it slowly downwards while the whole of my body ached with longing for him.

'I want you to come.'

He grinned. 'I knew you would like this, my sweet Alys,' he said. nibbling the lobe of my ear. 'You thought you didn't care for bed sport, but see how mistaken you were. I know you better than you know yourself. I always have.'

I supped in silence, picking at my food, while John carried on a conversation with John Worthe, the steward. My mother-in-law had warned me of the perils of temptation, of how a wife could be seduced by the allure of a forbidden love and not recognise the danger until it was too late. She had described the flames of passion which blazed as bright as the noonday sun and how if you stretched out your hand the heat would scorch your fingertips and fire would burn you up.

But I had not listened. I had ignored her warnings. She was barely cold in her shroud and I had indulged in the worst of all sins in one of her beds with her own son, a man who was not my husband. I was the lowest of sinners known to God: a woman caught in adultery.

That night I determined to be resolute. I had sinned but would not sin again. I would not repeat my folly. I was no foolish woman like Dame Alice Perrers who had indulged in unbridled lust with the old king. Nor was I was like Lady Swynford who chose to throw away her reputation, condemning her children to a lifetime of bastardy, all for love of a man who was not her husband. I was better than either of them. I understood my duty as a wife.

I told myself I was strong, I would refuse further dealings with him. I was Thomas's wife. John was my brother-in-law and could never be anything more. What we had done was wrong but there would be forgiveness. Our coupling had been the result of our overwhelming sadness at the princess's death but it would not happen again. We would set aside our desire for each other and recognise the encounter for what it was: a moment of passion released by our mutual need to countermand our sorrow.

I sent my maid away and waited until the door creaked open. I was perfectly calm. I had made my decision. If John wished he might speak to me of love, he might write verses the way other young men did. I might yearn for him but I would not yield to carnal pleasure.

I should have known myself better. One look, one touch and I was undone. Within a heartbeat I was in his arms and beyond that it was but two steps to the bed and all was lost. He made love to me until I was dizzy and exhausted by desire. My limbs ached, my lips were bruised and when we finally fell asleep we lay damp and exhausted, entwined in each other's arms.

I awoke at cockcrow, realising with dismay that sunlight was already creeping round the edges of the shutters and advancing across the floor. John turned and, with his eyes still closed, began to make love to me again.

I forgot the hour, the order of the day and abandoned myself once more to the joy of his caresses.

'This can go nowhere.' I said later, half-wanting him to disagree, to tell me we could continue like this forever, that we could escape into the greenwood and live in some distant unknown place where no-one would ever find us.

'No,' he agreed pleasantly, stroking my breasts.

'What shall we do?'

He rolled over onto his back and pulled me on top of him. 'What do you think, sweet Alys? Will my brother agree to share you with me? Shall I come to your bed each Tuesday and Thursday?'

'He would kill you first.'

He laughed. 'He has already tried once.'

'Perhaps when I return to Woking you could visit me there?' I said wistfully, thinking as I spoke of my inquisitive women, my children and the lack of opportunity to be alone.

'I do not think that would be a good idea, do you?'

'But where shall we go?' I cried.

He stroked my hair and idly wound a strand round his little finger.

'I shall go to Westminster and make my peace with Richard. With our mother dead, God rest her soul, he will wish to make amends.'

'I cannot come to Westminster.'

'No, you cannot.'

'So what shall I do?'

He smiled lazily. 'Return to Woking. Become a chaste wife once more. It is a part you play most delightfully.'

I felt near to tears. 'But I shall not see you.'

He put his mouth to mine. 'We shall see each other often. You are my sister. What should prevent us from being friends?'

'But this?'

'Ah yes – this. Yes, I see the difficulty.'

It was impossible he did not care, not after last night and all the words he'd spoken.

He pushed me off him, sat up and started pulling on his clothes.

'Do you not want me?' I asked in a small voice.

'What d'you think?' He sounded distant, as if having eaten and drunk his fill, he would rise from the table and leave without a backwards glance.

But when my lips trembled and tears began to fall, he took me in his arms and kissed me gently. 'Of course I want you, sweetheart, but we must be careful. It will serve neither of us well if our dalliance becomes common gossip. I shall think of something, never fear. Now come, Lady

Holand! We have duties to perform and I'm as hungry as a beggar in Lent.'

Why? That was the question I asked myself as I fled the castle at Wallingford. Why had I, who knew perfectly well the difference between right and wrong, done something so wicked? Because wicked it most certainly was. Not just a sin against my marriage but a sin against God.

Like all women, I had been taught as a girl about a wife's duty and there had been no expectation that lies and deceit would form any part of my married life. Yet I had not behaved as I should have done.

My mother-in-law would have had no difficulty in answering the question; she would have said it was passion. But I had never been a passionate woman. I was sensible, perhaps sometimes a little foolish, but never passionate. So why had it happened?

'Are you sick?' asked my daughter, Lizzie, a child of exhausting curiosity.

'No,' I said. 'I am not sick; I am sad.'

'Because our lady grandmother is dead?'

'Yes.'

On my return I had admired my son and how much he'd grown and had hugged my three girls tightly, praying their closeness would protect me from the burning of the noonday sun.

'Will the king bury our lady grandmother here, beside our baby who died?' asked Joan, who, this last year, had become overly interested in the processes of death.

'Hush child,' said the nursemaid.

303

'No, Joan, your grandmother will not be buried here. She has asked to be buried beside your Grandfather Holand.'

'Do I know him?' piped up four year-old Margaret.

'No, you don't know him,' I said gently to this littlest daughter of mine. 'He died many years ago before any of you were born.'

'Why does she want to be buried beside him if he died such a long time ago?' puzzled Joan.

'Because he was her first husband and she loved him very much.'

'Did she love me?' asked Margaret, pulling on my skirts.

'Your grandmother loved all of you. She was a good, loving woman.'

'Will you be buried beside our father when you are dead?' asked Lizzie.

'Of course she will,' said Margaret dismissively, giving her sister a push. 'She loves him best. You do, don't you, lady mother? You love our father best.'

I turned away, dangerously close to tears at the simplicity and honesty of my daughters whose innocence knew nothing of the dangers of temptation and the sins of the flesh.

When Thomas returned, a week later, I welcomed him with my three girls placed in front of me, arrayed like a defensive wall. I was frightened in case he knew, lest someone had told him his brother and I had been alone together. But he greeted me as kindly as he had ever done and then bent down to kiss his daughters.

Later, after supper when we were alone, he told me he had just come from Wallingford where he and both his brothers had gone to see their mother's body and have a mass said for the repose of her soul.

'It was a sad occasion; but my other news is good: John is no longer facing the executioner's axe. Richard knows his refusal to listen to our mother's words caused her great sorrow in her final hours. He cannot forgive himself so he is trying to make amends.'

I said nothing, too frightened to utter John's name.

Thomas looked perplexed. 'I thought you'd be pleased?'

'I am, Thomas.'

'Of course John is not yet back in Richard's favour, he will have to work hard for that. And there is much royal displeasure at our mother's request to be buried beside my father.'

'He will surely not go against her wishes?'

'No, he has agreed the burial will be at Stamford, but he is angry. He regards our mother's choice as an insult to his father's memory despite my telling him that it is not. Though I have to admit I do not understand her reasons. I thought, as did we all, that she would lie beside the prince in death.'

'She loved your father. That is why. It is really very simple.'

Thomas moved closer and placed a hand on my sleeve. 'I gained no enjoyment from the campaign, Alys. There was no glory for any of the men and I missed the pleasure of your company.'

His hand lay hot and heavy on my arm and I longed to move away but willed myself to remain still and quiet.

I knew what he wanted and had prepared myself to be dutiful. I had done this a thousand times before but this time would be different and I was filled with inner panic.

'Alys,' he said quietly. 'Send for your maid and we shall go to bed.'

He didn't know. I thought he might guess. I thought I would betray myself. But he went about his business as silently and as efficiently as ever. When he had finished, he kissed my cheek, thanked me and closed his eyes. Within moments he was asleep leaving me alone and trembling.

I could not do this but I must. Thomas was my husband and had the right to treat me as his wife. A wife's duty was to serve her husband in whatever way he wanted so I had to accept this burden no matter how hard it was.

I fell asleep with tears trickling from beneath my lashes, wishing with all my heart that the man beside me was someone else.

I declined Thomas's invitation to return with him to London, citing any excuse I could think of: Edmund's slight cough which required a mother's care; a promise I had made earlier to visit the elderly prior; a duty call upon our neighbours who had not seen me all summer.

'I shall come later,' I said, filled with guilt at his disappointed face. 'When my duty here is done, I shall come.'

But I didn't. I wrote letters: Edmund was sickening with a fever, Margaret had fallen and I was worried; her ankle was badly swollen. The children's governess had failed to teach the girls their prayers and the prior had asked me to visit a widow at Pyford. But yes, I would come soon.

It was easy enough to evade my husband's invitations, that merely required a little ingenuity. But a royal command to attend the Christmas festivities was another matter entirely, one that could neither be ignored nor declined. As the days shortened and the nights grew cold I ordered my gowns packed, bade a tearful farewell to my children and set out for the king's palace at Eltham.

19

THE AFFAIR 1385-6

Three years before when I'd last seen Eltham it was summertime and the gardens were in bloom. Today the moat was frozen. It had snowed in the night and the king's palace resembled nothing so much as that triumph of the master confectioner's art, a sugar-powdered subtlety. Below the snow-covered rooftops which sparkled in the winter sunshine, a dozen frost-brushed windows blazed as if they were on fire. The king's men had swept the paths but the gardens and the park beyond lay silent, smooth and glistening, every tree laced with white as if an angel had delicately applied a paintbrush to their canopies. It was bitterly cold.

If outside was still and quiet, inside proved to be a riot of noise and gaiety. Branches of winter greenery hung on every wall, the hearths were piled high with burning logs and great stands of beeswax candles lit the rooms. The sounds of minstrelsy were everywhere and the chambers set aside for entertaining were crowded with hundreds of people. From the little I could see, every one of Richard's friends was in attendance as well as most of his enemies.

As I entered the hall I saw my brother; he was forcing a smile at some joke of Simon Burley's which had made the assembled company laugh. There was little laughter in the group which surrounded the youngest of the king's uncles, my sister's son-in-law, young Woodstock, now newly titled, duke of Gloucester. His circle of friends had long faces and were muttering to each other in low angry voices.

'I thought you'd met with an accident,' said Thomas, taking my arm and pushing a way through to the presence chamber.

'I am sorry,' I said politely. 'I was delayed on the road.'

'No matter. You are here now. You must make your greetings to Richard before he learns of your arrival and wonders what you're doing.'

I raised an eyebrow. 'So suspicious?'

Thomas shrugged. 'He is a boy trying to fill a grown man's boots. Naturally he is suspicious. He sees plots everywhere.'

'He is nineteen.'

'Our mother kept him a child too long. Kingship is more difficult than he believed it would be; he has a fear of making mistakes.'

'His campaign was not a success.'

'A waste of money. It gained him nothing, not even his spurs, and the failure has made him doubly suspicious. He is turning more and more to de Vere and Burley and the others he favours and listening less and less to those with experience.'

The guards at the entrance to the royal chamber stood back as we were announced. I looked for my little Alianor but could not see her anywhere.

Richard and Anne, sitting on their matching thrones, looked magnificent, clothed from head to toe in crimson, white and gold with enough jewels to purchase a small kingdom. The silk of Anne's crimson gown was smothered in thousands of tiny diamonds and her robes were trimmed with that most costly of furs, snow-white miniver. On her head she wore her favourite crown, an elaborately twisted golden diadem studded with rubies and pearls. My mother always said that fine clothes made a fine woman and this was certainly true for Anne; she looked almost beautiful.

I received a few curt words from Richard and some kinder ones from Anne and was then ushered to where the ladies had gathered near to the elderly dowagers. The old ladies sat on cushioned benches peering vainly through their old rheumy eyes. They reminded me of Aunt Wake who claimed till the day she died that she could see perfectly well when we all knew she was nearly blind.

I didn't want to look around me in case my brother-in-law would see me looking because if there was one person I was afraid to meet, it was him. I hoped he would not be here, that Richard had not wanted his unwelcome presence. Yet I could not prevent myself from looking, trying to seek him out, wanting him to be wanting me. My throat was dry, my lips trembled and my heart hammered so loudly I thought the woman next to me must surely hear.

'Deaf as well as blind, it would seem.'

The voice came from my right. I started, but it was only my sister. 'I didn't see you,' I said in relief.

'So I observed,' she said drily. 'Who were you looking for?'

'Nobody,' I lied quickly. 'Well, the duke if you must know. I wondered where he was.'

'Leicester.'

'Why Leicester?'

'Celebrating Christmas with his family and keeping out of Richard's way.'

Joan always knew where everyone was. I suspected she kept a tally of our movements and doubtless had them written on a lengthy roll at Pleshy.

'And you?' she said. 'Where have you been all autumn for you have not been in London?'

'Woking; caring for my children.'

She gave me a disbelieving look. 'Alys, you have a dozen women in that nursery of yours at Woking. They can care for your children. You should be with your husband.'

'My children need me.'

'Not as much as your husband does. A mother's duty is to employ suitable women for the nursery; a wife's duty to be at her husband's side. I have told you this before and I should not need to tell you again. You shame our family by your neglect of Thomas.'

'I do not neglect Thomas.'

'So why has he been alone in London while you skulk down in Woking and why is he so miserable?'

'Thomas is not miserable. I would know if he was.'

'Alys, you know nothing. You never have.'

I glared at Joan. With both her daughters married she spent her time poking her nose into other people's business.

'I wish you would get married again,' I said crossly. 'Then you could attend to your new husband's affairs instead of interfering in mine.'

'Marry again?' she looked at me as if I had said something particularly stupid. 'Why would I do that?

Women who remarry take lesser men as their second husbands and lesser men still as their third. Why would I wish to descend to the position of a cloth merchant's wife? No thank you, sister. I shall remain the dowager countess of Hereford until the day I die.'

At that moment there was a loud braying of trumpets from the minstrel's gallery. It was time for the frost games to begin. There was an immediate flurry of grooms and maids, all scurrying about bearing cloaks and gloves and boots. Everybody was laughing with excitement at the thought of the fun we were about to have. Frost games were always fine entertainment.

The women's procession was led by Joan's elder daughter, now duchess of Gloucester. She was followed by my sister and then by everyone else. We were all wrapped in our fur-lined cloaks and wearing our warmest boots.

Once outside, in spite of the hundreds of flaring torches which lined the paths and terraces, it was impossible to tell who was who amidst the crush, what with hooded cloaks, the darkness and a tangled mass of laughing, chattering people. I caught an occasional glimpse of a familiar pale face shrouded in black and once or twice saw the sleeve of a gown I recognised, but mostly we were anonymous shadowy figures, mingling with each other in the dark.

A hand plucked at my sleeve and a whisper slid out of the darkness. 'There is a set of stairs by the buttery. I'll meet you there.'

I turned. There was no-one.

But my lover's voice was like music to my ears, a well-remembered tune sending shivers up my spine and melting oceans in my heart. I was frightened, but measured hand in hand with fear was joyous anticipation. No-one would miss me. It would be easy to creep away. There was laughter and shouting and singing and dancing and, amidst the melée, no-one to notice I had gone; not even my sister. I would be perfectly safe. I knew that to go was very, very wrong. But I would be perfectly safe.

I hesitated no more than a moment then slipped away, lost in the crowd, edging into the gloom of an ill-lit cloister. I ran quickly back to the house, through the public rooms, past servants startled at my enquiries for the whereabouts of the buttery, until I discovered the stairway hidden within an archway. There, waiting for me in the shadows was my brother-in-law. He grasped my hand, dragged me up the steps and into a tiny room set under the eaves. He closed the door and bolted it, then took me in his arms. He did not speak. My lips were cold as ice but his were warm.

It was not like the first time, nothing could have been as sweet or as tender as our first encounter. Now he was in such a fever to possess me that he could not wait to unlace my gown or remove my stockings, he simply lifted up my skirts, pulled aside my linen and, pushing me back against the wall, thrust himself into me.

I felt nothing. I was far too nervous.

'Oh Christ Jesus!' he groaned as he shuddered and collapsed into my arms. 'Oh my sweetest, sweetest Alys.'

He had been without me for several months and I knew enough about men to know how much he had suffered from the deprivation. Perhaps there had been other women but I thought not; not if he loved me as he did. I was certain he loved me because he was very good to me afterwards, laying me down carefully on the pallet bed and taking the trouble to unlace the top of my gown and stroke my breasts. The touch of his fingers on my naked skin made me so unbearably excited that I began to gasp with pleasure and, once he had recovered himself a little and regained some strength, he enjoyed me for a second time.

Afterwards we lay in silence.

'Where is your bed with the red silk cover?' I said at last, thinking perhaps I was being dull and should make a little conversation.

'At Wallingford.' He seemed disinclined to talk and I did not know what else he wanted.

I lay quietly at his side wondering if what I had given him had been enough and if I still pleased him.

'You should go back,' he said. 'Before you are missed.'

I did not want to leave. I knew it was foolish, but I wanted to stay.

'Can we meet again like this?' I asked shyly. 'Perhaps tomorrow?'

He reached for my fingers. 'No.'

'But if you have this room?'

'I said no, sweetheart. I cannot return to serve Richard so I must find a place elsewhere which means making myself pleasant to others, and the king's rooms are the best places for me to find employment.'

I knew little about his situation except that Richard had stripped him of his offices and left him virtually penniless.

'Cannot Thomas help?'

He grinned. 'I already live on his charity and as I have his wife in my bed it hardly seems a fair bargain.'

'I will always be in your bed when you want me,' I said quietly, wishing he would kiss me again.

314

'I know, sweet Alys. You have no idea how much comfort that gives me. But I do need money.'

'Who will you ask?'

'I would have asked the duke, but he is in Leicester. I cannot ask his brother.'

'Obviously not.'

I could imagine Isabel's husband punching John if he so much as dared to ask for a favour.

'It is a pity. Isabel would have persuaded him but these days, Constanza guards her like a hawk guards its meat.'

There was an awkward silence.

'John?'

'Mmm?'

'You and Isabel; you do not still … do you?'

He smiled lazily. 'Would you mind?'

He must have seen the stricken look in my eyes because he gathered me into his arms and kissed me gently. 'There is no-one but you, sweet Alys. Be assured; no-one but you.'

Two weeks after the end of the Christmas festivities, we gathered to say farewell to my mother-in-law. The princess's body, covered in black cloth-of-gold, was carried to London on her barge. I was told there was nowhere on either side of the river that was not lined with mourners. All the way from the castle at Wallingford, past Reading and Great Marlow, past Windsor and Walton to Kingstown and the king's palaces at Sheen and Westminster, people turned out in their thousands to say farewell to the princess because she had been greatly loved. After a solemn ceremony in the abbey at Westminster, insisted on by Richard, her family followed her coffin to Stamford where she was finally laid to rest beside the man she had loved best of all: Thomas Holand.

The chapel was not grand like the chantry chapel the prince had endowed at Canterbury but at the end she had craved the simplicity of the life she had lived when she was a young wife, a life built on love.

'I understand her better now than I did,' I said to Maud, thinking how much loving John had changed my life. 'For a long time I was very muddled but I can see clearly now.'

Of course I could not see clearly. No woman in love sees clearly. Unwittingly I had become caught up in those flames of passion my mother-in-law had warned me of, dazzled by the delights John offered, barely able to tell right from wrong. But it was not my fault.

I tried not to think about him, put him completely out of my mind but I failed. So throughout the long bleak months of winter I determined to arm myself. I prayed to Our Lady to help me find the strength to resist this temptation that had come disguised as my brother-in-law. He was the serpent in my garden and the joy he offered was the forbidden fruit.

Winter lasted forever and spring, when it came, was accompanied by a cold dry wind from the east which shrivelled grass and caused beasts in the byres to sicken and die. By the time I travelled to Sheen for the Easter celebrations there was no sign of buds or leaves on any of the trees and even the king's pleasure gardens looked dull and devoid of colour.

In the last two months I had seen little of Thomas who had been visiting his new manors in Rutland. I had wanted to ask him if John had been given a position but on the two occasions he came home I did not dare. I was sure I would blush and stammer if I so much as mentioned his brother's name so I said nothing. Thomas was too busy telling me of a problem with his manor at Ryhall and reclaiming his rights as a husband to notice my reluctance to talk.

The first person I saw on my arrival at the royal palace was that fussy little woman, Dame Chaucer, Lady Swynford's sister, who served Constanza.

'Ye'll have heard my mistress is bound for Spain?' she said, sidling up to me.

'No, Dame Chaucer. I have not heard.'

She smiled at my ignorance. 'I thought your husband would've told ye. It's off to claim her crown, they are.'

I felt a stab of annoyance that I'd not known but swiftly realised it was my own fault for hiding myself away at Woking and refusing Thomas's pleas for me to join him.

'And your sister, Dame Chaucer?' I enquired. 'How is Lady Swynford?'

'She is well, I thank ye.' She paused and then, looking about her to make sure no-one could overhear, whispered, 'He still sees her, y'know. But there's none of that other nonsense, not now. They learned their lesson and it was a hard one for my sister. She's sworn an oath and she'll not break a holy vow, not even if he were to get down on his knees and beg.'

The woman was nothing but a kitchen gossip. I smiled distantly and turned my back. When I reached the women's rooms the talk was all about the duke's planned expedition

317

and how Pope Urban had declared it a crusade. I was told by at least three women, who were well-placed to know such things, that the Holy Father had sent a banner and how his support had opened men's purses. Offerings were pouring into the Lancastrian treasury. The king's council was completely won over by the idea and had granted the duke fresh funds in the renewed hope that, with the help of King Joao of Portugal, Castile could at last be defeated.

Constanza would be well pleased. She had waited a long time for this.

On Sunday we celebrated the risen Christ with a grand feast and the usual vast array of dishes which tried my stomach dearly after months of simple fare at Woking. To my delight I found myself seated, not beside some mumbling old dowager full of aches and pains, but next to the duke's daughter, Elizabeth. It was a long time since I'd had the pleasure of talking with her, not since her marriage to the Pembroke heir, little John Hastings, some five years before.

'You should take some of the figs in ale, Lady Alys,' she said politely, selecting one of the paste coffins filled with fried cheese for herself. 'They are very good.'

'Thank you,' I said, noticing how, under the table, her elegant feet were tapping to the rhythm of the minstrel's tabor. 'Do you still like to dance? I remember how much you enjoyed it when you were a little girl.'

'Oh yes,' she said gaily, her eyes lighting up with laughter. 'I like dancing best of all and I am very good at it, even my sister says so. But our stepmother disapproves of dancing as a pastime for young women. She would rather have me at prayer.'

Constanza's preference did not surprise me one bit.

Elizabeth leaned closer and whispered confidentially, 'I miss Lady Swynford. She liked dancing.'

'But you are a married women with your own household. You can do as you please.'

She twisted the ring on her finger and pouted prettily. 'I ask you, Lady Alys, what good is a thirteen year-old boy to me as a husband? I shall grow old and ugly waiting for him to become a man.'

Poor Elizabeth. She was past twenty and had been waiting a long time. She was such an attractive young woman, it seemed a shame for her to waste her youth in this way.

I put my hand on hers and said kindly. 'It will not be long. Be patient.'

'I have been patient, Lady Alys. I have been patient for five whole years and I am tired of being patient.'

The following day was the annual giving of Easter gifts and bestowing of good wishes for the year ahead. As usual the duke was immensely generous presenting me with an illuminated copy of the *Roman de la Rose* which I had long coveted.

'Lady Alys,' he said gravely. 'I want to give you my thanks for the special kindness you have shown to my daughter, Elizabeth.'

He was as tall and lean as he had ever been, but there were white threads in his hair and lines etched into his cheeks which had not been there before. He looked like a man well gone into middle age, no longer the handsome young chevalier my cousin, Blanche, had married.

'She is a lovely young woman,' I said, unaware I had given Elizabeth any particular kindness other than talking to her the previous day at dinner.

'Do you think her mother would consider I had done well with our daughter? I worry, for the girl is not content.'

So he had at least noticed Elizabeth's misery.

'If I may be permitted to offer an opinion, your grace, I think the Lady Elizabeth will be happier when she and her husband can live together as man and wife.'

He smiled thinly. 'I know, but his tutor tells me the boy is not yet ready for marriage. So much goes not according to plan. I sometimes despair of God's designs. What does He want from me?'

'You do what you believe is right, your grace. It is all that any of us can do.'

We talked a little of the days we had shared when my cousin had been his duchess and I had been just a girl, then he made his farewells and moved away to speak with Senór Gutierrez, his Spanish secretary.

I was not doing what was right and I knew it. I had managed to avoid speaking to my brother-in-law but was unable to keep my eyes off him. I watched hungrily as he flirted with Anne's ladies and made the middle-aged countess of Warwick blush to the very roots of her greying hair. A little later he made himself pleasant to Constanza and then spent a long time talking to the duke's three daughters. The eldest said very little as he tried to engage her in conversation but the jokes he told made Elizabeth laugh and reduced young Catalina to a state of helpless giggles.

He was handsome and charming and, seeing how clever he was with women, I wondered why it was me he wanted. I was no longer young and always found myself hopelessly inarticulate in his company. I never knew what to say or do and by now was convinced, despite his protestations, that there must be other women. He was far too attractive to spend his nights alone. Jealousy gnawed relentlessly at the edges of my mind when I should not have been thinking of him at all.

At last, unable to bear my misery a moment longer, I went outside and walked down the path to the river where the water races were taking place. It was still cold but today the sun shone on Richard's celebrations. Further along the bank, dozens of people cheered and shouted as two boats sped across the river, oars flashing in the sunlight. The duke's boat won and his brother Gloucester's oarsmen were well and truly beaten. Men surged down the bank to help the laughing winners ashore while the losers were left to console themselves as best they could.

Then, as if I had conjured him up, John appeared at my side. He placed his hands on the rail so that our fingers almost touched and together we stood in silence, staring out at the dark flowing current. My heart hammered painfully against my ribs and my legs, beneath my skirts, trembled. I knew I should say something witty or clever but could think of nothing.

'You remember the sisters of the house of the Grace of the Blessed Mary outside Aldgate?' he began.

'Yes,' I said, startled into a reply.

'I believe next Tuesday you will set out from your house at noon to visit them.'

'But why?'

'Hush! You will take with you one maid and a man, preferably an oaf of little intelligence. You cannot go alone, you would not be permitted to ride out without an escort.'

'Thomas would not allow it.'

'You know the street of the church of the eleven thousand virgins?'

I nodded.

'Opposite is Lime Street and on the west side of Lime Street is a great house with a chapel and a green garden which belongs to Simon Burley. If you take the lane on the other side by the church of St Denis, you will find an inn. It is called "The Lily". In the yard they will take your horse and show you upstairs.'

'And you will be there?' Even I could hear the doubt in my voice.

'If you come.'

This was lunacy but I could not prevent myself from smiling. He had not forgotten. He still wanted me.

I was well used to the stench and muck of London's alleyways and fully expected Lime Street to be squalid and unattractive, but it wasn't. The lime burner's yards were tucked discretely behind high fences and the only smell was that of domestic fires and an occasional unpleasant reminder of Eastcheap butchers. Outside an imposing arched gateway a man was shovelling what dirt there was onto a cart, beyond him a glimpse of ordered greenery. This must be Simon Burley's house. From what I could see it was a handsome stone-built dwelling, three storeys high with beautiful dark red tiles on the roof and two large oriel windows jutting out towards the street.

I looked to my left. There was the little church of St Denis with its squat tower and carved wooden saint. I turned into a lane which was narrow, barely wide enough for our horses. Here, houses were mostly one or two storeys, built of wood with closed shutters and tiny doors. One boasted a battered sign of a painted snake coiled round a rod but the house was dilapidated and probably let to poor families who hadn't bothered to remove evidence of a past tenant's occupation.

The inn was the largest and most prosperous building in the lane with an upper room and a yard for travellers' horses. I edged my mare into the yard. There was an open stable building, a great tub of putrid water, a boy carrying an armful of straw and an old man leaning against a wall. There was no sign of John and I wasn't sure what I should do. Noticing my hesitation, the old man ambled over and took my reins. Without saying a word, he helped me down and calmly pointed to the steps as if he welcomed a woman like me to the inn every day of the week.

I climbed the steps, fear slowing my feet, half-hoping John would not be there and I could run home to safety. But he *was* there and the minute I saw him I forgot my fear and walked straight into his arms.

'I knew you'd come,' he said, smiling.

He kissed me, then drew me down onto the pallet bed. I was a little nervous but between us we managed to remove most of my clothing until I was all but naked and shivering with desire. Then slowly and with the greatest deliberation he began to make love to me.

Later, as I lay in his arms, he told me how much he liked my breasts.

'They are wonderfully soft,' he said, allowing his lips to drift across my pale skin.

'Do you not think they droop too much?'

'No,' he said, taking a mouthful of soft flesh and nipping it gently between his teeth. 'I don't.'

'I have a corset which my sister gave me,' I said shyly. 'It is designed to make my waist smaller but it also pushes my breasts up so they appear more rounded.'

He glanced up from his preoccupation with my body and grinned. 'You do?'

'I could wear it one day if it would please you?'

I wasn't very experienced in love-making, I'd had no instruction and didn't know what words to use or what to do with my hands, but it was clear my offer excited him. He pressed himself even closer so that every inch of his body was moulded against mine and told me other ways in which I might give him pleasure. He laughed when my cheeks grew hot and my eyes widened in horror at one of his suggestions.

'Do women truly do that?' I said as his fingers began an exploration of the soft skin at the top of my thighs.

'They do.'

'English women?'

He paused for a moment, considering the question and then slowly slipped his hand over my hips.

'Yes.'

I was certain that none of my friends would entertain doing such a thing. But I did love him and I did want to please him.

'Is it allowed?' I asked.

'By whom?'

'The Church?'

He laughed. 'What does the Church know? They are nothing but a bunch of old cardinals who've never had a woman in their life.'

His eyes were challenging, daring me to refuse, daring me to ask if any other woman had ever done such a thing for him.

'And you would enjoy it?' I said uncertainly.

'Oh sweetheart, if it was you I would enjoy it more than anything else I can possibly think of.'

I thought fleetingly of Isabel and her strange foreign ways and that decided me.

He was watching me closely and must have seen capitulation in my eyes because he leaned forward, touched my lips with his and whispered, 'You are delicious.'

We met every Tuesday and every Thursday just as he had once said we would. Two afternoons each week my husband unknowingly shared me with his brother; two afternoons when I told my household I was visiting the sisters of the house of the Grace of the Blessed Mary; two afternoons, no more, no less. I thought he might tire of me, that his desire would become dulled. But it didn't and I came to believe he wanted me every bit as much as I wanted him. And I wanted him every moment of every hour of every day.

I lay quietly on the tiny pallet bed watching him sleep. He looked younger when he slept, his mouth softer, his lashes brushing his cheeks, his hair tousled and damp on the pillow. The pillow was not very clean, indeed the more I looked, the more I noticed that none of the bedding was very clean. There were grease stains on the rough woollen cover and marks of dirt on the edges of the coarse linen sheet. I hadn't investigated the mattress but could smell mouldy straw and had a suspicion that a number of crawlers lived inside the heavy canvas. There were definitely fleas; three bite marks in a neat red line across my belly were testament to that. By the covered slop pail in the corner I could see evidence of mice. It was not the sort of lodging house I would have frequented by choice.

But I had no choice. If he was there, I had to come.

The first time I hadn't noticed the squalor. I had been so nervous and desirous of seeing him, I'd fallen into his arms and onto the bed without a glance at my surroundings. Now I had the urge to bring fresh strewing rushes, clean covers, a goose-feather pillow, a hanging for the wall, linen, cushions and a mattress stuffed with duck down and scented with bedstraw. If I did that, this room would feel like a home.

He stirred. I leaned over and kissed his mouth. It was warm and tasted of the wine we'd drunk. The touch of my lips on his made him smile.

Slowly, he opened his eyes. I could see a face reflected in the depths and didn't recognize myself.

'Do you want me again?' I asked, stroking the dark golden hairs on his chest.

He put out his hand and cupped my breast.

'Very much.'

I felt again that leap of pleasure which always filled me when he expressed his desire.

Today I had worn the corset. My maid had hauled the laces as tight as she could and I had felt my breasts constrict as they were pushed high over the top of my kirtle and when I had opened my cloak for John, he had smiled.

I quivered as he began to unlace the ribbons of my gown and by the time he had reached the corset, where my breasts spilled out above the satin binding, his fingers were fumbling and neither of us could contain our growing impatience.

'Why do you women truss yourselves up like hobbled sheep,' he had complained.

'To give you the pleasure of untying us,' I had said, kissing his ear.

And I had given him a great deal of pleasure once he had finished undoing the ribbons and released my breasts from their captivity. We had made love all afternoon until the light began to fade and I knew I had stayed too long.

'I do want you very much,' he said, raising himself onto one elbow. 'But it is late and you ought to go.'

He watched me dress, helping me with the lacing and tying the ribbons of my cloak. He wrapped his arms around me and held me tight as if unwilling to let me go.

'Alys,' he said quietly. 'There is something you need to know.'

I tipped my face to his and kissed his mouth. 'I know everything,' I said.

'No, you don't.' His face was shadowed. 'I am going away.'

'Will we not meet on Thursday?'

'No, not Thursday, not next Tuesday, not ever again.'

I stared at him in disbelief. At first I thought he was joking but this was no joke. He was serious.

My lips trembled. 'Not ever?'

'Not ever.'

'Where are you going?'

'With the duke to Portugal. He has appointed me his constable.'

Portugal? Across the seas. Weeks away. A foreign place full of strange foreign people. Surely not Portugal.

His eyes were perfectly steady and I knew it *was* true. He really *was* going.

'When do you leave?' I whispered.

'Tomorrow. I ride for the West Country. We sail from Plymouth.'

Tomorrow! He was going tomorrow and he'd said nothing, not a single word.

'How long have you known?' I was trying to quell my mounting panic.

He hesitated. 'Since February.'

'Why did you not tell me?'

I had no wish to distress you.'

All those times I had come to see him, he had known and yet said nothing. I wanted to weep and rage in fury at his leaving me but I could not let him see me weep.

Alys, sweetheart.'

'When will you come back?'

'Maybe never.'

At that, the last remnants of my pride gave way and I began to weep.

'You cannot leave me,' I cried.

He stroked my head as I clutched at him, sobbing against the front of his shirt.

'Sweetheart, this could not have lasted forever. I have

to find a new life for myself away from Richard and you must go back to being my brother's wife.'

'But I love you,' I cried, saying the words I should not have spoken.

'I know,' he said gently. 'But love is fleeting. By next spring it may be we shall have forgotten each other. Believe me, for I have seen more of the world than you and I know that this is true.'

Later when I lay sleepless in my own bed, wrapped in utter misery, I remembered that of all the words he'd spoken he had never once said that he loved me. He had talked of need and gratification, desire and pleasure but never of love.

Days passed and in my distress I had no appetite. At supper I ate little but each morning found me retching over a bowl. My ladies kept their distance, fearful of what afflicted me, while my ever-faithful maid applied damp cloths to my face and sat me in front of the hearth. Thomas, convinced I was sickening, insisted on having our physician come. The man took one look at my flushed face and red-rimmed eyes and didn't move from the doorway. He questioned my women as to what I had eaten and whether I had bathed overmuch and recommended I should be removed to the country.

'I shall send you to Woking,' said my husband firmly. 'When you are recovered we shall travel together to Castle Donnington.'

I nodded my head in assent, closed my eyes and wished I could sleep forever.

I returned to Woking and found the company of my children better medicine than anything our physician could have prescribed. It was not possible to drown in grief with four small children in the house and gradually as the weeks passed I began to emerge from my misery and see myself for what I really was: a foolish and thoroughly misguided woman; a woman who had wronged her husband grievously, imagining a great and undying love where none had existed. I had been used by a practiced seducer and yet could not quite bring myself to believe John had felt nothing for me.

My sister came to visit and chastised me roundly.

'What is the matter with you? Are you sick?'

'No, I am not sick. I am perfectly well.'

'You're as pale as a corpse,' she said peering at me. 'Are you sure you're not sick?'

'No, I am not sick and you can stop bullying me.'

'Is it Thomas?'

'No, it is not Thomas.'

'But it is someone?'

'There is nobody,' I lied. 'And you can leave me alone because I shall tell you nothing.'

'So there is someone,' she said triumphantly. 'I knew it.'

Eventually, tired of her interrogation, she resorted to whispering of Richard's latest folly.

'He has made William de la Pole, earl of Suffolk and given him the Ufford estates. It is disgraceful. He is a fool because the others will not stand for it. Sooner or later there will be trouble.'

'And what of your son-in-law, Harry?'

She smiled fondly. 'Not high in Richard's favour but

that is no surprise, they were never friends. He is taking Mary to Monmouth and then rides to Plymouth to say farewell to his father. You heard the duke is for Portugal?'

Mention of the duke's campaign caused my treacherous heart to flutter and die. Plymouth was so very far away, and Portugal, even further.

Joan stayed for three days and then left for Pleshy, still railing at me for being a fool. But I already knew I was a fool, I needed no-one else to tell me.

Three weeks after May Day, Thomas returned, sweeping into my rooms in an uncharacteristically ebullient mood.

I looked up from my sewing, wondering what had occurred.

He sat down beside me. 'I have an important commission. The duke has asked me to escort the duchess and his daughters safely to Plymouth.'

I felt my heart begin to race. 'Plymouth?'

'In the furthest reaches of Devonshire. The ladies are to rest at a nearby priory until the duke's fleet is ready to sail. Will you come with me?'

'To Devonshire?'

'Yes. It would please me greatly to have you at my side. It has been lonely these past weeks. And we shall be able to say farewell to my brother. You recall I told you John has been made the duke's constable.'

'I remember,' I said, trying to quell the joy I felt.

I would see him one last time. A bitter crumb but better than this present starvation. I knew I was a fool thrice over but was unable to stop myself from smiling and a peculiar lightness filling my heart. One last time.

20

Constanza and Catalina travelled in the larger of the two ducal carriages, while Elizabeth, her elder sister and I were squashed into the other. It was a long, tedious journey and by the time we entered the wildness of Devon we had exhausted most of our conversation. Elizabeth was moody and restless, constantly asking how much further it was, how many more days, in the manner of a small child. There were several occasions when I longed to slap her. Her sister mostly sat in silence and our conversations were restricted to the little she knew about her father's plans for her.

Our cavalcade was vast. Constanza was taking her entire household to Portugal. As well as her ladies, her maids and other female attendants, she had clerks, chaplains, minstrels, grooms, her tailor, her goldsmith and her cook. We were accompanied by Thomas's men and a large escort of Lancastrian men-at-arms. Behind us came a straggling contingent of excited Spanish exiles who couldn't wait to leave what one of them rudely called "this wet little country".

After a night spent at the bishop's palace at Chudley, we set off along a muddy track which skirted the edge of a great moor. This was a brooding mass of bleak upland, a wild and mysterious place of hidden bogs and huge boulders, once inhabited by a race of giants. There was nothing gentle about the moor; it was a harsh country.

Our progress was slow. We passed an uncomfortable night at the abbey at Buckfast where the brothers were very kind but had little to offer in the way of comfort for our vast numbers. Next morning, as we left the abbey walls, a mist descended, creeping through the trees, wrapping us in its damp grey fingers. As the mist became thicker, I very much feared we would become lost.

'Lady Alys?' Elizabeth said in a quiet voice, nodding in the direction of her sister who had fallen asleep. 'May I ask your advice?'

She appeared slightly flushed as if embarrassed. I was ten years older than her and she had mostly kept her distance during the journey, preferring the company of young women of her own age.

'Certainly you may,' I said, curious as to what it was she wanted.

She was sitting beside me so we were able to whisper with no danger of disturbing the others.

'Lady Alys, I have missed my course.'

How odd she had turned to me on such an intimate matter. Why not one of her maids or her sister?

'You must not worry, Elizabeth,' I said kindly. 'It will be the excitement of the journey. Your course will come in a few days.'

'No, you don't understand, Lady Alys. I have missed three times.'

'Three times? You are surely mistaken?'

She looked at me as if to say how could any woman be mistaken when our lives were governed by the rhythms of the moon.

'I am certain.' She paused. 'Lady Alys, I think I may be with child.'

I tried not to show how shocked I was. Apparently the Hastings boy was not such a little boy as everybody thought. Elizabeth and her young husband had taken matters a step further than the duke's imaginings. Looking at Elizabeth's prettiness, her reddened lips, her copper-coloured curls and her womanly figure, I was not surprised. She was beautiful and was ripe for bedding. Clearly her husband had looked and liked what he'd seen. For once it was the duke who was mistaken.

I smiled at her. 'Elizabeth I am so very happy for you. This is wonderful news. Is your husband pleased?'

'Is not a husband always pleased?'

'Certainly he is and I'm sure yours is hoping for a son.'

'Lady Alys, I do need to be certain and I have no-one else to ask. My sister knows nothing about such matters nor do any of my own women. I wish Lady Swynford was here. She would know. You understand, I would not wish to make a fool of myself. I cannot afford to make a mistake because this is very important. I must be certain.'

Naturally she needed to be certain. It was usual for a woman to wait until she felt the child move before she said anything but with Elizabeth about to sail overseas she clearly needed to know before she left. Perhaps the duke would prefer her to stay in England with her young husband.

'You have missed three times?'

'Yes.'

'Have you felt unwell?'

'I have vomited in the mornings.'

'But the child has not quickened? You have felt no fluttering in your belly? No movement like a gentle tapping?'

She shook her head. 'No.'

'Your breasts?'

'Larger.' She smiled as if remembering a private joke. 'Heavier, a bit more tender.'

'And your waist?'

She held up her first finger and thumb to show me how much she had thickened. 'Nobody has noticed yet.'

'Then I think it is almost certain, Elizabeth. Of course until you feel the child move you cannot truly be certain, but you have all the other signs. Any woman will tell you the same.'

'Thank you, Lady Alys. You cannot know how grateful I am.'

I thought how pleased the duke would be but felt sad my cousin was not alive to see her grandchild. I doubted Elizabeth remembered her mother. It was a long time ago and she had been only a little girl when Blanche had died.

'Lady Alys, may I ask you something else?'

'Anything, Elizabeth.'

She bit her lip and looked more uncomfortable than ever.

'It is about marriage.' She blushed most becomingly and I wondered what else she could possibly want to know. 'Lady Alys, I know a girl may freely consent to marriage once she is twelve years of age. We were taught that by Lady Swynford. But I have heard – that is, someone told me – it is different for a boy. I thought that you, with your brother being a bishop, would know. The difficulty is that my husband is only …' She was twisting her fingers into knots and looking more and more embarrassed at every word.

I felt very tender towards her, smiled and patted her hand. I could understand her difficulty only too well. I recalled Tamkin's words that winter when our father died, of how a boy could not consent to marriage until he was fourteen years of age; how any marriage contracted before then was not a true marriage and could be set aside until there was proof of the boy's later consent. A child born of the so-called "marriage" would be illegitimate.

The Hastings boy was still just thirteen years of age. A lusty potent thirteen it would seem, but thirteen nonetheless.

'Please do not concern yourself, Elizabeth. I am certain this will be easily settled.'

'It must be. You understand, I could not bear the shame otherwise.'

'In which month does your husband celebrate his birth, Elizabeth?'

'October,' she said in a very subdued voice.

'When October comes, you must ask him to lie with you. Pay no heed to your midwife, who will tell you foolish stories about how the child might be damaged. I assure you that will not happen.' I gritted my teeth remembering the times Thomas had lifted up my nightgown when I was heavy with child and would rather he had left me alone. 'Once your husband is fourteen, any commerce between you confirms your marriage. My brother told me the rules but they are very complicated and need not concern you. Just rest assured, if you do as I say it will be a true marriage in the eyes of the Church and your child will be born legitimate.'

She sat back and sighed happily. 'Thank you, Lady Alys. You do not know what a burden you have lifted from my mind. To tell you the truth, I was very worried.'

We sat in silence for a while, listening to the churning of the wheels and the rattling and creaking of the coach.

'Lady Alys,' she said suddenly. 'Please say nothing to my lady step-mother or to his grace, my father. I would rather they did not know yet.'

'I promise not to breathe a word. But you will have to tell them soon.'

She smiled broadly. 'I shall tell my father when we get to Plympton. Is it far?'

It wasn't far. Three more days took us past several tiny villages, mere huddles of mud hovels clinging to the edge of the moor, through steep-sided combes thick with trees, down to the narrow Ivy Bridge where our track crossed the rushing waters of the River Erme. Here, our hosts informed us, it was only another half day at the most until we reached our destination: the priory at Plymton.

I knew immediately it would be a comfortable place. The priory was built like a little palace, grown rich on the patronage of people like the duke. I was told noble guests were commonplace and the princess, God keep her, had rested within its walls for several months when she and the prince had returned from Aquitaine.

After prayers to give thanks for our safe arrival, we retired to rest in seclusion for two days to recover from our journey. Thomas disappeared to lodgings in the town and I saw no more of him until the third day when the duke decided to give a feast to welcome his family.

From my seat at the table I kept my eyes lowered with only occasional glances at my brother-in-law, thankful I was not seated beside him. The temptation to touch him, even something as insignificant as a thread of silk from his sleeve, would have been too great to resist, in my foolishness I would have given myself away. But he made no effort to pay me any particular attention. Naturally he had to be careful but all I needed was a secret smile, yet there was nothing: not a note, not a glance not even a nod of greeting.

The food, as always with the duke, was plentiful and after our meal there was a little entertainment for us to enjoy before the duke said he would retire to the chapter house to discuss business. Constanza led the women back to her rooms where she invited one of her Spanish ladies to read.

The text was dreary and I wished I'd had the good sense shown by Elizabeth who had slipped out before the reading began. As the woman's nasal voice droned on, detailing the martyrdom of the blessed Saint Agatha, I allowed my mind to wander, thinking with pleasure of Elizabeth's forthcoming child. Blanche would be a pretty name for a daughter and would surely please the duke.

I was suddenly aware Constanza's lady had stopped reading. One of Thomas's young pages stood in the doorway, awkwardly apologising for disturbing the duchess. He bowed to me and said my husband wished for my company. Rather surprised, I begged leave from

Constanza and followed the boy out of the room. The lord, he said, was waiting for me in the cloisters.

Thomas stood on the flagstones staring blindly out through one of the arches at the neat pebble paths winding in circles round the cloister garden. He was alone, his face ashen.

'Thomas?' I said. 'What is wrong?'

He turned, his eyes huge and full of sorrow.

'It's John.'

My heart lurched and the pillars swam in a blur. My greatest fear had materialised. Thomas knew.

I said nothing, just stood frozen with terror, wondering what he would do. Where would he send me and would he allow me to keep my children?

'Did Elizabeth tell you?' he said.

'Elizabeth?'

Why had he mentioned Elizabeth? She knew nothing about John and me.

'Did she tell you she was carrying a child?'

I felt the most overwhelming relief. So that was what this was about. Elizabeth had confessed her condition. Thomas didn't know anything about what I'd done. I waited while my heartbeat slowed and the colour flooded back into my cheeks.

'Yes,' I said, composing my face into one of serene womanly pleasure. 'She told me a few days ago. She wanted it kept secret until she told her father. Is the duke pleased?'

Thomas shook his head and ran the fingers of his hand through his hair. 'Pleased? He is beside himself with rage. He has threatened to have my brother killed.'

'Killed?'

'Yes, killed. What else would a father do to a man who has violated his daughter?'

'I don't understand. You said he had threatened your brother'

'Yes, my brother.'

'John?'

'Yes, John. What other brother do I have? Apart from Richard.'

'But why? What has John got to do with Elizabeth?'

Thomas took me by the arms and said slowly and clearly so there was no possibility of my not understanding, 'Elizabeth is carrying John's child.'

'No!' I protested. 'That cannot be so. It is her husband's child. She told me. You are mistaken.'

Ice-cold terror flooded my veins as I felt my world begin to crumble.

Thomas said flatly, 'It is you who are mistaken. The child is John's. Elizabeth has admitted as much to her father.'

A great chasm opened up before my feet and I stood staring uselessly across the void at my husband.

'But he doesn't know her.'

'It seems he knows her well enough.'

'She said ...' I flailed uselessly, looking for answers to the impossible.

'Alys. The child is John's. I don't care what Elizabeth said to you. She has told her father the child is John's.'

'She is lying.'

'Why would she lie? They have both confessed to secret meetings. Now she is carrying John's child, they wish to marry.'

I clung to the one certainty I knew.

'He cannot marry her. She is already married.'

Thomas leaned his head against a pillar.

'Elizabeth wants her marriage to the Hastings boy set aside.'

'Impossible.'

'He is thirteen. She says they have not yet shared a bed.'

'No!' I crammed my fist into my mouth to stop the pain.

'Alys! What is the matter?'

'She asked me. She asked me and I told her.'

'Told her what?'

'Tamkin told me how it was. But I didn't know, I didn't know.'

'Alys, you're not making sense. What did your brother tell you?'

I raised my face to his, wanting him to say that none of this was true.

'I told her how it could be done,' I whispered. 'How her marriage might be ended. But I didn't know. Truly, I didn't know.'

And then I began to weep.

Thomas slipped his arms round my shoulders and held me tight against him. My face was hidden in the rough warmth of his jacket and my tears soaked the dark woollen cloth newly purchased from Flanders only last month.

'Don't cry, Alys,' he murmured, his mouth soft against my hair. 'This is not your fault. Nothing is your fault, dearest. This tragedy is not of your making.'

Oh, but it was. It was.

For two days the duke's fury resounded through every corner of the priory and there was nowhere for me to hide. His harsh words, cursing and crashing of things hurled across the chamber, frightened everyone. But Elizabeth's screams as she roundly abused her father, were worse. There was nothing he could do, she shouted. She was going to marry John Holand with or without his permission and if he wanted to avoid a scandal he had best give them his blessing and arrange matters with that boy he pleased to call her husband.

Inside, I was as cold as ice and utterly empty. I felt nothing. Elizabeth had told me all I needed to know. She had missed three courses and it took no more than a moment to realize that John had been lying with her in those weeks after Easter when he had also been lying with me. Those sun-filled afternoons when he and I had made love in the upper room at the inn, when I believed he was mine – they were a lie. He had praised the curves of my lips, my neck, my woman's body, saying how desirable I was, how much he adored me – but the words were false. They had meant nothing. They were just words. I had been deceived. Each time he had sent me away with a Judas kiss and gone straight to her bed. And the betrayal of getting her with child was more than I could bear.

'Would you like me to read to you, Lady Alys?' Elizabeth's sister was very kind but I shook my head and turned my face away. All I wanted was to be left alone, to grieve for the loss of a love which had never existed.

But I was not allowed to be alone. Harry arrived from Monmouth and had to be entertained and in the scandalised atmosphere of Constanza's rooms, where her

Spanish ladies were speechless with disapproval, hasty arrangements were made for a wedding which nobody wanted – nobody apart from John and Elizabeth.

Within the week I joined with the others in a pretence of joyfulness to watch the man I had once loved, marry my cousin Blanche's daughter.

'They're all the same,' said Amy Melbourne who, with another of Constanza's English women, Aline Gerberge, had come to gossip. I'd known them a long time which they believed gave them licence to prattle in my presence. 'Break a woman's heart as soon as look at them.'

'He'll not make her happy,' prophesied Aline.

'I doubt he'd make any woman happy,' said Amy. 'Look at the Lady Isabel. Used her like a common whore and when her husband turned nasty, cruelly cast her aside. I never saw a young woman so destroyed as she was.'

'All that wailing and our mistress with not an ounce of compassion, no matter the Lady Isabel was her sister.'

'And him walking away whistling a pretty tune.'

'But you've got to admit he's right handsome,' said Aline. 'And those legs! No woman would say no to a man like that in her bed. I certainly wouldn't.'

'Your Edward would give you a right wallop if he heard you say that.'

'If my Edward did his duty by me a bit more, perhaps I'd not be saying it,' Aline said tartly. 'What do you think Lady Alys? He's your brother-in-law. You'd know.'

'Know what?

'What is he really like? Has he ever made advances?'

I looked at her with empty eyes.

'He is my brother-in-law. Why would I let him touch me?'

343

A week later, the Portuguese galleys arrived and at last it was time for embarkation. The pride of the English fleet in all their painted, round-bottomed magnificence lay anchored offshore and in Plymouth thousands of men surged through the streets like the vanguard of an advancing army. Beyond the sound of marching feet and bawdy songs, the harbour was alive with noise and movement: a multitude of little boats scurrying to and fro as men, their horses, their arms and their equipment were ferried out to the waiting ships.

I stood on the steps, sheltered by the doorway of Thomas's lodgings, with the sea breeze softly brushing my face, watching the last of the day disappear. A sharp tang of salt assailed my nostrils and from below the harbour wall came the relentless crash of surf and the raucous cries of swooping gulls.

'I wish you would go back,' urged Thomas, but I stubbornly shook my head.

I would wait out the passing days like the watcher of a marked candle burning the hours away. Six days, five, four, three, two and then only one more day until he was gone. The ship's captain reported a favourable wind with all set fair for the morrow. A procession of ladies arrived from the priory. The holy flag was kissed, the duke and his family blessed and prayers said for a safe journey and glory on the battlefield. The duke said farewell to those who were not sailing with him and escorted his duchess onto the gilded barge.

'We'll row out with Harry,' said Thomas. 'There's a private dinner for the family aboard ship. The duke has said he wishes you to be there.'

I didn't want to go but what reason could I possibly give for refusing? So I nodded my head dully and prepared to accompany my husband down the steps.

Our little boat rode the waves well, skimming lightly across the water and in no time we were nosing our way in amongst the hulls of the great ships which would carry the duke, his family, his household and his five thousand strong army all the way to Portugal.

The meal was an intimate affair, only nine of us at the candlelit table. Throughout the serving of the dishes I ached in an agony of longing and despair with John just an arm's reach away, listening to the warmth of his voice, remembering the words he had spoken across the pillow, watching his eyes light up as he smiled at Elizabeth, the way he had once smiled at me. I said nothing but there was no need as the men found plenty to say.

'We'd better go,' said Harry at last, alert to a change in the movement of the ship. 'If we stay much longer we'll be half way to Spain.'

Chairs were pushed back and, in the cramped confines of the duke's cabin, we made our private farewells.

'Thank you, Lady Alys,' said Elizabeth as she kissed my cheek, her silk clad body with its precious new life pressed up against mine. 'John and I owe you a debt of immense gratitude. It was your advice which made this possible.'

I said little, merely kissed her with my cold dry lips and murmured a few meaningless words.

When it was time to say farewell to my brother-in-law I was unable to form any words at all. He kissed my lips and then my cheeks. holding my hands in his.

345

'I didn't want to hurt you, Alys,' he whispered, his face warm against mine, his body treacherously close. 'But you must understand this: Elizabeth will be my duchess.'

How could I have forgotten? He had always wanted a duchess and when he found a willing young woman whose father was a duke, what better wife could there be. Elizabeth wasn't a middle-aged fool with six children and a husband in her bed, she was young and merry and very, very pretty; and her father was the richest man in England after the king. No wonder he wanted her.

I stood in silence, blinking back the tears. This would be the last time, the very last time I would ever see him.

'Come along, Alys,' called Thomas. 'It is time to go.'

By then, everyone was weeping so nobody noticed tears spilling down my cheeks.

We clambered back into the little boat and, with the wind rising and the tide about to turn, the oarsmen hurried back to shore. There, the three of us watched from the landing stage as the signal was given to raise the sails. The great squares of canvas filled and bellied, and slowly, one by one, the huge ships began to move out towards the open sea. Too soon they were nothing but dark shapes on the horizon disappearing round the headland into a blaze of shimmering golden light.

'Wind is set fair,' said Harry. 'Should be a speedy voyage. Let us pray God continues to smile on my father's venture and they come safe to shore. And now I must bid you farewell. I am for Monmouth and my wife. It will be a merry gathering. My father has requested I invite Lady Swynford and her daughter to join us there.'

He walked swiftly away while Thomas and I remained

for a little while, staring out at the emptiness. I thought of Lady Swynford and wondered at how her story was ending more happily than mine. She might not be in the duke's arms but she was clearly in his thoughts.

We turned our faces towards the town and began the slow walk back along the weathered boards. A man was busy with his nets and nodded as we passed. Thomas began talking about his brother and how much he would miss his company but how with Richard in his present mood this journey overseas was for John's own good. And wasn't marriage with the duke's daughter the most fortuitous piece of luck?

'He took a great risk. I wasn't aware they were close but I've not seen him so smitten with a young woman in a long time. Last night, when we shared a cup of wine, he talked of nothing but the Lady Elizabeth.'

I couldn't bear it. I picked up the skirts of my gown and began to hurry. Before I knew it, I was running. I didn't look where I was putting my feet. I didn't notice the coil of rope. I tripped.

I put out my hands to save myself and grasped nothing but empty air. I crashed onto the boards and found I was tumbling over the edge. The fall through the air lasted an eternity. I hit the water. The shock was immense. Water rushed through my clothes and in that instant I knew it was icily cold. I bobbed on the heaving surface with my skirts spread out around me, waves crashing against the wooden uprights. Seawater engulfed my face, my neck, my hair, my boots. It swept into my eyes and I was blinded. I thrashed with my arms and kicked with my feet but the waves rose higher and I screamed as water filled my mouth. I fought against the cold dead fingers dragging me down. I tried to grab hold of something, anything, but there was nothing there. Nothing but dark icy water.

I sank down and down and down.

I knew water was supposed to cleanse the body of sin but nobody said it would be like this. I thought of my children. I thought of my home, my husband, my sister. I thought of my cousin, Blanche, and the sunlit days of my girlhood at Kenilworth. I thought of my mother and how much she had loved me.

I knew this was death and tried to pray. In the darkness I could see the blessed Virgin in her radiant glory, her gentle smile, her blue robes swirling around her slippered feet, her slender hands outstretched towards mine. I tried to grasp her fingers but dark water slid between us like a closing gate and I could no longer see the light. I tried to breathe but the pain in my chest was too great. Slowly everything became black.

All of a sudden I felt a violent tugging. Something had hold of my hair and was pulling at me. *Sainte Vierge*! A sea monster! I tried to fight but had no idea where it was. My arms and legs refused to move. The tugging became more insistent and I felt myself dragged upwards. Then my face burst above the surface. I gulped and spluttered and gasped and tried to shout. I could see nothing but oceans of water and the brightest of lights. I seized hold of something by my side and discovered it was a man. I clawed at his face and clung to him, desperately frightened lest he should disappear. He pushed my hands away. I screamed. His fingers grasped my head and held it firmly against his shoulder. A voice told me to stop struggling. It was Thomas.

I cannot remember how he got us both to shore but when I next opened my eyes I was huddled on the shingle with little waves splashing merrily around my feet. My clothes were soaked, my throat was raw and my eyes stung horribly. Next to me, Thomas was on his hands and knees, vomiting onto the ground.

The sun sparkled and people came running. There was shouting and the sound of gulls mewing and Thomas was still crouched beside me, retching. Someone lifted me up and I was tipped onto a makeshift litter of coarse sacking. I was barely conscious of the bumping and swaying as I was carried to Thomas's lodgings. There, the woman of the house took my arm and led me upstairs to a tiny room where a sulky fire had been lit. She asked if I had a maid or would I let her help me out of my wet clothing. I was shivering with cold and the remnants of fear and was careless as to who stripped off my sodden gown.

Soon I was wrapped in a dry woollen blanket and placed on a stool in front of the fire. The woman put a cup of strange-tasting fiery liquid into my hands and encouraged me to drink. She kept up a continuous flow of chatter so I was required to say nothing.

After a while, Thomas came. He was wearing dry clothes and apart from damp hair, sleek against the curve of his head, he looked no different from usual. He waved the woman away, leaving us alone together in the tiny smoky room. He pulled up a stool and sat beside me. For a long while nothing was said, we simply sat there in silence like an old poor couple, watching the blue spitting flames and the hiss and crackle from the salt-encrusted logs.

'You should have left me,' I whispered.

He made a harsh noise like a half-strangled sob. 'And let you drown?'

'Perhaps it was God's will.'

'I doubt that.'

'But you cannot swim.'

I sensed the relaxing of his muscles, the familiar twist of his mouth.

'There is a little place in Normandy where the village saint protects those who find themselves in dangerous waters. I heard his story once and visited his shrine. He is much venerated. It must have been he who told me what to do. Besides, we were close to shore. I only had to drag you a little way.'

I sat there thinking how odd it was that my husband, whom I had privately thought a coward, was the one to risk his life for me, whereas his brother, whom I thought brave and resourceful and had loved with a passion, had brought me nothing but grief.

'I have not been a good wife.'

'No,' he agreed. 'You have not. I hoped for your loyalty and your discretion. But it seems I got neither.'

Of course he knew. I'd realised for some time that he must. I bowed my head, wondering how he had found out.

'I did not mean to hurt you.'

He stared, unsmiling, as if he didn't believe me.

'Why did you do it? You must have known it was wrong.'

Yes, I knew it was wrong.'

'So why? Did I neglect you?'

No.'

Was I unkind?'

'No, you have always shown me the utmost kindness.'

'So why? What drove you to something so foolish and so dangerous?'

I considered when the candle flame had first flickered in the dark, when I'd first yielded to temptation.

'It was vanity.'

'Vanity?'

'He made me feel desirable and for a woman that is no small thing. It was like a fever, like burning up in a wildfire. '

'Then it's as well the source of your conflagration has been removed,' he said drily. 'Who knows where it might have led you otherwise.'

'How long have you known?'

'Long enough.'

'My maid?'

'She proved remarkably stubborn, completely faithful to her mistress. It was the groom. After a little persuasion he was only too eager to tell me where you'd been and who you'd met. Can you imagine the humiliation I felt? At that moment I would willingly have killed you both. No man wants an unfaithful wife and to know it was my own brother made the betrayal doubly painful.'

'Why did you not stop me?'

He gave the smallest sliver of a smile. 'I thought of sending you to a nunnery but could not bear to part with you.'

I shook my head uselessly, aware of the dreadful damage I had done, the immense hurt I had caused.

'I should have protected you. I failed in my duty to keep you safe and for that I am more sorry than I can say.'

'It was not your fault. Not in any way.'

'A husband must bear some responsibility for his wife's actions.'

'I am the one to blame,' I sobbed.

He did not take me in his arms, that was not his way, but he slipped his hand over mine where it lay in my lap.

'He is not worth your tears, my dear. You are not the first woman to be tempted by a handsome rogue and you will not be the last.'

'He is not a rogue.'

'Oh, but he is. You forget, I know him very well, better than you. He has ruined dozens of women: wives, daughters, my mother's serving women, pretty wenches; all seduced and carelessly tossed aside. You must know there are men skilled at hiding their true natures, who weave lies into truths so that when the cloth is made whole a woman cannot tell the difference.'

Yes, I knew. The stories of my girlhood had been full of such disguisings, of men pretending to be what they were not, stitching themselves into bearskins, dressing themselves in rags, and all for the purposes of deception.

'It was not only him,' I whispered. 'I was as much to blame.'

'You were deceived.'

'Oh Thomas, I would not have you believe me innocent because I am not. I could confess a dozen sins against our marriage and that makes me truly ashamed. If you wish, I will tell you everything but please, I beg of you, do not take away my children.'

He lifted my hand from where it lay and raised it to

his mouth. I felt the soft brush of his lips on my fingers, a gentle husbandly kiss.

'You may tell me if you wish, but there is no need.'

I knew he would find my actions incomprehensible. He was too uncomplicated. He could never conceive of a passion like the one I had felt for his brother.

'I doubt you would understand.'

He gazed at me with sadness in his eyes.

'You think I know nothing of temptation?'

'I think it too horrible,' I said quietly.

He gave a short laugh. 'Let me tell you a story. You remember the year I accompanied the duke on his long march from Calais?'

I nodded.

'That winter in Bordeaux, I was miserable. You and I had parted badly and I found very little in the thought of going home to bring me comfort.'

How young and thoughtless I had been, sending my husband off to war from a cold bed. I understood better now how much that must have hurt. But regret is pointless, we cannot undo past harms we have done.

'One day I met a young woman, a widow. She was not particularly beautiful but she was kind and she was educated. I would visit her house and we would talk. I would read to her and she would bring me wine and cakes. I thought nothing of it. I was lonely, she was lonely, and we enjoyed each others company. And then one evening she invited me into her bed.'

I remembered the bitter taste of a suspected betrayal from long ago.

'Did she have cherry-red lips?'

He shrugged. 'I have forgotten what she looked like.'

'You were tempted?'

'I was. I knew it was wrong. Most men would have taken what she offered and never once considered their marriage vows; they would not have hesitated.'

'But not you?'

'He looked at me, his brown eyes misted with tears. 'I was the worst of sinners. I not only considered the vows I'd taken on my wedding day, the promises binding me to you, but swiftly set them aside because the temptation was too great. I lay with her that night and every night for the next two weeks.'

I was surprised how much the knowledge hurt. I could not understand why it should. There was no reason for me to be jealous of an unknown woman my husband had once desired when I had not desired him in that way myself.

'I was burdened with shame,' he said quietly. 'I prided myself on being chaste yet found I could not be. After I had taken my pleasure, I turned my face to the wall, refusing to look at her because she reminded me of my failure. Yet each day I was tempted again and returned to her bed. When it was time to return to England, she begged me to stay. She said she would ask for nothing other than what we had; she would be my concubine, her good name was of no importance, I was all she wanted.'

I saw myself in this unknown woman: that last time at the inn, begging John not to leave me, clinging to him, offering my body like a common whore, telling him that nothing mattered but our love.

'What happened to her?'

'I heard she married an elderly neighbour.'

'And you came home.'

He smiled, properly this time, the light from the fire illuminating the contours of his face, making him look younger than his years. 'I remember riding up to our house at Woking and finding you waiting for me. I felt like a man reborn. Here was everything I wanted: a home, a beautiful wife and two wonderful children. But the shame of what had happened in Bordeaux lived with me for many years, making me more sober than was good for me. It is a hard thing for a man to acknowledge that he has not lived up to his own ideals.'

'You were a young man far from home. It was natural.'

'Because an act is natural does not make it right. It is what separates us from the beasts in the field.'

That night, safe in our curtained bed, he held me in his arms and, with an unusual determination, began to make love to me. I felt his anger in every thrust but allowed myself to be willing. Although the encounter was awkward, with many unspoken words lying between us, I found it oddly satisfying. I enjoyed the firm warmth of his body, the roughness of his caresses and the closeness of someone who cared for me. I offered him my mouth, not as a wife's duty, but because I wished to feel the familiar taste of his lips.

When it was over he gave a satisfied sigh and rolled off, lying so that he could look at me through the haze of one who has gratified himself well and enjoyed the experience.

'Thomas, there is something I must tell you. I am carrying a child.'

355

There was silence: nothing to hear but the banging of an ill-fastened shutter and the sound of my husband's ragged breathing. We lay like a prisoner and her gaoler in a cushioned cell, the confession half-made, the possibility of deceit still lingering in the air.

'Is it mine?' he said at last, his voice perfectly steady.

'Yes,' I whispered, without a moment's hesitation. 'It is yours.'

I heard a slight exhalation of breath and saw relief flooding his face.

'That is all that matters,' he said.

Whatever anxiety he felt, whatever doubts he'd entertained, they were all swept away by my swift reassurance. I'd known he would ask, because Thomas was not stupid, and I'd prayed long and hard as to what my answer should be.

There was the tiniest pause when neither of us said anything. I prayed to the Blessed Virgin to give me courage.

'Thomas, I would not want you to think …'

He placed his finger on my lips. 'I think nothing.'

But my eyes must have betrayed what I was too frightened to put into words.

He gazed at me, steadily, and said, 'Alys, I shall say this once and we shall not speak of it again. I am not a selfless man, I have many faults. But I want you to know that whatever sins you have committed, however much hurt there is between us at this moment, you will always be my beloved wife. And even if this child were not mine, I would welcome it because it is *your* child and you are the woman I prize above all else.'

A sudden gust of wind rattled the shutters. Rain

began splashing onto the cobbles outside our window. Then came a brilliant flash of light and a distant growl of thunder. Thomas raised his head from the pillow.

'Don't be afraid, dearest. It is only a summer storm. It won't last forever.'

EPILOGUE 1397

God in His mercy has granted us ten more years: ten years to build this loving trust between us; ten years in which my husband has become so very dear to me. I do not love him with the same dangerous, heart-stopping passion I once felt for his brother but I value his kindness and find a surprising pleasure in our intimacy. He is a loving husband and I see him now for the truly good man he has always been. My foolishness nearly destroyed our marriage but God has given me a second chance. I hope I have used these years wisely.

To our joy, the baby born to us that December, ten long years ago, was a girl. We called her Nell: partly for my mother, a woman who knew the folly of committing a sin in the name of passion, and partly for our eldest daughter, Alianore, who, as the Mortimer countess of March, is now too grand to answer to such a childish name. Thomas loves our second little Nell with a great tenderness, confessing to me that he finds her the most delightful of all our children.

He rarely goes to court these days. He is no crusader and believes Richard increasingly rules through the use of terror. If he could prevent it, he would expose none of his family to the horrors that are unfolding around the king, so we spend the time we have left together, enjoying a quiet life with our youngest children.

Thomas sits by the fire, wrapped warmly against the chill and says he will not live to see another summer. I pray he is mistaken. I laugh at the way he pats my hand and accuse him of becoming an old man before his time. But this winter his lips have acquired a bluish tinge and his skin has become more transparent. His breath comes short and although in our bed he holds me as tenderly as he ever did, he rarely manages to be a husband to me in that way.

I fear I am losing him and the loss will be more than I can bear.

AUTHOR'S NOTE

Thomas died on 25th April 1397. His will, written in English, says of Alys – *"praying for my wife for all the love and trust that hath been between us."*

The duke of Lancaster's Spanish adventure ended in failure. He and Constanza relinquished their claim to the crown of Castile to their daughter, Catalina. Constanza died in 1394. Two years later, the duke married his mistress, Lady Katherine Swynford, and made her his duchess. In 1397 Pope Boniface and King Richard agreed to the legitimising of their four bastard children.

In November 1386 Richard's power was revoked by a group of his nobles and later, several of the king's associates were convicted of treason. Robert de Vere and Michael de la Pole fled abroad; Simon Burley was executed. A furious Richard swore to have his revenge.

John and Elizabeth returned to England in April 1388. Richard gave his brother the earldom of Huntingdon and later made him duke of Exeter.

Queen Anne died in 1394. After two years of mourning his wife, Richard married Isabel, six-year-old daughter of the Valois king of France.

ACKNOWLEDGEMENTS

There is very little written about Alys and her marriage to Thomas Holand. I searched hundreds of books and websites looking for clues to her life. The birth order of her children proved extremely difficult to unravel. Below are some of the books I found useful.

Penny Lawne	Joan of Kent
Ian Mortimer	The Perfect King: The life of Edward III
Joanathan Sumption	Divided Houses: The Hundred Years War III
Kathryn Warner	Richard II
Kathryn Warner	Blood Roses
Alison Weir	Katherine Swynford: The Story of John of Gaunt and his Scandalous Duchess

My thanks go to the writing group: Jackie, Jane, Kat and Ken and, as always, to my husband, Richard, for his help, advice and support. My thanks also to the team at Matador. And a special thank-you to Pip, my silent, unpaid walking companion who allows me time and space to plot my stories.

COMING SOON

The Epiphany Betrayal

By 1397 Richard II's reign has descended into a nightmare world of execution, banishment and murder. Only those whom the king loves are safe and much of his fury is directed at the Arundel family of Nell Holand's mother.

When Henry of Lancaster seizes the throne from his tyrannical cousin, no-one could be happier than Nell. But her Montagu father-in-law and her uncle, the dangerously ambitious John Holand, are plotting to restore Richard to his throne.

When Nell is entrusted with delivering a secret message, she must decide which of the players in this dangerous game are to be trusted and who most deserves her loyalty. Whatever she does, whoever she confides in, she knows people are bound to die.

From the shadowy streets of London and the king's magnificent palace at Windsor to the wilds of faraway Devonshire, *The Epiphany Betrayal* is the story of a young woman who faces hardship and danger when her life is turned upside down, and of the secret she must keep from her husband if she is to remain safe.

ABOUT THE AUTHOR

Caroline Newark was born in Northern Ireland. She has a degree in Law from Southampton University and her career spans such diverse activities as teaching science, starting a children's nursery business and milking Jersey cows.

Caroline's series of books is based on the women in her mother's family tree. There is one book for each generation, beginning in 1299 with *The Pearl of France*, the story of Marguerite, sister of the French king who marries the elderly Edward I as his second wife. Marguerite is Caroline's 19 times great-grandmother.

The Queen's Spy tells the story of Marguerite's daughter in-law, Margaret, and *The Fair Maid of Kent* that of Marguerite's granddaughter, Joan, the first English Princess of Wales. *An Illegitimate Affair* is the story of Alys who marries Joan's son and *The Epiphany Betrayal* (to be published in 2020) that of Aly's daughter, Nell.

Caroline Newark lives in Somerset with her husband and their border collie, Pip. She has two daughters and five grandchildren.

Website:	www.carolinenewarkbooks.co.uk
Contact:	caroline@carolinenewarkbooks.co.uk
Follow:	Caroline Newark on Facebook
	@caronewarkbooks on Twitter